ERIK L. WELCHOFF

ENTER: THE CHAMPION

tales of a methonian warrior chronicles of anton seven

BLUEPRINT PRESS
INTERNATIONALE

Enter: The Champion
Copyright © 2023 by Erik L. Welchoff

ISBN
978-1-959365-56-3 (Paperback)
978-1-959365-57-0 (eBook)
978-1-959365-55-6 (Hardcover)

to Lorien Welchoff.

> *the very best daughter a man could hope for. Both her love, and her smile, push me onward to accomplish my every ambition; she would make any father proud.*

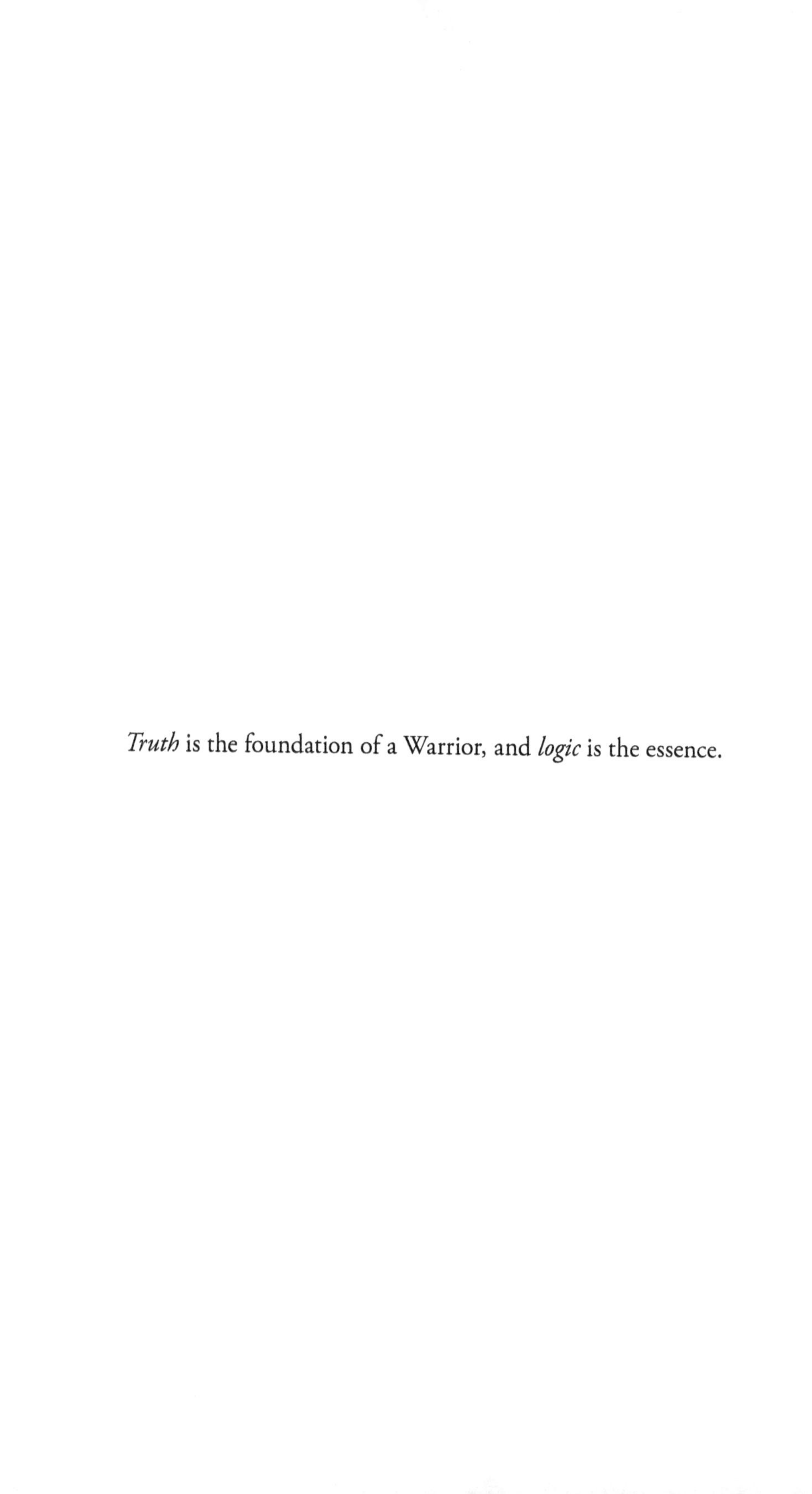

Truth is the foundation of a Warrior, and *logic* is the essence.

TABLE OF CONTENTS

PART 1

"Enter: The Champion" 1
Assignment: Tooloo 3
Encounters and Conflicts 15
Changing of the Guard 38
A Warrior's Tale 67
Erudition 104
The Tragedy of Love 124
Pain and Comfort 157
Of Lab Mice and Masters 172
Au Revoir Methonias 194
Secrets of the Methonian Masters Revealed................................215

PART 2

"The Interdependence of Magic and Science" 235
The Summoning... 237
The Primords.. 254
Those Who Mourn the Damned 268
Gifts from the Magi 285
Glory and Folly..310
An Audience with the King.. 330
Celestra and the Universe...346
Bane and Despair 370
The Portal Opens..386

Glossary...404

PART 1

"Enter: The Champion"

Assignment: Tooloo

ANTON SEVEN LOOKED AT HIS left hand and noticed his ring had turned black, signifying he'd made a terrible mistake. His eyes suddenly widened, his mouth hung open, and a look of horror covered his face.

"Oh my God!" he exclaimed with a gasp. "What have I done? This can't be!" A crushing feeling of dread filled his heart, and tore at his soul, sending a tingling sensation through his nervous system. The dreadful feeling of shock nauseated him, and made him giddy. His mind raced from thought to thought. Several moments passed before his mind cleared enough to collect his thoughts, manage his current predicament, and accept responsibility for his devastating failure. "How could I have been so blind?" he shouted into the air, but nobody heard—all of the villagers' ears were incapable of hearing. Grief filled his heart beyond his capacity to contain it, and he continued to stare at the coal-black ring on his hand as he clenched his teeth.

He thought about how his Masters had entrusted him with the responsibility of protecting the lives of an entire village, and how his decisions and choices had resulted in their gruesome demise; he'd inadvertently permitted the entire village to be murdered.

"Black," mumbled Anton. "That's something my ring *never* did before! That's a color *nobody's* ring has ever been before! How can it *possibly* turn black! What *caused* it to turn black? My *decisions*? My *choices*? Did I *miss* something? Maybe it's worse; could it possibly be my... *emotions*? Oh my God, it *is* my emotions! This can't be! I can't *feel* this way! I shouldn't *feel* at all!"

His whole life, his ring had always appeared clear, or in shades of pale yellow, soft, and pastel—never a midnight black so absolute it seemed to mock the darkness of deep space. Anton continued to stare at his ring as he recalled the day his Masters had given it to him. He was much younger and smaller then, and the ring had seemed so much bigger. It seemed like only yesterday, yet from his youthful perspective, it had been a lifetime. He was but a mere child then, with much to learn, yet he'd never forgotten that moment. It seemed so important at the time, as if he'd finally achieved a milestone in his life—but now the memory tore at his heart.

The ring was made of a special living crystal that came from a *Lapillusaurus*. It was like the pearl of an oyster and it had special properties he still didn't fathom. When he put it on his finger for the first time, it was clear, indicating his youth, innocence, and naivete. He remembered how it had changed from clear to milky white and then pale yellow—a slow process that had taken most of his life. An endless amount of work training his mind and body led to the honing of his heart, triggering the crystal's gradual transformation into its current color; it had only to change to gold, and then, finally, his Masters would allow him to graduate. He had just turned twenty-one, the age that most Warriors graduated, and he didn't want to face disintegration as a failure. Those Warriors that didn't complete their training by twenty-two were eliminated.

Anton's Masters had determined this would be his final mission— the one that would coax his ring into completion, indicating he'd accomplished everything a Warrior was to achieve. Or perhaps he'd merely convinced himself of this, and his Masters' motives were less trustworthy. They had alluded to this, hadn't they? Now he wasn't so sure he'd determined the correct conclusion. He'd always felt in his heart that there was a greater purpose for him—a reason why now was the crucial moment to finish his training. But somehow, he didn't fully understand it.

Before he had left the Temple that morning for this mission, the Masters simply told him: "This mission may provide a promising conclusion for your future. Either way, it will be a conclusion."

The Temple Masters had sent Anton not only to assist and support the villagers of Tooloo, but also to test nearly twenty years of the most extensive martial arts training that had ever been available anywhere in the universe. His special skills were the culmination of all the physical arts welded together to create the ultimate offensive and defensive style of fighting ever known. His body was capable of these great physical skills due to the genetic alterations performed by the Methonian Cloning Labs; he was quite literally a perfect human.

This mission had provided Anton with the opportunity to apply all of his special skills in a practical test environment. The planet of Methonias was the only place in the universe available for the Warriors to develop their knowledge and skills. The Masters would send the Warriors-in-training into various regions of Methonias, each designed for specific training and development purposes.

"I sent them to their *graves*," Anton moaned. "What will become of me? Assuredly, the Masters will see fit to terminate me for my insurrection. They could only conclude I'm no longer trustworthy, or capable of finishing a mission on my own—or worse, that I'm an inferior product!" He may have exaggerated his guilt, as was his way; however, he realized the truth of his fears. His Masters didn't permit Warriors to fail. Most of all, he knew they were supposed to be incapable of feelings. Feelings, in fact, were impermissible. Yet Anton did feel.

"I need to meditate," he mumbled to himself; deep meditation always seemed to help him through his personal concerns, allowing him to review his mistakes objectively. Right now, he hoped it would wash his emotions away. "My assignment was to *help* these people—to *prevent* their deaths," he moaned. "I'm a failure."

Anton adjusted himself into a comfortable posture to meditate; in this way, he could contemplate the pain he felt, and attempt to reason his way out of his current predicament. As always, he preferred the classic lotus position—legs crossed, eyes closed, head slightly tipped back, and the back of each hand positioned upon his knees, with thumb and middle finger making a circle. Contemplation and meditation always gave him a structured self-induced feeling of relief from his troubles. He used this technique whenever possible as a release from his emotions, a way of cleansing his heart in order to understand the things that troubled him most. He gained strength and insight by doing so, and periodically he used meditation to replace sleep. Carefully, meticulously, he evaluated the events leading to this grievous and troubling dilemma.

THE FATEFUL MISSION HAD STARTED a few days earlier when the Temple Masters assigned him the task of single-handedly defending a small village far inside the tropical region of southern Methonias. An Aerocraft transported him there and dropped him off a couple of miles north of the inhabited territory.

There were few places that an Aerocraft could land safely deep inside the jungle—the dense foliage was too impenetrable and the terrain too uneven; rocks jutted randomly from the ground, and loose soil covered most everything else. The Aerocraft pilot was forced to find an open area just to the south of a rocky upheaval that was as large as a small mountain. From a distance, the upheaval looked like a large portion of the plateau— nearly a mile long and a half mile wide—was supported by a humongous pile of massive boulders. It was covered with the same dense jungle foliage Anton was about to enter.

It was rumored that this formation was home to a small group of people that repeatedly ravaged the realm. Each had committed unspeakable crimes of various types, forcing the nearby villages to defend themselves as best they could. Being a peaceful people, the villagers considered killing abhorrent, and never used it as a deterrent. Banishment wasn't the best of solutions, for the offenders might return to do more harm later, but such was the villagers' way. However, these less effective peaceful methods provided opportunities for the Warriors to perform training missions at needed intervals, as determined by their Masters.

Since it was the custom of all Warriors to embark on a mission on foot, Anton expected the traditional long hike to his destination. After examining the satellite imagery of the area while in flight, he determined that he had at least an hour's journey to traverse through dense jungle growth before reaching the nearest village. This put a smile on his face as he exited the Aerocraft; he enjoyed exploring new places and liked to test his skills in an unfamiliar region—like any young Warrior his age.

Looking over his shoulder as he reached the jungle's edge, Anton watched the shiny metallic craft that had brought him here rise with a modest but shrill whine of engines, and then suddenly burst into an impossible arch of speed as it accelerated away. Turning his attention back to the jungle, he suddenly felt quite alone, something he'd never really felt before. He'd always shared his training missions with his fellow Warriors-in-training. Only the oldest Warriors-in-training attained permission to test alone.

Uncertainty filled his heart as he wondered into the unknown. Having the support of his brother Warriors always gave him a sense of security and confidence. Now every small decision was his and his alone. Group decisions were something he'd always shared in, or the decisions were determined for him without his input. For the first time in his life, he was completely self-reliant.

Large tropical trees laden with hanging vines and surrounded by heavy underbrush were everywhere. Outcroppings of rock hanging over concealed edges of deep valleys that suddenly revealed themselves made travel difficult and hazardous. Anton had extraordinarily enhanced physical abilities, and his senses were acute to every tiny detail of the terrain—but more than once, he found himself an instant away from terrible peril. Only at the last second did he notice subtle changes of the foliage and terrain that saved him from an untimely demise. To anyone unfamiliar with this region, death would come swiftly. His progress seemed slow, but he covered the distance to the village at a steady pace, and managed to avoid all of the concealed pitfalls in his path.

He found the abundance of pestering insects incessantly irritating; they were a constant reminder of the region. Large bees, flies, poisonous centipedes, and many other creatures he had forgotten the names of crept or whisked past him constantly. Beetles, scorpions, spiders, and ants never gave him a moment's rest. Anton hated insects; they vexed him with their constant distraction. He was continually swatting at them, and he was bitten and stung many times. Many of the insects were venomous, and he despised having to keep a close eye out so as not to succumb to their attack; he didn't need the additional encumbrance while he performed his job.

Aside from this, he continued his journey undiscouraged as he traversed through the jungle's dense undergrowth. He moved stealthily, and his motions were utterly silent; no creature took enough interest even to acknowledge his passing.

After nearly two hours, not the one hour he had anticipated, Anton finally arrived in a tiny village. It was just before noon. The primitive thatched-roof huts were made of tropical timbers. As he entered the center of the village he immediately attracted the villagers' attention. Not knowing who he was, the villagers—mostly women and small children—scurried off for the cover of their primitive dwellings. The only one who remained was a huge man, who seemed made of nothing but muscle. He wore had a heavy scowl as he watched Anton's approach.

Walking straight toward him, Anton was entirely indifferent; given his own strength, he felt no fear of anyone. As he drew closer and realized the sheer magnitude of the man, he began to calculate what the best combat tactic for the situation would be, should he suddenly need to defend himself.

"Halt!" ordered the brute. "Don't come any closer or I'll turn you into food for the dogs!"

It was immediately apparent to Anton that this was a likely probability for any normal human. The man was obviously more than a match for several average-sized adversaries simultaneously; however, he posed no threat to a Warrior. Besides, he saw no hazard from any dogs.

The man stood nearly seven feet tall, with a build worthy of a Titan, all of which was highly toned muscle, and he easily outweighed Anton two to one. Anton knew he could easily dispatch such a large and fit man; his size didn't intimidate him, although his confidence wavered for a brief moment. "I'm curious—what is he hiding? What is he protecting?" Anton mumbled to himself. Anton's enhanced body design gave him increased flexibility and leveraging capabilities, even against such large opponents, yet this giant seemed to have immense confidence in the presence of a Warrior.

Putting his thumb and forefinger to his lips, the man whistled sharply, and within seconds, two large animals raced to his side, growling at Anton. They seemed prepared to do the man's bidding.

Taking a step back, Anton decided to be diplomatic. "I've come in peace, to help the people of your village," he said unconcernedly. Eyeing the dogs, he reasoned that negotiation was his best approach, and spoke with a gentle voice, hoping this would somehow appease the barbarian. Besides, his true mission lay in helping the village, not fighting their champion and his pets.

"How do I know that you are not lying? You look like an *outlaw!*" The man gave a disbelieving snarl, and opened and clenched his fists; it was evident he didn't wish to discuss the matter and would prefer a fight.

Anton held up his left hand so that the man could see the glowing yellow ring of crystal that sat upon his finger. Immediately, the man's face became respectful. Only Methonian Warriors wore a ring of crystal; it was the indication of their heritage.

"You're a Warrior? No! Perhaps you are a thief! I believe you *stole* that trinket from somewhere! You look like one of the outlaws that plague this region," he sneered. "Tell me why you are here; I believe you came to *plunder* my village! Answer me quick, or you will feed my pets!" The man seemed unsure of Anton—however, it was obvious he was less inclined to pick a fight now than he had been just moments before. Still, he firmly asserted his threats with a snarl.

"My Masters assigned me to protect your village, and I have come to rid the area of your troublesome outlaws." Anton bowed, demonstrating his Methonian desire to help. This act added an additional softening effect. "I wish to know if this is the village of Tooloo."

"No!" the other man said. "You have come to the wrong place. The outlaws you speak of will not be found in *my* village." A large grin covered his face. "*I* am *all* the protection *my* village needs!" He pounded his chest once with his huge fist, and a resounding thump filled the air like the striking of a drum. He looked down at Anton through the slits of his eyes, as if this young man was merely a child; he was ready to challenge any argument with immediate action.

"Then where might I find these outlaws I seek?" Anton asked, hoping that finally he'd softened the giant's disposition. "How far away is Tooloo?"

"Tooloo is three hours' journey to the south; for a Warrior, maybe less, but you need to *know* the trail or it could take you longer. Find Mahkeetah, he can tell you how to find the outlaws. Come, I will show you the path, and then you will leave and not return." The large man motioned for Anton to follow him, and quickly walked toward the far side of the village. They passed many primitive huts made entirely of fresh timber and thatch;

it was obvious they were recently constructed. The smell of freshly cut grass and wood filled the air, stimulating Anton's senses with its distinctive aroma, and he could see that the new huts were built over the remains of several destroyed by a recent fire.

"My name is Thorik," the large man said. "I am the chief of this village, and I am glad that I can help a Methonian Warrior."

The tone of Thorik's voice had changed considerably, as if he had accepted Anton for who he was, and therefore expressed a desire to help him rather than protect his village—or perhaps he simply wished to see Anton leave as quickly as possible.

"Just so you know," Thorik went on, "this is the village Picuris. As you see, the outlaws have visited us recently; they destroy everything they can if they don't get what they want." Pointing at several burned huts, and at the recently constructed huts, he drew Anton's attention to an area of recent devastation.

The villagers, not hearing the expected scuffle between Thorik and the stranger, slowly emerged from their huts, or timidly peered through the doors and windows as the men headed to the far end of the village. When he and Anton reached the border, Thorik pointed at an opening in the dense jungle undergrowth.

"This is the trail to the village of Tooloo. After a time, you will come to a wide river. Follow it downstream until you reach the point where the water falls into a valley; Tooloo rests at the base of this water. Beware, there are many dangers along the way. The jungle has many eyes, and it sees all!"

Nonchalantly, Anton responded: "I shall heed your advice." His inflection was arrogant, as if he were more than a match for anything he may encounter along the way. Quickly he turned around and trotted down the trail, leaving the village behind.

Thorik watched Anton as he left; shaking his head in disgust, he mumbled to himself: "That one will have many troubles with people. He is hard to like." Turning back toward the huts, he shrugged and heaved a sigh.

IT WAS OBVIOUS TO ANTON the journey would take quite some time, so he hurried along at a pace few could hope to match, and as comfortably as if he had lived in this region his whole life and knew the way by heart. Scanning the terrain with great caution, and carefully assessing everything he saw, he was always on the lookout for the unknown dangers Thorik had warned him of—just as any Warrior would be. Other than the natural hazards of the region, he didn't find anything out of the ordinary.

The jungles of Methonias were lush with vegetation. It was thick and beautiful, and dangerous and alluring. Potentially, an unwitting traveler might find himself enraptured by the tremendous fragrance and remarkable beauty of the many exotic flowers. Some flowers were as large as a human, or as tiny as a dewdrop. Anton, however, gave little notice to such distractions. His only concern was arriving at his destination quickly and safely.

The trail required little effort to follow; signs of heavy use defined it well. Anton hurried along for quite some time until he finally heard the sound of rushing water in the distance. For a moment, he stopped and tried to imagine what might lie before him; as he did so, he rested for a minute or two and allowed himself to enjoy the shade under the dense canopy of trees. The sounds of indigenous animals crying out pervaded the atmosphere, and he listened attentively to the sounds of their activities and purposes. Suddenly, the vocalizations and activities seemed to escalate, making it more difficult to hear the sound of any nearby water. Monkeys swung from branch to branch and tree to tree. Birds screeched and cawed relentlessly, declaring territorial rights and displeasure with the unknown intruder. The growls of unknown predators left Anton with an uneasy feeling that he might have to defend himself at any moment.

After catching his breath for a few minutes, Anton again continued his journey. It didn't take long before he reached the river's edge, just as Thorik had said he would. The river was wide like the chief had said; it was nearly fifty yards across and it flowed swiftly in the center; rapids caused by huge boulders lying under the water's surface suggested an additional hazard. Anton determined it to be rather deep where it ran the fastest. It would prove a considerable challenge to cross if he needed to, but crossing was not impossible. Being thirsty, he looked for a suitable place to take a drink. Wading into the water to refresh himself, he was surprised to find it colder than he'd anticipated. But it felt good, and gave him a little bit of relief from the tropical heat.

Many exotic tropical birds flew past Anton; they dove into the water, occasionally catching small fish, or scooping up an insect for a quick snack. The little pests covered the surface of the water in places, skipping along and going about their business, providing the easy meal for both the birds and the fish.

Anton enjoyed watching all of these activities; he was thankful for this particular assignment, more so than any of his previous ones. A morning of solitude in paradise satisfied some inner yearning he felt inside his heart. He couldn't identify it—it was a sense of personal release that allowed his inner stress to dissipate in a way even meditation hadn't fulfilled. He felt more attuned to this ecosystem, and more comfortable with himself than ever before.

Once he'd completed his absorption of the natural beauty and refreshed his thirst, he decided to continue his journey.

The trail remained well-defined as Anton followed the river downstream. By early afternoon he could hear the roar of the waterfall Thorik had described; the sound grew louder as he continued along the path. Soon he came to the edge of a cliff. Looking down, he could see a village near the base of the immense falls and a picturesque valley stretching beyond. Without question, his destination lay just below—yet again, he stopped for a few moments to enjoy the scenic view and absorb this new sensation of complete freedom. He savored the beauty of the trees, the smell of the fresh air with its abundant fragrances, and the sound of birds chirping wildly nearby. But duty prevented him from succumbing to the sensory input; he refused to allow it to distract him indefinitely as he observed his destination.

Anton's thoughts and instincts rarely swayed from duty and service; they precluded him from simply immersing himself in destined obligations, and digesting the beauty of the region. Yet he permitted himself a small indulgence anyway; the scenery elated him, the smell of exotic foliage exhilarated him, and the fauna enlivened his ears, giving him an awareness of self-mastery. He wished to embrace the sensation if only for a few moments. Having genetically enhanced photographic memory capabilities that exceeded a normal human's, he made a clear mental picture of everything around him for future reference, thus justifying the personal time in his trained Methonian way. As he did so, he felt as if he were the master of the valley below and the entire region.

Military strategy and training governed Anton's thoughts and actions. He continued to take great care to memorize the strategic placement of the village and its surrounding topography, diligently studying its exact position at the base of the falls, and how the steep cliffs surrounded three sides of its perimeter. The topography gave an excellent natural defense from wandering people who might wish to enter. But it had a terrible deficit: there was only one easy way in and out; it was as much a trap as it was defensible. Where the two sides of the valley converged together, the waterfall flowed over its edge, dropping nearly three hundred yards and creating a spectacular view; water splashed everywhere as it fell across enormous boulders and large stones that jutted outward from the cliff.

Mist filled the atmosphere; it made the tropical temperature more pleasant and nourished the lush vegetation and unusual gigantic flowers that lined each side of the falls. These flowers grew from every crevice, ledge, and crack between the stones that jutted out along the way. At the bottom, the river again coursed from a large pool created by the falls. Beyond this, Anton could easily see the far end of the valley, which was more than two miles distant. There it opened to a tropical jungle that seemed to stretch on endlessly. The width of the valley at the far end was over a quarter mile, and the river flowed down its center, winding between the cliffs.

Needing to rest before making the challenging descent into the valley, Anton sat on a rock that jutted out over the edge of the falls, looking downward. His long run had left him both hungry and out of breath, and he needed to be at his best for the final leg of the journey. Looking around, he found a weighty moss-covered rock under a nearby tree. It appeared to be relatively bug-free, and nothing seemed to be crawling about that might disturb him, so he sat next to it, crossed his legs, adopted the lotus position, and meditated for a few minutes. This revitalized his muscles and sharpened his mind enough to continue without the need of sustenance. It also fine-tuned his senses to everything around him.

By reaching out and feeling with his mind, and gathering as much information as possible with all of his senses, it was as if he had become a part of the region; this changed his initial impressions of the region's topography significantly, and he felt as though he had become one with his environment. He felt as if he'd spent a great deal of time here, though in fact it had only been a few minutes.

After a short time to rest, Anton sought the easiest path down the nearly sheer cliff. The trail wasn't entirely obvious, but to his trained eye, it stood out quite clearly. He easily located a narrow set of stairs and a steep path cut into the granite wall just below where he'd taken his short break. Quickly he climbed downward and hurried as fast as he could. The descent into the valley was arduous, but the steep angle gave the illusion that he traversed the distance quickly. The complexity of the path would be quite hazardous for any average person, but it presented no particular difficulty for a young Warrior. Stopping only once for just a moment to look at an interesting flower that grew near the falls, he intended to make his descent without further delay, and continued on. Finally, Anton arrived at the bottom without an incident.

The trail down the cliff had lead Anton quite a distance down the valley, therefore he had to follow the river back upstream toward the falls. The water looked cold and inviting, and he was tempted once again by the thought of its refreshing embrace. At his feet was the large pool of water at the base of the falls that he'd observed from far atop the cliff.

The beauty of the valley was immense; the most aromatic scents of exotic flowers filled Anton's lungs and his nose, intoxicating him; he felt as though he'd entered the Garden of Eden. As he partook of the enhanced atmosphere of the valley floor, he slowly strolled along, seemingly lost in the environment as he headed toward his destination upstream. It didn't take long before he finally arrived at the village of Tooloo.

CHAPTER 2

Encounters and Conflicts

AS ANTON ENTERED THE VILLAGE of Tooloo, the effect was much the same as when he had entered Picuris. Mothers grabbed their belongings and children, and people scurried in all directions, disappearing into thatched huts. No men were visible anywhere; Anton thought this peculiar. Genetically engineered into the DNA of the indigenous people, this predesigned illogical behavior still baffled him. He knew that genetic engineering drove the behavior of everyone on Methonias, and these villagers were no exception. That meant these people couldn't alter their conduct any more than he could alter his own without some mutation in their DNA, yet their behavior still toyed with his logic; it mystified him why the Clone Masters had chosen this characteristic for them; he had none of these traits designed into him.

In less than a minute, not one villager was visible anywhere. Anton quietly chuckled to himself and shook his head; the natives' timid behavior amused him. After everything was quiet, he walked to the center of the village, where a tall pole stood with a weather vane on top. He leaned against it and casually examined his surroundings, exhibiting an attitude of indifference as he waited for someone to show up, or something to happen. Nothing did; not one man appeared, the way Thorik had in Picuris.

After a few minutes, Anton's hunger seemed more important; not having eaten for hours, his stomach gnawed at him, so he looked around, searching for something edible. In front of a nearby hut, he noticed a large basket, laden with oddly shaped fruit. He quickly approached it, to inspect it more closely. It was yellow-skinned, and fluted like an acorn squash, and it looked quite appealing. Flies buzzed around him annoyingly, and he swatted at them relentlessly. Quickly, he reached down and selected a suitable-looking fruit, and proceeded to satisfy his hunger.

Next to the basket sat an urn of water with a long-handled ladle hooked on its lip. It was blighted by various insects—some drowned and floating, and some flying about. However, he was feeling dehydrated from the tropical heat and his hours of travel, so he scooped away as many of the pests as he could, ignored the rest, and then quickly refreshed his thirst.

"Maybe I can stir up some action," Anton quietly thought to himself, and then walked toward a nearby hut. He wondered what might be going on inside the many structures as he quickly finished his fruit; he did so because he wished to be free from the persistent insects buzzing around him. His disgust for the pests pushed him to swallow the tangy-sweet fruit nearly whole.

One of Anton's Masters' old phrases came to mind: It's difficult to guess your opponent's next move when he cannot be seen. If the opponent doesn't show himself, give him a reason to. He reasoned that this advice was appropriate to his current situation.

"Now, how can I get a reaction out of you people?" Anton said aloud. But nobody responded. In a dispassionate tone, he shouted: "Where is your chief? I would like to talk to him." He tossed the pit of his fruit to the ground. "Are you all so *afraid* of one man that you hide like *children*?"

"I'm not afraid of the likes of you, boy!" said a stern deep voice from behind.

"Damn it!" Anton cursed himself under his breath as he whirled around on one heel to face the man; he immediately adopted a defensive stance and prepared for battle. He couldn't believe he'd allowed someone to sneak up on him so easily; only fellow Warriors had ever done that in the past. Anton had dropped his guard for only a split second as he ate the fruit—yet it had been just enough to allow the mistake.

"Who are you, and what do you want of this village?" the man asked, while brandishing a katana menacingly. He exhibited no fear of Anton, and displayed complete control of the situation. "Be quick or you won't live to see the setting of the sun!" he said as he slashed his blade to-and-fro, with more than a simple villager's skill; the man was obviously challenging him.

It was immediately evident to Anton that this man was an expert in the uses of his weapon; his training appeared to be the equal of any Warrior, and surprisingly, his katana looked identical to those used at the Great Temple. It was about three feet long and had the Temple insignia built into the Supergrip Tsuka below the Tsuba; the weapon could only have come from the Methonian Temple.

"Are you here for good, or for ill? Ward yourself—I'm prepared to do battle!" threatened the man.

Raising his left hand, Anton responded to the tall man's advance. "My name is Anton, and my Masters assigned to me the task of ending your problems with the outlaws in this region. It surprises me to see you require any help at all, given your obvious skills! My Masters are wise to all the local troubles of this region, and deemed your burden worthy of my service. I'm not your enemy, I'm here to help!" Anton bowed slightly but did not take his eyes off the weapon or his opponent's eyes.

The man stood before him with an air of readiness, carefully sizing up his opponent. Then he noticed Anton's ring and he realized the profundity of the symbol. Suddenly his attitude changed, from combative to tolerant. Slowly lowering his katana, he knew it would be useless to engage in melee.

"You're a Warrior!" he conceded. "End my vexations indeed! Perhaps we'll see salvation yet! Come quickly, we've things to discuss before it is dark!" He waved for Anton to follow him toward the village center.

Cautiously, the villagers began to emerge from their hiding places as the two men walked across the center of the village and entered a nearby hut, quickly disappearing from view.

"You came at a very opportune time for Tooloo; it's true, we need your offer of help. The outlaws have terrorized us for a long time now, and life here is very difficult as a result. Why were you the only one sent to save us? Surely one *boy* isn't enough for our need! Most of all, can we trust you?"

"It was the choice of my Masters to send one." Anton bowed his head slightly, never removing his gaze from the man. His voice was gentle and reassuring. "It's the great wisdom of my Masters that one Warrior is more than sufficient to handle nearly any situation. It's their prudent vision that I should complete my training through this exercise, however long it may take. And I must complete it alone. Now, tell me of the predicament you face, so that I may best conceive a course of action."

The man gazed at Anton with a pronounced expression of disgust. Anton puzzled him and the man found it difficult to articulate any further response. As he listened to Anton's arrogant confidence, and realized the significance of his youth, a feeling of disillusionment marked his face. All he could see was a boy who admittedly hadn't finished his training. "Complete your training *alone?*" he echoed, with a scoffing tone. "*You* will decide what to do here? *You're* not *needed* here! We need a *real* Warrior—not some *boy* in training!" Again, he scoffed but said nothing more.

Gradually taking a deep breath, he gritted his teeth, and stifled his feelings as he slowly exhaled while leisurely circling around Anton.

"I wish to be straight with you, *Warrior*. I don't particularly like *any* of you—you disgust me!" He gave Anton a scowl then continued. "You always bring undesirable conflict. You aren't any different from the outlaws we have to face; the only significant difference is that you intend to help rather than harm—but you use *violence*, just as *they* do!" He looked long and hard at Anton and waited for a reaction. It was as if he was offering a challenge, or at the very least attempting to intimidate him to prove himself justified in his contempt.

"I think anyone raised without true parenting or real parents has absolutely no business making decisions for real people." He pointed his finger at Anton, as if accusing him of a crime, and wanted to be undisputed about their genetic differences. It was obvious that he had no respect for the product of the Clone Masters back at the Great Temple, and he wished no part in their involvement.

"Furthermore, I'd like to add that you Warriors are artificial. You're not really human! You lack ancestry, you lack the proper nurturing during your youth, and you lack feelings, *all* feelings—this is your greatest weakness and your ultimate flaw."

Anton just stood there and looked at him through narrow eyes, saying nothing at first. "I don't care if you like or dislike me," he replied. "I have a job to do and I intended to complete my mission, and then report back to my Masters. Nothing else matters to me except completing this mission and my training." He knew he was only antagonizing the man, but he didn't care for the accusations of inferiority. He didn't think he needed to defend himself or justify his heritage in any way.

With an angry look, Anton continued, arrogantly: "Just to clear things up a little, *you're* just as artificial as *me!*"

Looking at Anton sardonically, the man didn't say a word. Once again, he took a deep breath and slowly exhaled; his consternation was obvious. Realizing he needed to change the subject, the man tried a different approach.

"Ahem, I've forgotten my manners," he said. "Please, sit, and we'll discuss this... *predicament* further." The tension in the air felt like a tropical storm was imminent, but the man pointed toward a beautiful woven rug that was just large enough for both of them to sit on.

The rug had an intricate design, depicting a man standing atop a tall spire-like peak, his hand raised over his head in a fist, grasping what appeared to be golden light or energy that escaped through his fingers as if grasping a ball of fire. The detail was incredible; it almost seemed to Anton as if he was looking at a photograph rather than piece of woven fabric.

Bowing slightly, Anton sat on the rug while continuing to give it a contemplative review. The design of the rug intrigued him in a way he couldn't explain; it gave him an inexplicable feeling of deja vu. He then examined everything in the hut with thorough Methonian scrutiny. The walls and roof were made of dried grass; small timbers supported the structure, and one large timber stood in the center to uphold the framework of the roof. Many artful handmade tapestries covered the walls, each obviously depicting a different story. Woven with the same extravagance as the rug he sat upon, they amazed him with their impossible attention to detail. He wondered how such incredible artwork existed in the hut of such a primitive people in the middle of a jungle.

Tied between two poles on the other side of the hut were two hammocks, hung in bunk-bed fashion. Each was woven with the same extravagant attention to detail. Yet the hammocks seemed to be such a primitive way to sleep and they contradicted the beauty and expertise of the tapestries; functionality for the environment was obviously the main purpose.

The thing that interested Anton the most were the primitive weapons stored near the hut's entrance. There was a pike, a hand ax, and a simple wooden handmade quarterstaff. When they entered the hut, the man added his katana to this collection, setting it in a special stand that made it easy to retrieve when needed.

"I noticed when you entered the village that you were hungry," the man said. "I shall send for food; talking can be hard work too!" He chuckled stiffly for a moment, and his eyes smiled at Anton as he attempted to reduce the uneasiness the two men shared. He motioned to an attractive young girl, about Anton's age, who knelt just inside the doorway.

Bowing her head shyly, the girl said nothing, and then quietly left. A moment later, she returned with the same bowl of fruit and container of water Anton had eaten and drank from a few minutes earlier. Flies swarmed around her as she walked toward the two men and offered it to them.

Very few of the villagers wore clothing above the waist, and the young girl was no exception; the villagers lived in a tropical environment, and clothing was non-essential. She wore nothing but a grass skirt that covered her from the waist to the knees. Since Anton had rarely seen girls, he savored her feminine attributes with youthful male appreciation. Involuntarily, his body responded as virile young men do, and he gently heaved a sigh, though not really meaning to; he felt a pronounced surge of excitement and desire course through his body as hormones triggered nature's involuntary reaction.

Smiling slightly, the young girl noticed Anton's spontaneous reflex as she placed the bowl between the two men. She was slight of frame and immensely beautiful. She clearly resembled the man. She appeared to be approximately Anton's age, and that further intrigued him. Her long straight black hair hung down past her shoulders to the middle of her back; two strands of it formed a ring around her head, and a bead of turquoise held them together in the back. A fragrant native flower was pinned over her right ear, and it gave off an intoxicating odor; it looked identical to the larger ones Anton had stopped to look at on his way down the falls.

Anton noticed how sweet she smelled as she set the bowl down between the men, and when she did so, her short grass skirt brushed against his shoulder, increasing his attention. His eyes remained transfixed upon her as she bent over. He particularly observed a necklace she wore—it had three unusual, yet somehow familiar-looking stones hanging from it. Something about their rectangular shape intrigued him, yet he gave it little thought; he only had eyes for her. The necklace looped down and swung gently from side to side, drawing his attention directly to her chest. He watched her firm youthful breasts bounce fluidly when she moved about, and his eyes never left her while she performed the simple service.

When she finished, she bowed her head and then backed away, never once looking directly into Anton's eyes. However, as she stood, the two of them held each other's gaze for a mere heartbeat. Then she smiled shyly and looked away. Her eyes were coal black, and they twinkled when she smiled; their color clearly matched her glistening black hair. Anton suddenly realized the man had the same exact color of eyes and hair.

Watching Anton's fervent interest in the young girl, the man interrupted his persistent gaze by drawing away his attention. "That's my daughter Nelda. She is my only child. My wife was the first villager killed by the outlaws—but of this, I do not wish to speak. By the way, my name is Mahkeetah; I'm the chief of this village. I seem to have forgotten my manners—please forgive me! Our awkward meeting must be the cause of this."

"Thorik mentioned I should seek you," Anton said. His tone was formal as he acknowledged Mahkeetah, but his eyes remained transfixed upon Nelda.

Mahkeetah watched Anton's intense interest in Nelda and decided to ask him a question. "Do you plan on staying long?" He was obviously trying to draw his attention away from her, as the question had no real relevance. He didn't mind Anton's interest, but wondered precisely what his intentions were, other than the obvious.

"I'm here at your service," Anton said. "When my mission is complete, I'll leave." His response sounded wooden, as if he were answering a test question back at the Temple. He turned his gaze toward him. "I won't stay any longer than necessary—the only thing that matters is that I resolve your problems, and complete my mission." He sounded completely indifferent as he coolly regarded Mahkeetah.

"Then this is my wish as well," Mahkeetah said. He pointed at the bowl of fruit and encouraged Anton to select one; he then quickly grabbed one for himself. Picking up a special knife that sat alongside the bowl, he slowly cut it open, and then carefully placed a bite into his mouth, as if relishing it for the first time.

It seemed to Anton as though Mahkeetah delighted immensely in the preparation and consumption of the indigenous fruit. The other man revealed his enthusiasm by carefully adjusting the arrangement of everything around him, making sure each item was just where it needed to be. He worked purposefully and skillfully at preparing the fruit. Another sign was the extensive number and variety of food preparation utensils that lined the back of the hut. This somehow seemed out of character for a village chief. Anton expected that the members of the village would provide all such services for him.

"This is tara fruit; it will sustain a man for long periods of time when nothing else is available." Mahkeetah skillfully peeled the skin off the fruit with a small knife, and sliced long strips as he ate. "It is one of my favorites; I hope you find it equally pleasing!"

Following Mahkeetah's example, Anton picked up his fruit and mimicked the chief's method of preparation. He used a small knife to first peel and then cut the fruit into strips. This was preferable to how he'd eaten the fruit earlier, since the skin was quite tough. Again, he enjoyed the delectable flavor, and savored every bite. It seemed more of a treat than a meal, and it seemed to charge his body with instant energy, as if it were some form of enhanced nutrition.

After eating his fill, Anton announced he was ready to hear Mahkeetah's story. "This fruit is really good; it prepares me for your report." Again, his words sounded wooden, as if he'd become bored of his host. Taking a deep breath, he looked directly at Mahkeetah and folded his hands in his lap.

"Very well, then," Mahkeetah said. "Prepare yourself. It isn't a happy tale; I'll try to be as complete as I can in its telling." Manifestly uncomfortable, Mahkeetah looked at Anton out of the corner of his eye, adjusted his sitting position, and cleared his throat.

"Two years ago, in the early summer, six men arrived in our village. These men all looked very different from the people of the jungle. They wore clothing we didn't recognize, clothing that we decided could only have come from your Temple in the north. They carried no weapons of any kind, but nonetheless, we were frightened of them. Yet they did not harm us. Oddly, they asked if they could stay with us and live here in Tooloo."

Taking a deep breath, Mahkeetah fidgeted for a moment, then continued.

"A decision such as this required a meeting of all the village elders to determine if this was prudent. Most were skeptical about them, wondering why several men from the Temple would suddenly appear and desire to live in our village. It was evident to most of us that something was amiss. Oh, they sounded sincere—their leader, Luthian, said many nice things about jungle life, and wanting to live in paradise. He sweet-talked our women, many of whom enjoyed his company, at first. They felt he was quite charming." Mahkeetah sounded disgusted as he spoke, and shook his head in disbelief. Heaving a sigh, he continued.

"This particular meeting was a long one. In the end, we decided to allow them to stay, as long as they did their share of the work. Things were peaceful for several weeks. However, Luthian eventually became aware of our village's fortune. Since he was from the Temple, we assumed it would be trivial. Yet he coveted it nonetheless. This perplexed the council. We were at a loss as to *why*."

Looking puzzled, Anton asked: "Just what was it he wanted? What do you have that they could want?"

"Patience, young Warrior, I'm getting to that," Mahkeetah said, sounding slightly irritated. "As I was saying, Luthian desired our meager wealth—a few jewels we have inherited. Truthfully, they're only simple crystals—not as nice as that ring *you* wear." Mahkeetah pointed at Anton's hand and held his gaze, making sure he was paying attention.

"My daughter wears these jewels as a symbol of her status among my people. In those days she generally wore them in times of celebration—however, she wears them more often now." Mahkeetah smiled slightly, closing his eyes and nodding once, indicating his pride for her.

"In addition, the strangers from the Temple—we call them the outlaws—coveted my katana, our only means of superior defense. Luthian demanded all of this from us, saying that harm would befall us if we chose not to comply. Instantly, we became slaves to their domination, as they threatened to torture my people if we didn't comply with their demands."

For a moment, Mahkeetah faltered. He tipped his head back and took a deep breath.

With a look of complete disbelief, Anton scowled at the chief. "How is it only six men could control the entire village? I saw how you handled that katana; only someone with extensive training wields it so! Where did you learn your skills? More importantly, why didn't you *use* them?"

"I was getting to that!" Again, Mahkeetah raised his voice angrily and stared at Anton for a moment. "We found out that the men *weren't* helpless. Tricky they were, not helpless. As I was about to say, they abducted my wife, and held her prisoner somewhere outside the village. Thus, they had the power to control us." Shaking his head, Mahkeetah had an expression of intense contempt.

Slightly embarrassed, but not shaken, Anton nodded that he understood. "I'm sorry, please go on."

With a stern look, Mahkeetah continued. "The katana is the strength and symbol of my people, so naturally I couldn't part with it. But most of all, giving it away would have given the other men complete dominance over us, and I feared for the life of my wife."

Mahkeetah's eyes darted around, as if the telling of his story distressed him deeply. His hands fidgeted in his lap, seemingly looking for a way to assuage his anguish. Yet they found nothing but air for comfort. It was as if he wished to fight, but had nobody to battle.

"Soon after taking my wife, the strangers again became restless, and started committing acts of violence against the people of my village, demanding we immediately give them all of what little we had, and to serve them as if they were our masters. Everyone abhorred them."

Taking a deep breath, Mahkeetah seemed to relax slightly.

"Then it happened—our chance for freedom. One particular day, these men drank too much tara wine as they meandered around the village, committing their offenses. Thus, we were able to capture them when they became too drunk to stop us." Mahkeetah seemed proud of the victory, yet he did not seem satisfied; an overtone of seriousness overshadowed him.

"We demanded to know where they'd taken my wife and held her captive. It took some... *persuasion*, but finally one of them gave in and told us where to look. With great speed, we hurried to this place, only to find her lifeless body. It was evident they'd killed her many days before, and there was evidence of… well, I won't describe to you what we found." Mahkeetah heaved a sigh and a tear ran down his cheek. For a moment, he fell silent, and then he gritted his teeth and growled angrily.

"We bound and blindfolded all six men, and took them many leagues north, abandoning them on a mountain cliff. This place has only one way up and down by the use of a platform that can be winched. There is no escape." A look of victory marked Mahkeetah's visage, and for the first time he smiled for a brief moment.

"Then, as we prepared to leave, we warned them never to return to our village, or we wouldn't be as gentle the next time. We're a simple people— we loathe even banishment. Yet the village elders decided it to be the best way we might free ourselves of these lawless men." Again, Mahkeetah seemed agitated, as if he had something even worse to tell, or was getting nearer to an important point.

"In our simple arrogance, we thought that would be the end of it. But about a month ago, they returned. We have no idea how they were able to escape, or find their way back to our village. Upon their arrival, they again demanded I give them the katana and my daughter's jewelry, or they would kill my people. As I said, without the katana, we would be at their mercy—therefore, I wouldn't give them what they asked for; I just couldn't. When they left, two of the men captured a very beautiful young girl named Naomie; she was my friend Tarna's daughter. This had a profound impact on everyone in the village; everyone naturally believed they'd kill her, and do even worse…" Mahkeetah adjusted his sitting position, revealing his discomfort.

"The next morning, as the girls went to the pool at the base of the falls to retrieve water, they found her; it was just as we'd feared, she was dead. It was a devastating blow to everyone, as we could not bear the thought of such evil. As I said before, we are a simple people. Evil thoughts aren't part of our lives—at least, not until the outlaws came!" Mahkeetah's deep voice became increasingly hoarse. Another tear ran from the corner of his eye, and he coughed violently for a moment. His hand shaking, he grasped the ladle of water and poured it over his head, and then rubbed his face and washed away his tearful convulsions; throatily, he continued.

"Each day after that, Luthian returned with his demands, proclaiming that more of us would die!" Tears now streamed freely down Mahkeetah's face, as the story became more difficult to tell. "That was *five* lives ago! I can never give in to these... *men*," he spat, "and I will *never* give up my katana! They'll have even *more* power over us if I do!" He was nearly hysterical at this point.

"They'll return tonight, and I fear yet another death. You must stop them! I cannot stand to see another one of my people die!" Mahkeetah rested his face in his hands for a moment, and then quickly removed them and looked at Anton, as if relinquishing the responsibility to him. "I cannot kill them, it is forbidden; I can only *defend* myself. It is our law," he mumbled.

Anton listened without emotion, and without saying a word. The death of these villagers meant nothing to him; he'd seen death many times before. As far as he was concerned, they were merely another group of primitive people in the tropics used as a test environment for his training. Yet somehow, the story touched his genetic code, striking a part of him he hadn't expected it to reach, something that existed deep inside him. It seemed to awaken an urgent need to fight for the village, to help the villagers even if it meant his own death. This was a sensation he'd never before felt. He knew what it was, it was the base DNA code built inside all Warriors; a spark of genuine need invoked its power over him.

As Mahkeetah fell silent, Anton finally spoke.

"One thing still perplexes me. It seems my help isn't needed here; you have a very good skill with a superior weapon! Again, I wonder why you aren't able to handle this problem yourself!" He looked at Mahkeetah with an expression of both curiosity and disgust, as if to say: "You haven't revealed the truth about yourself."

"It is paradoxical to possess a weapon such as yours without using it for its designed purpose. Your problem was destined by your inaction and your ludicrous laws; your lack of initiative perpetuates their desire to continue killing. You should stand up for yourself, like a man. You disgust me! What I find most disturbing is that you still haven't answered my question: How did you learn to use your katana with such skill? Only Warriors have this expertise! In reality, this whole problem is *your* fault!"

Mahkeetah fell silent. He looked at Anton for a moment with contempt. His hands continued to fidget in his lap, and then, hesitantly, he replied. "I cannot take a life; I haven't got what it takes to do so. Our law states that I must forfeit my own life if I should intentionally do so, even in my own defense, or that of the villagers. Our laws confine me."

This contradiction flummoxed Anton. To him, it was completely illogical. His training taught him to care little for the life of an enemy, and to defeat the opposition as quickly as possible, and by any means necessary. As a rule, this meant simply to kill the opponent. Why would anyone learn to use a weapon such as Mahkeetah had, and then never use it for its designed function? Why would anyone invite this very predicament? The paradox grew with each query, but Anton let his questions and these contradictions go unanswered. He needed to concentrate on completing his mission, and for now that meant gaining pertinent intelligence.

"I won't pretend to understand you, Mahkeetah. The training a Warrior receives mandates we *use* our skills, not *squander* them the way *you* do. So, allow me to ask: will all six men be coming tonight?" Anton's tone was indifferent again.

"I'm all too aware of your *rules of training!*" Mahkeetah snapped. Then he caught himself and pinched his lips together, holding back what he'd intended to say. For a moment, he sat there silently.

"They always send three." Slowly, carefully, Mahkeetah observed Anton's quizzical expression. Clenching his teeth together, he shook his head; it was obvious he was angry with himself for his sudden lack of restraint. He waited to see Anton's reaction.

Anton's eyes darted at Mahkeetah's and narrowed. He noted the other's carefully stated reply; for a moment, he stared at him. Then he shook his head and dismissed his response as irrelevant. Again, his logical reasoning left him perplexed and confused. How was it possible that three men would be more than a match for an entire village? This situation seemed completely ridiculous. They didn't need a Methonian Warrior to solve their problem—they simply needed courage! Taking a deep breath, Anton set aside his disconcerted feelings and continued.

"Three? It seems to me that this is a simple matter to handle. When they arrive, I'll greet them alone. Make sure everyone is out of sight— this seems to be what you people do best anyway." He gestured with the back of his hand, as if dismissing Mahkeetah and his fellow villagers, and saying that the encounter would be of no consequence to him. Yet somewhere in the back of his mind, the question of self-reliance nagged him. Why couldn't these people handle the problem for themselves? They were armed, and there were many of them! Nevertheless, he knew that the intent of his mission was to complete his final training—that was the only important point.

"Just as you determined when you entered the village, everyone who comes here decides that Tooloo is a safe place to live," Mahkeetah said as he looked at Anton with uncertainly. A certain amount of distrust arose within him, and an impression that the young Warrior was overconfident overwhelmed him. He knew Anton didn't really care about anyone—he was, after all, a Warrior, and his attitude was common for all Warriors of his age. Anton's cold detachment worried him.

"Do you require any assistance?" Mahkeetah said. "If there's *anything* we might do to *help...*" His slight sarcasm was meant to prompt Anton into revealing what he was thinking. A feeling of disgust shot through him like a jolt of electricity, and he held his tongue so as not to reveal his mistrust.

"I can handle these three; they're foolish men," Anton said, arrogantly. "Foolish men make elementary mistakes; I'll exploit this, and I'll defeat them."

Anton's arrogance and indifference intensified Mahkeetah's apprehensions. "Very well, then," he said. "We've settled this matter. It will be dark in a little while—let us prepare for their arrival." Standing up, Mahkeetah walked towards the exit. He knew time was growing short, so he motioned for Anton to follow. Together they quickly exited the hut. He couldn't get over how young and overconfident Anton was, and how easily the danger he faced could escalate. Yet he knew he had no other choice but to trust him for now.

Together, they walked toward the village center, and many of the villagers suddenly appeared and gathered around them, anticipating an explanation. A sense of urgency filled the air, and a concerned chattering erupted. Mahkeetah held up his left hand to draw attention to himself, and immediately everyone fell silent.

"Tonight, there will be no death! This young Warrior has come from the Great Temple in the north to end our fear of the outlaws!" Mahkeetah spoke loud enough that everyone could hear him, but not so loud that his voice would carry out of the assemblage and beyond the village.

A cheer from the congregation rang in the air; the prospect they might soon be free of the outlaws' tyranny made the crowd mumble, giddy with anticipation. Mahkeetah quickly raised both hands and motioned for everyone to quiet down.

"For this to be accomplished, all of you must remain in your huts until the confrontation is over. If everyone will disperse, nobody will be harmed today by the outlaws." He attempted to convince the villagers to put all their trust into the arrogant boy, even though he himself did not share that trust.

A loud rumble of concern arose among the adults present; it was as if the villagers also lacked confidence in the strange young man, or mistrusted his methods. He was unknown to everyone in the village, and they hadn't yet measured his character, capabilities, and capacity for violence. The young girls, however, looked upon Anton with favorable smiles; they seemed enthusiastic to see him, as if he offered them something he'd yet to comprehend.

Glaring at the young girls, Mahkeetah silenced their giggles and smiles; he had a natural ability to command, and it was obvious why he was the Chief of Tooloo. His temperament easily inspired confidence in his decisions, and quickly swayed people to accept them. After a moment or two, the villagers dispersed and quickly vanished.

Once again, Mahkeetah and Anton stood alone in the village center, looking at each other. They had a shared understanding of commitment and of the imminent finality to their problem, and they clearly had opposing perspectives on the agreement they'd made. Mahkeetah felt as though the fate of the village was in jeopardy, and Anton felt as though his assignment would soon conclude. Either way, they'd committed themselves, for good or for ill.

"I would like a few minutes alone to prepare myself mentally for the arrival of the *barbarians*," Anton said, emphasizing the word to demonstrate his superiority. He was aloof, as if knowing he was more than a match for the coming danger. "I'd also appreciate it if you didn't show yourself when they arrive, no matter what happens. Do you agree?"

"I will, as long as you remain alive," Mahkeetah said, giving Anton a sardonic look, wondering if he'd made a grave error. With a slight nod of his head, he held Anton's gaze for a moment longer, emphasizing his mistrust. Then he departed.

Shrugging Mahkeetah's attitude aside, Anton sat with his back against the pole in the village center and concentrated on the upcoming ordeal. Mental preparation before a battle was as important to a Warrior as the combat itself, and he used his time to formulate a strategy. A calming sensation filled his thoughts, and he relaxed every muscle of his body, cleared his mind of unnecessary thoughts, and sharpened his perception, focusing his awareness on his surroundings. He then mentally prepared his body for each movement he would make. A calmness and clarity filled his mind and body; it echoed so strongly that his muscles felt as if they were about to explode into a fierce frenzy of combat; he was completely ready for battle.

About a half an hour later, he heard voices in the distance moving closer. Fine-tuning his Methonian hearing, he precisely singled out the exact sounds he wanted to hear; he screened out all the jungles sounds, ignoring the wind, the loud chatter of the birds, and, with a certain degree of difficulty, the insects. Then, suddenly, he identified three distinct and separate people approaching; a few moments later, he watched them enter the village. Slowly he stood up and waited for them to make a move.

"Well now, are *you* tonight's offering?" asked the first man. The two following behind him laughed as if they had no other thoughts but his.

"Looks like we'll have some *fun* with this skinny little boy they've left as a... *sacrifice!*" responded the second man, and a roar of laughter erupted from the three men.

"Wait, I don't remember seeing him before. Who are you?" asked the third man guardedly.

Anton recognized the men's clothing. Without question they were from the Temple's taxi service; they were Aerocraft pilots and crew. This surprised him, yet he didn't flinch from his ready stance. The three men slowly moved closer until Anton could smell the putrid breath of the first man. Another small round of serious laughter rumbled from the three. The first man quickly threw a punch in Anton's direction.

That was all Anton needed. As the man's fist flew toward him, he bowed backwards, grabbed the moving arm with both hands, forced the momentum of the intended punch away from him, and twisted the arm behind the back of the man, pushing it beyond its limit. A distinct popping noise filled the air. The man's clavicle suddenly projected through his skin, and blood flowed freely from the wound.

Simultaneously, with a skillful fluid motion, Anton kicked backwards, catching the second man's jaw with the heel of his foot. There was another sharp pop as the jawbone shattered beneath the skin. The man fell sharply to the ground, grasping at his face. He wailed an earsplitting shriek.

Whirling around, Anton shifted his weight from one leg to the other. He stood facing the third man in a ready stance and waited for him to make a move. The man threw a punch. Anton avoided it by tilting sideways, and the man's fist completely missed him. Anton delivered a kick to the man's chest. His heel connected with the man's sternum, shattering it inward. Blood oozed from the man's mouth as he fell to his knees, lay on his side, and writhed on the ground, clutching his chest. His breath, inhibited by the blood and pain, came in gurgling gasps. Anton pivoted around, looking for any sign of continued aggression. Then he stood in a ready stance over the three men, making sure the fight was over. It was evident they were unable to continue. A Warrior's training didn't allow him merely to win a fight; he had to destroy his enemy to prevent any further action. Slowly each outlaw forced himself to his feet, clutching the damaged part of his body. Their eyes pleaded for him stop.

The ring of crystal on Anton's finger glowed brightly; its luminescence permeated the atmosphere, revealing who Anton was. He was suddenly the center of everyone's attention. Taking a quick glance at it himself, Anton felt as though it was just a shade darker than it had been earlier that day. But it hadn't yet turned gold. He was sure it appeared darker—or had it? How else should he measure his success after a victorious fight? A slight shiver ran up and down his spine at the idea that it had changed. Maybe it was just his desire to see it change, or maybe he perceived something new about himself—he wasn't sure.

Suddenly sagacious, Anton realized that using his special skills to defend these people gave him a sense of purpose. Perhaps his creators had intended this from the beginning—for him to enjoy helping people with his abilities. His confidence grew as he considered his importance, and his heart filled with pride.

The three injured combatants stared at his hand, and the ring glowed more brilliantly, imbuing the atmosphere with its yellow luminescence. The day was waning into evening, and darkness was not far off. Anton's ring radiated as if it was an artifact of magical power, and he stood dominantly over the three destroyed men.

Fear stretched across their faces as they realized that Anton was a Warrior from the Great Temple—not a simple villager. Their failure to recognize his garb, unique physical appearance, and the symbol of his origin had given them a false sense of security. Perhaps they had been away from civilization for too long, or maybe they hadn't expected a Warrior would intervene in their small part of the planet, or perhaps the differences of Anton's particular clothing from years gone past had prevented their ability to see him for who he was. Most likely it was the late evening shadows that precluded their lack of recognition. But Anton recognized what the real reason was—these men were entirely ignorant.

"You're a Warrior!" the man with the broken arm said, straining to speak through his severe pain. He gasped as he realized the predicament the three of them faced. All the confidence he'd had just moments before changed to fear and repulsion. "I didn't recognize you!" Shock covered his face.

Quickly returning his attention to his enemies, Anton extinguished the glow of his ring. Bowing slightly, he kept a close eye on each of them. "You're correct, and I have a message for your leader, Luthian," Anton sneered. "Tell him not to send his servants tomorrow, tell him to come himself. I wish to negotiate his future activities here, in Tooloo. You're dismissed!"

Hobbling away as quickly as their crippled bodies allowed, the three men obeyed Anton's command. Blood marked the area of combat, and they left a trail of it as they left. Anton watched as they disappeared from view. Then he returned to Mahkeetah's hut. As he entered, he looked for something to drink, and took a dip of water from the nearby urn.

A feeling of transcendence flowed through him, and he exhibited a smirk of self-assurance as he nonchalantly gazed at the chief.

"They may return tonight," he said, "but I doubt it. I'm sure that *someone* will return by tomorrow evening." Dipping the ladle again, he quenched his thirst, and then seated himself on the rug next to Mahkeetah, just as they'd done before.

Picking up another tara fruit, Anton returned to eating, as if nothing had happened. Immediately his attention fell upon Nelda, who sat quietly in the corner of the hut, motionless; she stared at the floor as if waiting for something. Hesitating for a moment, he gazed longingly at her beauty. He was filled with intense desire, and then he realized Mahkeetah was watching him very closely.

With a huff, Mahkeetah offered some bread from a basket. Just as Anton reached for it, the other man quickly withdrew it for a moment, glaring. After their eyes made contact, he again offered the basket. The bread was still warm and fresh, and Anton unconcernedly helped himself to a small loaf, completely ignoring the other man's mood.

"Please, *enjoy*!" Mahkeetah said to Anton, sarcastically. Sighing, he then nodded toward Nelda, as if asking her to do something.

Quickly, she left the hut, and then returned a moment later. Looking at Anton out of the corner of her eye, she added a plate of dried meat to the selection of available entrees, and bowed her head toward Mahkeetah.

Snatching a rather large morsel, Anton worked at softening it with his teeth. It was tough and salty, but had a nice flavor. He wondered what type of creature it came from.

"I disapprove of your callous brutality, Anton," Mahkeetah scolded, looking upon him with disgust. "I fear you've escalated the problem rather than solved it. If you were a member of this village, you too would be banished as an outlaw for such aggression. You Warriors solve all your problems by being as bad as *them*." He stabbed his finger toward the village square. "I disapprove of your training and your Masters. The end doesn't justify the means!" He hesitated for a moment, then added: "Don't you believe you may become what you hate? Doesn't violence beget more violence?"

"We fight for what's right," Anton said. "We fight the good fight on the side of justice. Sometimes you have to stand up to evil, and cast it down. If you're unwilling to, evil will surely prevail and imprison you." Anton sounded as if he were reciting the words of his Masters. He did not look at Mahkeetah as he spoke, and he continued chewing on the dried meat, trying to soften it.

Swallowing, Anton went on. "In order to defeat your opponent, you have to use the same tactics—or violence, as you put it. This is how freedom is won. Oh, and by the way—those men wore the uniform of the Temple's air taxi service. Didn't you recognize that?"

Looking directly at the Warrior, Mahkeetah was silent and anxious. He considered Anton's question, shuffled his feet, and then heaved a heavy sigh and bit his tongue.

In an attempt to change the subject, Mahkeetah continued cautiously. "Just what do you think we should do when they return? Don't you realize that now they have an even *greater* reason to harm us; as you pointed out, they worked for *your* Masters!" He needed Anton to understand that his actions had escalated their predicament; he knew that winning the battle was a declaration of war, not just a simple engagement with the enemy. More importantly, he had known all along that the outlaws had come from the same place Anton had. This point only intensified his personal misgivings.

"We've debated that there might be more than the original six of these outlaws," Mahkeetah continued. "This question haunts us. We know that they could *never* have escaped from the prison atop the mountain without help. It stands to reason that someone else must have aided them in some way, therefore it's only logical there are more of them."

It was apparent to Mahkeetah that Anton hadn't thought of every consequence yet, and that it was just as the village elders had feared— that Anton wouldn't consider all aspects of his actions, and that he was too young to understand what he was truly up against.

"I've been thinking about that—it isn't important," Anton said, continuing to stuff his mouth, and speaking between bites. He smacked his lips, and saliva ran from the corner of his mouth, and then down his chin. Wiping it away with the back of his hand, he continued. "It's time for a plan, and I have some ideas; is there some place that the villagers can hide nearby, outside the village?"

Anton seemed more intent upon filling his stomach than actually listening to the magnitude of Mahkeetah's words, and this infuriated the other man. With another heavy sigh of antipathy, he responded firmly.

"*No!* Wait, perhaps there is. There's a cave in the hillside under the waterfalls. The water conceals it, and I'm sure the outlaws are unaware of its existence; we keep it a closely guarded secret. Due to the shape of the bedrock, the untrained eye can't easily discern it without some knowledge of where to look. I must tell you, though, this cave isn't a safe place to hide and we *will not leave* our village. To conceal ourselves in that cave is madness; don't expect anyone to agree to it, it will not be done! Besides, it's *far* too small!"

"But you *must*," Anton responded. "The outlaws will be looking for vengeance when they return, and you'll be safer if you hide. I'll handle the rest myself. I met Thorik, and I saw how several of the huts in Picuris were burned; I believe Tooloo isn't the only village these outlaws pillage."

"I don't *care* about Picuris!" Mahkeetah said. "We *will not leave!* We'll die *in* our village rather than *cower* in fear!" Mahkeetah slapped the ground with the palm of his hand as he spoke. He didn't like handing his responsibilities over to a boy he didn't know or trust— especially a Warrior from the Temple. His anger flooded his heart as they discussed the villagers' fate.

"If you aren't here when they return, they won't be *able* to harm anyone," Anton argued. He wanted to handle things his own way, and he didn't care about Mahkeetah's objections. The fact that this primitive villager was arguing with him at all showed his obvious ignorance, and his lack of Methonian training.

"I want them to be focused on me," Anton went on, "and I don't want them to be able to harm anyone else. This will make my job much easier. I'll finish this once and for all, and then I'll leave."

"You mean you want to *kill* them! And you don't want any witnesses! This is *deplorable*, and it's unacceptable! They'll burn my village down; you can't stop them from doing that! They'll take what they want! This they've threatened before and done! It is a simple equation!" Mahkeetah slammed his fist on the ground again, making a dull thud. Anger showed like fire in his eyes. He looked determinedly at Anton, trying to assess just how much to trust him. What little he had was fragile at best—he didn't like a young, brash, and arrogant boy trying to tell him what to do with his village, and with the lives of his villagers.

"I'll remain here to prevent any harm to your homes," Anton said. "I'm more than a match for these simple barbarians." His response was nonchalant, conveying his complete confidence and dismissing ahead of time any argument Mahkeetah might choose to make. He continued to chew on the last bit of his dried meat, evincing little interest in continuing the debate.

Gritting his teeth for a moment, Mahkeetah restrained any further response. His face turned red as his rage escalated; he couldn't believe how this conversation had progressed, and it left him at odds with himself. On the one hand, he knew Anton could likely handle any further violence from the outlaws. On the other hand, he despised the use of the violence, and there was always the risk of the village being set on fire.

"I will sleep on your words, Warrior," he said. "I'm reluctantly grateful for your service today. However, as I said, I disapprove of your methods; I'm just glad that there were no deaths. You're asking much of me and my village. Your actions have raised the stakes, and now I fear for *all* of our lives. Don't you start to thinking that merely breaking a few bones will be enough to save everyone! You don't realize who these people really are..."

Mahkeetah closed his mouth, stood up, and walked over to the doorway of the hut. Taking a deep breath and letting it out slowly, he lowered his gaze to the ground outside and shook his head. He put his hands on his hips and pressed his lips together. After a few moments, he returned to the rug, but didn't sit. He looked pleadingly at Anton, as if he had something important to say, yet was at a loss for the words. At the same time, he needed Anton's help, though that help came at too steep a price, and he feared the problem had escalated beyond his ability to pay it.

Anton sighed heavily. He was tired of the conversation, and increasingly anxious. His demeanor, and the look in his eye, stated clearly that he didn't like Mahkeetah's refusal of implicit trust. He believed the chief should unquestioningly accept any advice he offered; furthermore, he felt in complete control of the situation, and impervious to failure. He knew he could handle any situation that might arise. Besides, nobody in this region of Methonias could match his abilities. Yet Mahkeetah didn't instantly accept his suggestions as he expected. This was irritating. Mahkeetah seemed very foolish.

The two held each other's gaze for what seemed an eternity, and then Anton broke the silence. "Very well—we shall discuss this tomorrow. Where might I rest tonight?"

"A hammock shall be brought in; relax while I send for it." Mahkeetah motioned to Nelda; with a slight nod of her head, she left the hut to accommodate her father's request. A few moments later, she returned, burdened with a heavy bundle slung over her shoulder.

As Mahkeetah and Nelda worked to secure the hammock between two poles in the back of the hut, Anton watched the young girl's breasts jiggle and bounce. His masculine urges filled him with desire. He longed for her, and his youthful body displayed his interests. Lustfully, he couldn't control his hormones as they boiled inside of him. Taking a deep breath, he shook his head slightly, and suppressed his urges as best he could.

After the others had finished tying the hammock into position, Anton realized just how much he needed to rest; this precluded anything else, even his lustful urges. He quickly resigned himself to slumber, and climbed into the makeshift bed. There he lay awake for some time, reflecting on the day's events; he had much to consider.

Settling into his own hammock, Mahkeetah followed Anton's example. He ignored his guest completely, and hoped his misgivings about him wouldn't keep him awake all night. He swiftly dozed off, filling the hut with the sound of unbridled snoring.

After the two men retired, Nelda also lay down to sleep, with a slight smile on her lips. She lay on her side with both hands under the side of her face, and fantasized about a future with a fit and handsome young Warrior from the Great Temple. Eventually, she too fell asleep, smiling.

CHAPTER 3

Changing of the Guard

MORNING ARRIVED QUICKLY; IT SEEMED to Anton as if it was within the wink of an eye. He woke up abruptly and swung his legs over the edge of the hammock. He noticed Mahkeetah was still asleep, and that Nelda had already arisen and left. Quietly, he stood, walked over to the window of the hut, and looked out at the magnificent morning. The sun was just beginning to tint the eastern sky; it highlighted the swirls of clouds from underneath with exquisite colors of pastel orange and light yellow. A feeling of peace filled Anton's heart as he admired the vestiges of the early dawn. Filled with anxiety, he could hardly wait to go outside for a better view of the natural beauty.

"Paradise," Anton mumbled to himself. "It's simply paradise."

The sounds of Mahkeetah's snoring filled the hut, distracting Anton from his peaceful mood; it spoiled the sensation that the beautiful morning yielded. For a moment, Anton stood and looked and the chief, who lay on his side, facing the back wall of the hut. An uneasy feeling about the conversation he'd had the night before continued to disturb him, so he decided to clear his thoughts and step outside.

Looking into the early morning atmosphere, Anton saw wisps of white and colored clouds littering the sky overhead, giving him a sensation of renewal. The cool morning breeze lightly caressed his skin and chilled him slightly; it felt good after the previous day's warmth. Anton was quite skinny, and therefore without any particular insulation—yet his genetically engineered constitution was superior to that of any normal human. He was able to endure and adapt to far more extreme temperatures. His muscles were highly toned, and when flexed, expanded beyond that of an average human—though they were not unnaturally enormous. The early morning sun gleamed off his tight and toned skin, giving him a lambent sheen, as if he had rubbed light oil over his body.

Might as well jog for a while, Anton thought to himself. Taking a moment to stretch his muscles, he placed the palms of his hands together and pushed, and then started to jog in place. The chill feeling of the morning air ceased almost immediately. With his muscles warmed, he headed north along the trail to the river, and looked for the cave Mahkeetah had described.

The trees were alive with macaws, parrots, toucans, and many other tropical birds; they were busy making quite a racket from high above, and flew about looking for a morning meal. It felt to Anton as if they led him down the trail toward the falls, guiding him with a winged rainbow of colors. As he arrived at the waterfall, he was quite surprised to see the air filled with hundreds of birds.

Anton also saw several of the young village girls there with urns; they filled them full of water from the large pool below the falls, and then carried them back to the village for the daily supply. Looking around he finally saw Nelda dipping an urn in the pool along with the rest of the girls. She wore a shawl tied over her shoulders to keep herself warm in the chill morning air, as did the other girls. This disappointed him for a moment. He'd hoped to catch a glimpse of all their feminine charms. Then he realized that as the day got warmer, their shawls would quickly disappear.

Casually, he walked toward Nelda as she filled her urn. She stood bent over the water, facing away from him. But she had noticed the eyes of the other girls looking in his direction, and understood that someone unusual had arrived at the pool. She knew it could only be Anton. When he neared her, she saw his turbid reflection on the water beside her. A slight smile extended across her lips, but she didn't acknowledge his arrival, and forcibly suppressed her delight.

"Good morning, Nelda," Anton said. "How are you this fine day?" He sounded awkward as he greeted her, shyly offering a warm and genuine smile.

"I am not permitted to talk to you," she said. "I must fill the urn with water and take it back to the village before breakfast." Her reply was dry and dismissive, but not displeased.

Anton had expected she would be happy to see him, but she sounded as if he were interfering with her responsibilities. He couldn't help feeling disappointed she had dismissed him so quickly; after all, he was a Warrior!

"When might I be... permitted to speak with you?" Anton tried to sound polite, yet his disappointment was evident. He really wished to have an opportunity to spend some time with her, since he had never been able to talk to a girl in earnest before. He ached for the opportunity, and wouldn't take no for an answer.

"I will be free from my duties in the early afternoon," she replied. "If you wish to talk to me then, I might return here when most of the children come to play. I can't stop you from doing as you choose." She hefted the urn and placed it on her shoulder, supporting it with both hands. It looked too heavy for such a slight woman. But surprisingly, she managed to carry it with grace and strength.

"May I help you carry the water back to the village?" asked Anton. He would do anything to get her to open up to him. He noticed how she leaned at an angle to balance the weight, and he knew he could impress her with his remarkable strength if given an opportunity.

"I must manage for myself," Nelda replied, and smiled at him for his proposal.

The men of the village never offered to do women's chores, and his offer of help was a proposition Nelda appreciated more than Anton could know. But the village's strict rules of conduct required her to decline.

"It isn't permitted for you to help me," Nelda added. "This is girls' work; you must allow me to do it alone."

Most of the village girls had already left the pool, and Nelda quickly followed them, trying to catch up. She secretly hoped Anton might continue to walk with her, ignoring her request. She knew she couldn't stop him from making his own choices. Soon, she caught up with the other girls, and was disappointed that he remained behind at the pool. In a heartbeat, she disappeared.

Scrutinizing the area around the pool carefully, Anton looked for any sign of enemies. His superior eyesight coupled with his extraordinary thought processes allowed him to delve deep into the jungle—beyond the normal range average humans could see. Satisfied that no threats were there, he continued with his search for the cave Mahkeetah had spoken of the night before. Casually, he made his way over to the falls, and found a path leading over some slippery rocks that went behind the wall of water. A normal human would miss the invisible path, but Anton discerned it with ease after having been told it was there.

Behind the falls, Anton looked around, marveling at what he'd discovered. The shape of the cavity resembled an amphitheater, and it appeared to be manmade. The sound of the falling water roared and echoed off the walls, making it nearly impossible to hear anything else. Anton wanted to examine it in depth, but he needed more time. After a quick but thorough inspection, he located the entrance to the cave; it was cleverly concealed in the back of the amphitheater and nearly indistinguishable in the dark wet rock wall. It was little more than a crack at best. It was naturally disguised, hidden from view to all but a trained eye, or someone who knew that it existed.

As Anton entered the cave, he carefully scrutinized it as quickly as he could. The light here was almost nonexistent and made it nearly impossible to see anything. The early morning sun angled through the waterfall from the east and illuminated the cavity of the cave; it provided light with long shadows from the trees that stretched over the pool, but by midday, the natural light would be at its best since it would shine directly from the south. He wished he had a glowrod, but quickly discarded the thought. In the end, he determined the minimal light would suit his needs.

"Might as well go back," Anton thought to himself. "That's all I can accomplish for now."

As he jogged back to the village, he had the strangest sensation that someone was watching him. He looked around as he ran, but seeing no one, he cast the feeling aside. Having examined the area earlier, he was satisfied everything was safe, and decided his feelings were perhaps misguided, yet the sensation nagged at him nonetheless.

As Anton entered the village, he saw people scurrying around, performing typical morning chores. Directly, he entered Mahkeetah's hut and saw him sitting and eating breakfast. Nelda too was eating her morning meal, and stood up to make room for Anton to sit upon the rug. She looked ravishing, and he smiled as she moved toward the back of the hut.

"You get up early, *Warrior*." Mahkeetah motioned for Anton to sit beside him and pointed at the bowl of food. His comment was dry and free of emotion, and he barely gave Anton a glance as he spoke with his mouth full. He seemed far more interested in eating breakfast than in administering social graces.

"I went to look at the cave," Anton said. "I believe it's sufficient for our needs. It appears there's enough room for the entire village to hide." He'd confidently concluded that his calculations were indisputable, and that Mahkeetah should blindly accept them.

"I've been thinking about that," the other replied. "Perhaps your idea is valid. We will try it if the village elders will approve it in council this morning." He gazed at Anton through narrowed slits. His eyes belied his trust in his plan, and a distinct lack of confidence marked his face.

"*Please*, I must insist, have some bread and some parita fruit. I noticed you had sampled some earlier." Mahkeetah again urged Anton to eat, and closely watched him as he complied.

In the bowl of fruit, Anton saw more of the wonderful parita fruit he'd enjoyed the day before. The bowl also included another fruit he hadn't seen, so he decided to try it. Picking up the purple pear-shaped specimen, he examined it with a look of bewilderment; it was about three inches in diameter and looked quite unusual. After a moment, he hungrily consumed it. He found the flesh soft and juicy, and entirely unlike the parita. Again, Anton felt surprised by this fruit's incredible sweetness. He looked at Mahkeetah, nodded his approval, and noticed the discerning look on his brow; he distinctly felt his tension as he ate.

"This is very good; it's quite unlike the synthesized tasteless food back at the Great Temple." Anton felt uncomfortable from the uncertainties he and Mahkeetah shared about each other. He decided that being as pleasant as possible might help avoid any arguments.

"One of these in the morning satisfies your hunger for hours." Mahkeetah's response sounded emotionless, as if he too were trying to avoid any disagreements. "It is one of our most important staples. We call them marpitas; they are plentiful, and grow the year 'round."

The two men finished breakfast with little more than awkward small talk. Mahkeetah stood and motioned for Anton to follow him. Nelda picked up their emptied bowls as the men left together. The sun shone brightly, and it warmed the cool morning very quickly; it was fast becoming another warm tropical day.

"I have business of my own to attend to. Feel free to enjoy the hospitalities of my people." Mahkeetah left Anton alone, and walked into the large community hut near the center of the village. Several other men had already arrived, and Anton deduced that the meeting of the elders was about to commence.

He wondered why they didn't invite him. For a moment, he stood there in silence, nursing his discontent. But soon he decided to find something else to occupy his time. Walking around the village by himself, he watched the women and children as they went about their business.

"I've been reduced to the duties of a security guard," he mumbled to himself. "Anyway, I needed some time to acclimate myself with the village layout, and familiarize myself with the villager's faces." He took a deep breath, forced a smile, and carefully inspected the area.

A sensation of freedom replaced his disappointment as he observed the villagers going about their daily routines; their mundane activities made him realize how simple and desirable life in Tooloo was. Never before had he felt as simultaneously needed and dejected as he did this day, although he grasped this feeling of satisfaction and fulfillment, ignoring all other negative thoughts. His disposition was obvious to those he chanced to meet; the villagers shared his friendly smile, and many of them took the time to talk to him as he wandered around. They wanted to know what the Great Temple was like, his personal interests, and how he planned to help them.

After enjoying the scenery and the friendliness of the natives, Anton spent some time trying to formulate an alternate plan of defense while he continued to survey the village surroundings. His mission was the most important thing on his mind, and he did not forget it for a moment.

The beautiful indigenous flora also caught his attention, as it had the day before. Flowers of all descriptions and sizes densely lined the edges of the village, creating a natural barrier. Their sweet fragrance permeated the atmosphere and nearly numbed his mind. It was so pungent and addictive; he found it pleasing to the point of near intoxication. Nothing like this grew around the Great Temple; it was located in the frozen mountains of the northernmost regions of Methonias, and very little could grow there.

The clever positioning of the huts held back the rapid growth of the jungle, and did so by clever design. It also required several of the village men to spend time each morning clearing away new growths of trees and underbrush, eliminating the encroachment on the village perimeter and the growth through the walls of the fragile huts. Everything in the jungle burgeoned forth so quickly that Anton could almost see the plants growing. The bioengineering of Methonias encapsulated every aspect of life, forcing it to grow at a torrid pace; this persistent marvel of the tropical flora's growth emphasized this capability vividly.

Small animals climbed and jumped through the surrounding trees, and they chattered and screeched to excess, making the jungle feel vibrant and alive. This was the healthy sound of the symbiotic existence of all things in nature, everything felt as if it were in perfect balance. Anton wanted to make sure that his efforts maintained that equilibrium and allowed the villagers to continue their lives in harmony without the destruction he'd seen in Picuris.

However, there was a negative side to all of this fantastic beauty. The insects here were far more abundant than back at the Temple, where the climate was much more severe. Anton hated the little pests. Everywhere he stepped he had to watch not to step on them. They flew around his head, constantly pestering him. Slapping at them frequently became a sport; his efforts to keep them at bay seemed more like practicing his special skills than a reactive behavior. After a short time, he knocked them from their flights with great precision, or scuffed them with his feet, tossing them far off into the jungle. A certain satisfaction came from the exercise, but the villagers thought his behavior rather odd, and chuckled among themselves as they watched him in action. They had learned to live with the insects, and seemed rarely disturbed by them.

As the morning wore on, Anton continued his surveillance, growing more content as he enjoyed the comfortable village lifestyle. It seemed to him unconscionable that the outlaws would have any reason to trouble these people. Why would anyone want to do more than enjoy the simple way of life this paradise had to offer?

Anyone from the Great Temple would be quite satisfied with life here, Anton thought to himself.

Afternoon approached, and Anton recalled what Nelda had said to him during their morning visit. It had now been several hours, and he decided it was time to return to the pool to discover if there would be an opportunity to spend some time with her.

When he arrived at the waterfall, he saw most of the village children playing in the pool, swimming, wading, and splashing each other, as children do. The older kids spent time watching and playing with the younger ones. All were happily frolicking to their hearts' content.

Looking around at the fun made Anton smile with delight, he'd never had such experiences when he was young, and for just an instant, he felt the child in him yearn for a little playtime. Growing up in the Great Temple had completely denied him of his youth; the entire focus of his upbringing was training and education—there was no time for play. Every Warrior spent their entire life preparing to fulfill their designed intent.

The children's lighthearted activities grabbed Anton's attention for a minute or two before he remembered why he'd come. When he looked across to the far side of the pool, he saw Nelda sitting on a very large rock that rested at the water's edge. She leaned backwards with her arms supporting her, looking out toward the falls, as if in reverie. Several children splashed below her, tossing water all about. The day was quite hot, and she'd long since discarded the shawl she'd worn in the early hours of the day. Her hair dangled backwards between her arms exposing her breasts to the direct sunlight. This provided him with an excellent view of her feminine charms.

Naturally, Anton's attention fixated upon her. He stood there for a moment longer, devouring her lavish beauty. He longed to touch her. Looking around, he noticed an easy way to cross the pool at its outlet, where enormous flat rocks created a natural set of stepping stones, allowing him to cross without having to wade through the water. It involved no particular skill for anyone—the stones were seemingly set there for this purpose. That didn't stop him from handspringing across, in acrobatic fashion—as if performing a carefully choreographed presentation. All eyes fell upon him as he swiftly crossed. Within a few seconds, he was standing behind Nelda.

"I thought I might find you here. How are you this afternoon?" asked Anton informally. "Umm, might I spend some time talking to you?" He felt nervous but exhibited complete confidence. Speaking to girls was something entirely new to him—tact wasn't a priority in a Warrior's education. He stammered a bit, trying to be as charming as possible.

Having noticed Anton crossing the water, Nelda was ready for him when he approached her. "You are welcome to sit with me if you wish, as there is plenty of room," she replied in a gracious tone. She'd placed herself in as prominent a location as possible; she was pleased that he'd fulfilled her indirect request. She hadn't wanted to disclose her personal desire for him outwardly, but inwardly she yearned to be the girl he chose to entertain while he stayed in the village. The afternoon was still young, and she was happy that they might have a couple of hours to share together.

"You are a bit of a showoff, aren't you?" Nelda said, prodding him. "Do all of you Warriors cross a pool like *that*? Or do you just need the attention and admiration of these children?"

"I—umm, I just try to stay in practice at all times," Anton replied. His face turned slightly red, and he felt uncomfortable. His response wasn't completely honest, but he knew he'd earned her critique.

"My father is upset with you," Nelda continued, and looked at Anton through narrow slits now. "I thought you two would have hit it off, but you didn't, and I'm surprised."

Again, Nelda's assessment caught Anton off guard; he hadn't expected she might bring up business when he was seeking pleasure. "Did he say something to you about me?" He didn't understand why she wished to discuss this; he thought it wouldn't concern her.

"A daughter knows what's in her father's heart, and I saw how you agitated him." She again put her finger on the sore spot that separated the two men. "Would you reconsider your plans? I know it isn't permitted for me to interfere with the decisions of men, but you have made my father upset, and I wish only for his happiness. He really deserves your respect! He really is a great man!"

Nelda appeared to be looking down into the water as she spoke— however, she was looking at Anton out of the corner of her eye, and she wanted to see how he would react to her forward remarks. Being the daughter of the chief permitted her to speak more freely than the other girls of the village when the opportunity arose.

"Is he upset with me protecting you people? Or is he unhappy with my decision to hide everyone?" Anton questioned.

"He doesn't like the way you're trying to make his decisions for him, rather than *offering* your suggestions." Nelda was quite direct. She looked straight at Anton for a moment and then quickly looked away, remembering her status as a young unmarried girl.

"I see. He doesn't appreciate the superior knowledge I offer him. I assure you that after I'm successful, he will be pleased with my choices." Awkwardly, Anton tried to reassure Nelda, and hoped she would relax and become friendlier with his advances. Her seeming lack of confidence in his abilities surprised him. He realized that he didn't understand how to talk to girls, but he desperately desired her attention and wanted the conversation to improve.

"Maybe we could walk over to the cave and see if it is safe for your people?" Anton said, hoping that would reassure Nelda. He meant only to help the village, not to make anyone angry with him, especially her.

"That sounds good. I like looking out from behind the waterfalls, even though we aren't supposed to go there unless we have a good reason."

Nelda understood Anton's actual intent. She'd hoped he might choose to leave the pool and go for a walk with her, away from the other girls. If they noticed them leaving together, it might instigate some jealousy, and this idea suited her; she enjoyed flaunting her status this way. Perhaps if word got back to Mahkeetah that she and Anton were becoming friends, it might help her father feel less angry toward him. Most of all, she hoped it would raise her status with her girlfriends. Besides, he was so attractive she couldn't resist some private time with him, and what it might lead to.

Anton held Nelda's hand, helping her down off the rock. Her hand's delicate touch surprised him—it felt so soft and fragile. Never before had he held the hand of a girl in this way, and the experience excited him, making his heart pound. He put his arm around her waist as they headed toward the falls, and she tenderly responded by placing her arm around his.

Anton's powerful body fascinated Nelda. His muscles felt tight and hard, even when they were at rest. His torso wasn't soft like her father's, and that excited her as she realized just how unique his physique was. She wondered what it would be like to be with a genetically superior human, and she squeezed his waist a little tighter as she pondered his distinctiveness.

Slowly they walked together toward the falls. Anton's desire boiled inside him. He enjoyed every touch, every moment, every sound and smell of Nelda; it was as if he'd achieved something greater than anything he'd accomplished before. He wanted to grab her in his arms and kiss her fully upon the lips, drinking from her beauty. But a strong sense of self-control bound him to politeness. Duty precluded any self-indulgence, and he was content with their simple contact, savoring it—at least for the moment.

Looking over her shoulder, Nelda noticed the other girls watching as they slowly walked away. A slight smile marked the corners of her mouth, her eyes glowed with delight, and she quickly looked down to disguise her contentedness from her friends.

The trail leading up to the falls was man-made and well cared for, and the jungle was carefully manicured back; trimmed grass grew around large flat stepping stones, with the feel of a beautiful well-kept garden in paradise. It seemed odd that the far side of the pool had a nicely tended path while the village side seemed far less kempt. This puzzled Anton as they walked.

It was not far to the falls, but the two lingered as they walked, taking several minutes to cross the short distance. They chatted casually as they walked, each wanting to know more about the other.

"I have a question," Nelda said, giving Anton a sly look out of the corner of her eye. "Why is it that there are no *female* Warriors? Why is it your Masters only create male Warriors?" She looked at him more directly, as if he was the one responsible for this condition. "Girls have special abilities too, you know!"

"They feel that the male body is stronger and less restrictive than a female's, and since a Warrior needs every advantage during combat, the male body is therefore the only qualified choice. This is the determination of my Masters." Anton mechanically recited the explanation he'd learned from his Masters, completely indifferent to Nelda's feelings.

The explanation left a frown on Nelda's face; she didn't like to hear that Anton believed men were superior to women. Taken aback, she prepared to lash out at him, as if holding him responsible for the logic of his Masters.

"I believe they're wrong," she said. "A woman's body is just as good if not *better* than a man's! Your Masters should reconsider." She thrust her nose in the air and turned her face away. She hoped Anton would try to defend himself; she wanted to hear him try to clarify his beliefs, giving her a second opportunity at argument.

However, Methonian training prohibited Anton from divulging his secrets. He wanted to disclose them to Nelda, but he realized it would only create more problems, and he knew it was an act of futility to argue with a girl. He realized the villagers had originally come from the same cloning labs as he, but many generations had passed since their inception and introduction into the region. Their offspring had inadvertently forgotten much of their origin, and perhaps this was the original intentions of the Clone Masters.

"It's truly beautiful here in your village," Anton said, attempting to change the subject. He didn't like the direction the discussion was going, and he thought that perhaps Nelda wouldn't understand or accept any truth, or any explanation. He was sure that he needed simply to tell her what she wished to hear, but he didn't intend to do that.

For a moment, Nelda hesitated. She huffed then, asking: "You like it here? This is good, I am pleased." She smiled slightly at Anton, and her eyes met his for a moment. Then she shied away.

Nelda's face glowed with youthful thoughts as she tried to maintain Anton's interest. She wasn't particularly angry with him, she simply wished to solicit any attention she could get.

"Maybe you would like to return here after your mission?" she asked. "Maybe you could *stay* with us! Wouldn't that be a *better* way to protect our village? You could *always* be here, and we would never be in danger again!" She hugged Anton tighter, attempting to sway him. "It would serve the village well to have the talents of a Warrior among us!" Secretly, she hoped for permission to be his mate; she knew his superior genetics would make excellent children, and her social status would remain above all others as a result.

"That is not possible; my Masters would never allow it," Anton replied, matter-of-factly, and looked down at the ground. He knew it was impossible to stay, and he didn't wish to explain what they both knew quite well. "No Warrior has ever lived anywhere on Methonias other than the Great Temple."

"I don't believe *that's* true!" she responded. "Maybe you can take me back with you to your Temple? We could live together wherever you go!" Nelda wouldn't let it go. "Don't you like it here?"

"Yes, it's perfect here, but it's not possible. As I just said, my Masters would never allow it." Anton faced Nelda directly, placed both of his hands on her hips, and then looked deeply into her eyes. They gazed at one another for a few seconds. Then Anton gave her a big hug, repositioned his arm around her waist, and continued toward the falls. Taking a deep breath, he decided once again to change the subject.

"Why is this side of the pool kept like a garden?" Anton asked. He wished to keep the conversation at a fundamental level; he was more interested in talking about her. "It seems strange you don't keep it as nice on the village side of the river."

His curiosity surprised Nelda. She figured Anton's interests were only about his mission. It caught her off guard that he wished to know more about the landscape surrounding the pool; she wanted him to think only of her.

"Our village was once on *this* side of the river. Many years ago, we moved to the other side of the pool so that we could better hide ourselves. But we couldn't forget our old home. If time permits, I will take you to the old location; it's quite beautiful there, and several of the elders still tend the gardens, even though we forbid them to. They still love the home where they grew up. This garden area around the pool was once even larger, but the jungle has taken much of it over. Only a small piece is left."

Again, Nelda looked into Anton's eyes. She wanted to see past his mysterious nature, to know what was in his heart, and to know how he genuinely felt about her.

Nelda's explanation fascinated Anton. He wanted to hear more, but they'd completed the short walk to the falls. Quickly he looked around, scanning the area for threats, and making sure nobody was watching. When he was satisfied, they continued.

"Come, the area behind the falls is beautiful." Nelda grasped Anton's hand and pulled him along the secret path leading behind the falls. It became nearly impossible to hear over the water's roar as they entered the secluded space.

Even for a trained Methonian eye, the path remained cleverly disguised, and it took an expert to climb over the wet stones and enter the large amphitheater behind the water. Again, Anton stood under the mountain stone and marveled at what could only be the skillful handiwork of the natives. Having a second look, he was certain someone had modified the stone to create this stage; the skillful workmanship of hammer and chisel had unmistakably created the amphitheater. More than fifty people could easily stand underneath the rock overhang and observe the rush of the falling water; it was as if the water created a shimmering curtain in front of a stage. The floor was quite wet, and the two walked carefully so as not to slip on the smooth slick granite surface.

They stood behind the thundering curtain and looked out from under the curved ceiling of stone. The sound was nearly deafening as it echoed off the walls of stone, and conversation was difficult. With their arms around each other's waists, Anton and Nelda enjoyed a private embrace, savoring the moment, each for their own reasons.

Nelda put her head against Anton's chest and clung snugly against him, entranced by the romantic feeling she desired to have; she'd waited her whole life for a moment like this.

"It looks as if your people excavated this space behind the falls," Anton said, casually hoping to gain knowledge of the handiwork. He pointed at the ceiling, slowly tracing its outline with his index finger.

Anton had a genuine interest in the villager's lives, and in particular, Nelda. His need to know more about her intensified with each passing moment. He had never had an opportunity to learn about a girl, and he relished his time with her. The only people he'd ever known were his Masters and his brother Warriors; he'd shared his entire youth with them. Women were still quite a mystery. This left him feeling clumsy, not knowing what to say to make a positive impression.

"Yes, we once stored food here," Nelda said. "As you noticed, it's much cooler behind the falls." Nelda liked the interest Anton gave her, and returned it with a smile. She wondered why he'd been so condescending to her father, and so nice to her. It pleased her to know she could draw out his good side with so little effort. She thought that in time, with her help, she could change him enough that both he and her father would become good friends; they were, after all, more alike than Anton knew.

"This is a clever use of the natural landscape," he said. "You are a clever people. I didn't know that you had the skills to modify your surroundings so creatively."

"What do you mean?" Nelda said, scowling at Anton suddenly. "Did you think we were a simple-minded people with no skills, unable to do more than *exist?*" Anton's statement hit a chord with her. She pushed away from him and took a step back. "Do you really think so little of us?" She looked hurt, and shook her finger at him.

"No, no!" he protested. "It's just that our Masters instructed us about the various people living throughout Methonias. Nothing was ever mentioned about what skills you people might have. I am very interested in seeing something that I didn't expect."

"I would think by now you could see we are every bit as clever as you *Warriors*. Just because we don't have some big fancy Temple to live in, and we don't have your technologies, doesn't mean we are less than you." Looking directly into Anton's eyes, Nelda continued to defend herself and her people. She felt upset that Anton would think of them as inferior.

"Wait, wait!" Anton snapped. "I'm sorry! I realize just how important you people are, and I see you have *many* skills. I also see you are very decent people, *worthy* of my help. Everything about life in Tooloo appears wonderful. It is paradise here, and you live happy lives. Now I know why my Masters felt I should come here to help you." With crude finesse, Anton was able to recover from his mishandled attempt at conversation.

Nelda looked directly into Anton's eyes as she listened to his awkward apology. When she was sufficiently satisfied, she put her arms around his waist and hugged him gently.

"I see. You didn't know anything about us. That is why you act the way you do." Her cheek pressed against his chest, and then she again looked into his eyes and held them seductively, as if offering him more. "I see you're a good man, you just need a little... fixing." Her eyes begged him to embrace her closely, and to take her.

Looking down into her eyes, Anton felt incapacitated with yearning, but he forced his hormone-driven desires to retrench, and then returned his thoughts to Nelda's implied request by embracing her with his strong

Methonian arms, and drawing her close to him. Her naked breasts pressed into his chest, a sensation he had never before felt. Then he kissed her full lips; he thirsted deeply for her passionate affection, and ached to take her right there.

"They are kissing! They are kissing!" a small boy suddenly cried out from behind Anton.

Quickly Anton turned around to see what the fuss was. The boy ran around in a circle with his arms spread out, as if imitating an Aerocraft in flight. Obviously, he'd hidden himself nearby and spied on the two to see what they were doing. He continued to giggle and run around, saying: "They are kissing!"

Anton and Nelda laughed at the sight; the young boy was far too much for even a Warrior's stoic demeanor. Then, unexpectedly, the circling boy came too close to the falling water. His outstretched arm dipped into the cascading torrents, which knocked him instantly off balance. The stone beneath his feet was very wet and slippery. He instantly tumbled, landing face-first on the chiseled granite, and sliding off the edge—into the deluge of the falls. It snatched him so quickly he didn't even have time to let out a scream.

Instinctively, Anton flew toward the boy like a streak of lightning. His genetic constitution, his conditioning, and his Methonian training forced his heroic response. Nelda screamed "No!" as he took three large steps and leapt through the air in an unbelievable arch, sliced into the falling water, and disappearing over the edge after the little boy. It seemed impossible that he would find him in the turbulent water below—the weight of the falls crashed and roiled so mightily no normal human could endure its concussion for long.

Swimming was nearly unmanageable as the water contained so much air from the agitated water that it had little buoyancy, and the cascading water hammered relentlessly upon any victim, holding them completely helpless; additionally, the frothing and pounding made it impossible for a person to see. Even with all odds against him, Anton used his quick reflexes and mighty strength to persevere. As he fought the cascading torrents, he simultaneously calculated trajectories toward the boy, the chaos of motion, and the possibilities of which direction he should force himself to move. Split seconds passed while his high-speed mental capabilities and reflexes worked their magic. Then, as he passed through the direct battering and buffeting of the falls, less turbulent water surrounded him, allowing him to see more clearly and move more freely; normal swimming became possible.

Quickly scanning around, Anton saw the boy pinned against a rock on the bottom of the pool behind the falls, and like an arrow, shot towards him. Grasping him in both hands, he pulled the boy free of the stone and pushed off the bottom of the pool. He had to return to the surface as quickly as possible, knowing the boy was nearly out of air. He could feel his own lungs starting to heave, and he too would soon take on water. Putting one hand over the boy's mouth, Anton prevented him from doing so.

With impossible speed and incredible strength, Anton ricocheted off the bottom of the pool and flew into the air like a dolphin breaching the surface of the ocean; only his feet remained in the water. As the two fell backward, Anton put his arm around the boy's chest and held him tight against his own. Quickly he swam towards the shore as the boy gasped for air and then coughed; within seconds, he'd pulled him to land and safety.

Nelda came running from behind the falls to watch Anton's heroism. Panicking, she screamed and held her hand to her mouth; suddenly she started flailing both arms, drawing attention to Anton's rescue.

"Help them!" she screamed, hoping someone would understand the plight of the child. She stood near the boulder at the edge of the pool where earlier she had warmed herself in the afternoon sun, and grasped at Anton as he made shore.

Both the adults and the children present in the immediate area around the pool watched and wondered what was happening. It didn't take long for them to realize something monumental had just occurred, and quickly they all ran toward the pool's edge, where Anton pulled the boy free of the water. The boy was still coughing, but his breathing seemed to be returning to normal. Nelda grabbed him in her arms, giving him a hug as tears rolled down her face. Her emotions overcame her composure, and she tried to comfort him as if he were her own child.

"Tok!" Nelda's tears poured freely as she rocked him back and forth. "I'm so sorry! Are you okay?" She seemed nearly hysterical. Tears streamed down her cheeks, and she hugged him tightly.

"He will be fine," Anton said. "He didn't take on any water; I pulled him free in time." He sounded dry and without feeling; several of the villagers looked at him as if he didn't care about what he'd just done.

One young man, about Anton's age, pushed his way over; he looked at Anton for a moment, then knelt before him and bowed his head.

"Thank you for saving my little brother," he said. "He's the only one I have; I couldn't live without him. He is only five, too young to know what he did wrong. I owe you a life." Standing up, he looked Anton in the eye. "I am your servant!"

"You owe me nothing," Anton responded. "I'm *your* servant; it's my duty to help this village with any crisis." He bowed graciously in full Methonian fashion, and then patted the young man on the shoulder and smiled. "I am here to serve! I merely performed my duty, upholding my design intent!"

"My name is Muzoke," the other said. "You honor us more than you realize. Let Nelda and the others care for Tok, there is so little room for all of us here. Besides, someone needs to report to Mahkeetah about what just happened. Will you return with me to the village?" Muzoke's eyes pleaded for Anton to come with him, and he grabbed his arm and gave it a slight tug.

"I would be happy to; it's about time to return anyway." Anton was hungry. Leaving Nelda and Tok behind, the two crossed the water over the large rocks at the pool's outlet and walked up the trail toward the village. Macaws called to them as they walked under the jungle trees, and Anton watched as the birds ate fruit high above their heads. He knew they felt safe enough to go about their business, so he knew it was safe to leave the pool unguarded.

"Can I ask you a question?" Muzoke asked, with a puzzled look. He clearly implied something else by the tone of his voice. "Just what were you expecting to do with Nelda behind the falls?"

"My intentions were innocent," Anton replied. "She was showing me the space behind the falls." A tone of finality resounded in Anton's response; it was clear he wouldn't answer any further questions on the subject, and quickly made his point absolute.

"I will take you at your word since you saved my brother and served my family, but the other girls think otherwise. Come, just as the birds are eating their lunch, food awaits our return!" With a smile, he led Anton back to Tooloo, running all the way.

As they entered the village, Muzoke ran over to his father, and quickly gave a recount of Anton's heroism. Before he was finished, the man jumped up and ran over to Anton.

"Young Warrior, my name is Tyrell. If what Muzoke says is true, we are indeed indebted to you. I must go to the pool now, but I shall return." He quickly shook Anton's hand. Then, with a look of concern on his face, he ran down the trail toward the falls.

Muzoke had already run off to inform more people of Anton's valiant deeds. The villagers ran up to him, offering food, a pat on the back, or praise for his heroism.

It felt odd to Anton that the mood of the villagers had shifted from a general distrust to that of honor and respect. He didn't quite know what to make of it, but his empty stomach was his main concern, and the offering of food satisfied him more than the honor and attention. Sitting at one of the tables near the village square, Anton decided to relax for a while and consume the offerings.

Within a short time, Mahkeetah approached him. "You are of greater value to us than we have given you credit for. Be assured, we didn't trust you at first, and even this morning I wasn't completely certain of your plans. In light of your unselfish acts this afternoon, it would be difficult for anyone to object to your proposal. Therefore, after dinner, the council of elders has decided to give you an opportunity to share who you are. They want to know better before they commit their trust in you and your plan."

Mahkeetah crossed his arms as he spoke, and Anton could still hear his misgivings. Yet everyone else smiled and patted him on the shoulder, or waved as they walked by.

"I suggest you prepare yourself," Mahkeetah said. "Our questions will be judgmental. This will be your only chance, and if you fail to convince the elders to trust you, you will be asked to leave!" Mahkeetah glared at Anton, pointing his finger at him.

"Now," the older man went on, "I am going to rest before this evening. I want my mind to be sharp and clear. Please enjoy yourself while I retire to my hut. It would seem that you have swayed many people to trust you today—therefore, the village is at your service." With that, Mahkeetah walked back to his hut and shut the door with a thud.

Offerings of food and fruit juice continued throughout the afternoon; Anton relaxed to a degree, and allowed his trained alertness to slacken.

The mood of the villagers made him complacent. Only Mahkeetah's temperament hadn't seemed to change. Nelda had returned from the pool, and shyly sat beside him.

"You are a great man," Nelda said. "There is more to you than I suspected. Forgive my earlier misjudgment of you." She put her head on his shoulder for a moment, and then slowly slipped her arm around his waist. "I cannot stay very long; I must attend to my father's needs. I want to spend more time with you later if possible. I know that you will convince both the elders *and* my father to trust you. Don't worry—he distrusts anyone he doesn't know. I'm sure he will realize you're a good man—you simply haven't convinced him yet." Nelda then stood up and walked toward Mahkeetah's hut; just as she entered, she looked over her shoulder and winked at Anton, and then quickly disappeared.

"I would like that too," Anton called after her awkwardly. He ached to hold her in his arms again. Her brief visit only left him feeling alone and frustrated.

Just as she closed the door behind her, Tyrell, Muzoke, and Tok returned from the pool. Smiling, they rushed over to where Anton was sitting. Tok was quite energetic and seemed completely recovered from his earlier mishap.

"Thank you, Mister Warrior!" he said, giving Anton a hug. Then he ran off toward an approaching woman—it was easy to deduce that this was his mother.

Looking at Anton, Tyrell mouthed a word or two, as if unable to speak. "I... umm, I cannot thank you enough. Is there anything we can do for you? After what you have done for my child I feel there is nothing sufficient we can do to repay your deed." His obvious emotions left him at a loss for words; shifting his weight from one foot to the other, he fidgeted with his hands, as if he intended to do something, but didn't know what.

"We *all* want to do something for you," Muzoke said, holding both hands out, empty palms turned up. His eyes pleaded for Anton to tell him what he wished of him.

"Please," Anton said. "I understand you are all grateful, but there is nothing I need. I was just doing what I had to do, what I was trained for." He looked at the family as if he was tired of their flattery. He didn't wish for them to worship him for saving their child. "It would please me if you would simply spend some time together," continued Anton, as if to dismiss them. He turned his face to the ground, took a deep breath, and then ignored them.

Just then, the woman gave Anton a big hug and kissed him on the cheek. "Thank you for saving my boy," she said. "We will leave you alone if that is what you wish." Looking at Tyrell, she motioned for them to leave. She then picked Tok up and headed back to their family hut, with Muzoke following closely behind, looking over his shoulder at Anton.

"I will find a way to repay you, young man," Tyrell said, with a smile and a wink. "I *know* what you want." Then he followed his family back toward his hut.

Feeling relieved that the incident was over, Anton stood up and walked away from the table. He needed some private time to digest the unexpected admiration, and he needed to plan how he would speak to the village elders later. Everything felt new to him, and he didn't know exactly how to deal with these people. He walked around aimlessly for a minute or two, and then decided to find a quiet place to meditate. It didn't take him long to locate a suitable spot just outside of the village perimeter. Crossing his legs and adopting the lotus position, he tipped his head back and reflected upon the events of the day. A sensation of peace filled him, and all of his stress evaporated.

The afternoon quickly waned, shedding its sunshine and warmth to the first signs of evening; ever-increasing shadows stretched across the village. The slight drop in temperature offered modest relief, and an intermittent warm breeze caressed Anton's skin. Feeling refreshed after an hour of meditation, he decided it was time to rejoin the villagers.

There were no incidents from the outlaws throughout the course of the day, and a feeling of contentment filled Anton's thoughts. It was an unusual day for him, since he'd never experienced close and personal contact with villagers before; it all felt so new and different. His perceptions about who he was and how he thought of other people were changing, in part due to his intimate experiences with Nelda, and in part due to the disagreements with Mahkeetah. It pleased him that the villagers had accepted him and appreciated him for who he was, and that they understood how important his special abilities were.

Like always, meditation did a world of good for Anton. He'd used his time to think of a way to convince Mahkeetah and the council of elders to trust him. He carried a small device in his tunic that allowed him to share his experiences from the past, and he intended to do just that. Reaching into a small pocket inside his tunic, he pulled out a tiny gadget, which was just big enough to fit into the palm of his hand. It was conical, and it looked like a jeweler's ring-sizing bar, made from a highly polished crystal. Gently hefting it in his hand a couple of times, Anton quickly returned it to his pocket, and gently patted it, making sure it stayed there.

"What was that you had in your hand?" Nelda asked, walking up behind him. She had seen him play with his crystal rod and then return it to his tunic and she was both suspicious and curious what he might be up to.

"It's a small device I will use this evening to share my past with all of you. I believe you will understand me better after I show you an experience I had about two years ago." Anton spoke softly, looking to Nelda with a gentle smile and a twinkle in his eye. "I'm pleased to see you again!"

"I am happy to see you too!" Nelda replied. "You're a great man, and I enjoy being with you. It's time for dinner. Everyone—the entire village—will eat together this evening. May I sit with you while we eat?" She smiled shyly and slowly looked up into Anton's eyes as she spoke.

"I would like nothing better than to be with you; I wish we had more time to spend together." Anton responded quickly. Normally, he wouldn't care about any girl at all, but he blurted out his feelings to her before he realized what he'd said.

Oh no, I shouldn't have said that! Anton thought to himself. *I have feelings for her? I can't have feelings; it isn't permitted!* He muttered to himself, and fidgeted as he did so; these were things he was unaccustomed to doing. "My Masters will punish me!" he mumbled under his breath.

It went against his training to have any personal interest in the indigenous people, and he couldn't afford to have his Masters discover he had feelings, particularly at the climax of his training.

"What did you say?" Nelda asked. "I didn't hear you." She heard Anton mumbling, and wondered why he didn't look at her or speak to her directly.

"Nothing," he replied. "I was just noticing how much I liked you." Again, Anton spoke before he thought; it was completely uncharacteristic of him.

"I like you too!" Nelda exclaimed. "I wish you would stay here and we could spend *much* more time together!" She smiled hugely and gazed longingly into his eyes, and then wrapped her arms around his waist. Pressing her head into his chest, she gently hugged him. "I wish we could spend our lives together!"

Returning her embrace, Anton took a deep breath and sighed. "That would be wonderful, but my Masters would never permit it. I must return to the Temple as soon as I complete my mission." His cold words were belied by his tone. He realized that if he shared his inner feelings with her, it would only complicate things beyond his control, yet he hungered for her in many ways, and wanted to elaborate; he hoped deep inside that she would try to convince him to stay.

"Your words say you must leave, but your heart says you desire to stay—I can hear it!" Nelda exclaimed. Grasping Anton's hands in hers, she again looked up into his eyes. "You don't have to leave; we can find a way for you to remain!" She gave him a reassuring smile, then placed her hand on his cheek, and gently caressed it. "Come now, it's time to eat!"

Leading him by the hand, Nelda headed toward the tables in the center of the village. Everyone had already gathered there, busily preparing the tables with food.

Mahkeetah sat at the head of the longest table and watched Anton and Nelda approach. He was talking to Tyrell, but paid careful attention to how the two held hands and smiled like a young couple.

"You will sit next to my father," Nelda said, gently squeezing his hand. "I will sit next to you. I think it would help if you said hello, *politely*." She hoped to influence him to gain Mahkeetah's respect; it was as much a test to see if she could influence him as improve their trust in each other.

"It's a pleasure to see you again," Anton said, bowing to Mahkeetah respectfully in Methonian fashion. But his words sounded indifferent.

"The pleasure is mine, young Warrior," Mahkeetah said, sardonically. "I see you have made a new friend with my daughter, and it would appear she has your ear." Mahkeetah looked directly at Nelda; his eyes narrowed disapprovingly, and he raised an eyebrow.

"We've had a wonderful time today, father," Nelda said. "Anton is a great man, and we wish to spend as much time together as possible." Smiling, she gave Mahkeetah a kiss on the cheek, and then motioned for Anton to sit.

"Spend as much time indeed!" Mahkeetah said. "All of us here today have witnessed you spending time together, and the benefit of genetic engineering! Great man, indeed!" Raising both eyebrows, Mahkeetah looked at his daughter and held her eyes to ensure she sensed his feelings; clearly, she didn't take his previous hint. He did not smile; he wanted her to think carefully about what she was saying.

"So, young Warrior, you desire my daughter," Mahkeetah continued. "You told all of us you came to do a job, to complete your training—and here, in front of *everyone*, you court my *daughter*!" Raising his voice, he made sure the entire village heard him speak. "It would seem you seek *pleasure* as well! Or was that your intent all along?"

Anton's mouth hung open, his eyes widened, and he looked directly at Mahkeetah. For a moment, he was speechless. Then he fumbled for a response. "My purpose here is to complete my training, as directed by the Temple Masters. And yes, it's true, I find in myself a strange longing to be with Nelda. It's a sensation I neither intended, nor comprehend. All the same, I... well... I'm both proud of, and embarrassed by this. I can't explain it, but I want to *be* with her!" His clumsy response struggled past his lips, revealing to all his heart's desire. He was incapable of expressing anything but the truth—his genetic engineering and mental training precluded lying. Thus, it compelled him to respond honestly, and everyone present understood this.

Mahkeetah stood up suddenly; with both hands on the table, he leaned toward Anton. "Do you know what you are saying, young Warrior? Do you realize that to state your intentions to me thus is a *proposal*? You have just asked for my daughter's hand in marriage, you unwitting fool! Again, you *confound* me! No Warrior should *ever* ask for a young girl's hand! Especially *my* young girl!" Yelling, he clenched his fists and raised them in the air, and then slowly, lightly, pounded the table as he tried to control his emotions. Anger filled his eyes—as if Anton had just harmed his daughter, rather than asking for her hand in marriage.

Everyone was silent during Mahkeetah's outburst. Then Tyrell addressed the chief. "I see this as a good thing, Mahkeetah. This village has accepted a Warrior before—have you forgotten?"

"I will not speak of this!" Mahkeetah said, glaring at Tyrell sharply. For a moment, the two held each other's gaze. Then the older man backed down, breaking eye contact, and shaking his head in disbelief.

"Do you think you can avoid revealing the truth any longer?" Tyrell went on. "It's time for you to cast off your anger just as you have cast off your past, and it's time for you to accept the greater good that can come of it. We all have mourned the death of your wife; now let us rejoice in the addition of a *son*!"

"Addition?" Mahkeetah screamed. Again, he pounded the table, this time with increased force. "There can be no addition! He is one of *them*! He is *emotionless*! He simply follows the predetermined biology built into him! Besides, they just met yesterday! How could you apply our laws to this... this... *transient*?"

Tyrell firmly stared into Mahkeetah's angry eyes. He raised both eyebrows and slowly opened his mouth, taking a deep breath. "*You* were one of *them*!" he said, sharply, pointing a finger at him accusingly. "You forget yourself! We all know *you* have emotions! However, and most importantly, due to the particular circumstances, bending the rules is irrelevant! You just protest because she is your daughter!"

Shocked, Anton watched the two men as they revealed Mahkeetah's secrets, unraveling his past, and answering many of the questions he'd had. It was now clear why he was so adept at using his katana—and more significantly, why he even possessed it. Why hadn't he guessed any of this?

Looking at Mahkeetah, Anton easily saw the subtle differences in his general appearance—deviations of genetic design that clearly indicated he wasn't born in Tooloo. Carelessly, Anton had determined that Mahkeetah came from another village. But now it was obvious he could only be a Warrior! It was now clearer why his Masters had sent him here; perhaps he was to address this issue too.

One thing that continued to nag at Anton the most was Mahkeetah's hair and eye color. Everyone in Tooloo had coal-black eyes and dark black hair that glistened in the sun. Mahkeetah did too; that was why Anton hadn't guessed the truth. No Warrior had eyes colored black, or hair any darker than a dark brown. The fact that Mahkeetah did was confusing to Anton; it was a contradictory piece of information.

"You withheld everything about yourself," Tyrell said to Mahkeetah, goading him to reveal more. "And you didn't inform him of *all* our laws."

"It wasn't necessary!" Mahkeetah responded. "I don't *have* to tell him—he's simply here to complete his training, and then leave! And I hid nothing—there was never a reason to tell him anything, or I would have!" Mahkeetah couldn't wait for Anton to leave; he wanted to spare his daughter from a future with Anton. It seemed as though his distaste for the Warrior increased with each passing moment.

"Your emotions are part of your failed development, Mahkeetah," Tyrell said. "We have all witnessed that Anton has emotions, but he seems to keep them under control. You don't! It's obvious for all to see that your Masters are busy at improving their designs, and improving the characteristics of their Warriors. Therefore, we will decide tonight whether we are to trust his help. I believe most of us here agree that he is quite capable of ending the troubles we face. As for you posing as the village chief, I believe it's time for that to change as well! We no longer need to hide this truth!" Tyrell held Mahkeetah's gaze and the two fell silent; the resentment between them was unmistakable.

"So be it!" Mahkeetah said, standing proudly and looking around the gathering, holding the gaze of each man in turn. "I officially release my claim to the position of chief and return it to Tyrell. I see now that I should never have held it in the first place—you people have no honor."

Dumbfounded, Nelda's face grew long, her eyes widened, and her mouth hung slack. "Daddy!" she exclaimed. A tear rolled down her cheek, and she looked at Anton for support—as if he would spring into action to repair the damage caused by her father's failure.

"Young Warrior—Anton," Tyrell said. "We are proud to have you among us. We are indebted to you for your unselfish heroism. It's beyond our ability to repay you for this. I swear that nothing but the truth shall be given to you from this point further." Standing, Tyrell walked over to Anton and put his hand upon his shoulder. "If you can prove to everyone here tonight that you understand our need precisely, we will carry out any advice that you propose. Furthermore, we will help you to spend more time with Nelda. A fair trade, is it not?" He smiled at Anton and patted his shoulder gently.

"Now, everybody, rejoice!" Tyrell continued. "A great meal is prepared—let us eat!" Holding his arms above his head, he looked around the village and smiled hugely, enticing everyone to respond with a cheer. Then he returned to his seat. The villagers reacted enthusiastically, filling the air with a felicitous sound that echoed off the valley walls.

"I warn you all," Mahkeetah said. "You're making a mistake! No good can come of this! Your plan may have worked once, but it won't work a second time!" He pointed a finger around the tables. Then he swiftly returned to his hut alone.

Nelda remained seated next to Anton, clinging to his arm with tears streaming. "Why didn't you do something to help my father?" she asked. "Why didn't you stop what was happening?" She looked at Anton, pleading for his help as if he were responsible for what had happened.

"This is between your father and Tyrell," he said, laconically. "I cannot interfere." Gently, he put the side of his finger under her chin, raising it so she could see his smile. "When the time is right, I will help you in any way I can; *you're* the only one who really matters to me."

Tenderly, Anton placed his lips upon Nelda's, kissing her passionately. An uncontrollable sensation of bonding suddenly overwhelmed his senses, making his head swim. He felt dizzy as the entire village seemed to disappear behind a misty veil.

Nelda slowly wrapped her arms around Anton as he expressed his intentions. Then, gently, she pushed him away. "We cannot do this here— the entire village watches!" With the back of her wrist, she slowly, gently, brushed his wet kiss from her mouth, and then shyly smiled, bowing her head. Wiping the tears from her face, she picked up a slice of tara fruit and placed it carefully between her lips, taking a small bite, and then placing the remainder in Anton's mouth.

"Save it for later, young ones—let us feast!"

Tyrell's voice brought Anton back from his fervor. Slowly the inner fog in his mind lifted, and his thoughts cleared. For a moment, he wasn't sure what had happened. But as his mind returned to clarity, he quickly forgot that his kiss of passion had even occurred.

"Yours is a true love," Tyrell continued, looking at Anton and Nelda. "They say when a Warrior falls in love with a woman, his need for passion rivals the intensity of his physical skills!" Then he winked at Anton, as if giving him permission.

Just moments before, Anton had wanted to object to Mahkeetah's declaration of his engagement. Yet now he found the concept inconceivably desirable—indeed, almost necessary, as if he were helping these people by accepting. He fought his conflicting feelings of desire for Nelda, and his obligations of duty to his Masters. He didn't understand his own thoughts. He looked around at all the faces watching him. Shamefacedly, he picked up a piece of bread and quickly chewed the hard crust, trying to hide his embarrassment behind his need for sustenance. An impassioned lingering desire continued to burn in his heart, and he fought to set aside his genetically impelled fervor.

"Everyone—a toast to our newly engaged couple. May they find happiness in a long life together!" a man's voice declared from the far end of the gathering, as he held up a goblet of tara wine. The entire village quickly responded, taking up their own goblets. Tapping sounds filled the air as toast after toast was made.

The meal went by hurriedly, everyone satisfying themselves with food, wine, and lively conversation. As the meal concluded, the women immediately cleared the tables, and the children rushed off to play. It all went by so quickly that Anton felt as if time had compressed somehow, and had then left him behind to wrestle with his uncontrollable feelings, feelings he should never have.

"We aren't sure if the outlaws will visit tonight," Tyrell said to Anton, nervously. "It's believed that they won't, due to your help yesterday. But we are on alert, watching, and will inform you of any arrival. As you know, they always come around dusk, and that time is nearly upon us."

"I shall patrol the village," Anton said. "All will be safe." Without emotion, he looked directly at Tyrell; in his Warrior way, he attempted to reassure him everything would be fine. He thought that duty might help to bring him back from his dilemma. Meditation was what he craved, but he knew there was no time for that.

For a moment Anton sat there frozen and silently considered something. Everyone quieted down and then Tyrell asked: "Is something the matter, young Anton?"

"I think it would be of interest to all of you if I shared something about who I really am, and what I've learned. I mean, I want to show you that I am ready to face these outlaws, and I will show you why." Then he stood and prepared to leave.

"We will build a fire," Tyrell stated with a smile, "so that all may witness your story. Everyone will gather around to hear what you have to say." Pointing toward the center of the village, Tyrell showed Anton where the fire pit was.

Anton acknowledged Tyrell's offer. "I'll be there." Hand over fist with a Methonian bow, Anton offered his respect to Tyrell, and then left the table and walked over to Mahkeetah's hut. Opening the door, he gazed inside and saw the fallen chief sitting in the lotus position on the tapestry on the floor, meditating. He stood there looking at him for a minute, and then, as one Methonian to another, hand over fist, he bowed to his brother Warrior as respectfully as he knew how.

Mahkeetah seemed to ignore him, and continued meditating. He was completely unmoved by Anton's show of deference, and continued his internal self-examination.

A Warrior's Tale

RETURNING TO NELDA, ANTON WATCHED as she helped to clear the tables with the other women of the village. Like Mahkeetah, her status had changed—and now she would have to perform equal amounts of menial labor alongside her peers. She had always helped in the past, yet as the chief's daughter, she had the right to skip responsibilities when it suited her. This had changed forever, and he could see the change reflected in her face.

"Might I help you?" Anton asked as he approached. "I'm willing to share in your obligations. I... I suppose, in a way, I'm responsible for this." It wasn't that he felt guilty, but he wanted to talk with her as she worked. He knew she blamed him to some degree for Mahkeetah's fall from grace.

"We're almost done here," Nelda said. "You have more important things to do. I will see you later, when the village gathers to hear your story." Forcing a smile, Nelda fought back her tears, hoping Anton wouldn't notice the turmoil of her emotions. Biting her lip, she turned her face away and wiped the corners of her eyes. "Please—men shouldn't involve themselves in woman's chores." Glancing up into Anton's eyes, she continued to gather the dirty dishes.

"As you wish," Anton replied. "I will use this time to prepare myself." With a half bow, Anton followed the procession of women to the pool to watch them cleansing the dishes in the stream below the pool's outlet. The efficiency of their teamwork surprised him.

Climbing the rock Nelda had sat upon earlier in the day, Anton adopted the Lotus position and meditated. It didn't take long for the women to finish their task, and soon they left the pool, leaving him behind. Evening turned to dusk, and the sounds of gathering people faintly challenged the roar of the waterfall, beckoning him to leave. As Anton slid down from the rock, Tyrell approached and waved for him to follow.

"All of them are gathered to hear your tale," Tyrell said. "Let us return to the village!" Tyrell patted Anton's shoulder with a fatherly smile, as if he were inviting him into his own family. "I believe Nelda is anxious to see you—come!" Pointing the way, he hurried along with almost youthful excitement, as if he anticipated something monumental was about to take place. It didn't take long to return to the village.

Near the pole in the village center, Anton could see a small fire burning; it was large enough to light the gathering. Everyone sat around, talking amongst themselves in anticipation of a marvelous tale. Pushing his way through the villagers, Anton looked around at them.

"I will need a small table; I will use a small device called a Crystallographic Holo-projector—or, as we refer to it, a CHP. It will help all of you see an experience from my past." He looked at Tyrell and raised his eyebrows, trying to encourage a swift response. Anton then reached into his tunic and pulled from his pocket the crystal rod he'd held earlier in the day.

Surprisingly, Mahkeetah appropriated a table and placed it next to him. "I've given today's events thorough consideration; I will consider you a son *if* you prove yourself worthy." With a Methonian bow, he swiftly returned to sit with Nelda. His temperament had changed considerably since dinner; it was almost as if he were apologizing, but with reservations.

Making short work of it, Anton placed his CHP on the table and removed the ring from his finger. Sliding it on the crystal rod, he activated the device. Instantly it produced tiny holographic images all around the table in the center of the gathering.

"I must ask for everyone to move back a small distance; the more room that's available, the larger the Holo-projector images will be. Oh, and it would help if the fire was put out—this too will improve the effect." Spreading his arms, Anton motioned for the villagers to move back; he then doused the fire with a nearby bucket of water, and adjusted the CHP. A holographic explosion filled the gathering, causing everyone to gasp. Enthusiastically, Anton began his presentation.

With a look of concern Tyrell asked: "just out of curiosity, if there is the possibility of an attack this evening, why are we having this presentation now? Wouldn't it be prudent to maintain a certain level of security rather than leave ourselves vulnerable?"

"I couldn't agree more," Anton responded. "Please, trust me; I know it is entirely possible the outlaws might disrupt my story. Actually, I hope they do! I'm prepared for them, and if this draws them here I will handle the situation."

Tyrell didn't seem convinced. With his hands on his hips he scowled at the young Warrior and heaved a sigh. "You gamble much with our well-being! I'm concerned for your reasoning; however, we've agreed to put our trust in you. You may proceed."

"Thank you," Anton replied uneasily, looking from face to face as he did so. He appeared contemplative for a moment and then continued.

"The Masters of the Great Temple assembled a seven-man assault force for a training mission to the Bad Lands. This is a large eastern region of the primary continent on Methonias." Anton narrated as the holographic images played out like a movie. The faces of the villagers revealed their awe. He smiled to himself as he continued. "The team included myself, Boris, Edgar, Luke, Tybalt, Duke, and Ivan." Anton pointed to each member as he spoke their names.

"This desolate zone obtained its name from the harsh arid climate and desert-like terrain; it's one of the least hospitable areas on our planet. As you can see, lofty mountains topped with plateaus throng the sky surrounding the region, and vast sandy deserts encompassed its entirety, making travel by foot in or out completely inconceivable. We traveled via Aerocraft to this area." A holograph of the Aerocraft's interior showed Anton and his six brother Warriors sitting patiently. The images adjusted to reflect his description.

"In this region, the vast and complex set of deep valleys are so rugged that passage on foot is difficult and very time consuming, and at times completely impossible. These valleys are quite often compared to the Grand Canyon on Ancient Earth, but are three times more extensive, being wider and deeper. They cover an area of nearly four million acres." Sounding like a teacher in a classroom, Anton walked slowly around the circle, pointing at various images as he spoke.

"In contrast, deep in the valleys are lush environments that support large populations of peaceful indigenous inhabitants. And just like all of you here in Tooloo, they are a beautiful people, and live in harmony with nature, in tribal groups completely isolated from the rest of Methonias." Smiling at Nelda, Anton was adjusting to his new role as a storyteller with ease. The entire village was silent as the images sped along, and Anton revealed facts about places they'd never known existed.

"As is true of all the peaceful tribal peoples, they are morally decent, gentle by nature, completely lacking in aggression. I'm not sure if you know, but there are the Jungle Dwellers in the southern regions of Methonias, the People of Ice in the northern polar cap, and the Islanders on the thousands of islands that dot the southwestern seas." Looking around at the faces, Anton noticed the interest in everyone's face; he was pleased they were interested in his presentation.

"Now I will show you my experience with caves. Contained within the canyon walls are a vast maze of caves and labyrinths. They occur both naturally and artificially, carved out over the years by a secondary group of indigenous people in this region. They are the most extensive manmade feature on the entire planet, going on for thousands of miles. This is where the Troglodytes live. This sub-class of humans has offered some of the most advanced training in the most primitive and remote region available on Methonias. They prey on the small tribes that inhabit the deep valleys below, where the rivers flow—pillaging and capturing many of the natives for slaves. Reportedly, they even use them as food—although that is as of yet unsubstantiated." Watching the reactions of the villagers, Anton decided to get to his point.

"Occasionally, the peaceful people of these valleys ask for assistance from the Methonian Masters, and thus they fulfill their intended purpose. The plights endured by the locals provide opportunities for teams of

Warriors to deal with—the same way that I'm here helping all of *you* now. On this particular occasion, the Troglodytes had nearly destroyed one of the larger villages, and had taken a high chief's daughter as a slave, as was their custom. This enabled the Troglodytes to negotiate for other things to supplement their decadent lifestyle."

Looking at Mahkeetah, Anton made sure he was listening to what he was about to say. He knew the former chief also needed to be educated on this subject; he was sure Mahkeetah hadn't shared his own training adventures with Tyrell.

"As I was saying—we were transported by Aerocraft, and then dropped off atop a plateau between the location of the abduction and cave's entrance. The valley below didn't provide a safe or expedient place to embark, since climbing the side of the valley wall was far more difficult than descending it."

Anton pointed at the Aerocraft as it landed, and then gestured, depicting the depth of the valley. Complete detail of the region filled the circle, giving everyone a new view of their world.

"To the west of the landing site, a snow-capped mountain range of Olympian proportions stretched from north to south, separating the desert plateau below. This desert contains Joshua trees, Yucca, sagebrush, and cactus of various types. This completely covers the vast span between the mountains and the valley." The recorded scenes continued to play out as Anton slowly adjusted the CHP to show one perspective and then another.

"Apparently, Anton, this is going to take some time," Tyrell said. "Could you please get to your point?" He seemed impatient, but the faces of the villagers appeared enthralled with the three-dimensional movie playing out in front of them.

"I'm sorry, but you need to know why I'm making this point," Anton responded. "I shall try to speed through or skip unnecessary parts as I can." He nodded and then continued.

"Quickly, one at a time, each of us departed the Aerocraft and prepared for the descent. It didn't take long to locate a hidden trail nearby, winding down the face of the sheer cliff."

As everyone watched, the Warriors gathered in single file and dropped nimbly down to the trail. It had loose rocks, an uneven footing, and immediately took a sharp turn downward, making the passage impossible for any normal human. Only the highly trained Methonian Warriors were skilled enough to traverse this type of terrain. Everyone in the village gasped as they watched the Warriors' acrobatic capabilities.

"Traveling was slow and dangerous, even for us, but we traversed the uneven surfaces, helping each other as we went." With a quick reflex, Anton changed a setting on the CHP, to increase the speed of the playback. Nearly an hour of time sped by in seconds.

As the team came upon a secluded and nearly imperceptible cave opening, Anton returned the CHP's speed to normal. The sun shone brightly, providing the only means to detect the cave's entrance; it was a naturally occurring crack in the side of the mountain with a sunlit circle in front of it. This fissure was set back behind a large boulder, making it nearly invisible, and difficult to detect. The team entered the circle and found the cave entrance on the far side of the boulder.

"As you see, the entrance to this cave is similar to the entrance to yours; it's disguised similarly." Anton pointed. "Here I will adjust the volume so that you will be able to hear the conversation of the team." Anton touched the CHP and stepped back. The Warriors' conversation immediately replaced Anton's narration.

"DISPERSE!" COMMANDED EDGAR SIX, THE team leader. Motioning with both hands, he watched his fellow Warriors carry out his orders, and then he too sought refuge behind a large rock.

Silently, each Warrior concealed himself with masterful proficiency. Quietly they waited, using their genetically advanced senses and perceptions for any sign of discovery. All was silent, so the team continued its advance.

Edgar waved his arm slightly to gain everyone's attention, and pointed to the cave entrance. "Luke inside!" he commanded.

Swiftly, Luke advanced toward the entrance, pausing for a moment to one side. With the speed and agility of a gazelle, he took another step and slipped inside. A few seconds later, he returned and gave the all-clear signal. Springing into action, the team entered the cave one by one. Once inside, they had strategic control of the cave's entrance, allowing them to proceed.

"AT THIS POINT," ANTON SAID to the villagers, "I felt uneasy about how we gained this tactical advantage; there wasn't anyone guarding the entrance. During our initial debriefing prior to the mission, there was no discussion of the enemy's tactical habits, so we didn't know what to expect. Part of our training is how adaptive and resourceful we can be in actual combat conditions."

"Apparently, the Troglodytes had no fear of intrusion from above, the entire population of humans lived below in the valley. Perhaps, since their eyes were accustomed to darkness, they only defended this entrance at night and rejected such activities during the day." Anton returned his attention to the presentation and the villagers continued to watch.

"GLOWRODS," EDGAR commanded, softly.

In unison, the team produced their glowrods—clear cylinders eighteen inches in length, made from a polymer that encased a core of Methonian crystal.

"THIS TOOL WAS THE ONLY weapon each of us carried. The crystal ring activates the weapon's functions, and the mind of the user controls the functionality. The glowrod can be fine-tuned to emit a variable amount of light as desired by the user, or collimated—that is to say, the rays can be made parallel—to emit a harmless beam of light from one end, similar to a laser. This can temporarily blind or intimidate an opponent; if necessary, the user can increase the intensity for cutting or other purposes. When used as a club, the rod shoots a cool neutral flame out one end, with enough power to turn solid rock to rubble; therefore, it can be used for a deadly attack at close range."

WITH GLOWRODS EMITTING A SOFT light—barely enough to illuminate the path—the group swiftly traveled downward through jagged rocks, and carefully maneuvered around and under the frequently changing ceiling heights. The floor of the tunnel was rough, and covered with small pebbles, like marbles. In places, this provided a challenge for the Warriors, yet they traveled skillfully, making only the slightest noise.

"After journeying deep into the mountain, we came upon a large semi-circular room with three additional tunnels converging at odd angles. A sentry guarded the entrance of each one, including the mouth of our tunnel. He became alarmed as we approached; the light of our glowrods apparently gave us away. Even the rock formations didn't provide enough cover to hide the light from eyes so accustomed to darkness." Pointing at the predicament, Anton continued to narrate.

"Edgar had anticipated this downside of using the glowrods, but he preferred the inevitable fight. He in particular invited battle, wishing to use force over stealth as his primary means to an end."

"TROGS AHEAD—MOVE!" shouted Edgar, and the group dispersed.

Launching himself into battle, Luke struck the first guard over the head with his glowrod, exploding his skull all over the cavern wall. Anton immediately rushed across the room to the far tunnel, where another guard raised his spear and prepared to fight, but turned around and fled as he saw his comrades helplessly slaughtered. Boris and Tybalt blasted the last two sentries with a shaft of light in the face. They fell to their knees, covering their eyes with both hands, and dropping their spears.

The Troglodytes had an advantage of speed in their natural environment, but Anton was much faster; he was tall and skinny, with long legs that had been genetically engineered for long-distance sprinting. Quickly, he overtook the fleeing cave dweller—but not before he'd let loose a cry for help. With one strike of his glowrod, Anton shattered the Troglodyte's skull. Grabbing his discarded spear, he returned to his comrades.

Duke and Ivan pinned the two survivors down as Boris and Edgar painfully extracted necessary information. Anton rejoined the melee after Boris acquired the location of the captured girl. Edgar drew his right index finger across his throat signaling to Tybalt to kill the two guards.

SUDDENLY, SEVERAL CHILDREN SCREAMED AS they witnessed the actions of the Warriors. It all happened so quickly that the village audience hesitated before they too gasped in horror as they realized the severity of what the children had witnessed.

"Anton!" snapped Tyrell. "We have children here! You must stop this!" Standing, the chief motioned for the women to take the young ones away from the presentation.

"You should use more discretion with your choices," Tyrell went on. "Did you think it was okay for the eyes of our innocents to witness such barbarism? I question your judgment! I see now that your choices may prove to be incompetent!"

Quickly Anton reached over and stopped the CHP. "Forgive me; I'm unaccustomed to editing my experiences, and I'd determined this mission to be significant. This is common for all Warriors to see, and to learn from." Clumsily, Anton attempted an apology. "Perhaps if the children went to sleep, I might continue? The answers to all your apprehensions, I believe, are contained within this mission; I'd like to complete my presentation." Pleading for a second chance, Anton looked at Tyrell, hoping the chief would understand.

"Very well," Tyrell answered. "I will trust you. We have seen enough that I believe in your... presentation. You may continue." He glared at Anton, as if to say: "This is your last chance."

Looking up at Mahkeetah, Anton saw a suppressed smirk; he pressed his lips together, holding back his thoughts. The former Warrior knew all too well that Anton's mission would inevitably include more violence, and he nearly chuckled outright as the story continued to unfold.

Touching the CHP, Anton set it into motion; it restarted where it had left off. Everyone's attention warily returned to the demonstration.

THE SOUND OF MANY FOOTSTEPS suddenly echoed from the tunnel that Anton had just left. The battle had consumed the Warriors' attention, and now they became stealthier as an unknown number of the enemy rapidly approached.

The seven Warriors proceeded down the corridor to the left of the one they'd arrived through. There was no cover available to shield their backs; the hand-hewn walls of this tunnel were nearly smooth, unlike the natural passages. They proceeded with added caution as quickly as possible, trying to stay ahead of the enemy's pursuit. Edgar led the way at a blinding pace, and the others followed tightly behind.

"AT THIS POINT, WE WERE desperately hoping for some type of refuge—an outcropping, an alcove, anything. As you see, all we found were occasional turns in the corridor." Anton looked at Tyrell as he spoke.

"Perhaps it would be expedient if you let everyone simply watch," Tyrell said. "Your comments only slow your presentation, and it's getting late." Tyrell stood up as he spoke, and looked around at everyone.

"Very well," Anton responded. "I will allow the projector to do its job." Looking first at Tyrell then at Mahkeetah, Anton sat next to the CHP and set it into motion. A smirk continued to mark Mahkeetah's face; he seemed content with Anton's awkwardness.

Since Anton had adjusted the CHP earlier, the less-eventful portions automatically sped up, playing through the scenes quickly.

THE TUNNEL SUDDENLY TOOK A sharp turn downward, making it difficult to keep a successful footing on the pebble-covered surface. Even the highly skilled Warriors had to slow their ferocious pace as the way became more hazardous; their feet slipped occasionally on the difficult surface. They traveled steeply downward through the tunnels for several minutes before arriving at a small chamber that seemed to serve as a resting point. In the center was a well, complete with a bucket on a rope and a crank-handle winch. Around the roughly circular room were crude benches cut from the cave walls.

"THE TREMENDOUS SPEED WE TRAVELED put us far ahead of our enemy," Anton said, "and this spot seemed an appropriate place for a rest; we felt grateful for the benefit of the well and of the seats." Pointing at the images, Anton again interjected a quick thought and then fell silent.

Mahkeetah gave Anton a look of disgust, as if to say he'd just promised to no longer interject. "Seems you can't keep your mouth shut," he mouthed at him.

"I DON'T HEAR ANYONE FOLLOWING," Edgar said. "We have time for a short rest." He motioned for Anton to operate the crank handle, and everyone sat and rested for a few moments as they waited for him to retrieve some water.

As quickly as he could, Anton produced a bucketful of water from the well. The well was very deep and required time to winch it. After careful examination, everyone agreed the water was safe for consumption. It seemed unusually warm, considering how deep it came from the ground. But it refreshed everybody's thirst.

As Anton labored, Luke scouted ahead for signs of the enemy. He wasn't gone long, and returned in time to drink his share and rest with the others.

From inside his tunic, Anton pulled out a few of his rations, and proceeded to eat. He was quite hungry.

"Good idea," Edgar said. "I will have some too. Who knows when we will have another chance to eat?" He also reached into his tunic, and everyone followed his example.

"WE ATE QUICKLY, SINCE NOBODY knew when we would suddenly need to depart. We assumed the Troglodytes pursuing us weren't far behind, and nobody knew how many of them there'd be. We didn't have time for a large-scale engagement, and we needed to use the lead time to find the captive girl." Anton pointed at the holograms as he quickly interjected once again.

"HOW MUCH TIME DO YOU think we have?" asked Luke. "The path before us looks easier but it will be much harder to traverse."

"Could you elaborate a little?" Edgar was never one for small talk, as was the way of all Warriors, but certain information required sharing. He wasted little time trying to keep everyone informed.

"The way is still down, the small pebbles are nearly gone, and crude stairs are cut into the floor. Overall, it's less hazardous—yet it will require more time to navigate the sporadic placement of the uneven stairs. They deviate in height from a couple inches to a couple of feet." Luke looked around at each of his comrades, making sure they'd all understood him.

"One more thing I noticed," Luke went on. "The smell of the air is changing; it's becoming acrid, and has the scent of sulfur about it." Concern covered his face as he watched everyone's reaction.

"It sounds like there's volcanic activity ahead of us—or perhaps worse." Tybalt seemed sure of his assessment and a silent curse passed over his lips. "I've dealt with subterranean lava flows before, and I don't relish another encounter with them."

"How long have we been underground?" asked Ivan. All of the Warriors had a remarkable sense of time built into their genetic makeup, but being underground for a long period always created a margin of error.

"Easily half a day," replied Duke. "And, by my calculations, we're perhaps an hour from our destination." Everyone nodded, concurring with his estimation.

QUICKLY, ANTON PAUSED THE CHP, and then raised his arm to get everyone's attention. "Every Warrior has a special knack at calculating time and distance, and we are trained for logical probabilities. Each of us shared a portion of Duke's particular calculative skills. It's never known precisely what special talents a Warrior might possess, and it is always a surprise to find out each one's unique talents. I personally excel at anticipating an opponent's next move, and it always aids me during combat." Looking around, he set the CHP back in motion.

"VERY GOOD, THEN—LET'S PREPARE TO move out." Edgar held up his hand, dismissing any further conversation.

Suddenly the sounds of footsteps echoed off the tunnel walls; the enemy was close behind. Instantly the Warriors bolted from their seats and continued their journey toward the bowels of the caverns below. As they entered the tunnel leading down, they discovered for themselves the truth about the air. It quickly became thick with the smell of sulfur, making it more difficult to breathe. The reason for the smell was obvious to all—it signified that lava was not far away.

The tunnel suddenly became more cave-like, having rough naturally formed walls and an inconsistent ceiling height, but the Troglodytes had chiseled the floor, creating the odd stairs that Luke had described. Each stair was uneven in height, length, and width, and roughly hewn. It was difficult to travel over the stairs quickly, especially given the darkness.

The cavern walls widened and tightened as the Warriors continued down. Finally, they came upon an enormous dimly lit chamber. It had the unmistakable red glow from lava far below. The air became even worse. Everyone coughed as they exited the tunnel. They walked out on a large ledge with a waist-high semicircular wall encompassing it. The outcropping stretched far enough that it allowed the Warriors easily to see into the depths below. The chamber ceiling was nearly a hundred yards above them, and the flowing lava was more than four hundred yards below.

"I hate the smell of sulfur!" Tybalt said, putting his hand over his face and trying to filter the air as best he could.

"We can't breathe this air forever, but we will adapt to it somewhat in a few minutes. Hopefully we can be clear of it before it overcomes us completely," Edgar said, trying to reassure everyone, including himself. He needed to keep everyone's attention focused on the mission, not their discomfort.

Looking down and far to the left, Anton was the first to see their destination. A large island of rock rose high above the river of molten lava. The flow split into two and oozed around both sides, making it a treacherous place to reach. On the island's surface Anton could see what appeared to be the captured slaves—but the distance was too far for an accurate verification. As best he could tell, the slaves appeared shackled to posts in a circle.

"I see them, over there!" Anton shouted, pointing. "It looks hopeless. There doesn't appear to be a way to get to them. Obviously, we can't cross the lava." Anton shook his head as he indicated the prisoner's location to Edgar. "It's going to be difficult."

"They were put there," Edgar said. "I'm sure we'll get to them the same way." He gave Anton a stern look; he disapproved of his inability to instantly draw a logical conclusion. "It's a fundamental concept even someone *your age* should easily realize."

"There's a ledge that follows the wall over here!" Luke said. "Follow me, it's this way!" He had again scouted ahead and found the path they needed to take. His special ability was proving essential for the team's success.

Quickly, each Warrior made his way along the ledge. There was barely enough rock to stand upon, but their superior Methonian skills mastered the challenge; it seemed to them as if the ledge were wide enough for an army. Clinging to the rock wall for additional support was difficult, since the stone was uncomfortably warm, but they pushed on around the chamber with inordinate speed. A misplaced step at this point would easily mean death—the fall was great and the flowing lava would unquestionably kill anyone. The expanse around the chamber was extensive, but it posed the sort of challenge the Warriors invited.

Occasionally, a foot would slip, or a handhold would give way, making the journey even harder. The Warriors' hands and lungs burned from the heat; their feet burned through their shoes, and everyone sweated profusely, making the effort increasingly difficult with each step. They traveled for nearly half a mile around bends, outcroppings, inlets, and the many irregularities created by the subterranean flows. At times, the cavern walls wound around backwards, and in all directions, but the ledge steadily increased in width, making the travel gradually easier. The ledge declined slowly downward and gradually took them closer to the lava. Finally, they reached the far end of the chamber and stepped onto another outcropping—much like the one they'd left behind. It too had a waist-high wall surrounding its edge, making it a safe place to rest and look around.

The vantage point allowed them to see far below; they could see the source of the lava. They watched as it belched high into the air and then fell back upon itself, reabsorbing into the flow. The lava's orange light was spectacular; it flickered and danced on the walls, making it difficult to see clearly.

As they neared the lava's source, the air felt even heavier, and the heat became completely intolerable. No average human could withstand these extreme conditions for long; even with their genetically superior bodies, the Warriors found it difficult to endure. They wore no special protection from these elements. They became dehydrated and fatigued.

As they left the outcropping, they looked back along the ledge they'd negotiated, and saw a long line of pale-skinned Troglodytes following them, traversing the ledge with an ease that rivaled the Warriors' skills. The distance between the two groups was quickly shrinking.

Anton felt disgusted at how inhuman and ugly the Troglodytes truly were; they had long unkempt dirty grey hair, and massive facial features, including a heavy brow. But the most prominent feature was an oversized mouth with very long razor-sharp teeth. Their skin was pale grey and rough to the touch. Their feet were twice the size of a human's. They truly were monsters.

"They're coming!" Tybalt yelled. "There must be nearly a hundred of them!"

"This isn't a good place for a fight," Edgar said. "We are at a tremendous disadvantage; let's find a more suitable spot!" Edgar urged everyone to push forward; the alternative was an unacceptably confined battle from a significant number of enemies.

"We must also find relief from this heat," Luke proclaimed, "and soon! I fear the air and these unbearable conditions more than the Troglodytes!" Everyone knew the overwhelming temperature and poisonous air could kill them if the enemy didn't reach them first.

"Things are about to get worse before they get better," Anton said. "The ledge is headed steeply down at this point!" He had sprinted a short distance ahead and was reporting over his shoulder. "We're in luck, though; the path leads toward an opening in the wall!" Quickly he sprinted further ahead, leading the way, hoping to discover the relief Luke had mentioned.

As if of one mind, the Warriors ran in unison, following Anton to the cave opening. It was small—little more than a narrow slit, but wide enough to allow a single human through. Anton hesitated as he approached it, and waited for his brothers to catch up.

"Luke—inside!" Edgar pointed toward the crack and quickly followed him.

In turn, each of the Warriors pushed through the narrow slit. Immediately everyone noticed the improved air, and the temperature dropped considerably. It was obvious that some other passage supplied the cooler atmosphere. Stalactites and stalagmites filled the ancient chamber; everyone stood in awe as they marveled at the natural beauty. It seemed in stark contrast to every passage they'd traveled through previously.

"Glowrods on full!" Edgar commanded. The smaller chamber they stood in adjoined a larger one, and it was full of Troglodytes, as far as their eyes could see.

Tybalt was the last to enter and fire up his glowrod, and he instantly came under attack, along with his brothers. Every Warrior fought for his life as the cave dwellers flung themselves from all directions at the intruders. But the Troglodytes didn't stand a chance against the superior fighting power and skills of the Warriors—even with the former's greater numbers. The glowrods blasted away at each assailant, and the room quickly filled with dead bodies.

"They're coming from behind, as well!" Tybalt cried, reminding everyone that reinforcements would soon arrive from the rear. "We'll be sandwiched in!"

"Leave none of them alive!" Edgar snapped, trying to keep everyone focused. It mattered little; they were preoccupied with the handto-hand melee.

The body count quickly increased, and bodies piled all around them, making it difficult to maneuver. If they couldn't push through the front line soon, the enemy would overcome them with overwhelming numbers from behind. But as luck would have it, the number of Troglodytes soon dwindled, and the remaining few fled for their lives. The ground was slick with blood, and the Warriors slipped on the dead bodies as they climbed over the survivors in pursuit.

However, the Warriors' luck soon ran out—the rest of the pursuing enemy finally pushed through the crack in the wall and into the chamber behind them. They found the bodies lying all around, and each Troglodyte let out a howl like the cry of a wolf as he entered and saw the fallen dead. Hate filled their eyes, and they craved revenge.

"Let's end this here!" Edgar pointed a finger at the largest caveman, offering a final challenge. Several had squeezed through, and they were ready for action. His own eyes held as much fury as the Troglodytes', and he spoiled to increase the body count.

"I'm tired of running from such pathetic creatures as you!" Edgar said, grasping his glowrod and standing in ready stance. He shot a bolt of light at the eyes of the apparent leader.

Instantly, each of the Warriors followed suit. Glowrods blinded the eyes of all the Troglodytes in the room, and they blasted their way through the enemy. Bodies shattered as the glowrods struck flesh; more blood spattered, covering the cavern walls and floor until it flowed in little streams. The enemy's cries of pain echoed off the walls in a frightful chorus of agony. Within moments, they were all dead.

Finally, the Warriors stood there looking at each other across the dead. They shared a mutual sense of loathing for the degenerative life forms they'd destroyed. Only Anton stood there displeased by their passion to kill; he felt offended by the satisfaction his brothers shared. He struggled with his own feelings and the contempt that filled his heart. Shrugging, he coldly turned his attention away from the carnage and tried to bury his emotions. Looking around the enormous chamber, he forced himself to examine the surrounding formations so that he might distract himself from his discomfort.

"Close the crack in the wall," Edgar said, pointing in the direction they'd come from. "We must slow or prevent any more of them from following us."

Everyone grabbed dead bodies and piled them against the crack in the wall. After several minutes, it was impossible for anyone to push through the opening from either side of the crack. For now, the passage was effectively sealed.

"Time grows short. The enemy must've received a warning. We must press forward!" Edgar spoke softly; he wanted to leave the chamber quickly. "A job well done. We had little choice." With an insistent look, he carefully caught the eyes of each of his brothers; he needed make sure they all agreed.

"I've had enough too," Anton responded; he needed to console his own feelings, which his brothers didn't share. "I feel as if I've committed some form of genocide." He was alone in his regret, and his brothers stared at him, perplexed. "I can't stand being here and seeing this." He retched as he spoke, revealing a forbidden aspect of his character.

Glaring at Anton, Edgar let him know he disapproved of his weakness; it was not how a Warrior was supposed to be. "They had it coming!" he said. "It was them or us!" Judgmentally, he stared at Anton, as if to say: "I'll report this when we return."

"I'm sorry," Anton said, defensively. "I didn't mean anything." He fumbled with his words.

"Enough!" Edgar said. "Let's go!" Pointing at Anton, and then motioning to the others, he led the way through the extravagant feature-filled room and down the next tunnel. It didn't take long before it opened into a colossal ancient chamber filled with gargantuan formations. This was a spectacular sight that left everyone in awe of its breathtaking natural beauty. The Warriors deployed their glowrods to see everything around them, but in such a large chamber, the light failed to reveal anything.

"There will be more of them ahead." Luke reminded everyone of the importance of keeping their attention focused on the mission. "We can't stop now—keep moving!" It was obvious they all needed a break, but they couldn't afford one now.

"He's right," Edgar said. "Keep your glowrods at a minimum—they need to recharge, and we don't want to alert every Trog in the area that we're here!" Edgar scowled at everyone and pointed his glowrod ahead of them, trying to find the best path through the labyrinth of formations.

Continuing on, they searched for an obvious path but found none; soon they wondered which way to go. Every Warrior had a genetically enhanced sense of direction, but there was no way to determine a path inside the natural maze. The multitude of choices wound through the formations inside the cavern, and quickly left the team disoriented. After a short time, they came to a halt and studied every aspect of their surroundings.

"I see footprints over here!" Luke abruptly yelled; his sudden excitement brought relief to the confused team. "They go in this direction." Quickly, he headed down the path. The others followed behind.

"Be careful!" Edgar yelled behind Luke as he pulled away from the others. "You don't know what lies ahead. We need to stay together!" Too often, one of the Warriors had separated for a look ahead, hoping to prove his own skills. But the potential of hidden dangers made this tactic inadvisable.

Hesitating, Luke allowed everyone to catch up. Edgar had good sense, and they all knew it. Soon the enormous chamber narrowed and they could see the dim light of the lava against the far wall. As they approached, he motioned for everyone to fall in behind him. A distinct smell of sulfur again filled the air, and the temperature increased proportionally—a sure sign they'd made the right choice. Looking through the crack, Edgar could see they'd arrived at the island.

"We're here." Edgar stated flatly.

The crack in the wall was larger than the previous one had been, and it gave Edgar a clear view of how to approach the bridge. There was a large semi-circular ledge just outside the small opening, and it had the appearance of a tiny beach, complete with volcanic sand. Jutting from the sand were large volcanic rocks, and fifty yards beyond was the stone bridge that arched over to the island.

However, there was one problem: there were fifteen sentries positioned along the rim of the ledge. Each one stood behind an oversized crossbow set upon a stand that swiveled around. They appeared oblivious to the Warriors' arrival, and they appeared unprepared for an attack from their direction. They randomly pointed their weapons, but could easily aim them at an approaching target if needed. The projectile atop the crossbow was as thick as a spear but considerably shorter, and a large stockpile of additional ammo was readily available nearby.

The bridge was nearly fifteen feet wide and had a waist-high stone blockade on each side—an unusual safety feature that seemed out of place. Four tall towers of stone nearly a hundred feet tall stood at each corner of the bridge. They were ten feet square at the base and tapering to nearly a point at the peak, resembling monoliths. Under the pyramid-shaped cap, a large hollow space contained an unusual green fire that burned furiously, as if some gas were under pressure and set afire. The torches' luminosity combined with the lava's glow from below, eerily lit the entire ledge; this provided enough light for the Warriors to see everything.

The walls surrounding the ledge appeared to be hand-carved from solid rock. To the Warriors' right was a raised platform made from heavy timbers. Several oversized drums sat upon this platform, obviously prepared for some unknown purpose.

The guards concerned Edgar the most; he knew if the Warriors charged the bridge they wouldn't all survive. But there seemed to be no other way to attain their objective than to expose themselves— therefore, they needed to formulate a plan of attack.

"This is a tricky situation," Edgar said. "It's unlike anything we've experienced so far." He looked at his brothers and motioned for each of them to assess the situation. "Let's put our heads together and see what we can come up with. What are *your* ideas Anton?"

Surprised, Anton gave Edgar a perplexed look. He hadn't expected he would be included in the planning of an attack. Since he was the youngest of the Warriors by more than two years, he relished the opportunity to share his opinion. He intuitively understood Edgar's concern and stood there for a moment as he calculated his response.

"I think surprise is our best tactic. We may have a chance if we wait until all or nearly all of them are looking away, slip through the crack as quickly as possible, and then blind them with our glowrods when they discover our advance. This should give us an opportunity to dodge their weapons as we rush them." Anton hoped everyone would quickly agree— but for a moment, nobody said a word. Obviously, everyone had their own opinion to share.

"I have an idea," interjected Duke. "We have the best runner in the universe—an Anton series Warrior. Have him run straight through to the bridge; its walls provide all the cover he'll need. The mounted crossbows won't have time to take aim at him, so I doubt they'd fire at him before he gets there. He will have the element of surprise, and will draw their attention from us, providing an opportunity for an attack."

"This is a good idea, but we haven't seen the area on either side of the crack," declared Ivan. "The large rocks and outcroppings could conceal any number of enemies; we need to have a look to each side before sending Anton out!"

"When Anton runs across the ledge I am sure he'll draw the attention of anyone concealed behind these rocks," scoffed Boris. He was one of the

Barbarian series, and he always preferred brute force over planning. "When they see Anton running, it's likely they'll come out in the open, and we can surprise them from behind!" As he grinned, it was clear he relished an aggressive battle.

"I agree with Ivan," Tybalt said. "We can't calculate what we can't see, we can only anticipate; there might be some other form of weaponry hidden from view. Anton may be in jeopardy if the bridge walls don't provide enough cover. That failure won't serve us." Tybalt always evaluated multiple possibilities. He was a Theoretician Series Warrior, and had specialized abilities for abstract computations. "At this point we can't afford to lose anyone."

Everyone knew he was right, and nodded. Then they looked at Edgar for his command decision.

"I agree with Tybalt," said Edgar. He knew Tybalt offered the best strategies, which he accepted without second-guessing. "I think we need a final strategy to manage the unseen." Looking at Duke, he encouraged his response.

"Allow Ivan and me to follow Anton out," Duke said. "He will cover the right side and I the left. We will deal with whatever we find. There is of course a certain amount of risk in this, but we have an excellent chance there is nothing there." Duke was always sensible, and only offered his opinion when he believed he was right. "After we've secured the sides, the rest of you can take out the guns."

"Very well," Edgar said. "It's settled. Everyone knows his job. Luke and I will handle the guns on the left, Boris and Tybalt on the right." The plan was now a command. "Okay, Anton, you're first—wait for your best opportunity when they're not looking."

Everyone made room for Anton's sprint. Duke and Ivan stood closely behind him, ready for their part in the attack, and the others prepared themselves to pull up the rear. Anton wondered why the Troglodytes on the crossbows seemed to spend more time looking out over the vast chamber of lava, rather than keeping an eye on the ledge, or even the crack in the wall. It was as if they were guarding the ledge from something else. It didn't take long to find the perfect opportunity to make his dash to the bridge.

"Here goes nothing!" Anton said. Quickly, he stepped into the narrow opening and passed through. With the speed of a cheetah, he sprinted toward the bridge in a desperate race for cover; the only protection he could hope for was fifty yards away.

Anton's heart pounded as adrenaline poured into his bloodstream, fueling his muscles with incredible acceleration. The distance flew by in a single moment—no more than two or three seconds—but to Anton it seemed like an eternity; every step felt in slow motion. Immediately, he dove behind the rock wall of the bridge; the cover was sufficient to hide from the Troglodytes.

However, something happened that none of the Warriors had anticipated. None of the Troglodytes noticed Anton as he flew past their ranks. He was so swift and silent that the guards simply missed seeing him altogether. The plan seemed in jeopardy unless he did something to draw their attention.

"Damn it!" Edgar said as he watched the first element of their plan collapse.

Suddenly Duke and Ivan bolted from their cover into the open—Ivan to the left and Duke to the right. They hoped to surprise any unseen opposition. Just as Anton's effort failed to gain the attention of the Troglodytes, Duke's and Ivan's plan too seemed in jeopardy. Not a single Troglodyte hid from view, as they had expected. Even the cover that the large rocks and outcroppings provided was insufficient to protect them from the mounted weaponry. To make it worse, they immediately drew the attention of the guards. The Warriors' plans had disintegrated.

Immediately, several of the crossbows whirled around, and the Troglodytes took aim at the sprinting Warriors; straightaway they fired their heavy bolts at them. Duke and Ivan skillfully dodged the first round of attacks, but more weapons swung around for a second volley.

"Run, quickly!" yelled Edgar. Pushing Luke through the crack, he followed him, with Boris and Tybalt close behind. The four ran out into the open, hoping to draw some of the attention away from Duke and Ivan.

Seeing what was happening, Anton realized that the plan had gone awry. He stood up, revealing himself to the cavemen. Attempting to confuse them, he jumped and waved his arms, yelling: "Hey, look over here!" Unexpectedly, his sudden improvisation was far cleverer than he'd anticipated.

Anton stood directly between the two Troglodytes closest to him. Surprised, they both promptly swiveled their crossbows around, aiming directly at him. Looking back and forth, he quickly realized his unusual predicament. Swiftly, he dove for safety behind the walls of the bridge, just as the Troglodytes fired simultaneously at him. The two bolts both missed him completely, and unintentionally struck each other; incredibly, the force sliced neatly through the first Troglodytes and continued toward the next two. Without giving the second pair a moment to react, the bolts struck them directly in their chests, like skewers. Four of the enemy tumbled and fell off the ledge into the fiery lava below.

Shocked, Edgar whooped a cry of excitement. "Woohoo!" he yelled. "That clumsy idiot—I've never seen such luck!" He dodged another speeding bolt by somersaulting, and returned to his feet with classic Methonian skill.

Duke and Ivan chased after their brothers as the team advanced toward the crossbows. Anton continued to distract the Troglodytes by attempting to cross the bridge and then ducking behind the wall; he acted like an easy target confusing the enemy, and it gave his brothers an opportunity for hand-to-hand combat.

Unexpectedly, two of the Troglodytes suddenly left their weapons and ran toward the drums. Quickly, they leapt upon the stage and started beating them. A distinct rhythmic sound filled the air, a rhythm that gave off a low sonorousness. The drums were enormous, and vibrated heavily when played, echoing off the cavern walls in deep reverberating tones; everyone could feel the sound waves vibrate against their skin.

"It's a signal! They're calling for reinforcements!" yelled Tybalt. "They must be stopped immediately!"

"Anton! Go!" Edgar shouted fervidly, with a wild look in his eyes; the passion for battle raged in him.

Instantaneously, Anton ran to the stage in the span of a heartbeat, following Edgar's command while the other Warriors quickly slaughtered the remaining Troglodytes and tossed their limp carcasses over the edge of the precipice. It only took a few moments to eliminate their enemies, and to bring the crossbows under Warrior control.

As Anton leapt upon the stage, he hurled himself at the first drummer. Feet first, he flew through the air, kicking the first Troglodyte's sternum, knocking the air from his lungs; he tumbled backwards, hitting his head on the floor of the stage. Rebounding off his chest, Anton did a backwards flip, and flew over the head of the second Troglodyte, landing lightly on his feet. Whirling around on one leg, his heel struck the other's cheekbone, shattering his skull and breaking his neck. Grasping the enormous and heavy drumstick in both hands, Anton twirled around, holding it like a sledgehammer. He then flung it with all his strength at the first Troglodyte, smashing his face and killing him instantly.

The Warriors looked at each other. Quickly they regrouped on the stage, examined the drums, and pondered their significance.

"There was purpose here," Tybalt said. "I believe our time is limited; more of the enemy will soon be upon us. I believe we are in for another onslaught." He spoke rapidly; adrenaline coursed through his bloodstream, and he fidgeted as if spoiling for more combat.

"Perhaps," Edgar said, "but the noise of the magma below may have drowned out much of drums' sound; I don't think it warned anyone beyond this chamber. I believe we're safe, at least for now." He glared at everyone in turn, as if making sure his word was final. He expected complete agreement. He wanted the team to focus on their mission. "Let's go get that girl and leave!"

Without hesitation, the Warriors hurried toward the bridge. It arched over to the island nearly seventy yards away, connecting forty yards below its surface; it attached to a small ledge recessed in front of a cave-like opening. The green fire burning in the corner towers lighted the ledge, casting an eerie flickering refulgence. The red glow of the lava from below accentuated the tomblike atmosphere, and added a feeling of inauspicious foreboding.

Oddly, there were no guards on duty outside of the cave's entrance on the island. Moments passed and still there was no response to the sound of the drums.

The Warriors quickly crossed the bridge and entered the cave-like opening. Inside, they discovered a series of prison cells, complete with iron bars that filled a rather large and dark dungeon. Torches inset in cubbies inside the walls lit the chamber; each burned the same inscrutable green fire as the monolithic towers at the corners of the bridge. Mysteriously, there was a reduction of the volcanic gases inside the dungeon, making the air inside easier to breathe. The green fire seemed to burn away the sulfur, improving the air quality. A flight of stairs at the far end of the chamber provided access to the island's surface. Most of the cells were empty, but one had a dozen men locked inside.

Frantic cries erupted from the incarcerated captives when they saw the Warriors arrive. However, the Warriors passed them by with hardly a glance. The men reached from behind the bars, grasping at the Warriors, pleading for their release.

"Free us before we're fed to that infernal beast!" the men shrieked frantically. "It will kill us *all!* You must *free* us! Only you *Warriors* can save us!"

Wild-eyed, they begged for salvation, but the Warriors continued to ignore their hysterical pleas, and remained focused on their mission.

They were entirely without feelings, only the objective to fight the monster and free the girl prioritized their actions.

"The girl must be above," Edgar said. "We observed a circle of people when we first entered the main chamber. If time permits after we find her, we'll release these men." Edgar coolly pointed up the stairs, toward the island's surface.

Without another word, the Warriors ran toward the surface and examined their surroundings. The island was entirely volcanic, its surface was very rough and uneven, yet relatively flat. It was three hundred by two hundred yards, and roughly oval-shaped; occasional jagged outreaches protruded around its perimeter. It appeared as though the molten rock that flowed around its perimeter had gradually worn it away unevenly.

The burning sulfuric air again burned the Warriors' lungs. The sound of people coughing indicated the location of the prisoners; a shocking sight awaited them as they approached the sound. On the far edge of the island was a circle of iron crosses sticking out of the rock, each jutted at a sixty-degree angle from the surface and had a prisoner shackled to it; there were ten in all. In the center of the circle was a pit nearly six feet deep, and nearly twenty yards in diameter; the crosses leaned in towards each other and the prisoners lay on their backs facing outward; the scene resembled a mass crucifixion.

A sense of confusion and horror filled Anton's heart as he gazed upon the prisoners; he'd never felt so distraught by anything before. He was bothered by the thought of torture, yet his brother Warriors seemed completely unaffected.

Then it happened—a low-pitched rumbling wail echoed off the walls of the enormous underground cavern. The horrifying sound came from beyond the circle—beyond the island and across the subterranean chamber. It was as if some angry creature was in exquisite pain. Everyone gasped at the sound. Instantly, the Warriors focused their attention on the edge of the island from which the sound emanated. They quickly ran to the captives and attempted to set them free.

Like a chorus, the prisoners screamed for their lives; their shrieks of fear indicated they knew precisely what was about to occur.

"It's coming!" yelled one man. He was hysterical, and he strained heavily against the shackles that bound his wrists and ankles. A look of pure horror marked his face—then he laughed hysterically.

"You didn't bring the keys!" screamed a second man. "You can't help us without the keys!" His voice was shrill and desperate as he realized his fate was nearly sealed.

"What keys—where are the keys?" asked Edgar. "We didn't see any keys." He looked from face to face, hoping someone would have an answer. But all he saw was horror, and all he heard were screams of fear.

"It will be here before you can retrieve them!" yelled a third man. "They're back there, below—with the other prisoners!" Uncontrollably, he shrieked his protest louder than the others, and struggled desperately to free himself from his shackles. "It'll kill all of *you* too! You don't stand a chance! Nobody does!"

Anton, Boris, Luke, and Tybalt all spotted a single girl shackled to one of the crosses. They raced over to free her as quickly as they could; it was obvious that she was the girl they sought.

"Are you the daughter of the chief?" asked Tybalt. "We're here to take you home."

"Glowrods!" Edgar commanded, sharply. Quickly each Warrior unsheathed their glowrod and brought it to full intensity. "We don't have time to retrieve any keys. "Anton, use your glowrod as a cutting torch!"

"It will only last a minute or two that way!" Anton stammered. "What will I do when it runs out of energy?"

"Quit your whining," Edgar retorted. "Do as I command! We don't have time for this!" Edgar was firm, and glared at Anton for his impudence. "Your comments burn time instead of those shackles! *Move* it!"

Duke, Ivan, Luke, and Boris sprang to perform Anton's job, pushing him out of the way. They burned through the fetters, freeing the girl. However, they'd run out of time. Just as the shackles fell away, the four glowrods ran desperately low of the precious energy that powered them; it would take time before they could fully recharge. The four Warriors pulled the girl free, and again they heard the strident trumpet of some unknown creature—only this time it sounded much closer, as if it were just below the edge of the island's surface.

"It's *here!*" shrieked the teenaged girl hysterically, and tears poured from her eyes. "Don't let me die! Not like this!" Boris picked her up and slung her over Anton's shoulder, as if she were no more than a toddler.

"Run to safety! You're the fastest, go!" Boris yelled his command, and Anton responded instantly, with a burst of incomparable speed. To him, it was as if the girl weighed nothing. He crossed the distance to safety in the blink of an eye.

"The gem lizard is here!" one of the crucified men screamed. "He will consume us all! We're as good as dead!" He pulled desperately against his shackles, vainly attempting to free himself.

A general yelling of all the men pleading for their lives filled the air, and the Warriors watched their wasted efforts as they frantically attempted to free themselves before the mysterious creature appeared; without the keys, they would swiftly run out of time before they could free them.

As Anton ran for the stairs, an enormous reptilian creature climbed over the edge of the island and stood next to the circle of captives. It let out an ear-splitting scream of rage. The magnitude of the sound reverberated and shook both the air and stone; pebbles vibrated all around, and the Warriors grasped their ears, to little avail. Suddenly, the creature pounded the volcanic stone with its massive front claws; everyone instantly knew what it was.

"*Lapillusaurus,*" Edgar muttered as he looked up at its humongous visage. "Ivan, Duke—stay!" Edgar selected these Warriors knowing their glowrods still had a full charge, and that they were going to need them if they were to have any chance at survival. He realized that for the rest of them to remain alive they needed to stall the creature. He knew he was sentencing his brothers to a certain death, but every Warrior was equal to a small army and he anticipated a major battle.

The *Lapillusaurus* had raptor-like talons on all four of its limbs; on its hind feet, they were like that of *Deinonychus*—a raptor from the late Cretaceous period on Earth—but its front claws had a few significant differences: they had massive long fingers, an unusual opposable thumb, and extraordinarily long arms. Its massive head sat upon almost-human shoulders; the head resembled that of *Tyrannosaurus rex*, only with a bony crest growing from the back of the skull like a *Parasaurolophus*. The body had mammoth bulging muscles, and its torso was vaguely human in shape. It had thick scales over its entire body that easily protected it from the extreme heat of the lava below, and razor-edged triangular protrusions that jutted from its spine the entire length of its body. A massive whip-like tail stretched nearly twenty feet, and it lashed to-and-fro like a cat's.

From the beginning of their training, every Warrior prepared himself to die so that another might live. Edgar showed no feelings for his friends, however he knew a Warrior's death was as important as his life—even during a training mission that seemingly had little import. In this way, only the top-notch fighters would survive the process of attrition; this guaranteed the finest ultimate product. If either Ivan or Duke survived, so much the better for the mission's success.

The young girl's scuffling made the escape difficult for Anton, and he worked extra hard to carry her swiftly to the refuge of the prison chamber. Even so, it only took seconds for them to reach the opening to the stairs. The opening was far too small for the creature to pursue them, ensuring their safety. Anton dashed into the chamber below—where the other prisoners were incarcerated—and waited for the rest of the team to catch up. He hadn't seen the *Lapillusaurus* as it reached the island's surface, but knew instinctively the moment it had, just before fleeing down the stairs.

The girl screamed relentlessly, and struggled to free herself as they entered the dungeon. Anton set her down and held her hands for emotional support. The girl's screaming changed to sobbing as she realized that though she was now safe, Anton had left her friends behind. She looked at him angrily and pulled her hands away. Realizing where she was, she suddenly ran over to the cell containing her friends and reached through the bars, preferring their emotional support to his.

"You left them *behind*; you Warriors left them *behind!*" She looked down at the floor and then closed her eyes as she sobbed. A moment later, she turned around and looked up into Anton's eyes, as if pleading for all their lives, and as if he were personally responsible for leaving them to die.

Never having any experience comforting a woman, Anton was at a loss as to what he should do. "My friends will be here soon; I'm sure they'll bring your friends with them; they are very good at rescues." He clumsily forced a smile for her, and hoped he'd said what she needed to hear. "You are safe with me; take comfort in your own rescue, and I'll see what I can do to free your friends here." Anton pointed at the confined prisoners.

The four remaining Warriors returned to the dungeon, joining Anton and the chief's daughter. Screams from the circle of crosses called after them as they fled down the stairs; it was obvious that they were about to pay an expensive price. Edgar had found it hard to leave two Warriors behind, knowing he would likely never see them again. It was a bitter pill to swallow, and he cursed himself as he made his escape.

Ivan and Duke looked up into the eyes of the towering *Lapillusaurus* as it studied the incarcerated men. Even though it was standing nearly six feet down in the pit, they had to look up into its face.

"Any ideas?" asked Ivan. "I'm at a loss."

Duke shook his head and heaved a nervous sigh. "Not a clue; our Masters didn't teach us how to fight this creature; I guess we weren't expected to."

Duke and Ivan turned to each other with a look of grim acceptance, knowing that neither would survive an encounter with the *Lapillusaurus.*

"Wait for it to look away, and then blind it while I climb on its back; I'll try to crush its skull with my glowrod." Duke's plan seemed futile, but they didn't have many options. Ivan nodded his agreement, and the two prepared to make their move.

"You realize that thing has no fear of us!" Ivan said. "Look how it ignores us completely."

A slight grin appeared on Duke's face as they both realized a possible advantage. "You're right. We *will* have an opportunity. The moment it turns its attention away, I'll make my move."

With a motion so swift that the eye couldn't follow it, the gem lizard snatched one of the crucified men in one of its massive claws; the talon was so hot it seared the man's skin instantly. With the precision of a surgeon, it used its other talon like a pair of scissors to snip each arm at the wrist and each leg at the ankle, and it held the man like a doll. The Lizard brought him screaming to its face and examined him carefully. Using a single razor-sharp claw, he neatly sliced through the man's clothing, removed it from his body like it was peeling a banana, and then proceeded to consume him as if he were the fruit inside. The distinct sound of bones crunching filled the air, and blood gushed from the corners of the Lizard's mouth, trailing down the side of its chin. The sight was horrifying—even to a Warrior.

The *Lapillusaurus* grasped another man and then suddenly gagged and coughed. Reaching delicately into its mouth, it drew out a large stone. The rock was translucent and roughly spherical, and it appeared to be a raw diamond-like crystal. Tossing it to the ground, the lizard snipped the limbs of its next victim and prepared it for consumption.

Facing away from the two Warriors, the *Lapillusaurus* ignored them completely. Seeing his opportunity, Duke lurched forward and leapt upon the back of the creature as planned. Its shark-tooth-like spine sliced his hands and legs as he climbed up the bony armor. Blood oozed from open wounds, making his efforts slippery and nearly impossible. Even worse, the creature's body was so hot that his flesh sizzled and smoked.

As expected, the *Lapillusaurus* didn't like the Warrior climbing on its back. As it turned around slowly and reached in vain to swipe Duke off, Ivan found his opportunity to strike. Grasping his glowrod, he shot a bolt of light at the lizard's eyes, attempting to blind it—however, his effort failed. Unbeknownst to anyone, the *Lapillusaurus* had an inner eyelid that instantly blocked the attack.

Blowing angrily through the horn in its head, the gem lizard bellowed forth a deep-pitched tone that resonated off the cave walls. The powerful audio vibrations blasted Ivan, knocking him off his feet to the ground. Then it shook back and forth, once again trying to dislodge Duke. Unbelievably, the Warrior managed to hold on firmly. Raising his glowrod, he struck at the base of the neck and shattered several of the creature's protective armor plates. Again, a mighty wail filled the air, nearly deafening everyone. Blood poured from Duke's ears; his eardrums had been blasted, and he'd never hear properly again.

Falling to all fours, the *Lapillusaurus* climbed from the pit and slowly shook its body like a dog expelling water from its fur, and then rolled over in Ivan's direction. Duke lost his grip and tumbled clear of the rolling monster. Returning to an upright position, it raised its head into the air, trumpeted in anger, and snarled at the two Warriors with a look of impending doom.

"Go ahead, you foul beast—do your worst!" taunted Ivan, even though he knew the creature couldn't understand what he said. Holding his glowrod ready, he prepared to strike the creature.

For what seemed like an eternity, the two opponents looked directly into each other's eyes, in a moment of mutual loathing. The *Lapillusaurus* instinctively knew nothing equaled it, and Duke knew there wasn't a creature anywhere he couldn't defeat.

With a sudden flick of its whip-like tail, the *Lapillusaurus* struck first. A sharp crack resounded as the tail slashed back and forth, trying to find its intended target. But Ivan was ready for this. He leaped into the air as it sliced under his legs, and then he rolled on the ground with a somersault as it flew over his head; skillfully, he evaded every strike the tail offered. Angrily, the gem lizard changed its tactics and leapt towards him.

Battered, sliced, burned, and nearly broken, Duke joined in the fray. The creature suddenly smashed Ivan beneath one mighty talon, crushing him just as Duke leaped upon the creature's back. This time it was easier, since the monster stood horizontally. Again, he saddled himself between two boney plates at the base of the neck, and grasped its snorkel-like tube. Wisps of smoke from Duke's burning flesh filled the air, yet he held on tightly. Striking the creature with his glowrod, he delivered a strategic blow at the base of the skull. Power detonated as it connected, and a flash of light exploded in his face. In an instant, the horn broke free, and the creature shrieked in agony, grasping its head on both sides. Then it rolled onto its back, trying to crush its attacker. Duke leaped from the creature's back and flew head over heels through the air, well beyond the island's edge, and disappeared.

Ivan had an opportunity to make a final blow. The last attack had left his sternum crushed, and blood oozed from his mouth; he didn't have much fight left. Nevertheless, his Methonian determination for success overcame any disability or injury, and he flung himself at the wounded creature. Raising his glowrod, he swung at the gem lizard's head.

The two combatants clashed; the *Lapillusaurus* opened his tremendous mouth and consumed Ivan past his shoulders just as the glowrod struck its intended target. An explosion of immense power blasted the enormous head of the mighty creature from inside, and it burst into a thousand fragments. Both man and beast fell silent together.

As the sounds of battle ceased, the rest of the Warriors freed the imprisoned people and prepared them to leave the holding area. The inmates, ignoring the urgency of their predicament, took time to comfort each other before departing.

Edgar looked at Anton and pointed toward the island's surface. Go quickly, and free any survivors left on the crosses." He continued to command his brothers into action and prepared to make a quick departure. Intuitively he knew Duke and Ivan were successful, and he also realized the Troglodytes would soon return in greater numbers to finish what the *Lapillusaurus* hadn't.

"As you command," Anton returned a full Methonian salute, and then retrieved a set of keys hanging on the nearby wall.

Racing to the prisoners, it didn't take him long to free the fettered men. Then he noticed the very large crystal that the *Lapillusaurus* had left behind. Without a second thought, he jumped into the pit, retrieved it, and placed it inside his tunic. It was heavy and sat awkwardly, but he tied the pocket closed and laced the tunic securely to his belt to keep it from swinging around as he moved.

Climbing from the pit, he helped the injured prisoners return to the holding area; they supported each other as they slogged along; their tortured incarceration impeded their capacity to flee. Beaten, given little or no food and water, and forced to breathe the poor atmosphere for an unknown length of time, they had nearly been killed by their imprisonment.

Directing his attention to Edgar, Tybalt shared his concerns. "I expect a trap on the way out—it's only logical. Therefore, we need to find another exit; the way we came in is no longer an option, especially with all of these injured people. It would be easier if we'd only rescued the girl, she was our only objective. Bringing all these people along is suicide."

With a glare, Edgar reacted to Tybalt's misgivings. "We've all considered this; our success will be greater if we retrieve them all. More importantly, these people should know a safer way out. And there may be additional benefits we haven't considered." Edgar looked around the room, hoping everyone would either agree with him or share their arguments. His Methonian nature begged for agreement, and he expected them to concur.

"We know the way we came in—it isn't far," one of the prisoners said, pointing across the bridge as he spoke. "We can lead the way if you

Warriors will permit. We're more than willing to risk death in order to escape; we would have died anyway if we'd stayed here. At least let us try."

"Very good, you lead the way," Edgar said. "Anton and Boris will be up front with you. Tybalt, Luke, and I will pull up the rear." Quickly, Edgar looked around at everyone, making sure they understood his command. Then he motioned for the group to leave.

Unpredictably, they encountered no opposition during the initial departure, and everyone quickly made their way through the crack in the wall. Following the lead villager, they struggled to climb a steep hand-carved tunnel. The weakened captives labored to climb their way toward freedom, and they slowed the Warriors, forcing them to support them as best they could. Progress was slow but steady.

An hour passed, and then another, and it seemed their escape would be uneventful—but then it happened. As they arrived at the cave's exit, a group of Troglodytes awaited them in ambush. They emerged in the dark of night, yet as the stars lit the sky it seemed bright after the many hours underground, inside complete and utter darkness. However, they were human after all, and the Troglodytes had the advantage of seeing in complete darkness. The stars were the only illumination, and it wasn't enough to see what awaited them on the ledge. The fleeing people unwittingly fell into the expectant enemy's trap.

Suddenly, a spear flew through the air and hit the lead villager in the chest, skewering him neatly to the ground. As he fell to one side, more spears rained upon the escapees; the Warriors grabbed survivors, pushing them to safety and knocking the heavy bolts aside as they showered down. The unexpected assault surprised everyone; they hadn't anticipated the enemy to lay in ambush outside the entrance.

"Behind the rocks!" shouted Edgar. The refugees scattered like scared mice looking for cover. "Use your glowrods!" Grasping his communication device, he pressed a series of buttons, requesting an Aerocraft to rescue them.

Glowrods fired shafts of light, and spears filled the air, raining down on the company in a tumultuous shower. Tybalt and Luke each took a spear in the chest; there wasn't enough room to deflect or avoid the impact with so many villagers restricting their movements. This made the odds of success even worse. Only three Warriors remained.

The large number of Troglodytes easily cut down all of the villagers except the chief's daughter, whom Anton protected above all others. They'd remained at the rear of the melee, and escaped the initial foray by sheer luck. However, a stray spear sailed toward Anton, but he parried and snatched the shaft from its flight as it ricocheted off a large boulder next to him. Just as quickly, he whirled around and returned the spear unsuccessfully; it failed to find a target through all the confusion.

Luckily, the glowrods had blinded several of the enemy, and they retreated to regroup. The nocturnal traits of the Troglodytes worked to the Warriors' advantage; the glowrods blinded many of them, providing an opportunity for escape.

"This way!" shouted Anton; he'd found a path leading to the upper plateau, and he motioned for everyone to follow, quickly leading the way.

The group hadn't traveled far before spotting more Troglodytes, just a few yards away. Once again, shafts of light and spears filled the air. Boris snatched the girl from Anton and assumed responsibility for her life; this freed Anton, and he quickly dropped to the rear. Edgar and Anton returned fire with the spears at their disposal, and decreased the enemy by another two; Boris also picked up a spear and prepared for combat.

"Trogs approaching from the rear!" Boris called out. He grabbed the girl and the team pressed forward to obliterate the last few Troglodytes standing in their way.

"Signal the ship with your glowrods," Edgar said, intending to finish their mission as quickly as possible. "There're more of them around here somewhere—keep your eyes open!"

With glowrods raised over their heads, the three Warriors methodically signaled the heavens to help guide the Aerocraft. Within seconds, they could see its lights as it speedily approached, and then it descended toward the plateau just ahead of them.

"Prepare for a final ambush!" Edgar said, sounding frantic as he barked commands. He knew the conclusion of their efforts was at hand, and he yearned for success.

Adrenaline coursed through Edgar's veins, and the effect made him far more aggressive and less attentive to detail. A moment later, with a dull thud, a spear pierced through his flesh from behind, and the point stuck several inches out of the front of his chest; blood spattered everywhere, splashing Anton,

Boris, and the young girl. Anton reached for Edgar as he sank to his knees, attempting to pull the other Warrior into the Aerocraft. But he was too late. Edgar fell to the ground dead, just a few yards from freedom.

Blood covered Anton's hands, making it difficult to grasp anything. He and Boris each grabbed one arm of the hysterical girl and sprinted toward the Aerocraft, dragging her between them. They reached the ship not a moment too soon, and Anton heaved the girl aboard while Boris turned around and pointed his glowrod at the enemy, hoping to stave off their final assault. Anton sprang aboard and beckoned Boris to follow, but fate again worked against them—just as he leapt aboard, Boris received the final injury. A spear pierced his leg. Anton reached down and yanked it out, tossing it to the ground. The door slammed closed and the sound of metal-tipped spears clanked against the hull of the Aerocraft. Firing its thrusters, the ship hastily streaked into the air at an impossible speed.

Reaching for a first-aid kit, Anton handed it to Boris, and then attempted to aid the girl.

"Thanks," Boris said, looking at Anton and then the girl as he quickly staunched the bleeding of his open wound. "We made it." Sighing with painful relief, he worked quickly to save his own life.

"Yes, we did," Anton replied. "But our friends are gone." He frowned at the girl. "I hope you appreciate it." His tone was harsh, but his eyes were sympathetic; he was never able to hide his true feelings.

"Appreciate it?" she exclaimed, as tears poured down her face. "You Warriors are a contradiction. You came to save us from that monster, and instead, you got everyone killed, including yourselves. What good are you?" She scowled at Anton, and shook her head in revulsion.

"Our mission," Boris said, "was to bring *you*, and *you* alone, to safety. We accomplished this. The mission was a success." Boris's reply was cold, and he shook his finger at her as he said it. He didn't like the fact that he'd risked his life for a girl who didn't appreciate it. "As for your friends back there, the ones that died—they weren't part of our plan, and they would've died anyway. We *fulfilled* our obligation; the mission *was* a success." His retort was straightforward and cold, without remorse or sympathy for the deaths and suffering incurred.

Anton watched the girl's expression as she listened to Boris. He saw the same look of horror in her eyes she'd had when the *Lapillusaurus* climbed up the side of the island. It was a mix of fear, panic, and abhorrence.

"I'm sorry; we just couldn't save your friends. When we embarked on this mission, we had no idea we would encounter the *Lapillusaurus*. We were only supposed to bring *you* back." Again, Anton attempted to console the girl. He had feelings of remorse for his comrades, and a sensation of pity for the loss of the girl's friends, and he only wished for her to realize it. Forcing a smile, he attempted to soften her mood.

"By the way, what is your name?" Anton attempted to console her further by being polite.

She looked at Anton with disgust and confusion, and then attempted to reply. But at first, she couldn't, and looked away, remaining silent. She took a deep breath, and then slowly let it out. "My name is Celeste," she snapped, finally, scowling at Anton with contempt.

Nodding his head, Anton replied: "Mine is Anton—pleased to meet you." This time he offered a genuine smile, and gently wiped the tears from her face with the back of his hand.

"Thank you for saving me," she said. Shyly, with effort, she returned his smile for a moment, lay down on her side, curled into the fetal position, and quietly sobbed.

WITHOUT WARNING, THE HOLO-PROJECTOR ABRUPTLY shut off, leaving the gathering without any light. It was very late at night— only the moon cast a faint glow on the villagers.

"We need light—light some Tiki torches," Tyrell commanded, pointing around the perimeter of the audience.

Nelda quietly sat closer to Anton, wrapped her arms around his waist, and leaned her head against his shoulder. "You are very lucky," she said. "You lived when all of your friends died."

"We will discuss this tomorrow, it's very late." Standing, Tyrell motioned for everyone to leave. Then he looked at Anton. Pointing his finger at him, he said, "You will spend the night with me—come!"

Within seconds, the village emptied; the show was over. A sense of impending doom filled the hearts of all who had attended Anton's presentation. The violence and the death of so many Warriors left them with a sense of despair. Many questions remained unanswered and the reality of their predicament seemed somehow exemplified by the presentation. Everyone recognized the eminent horror they were about to face. It would be a very different day in the morning, and everyone knew it—all except Anton.

CHAPTER 5

Erudition

MORNING CAME IN THE BLINK of an eye for Anton. The late-night activities had left him inexplicably unsettled.

Tyrell's reaction to the previous night's presentation was less than enthusiastic at its conclusion, and Anton desired to meditate, but there was little time for that now. Being a Warrior, a few hours of sleep normally refreshed him—but today his thoughts were troubled.

It was early when he awoke to the sound of tropical birds going about their business. The sun had just peeked over the horizon, and he quietly left the hut and looked around aimlessly, watching the sunrise lighting the village in long shadows. Nobody else had yet arisen, and he decided to wait at the falls for the young girls to arrive for their morning chores.

Crossing to the far side of the pool, Anton climbed upon the sitting rock and crisscrossed his legs as if to meditate. But instead he watched the activities of the birds winging across the pool, cawing at each other as they went about their morning routines. It didn't take long for the girls to arrive, filling the large urns with water for the village's daily supply.

As Nelda arrived, Anton slid off the rock and approached her. "Good morning," he said. "How are you today?" Smiling hugely, he helped her dip the urn into the pool. As they worked together to fill it, his muscular arm rubbed lightly against hers. She drew in a sudden deep breath.

"You may be my betrothed," she responded, "but this is women's work. You shouldn't be helping me." Nelda looked up into Anton's eyes and smiled shyly as she caught them for an instant. Then she lightly slapped his hands with the back of hers, gently shooing him away. "Go—I don't want people to say I need help to do the simplest of chores, even though they know we are to be married soon."

Anton straightened up, and then bowed. "I am at your service, milady." Without hesitation, he quickly turned away and sped down the path towards the village, hoping to find Tyrell awake; he wanted to talk to the chief.

As he entered the village square, Anton saw the usual bustle of activity as breakfast was prepared. Tyrell was busy talking to several of the elder men, including Mahkeetah. As they noticed his arrival, they suddenly disbanded, heading for the tables, which were laden with the morning's repast.

"Please, young Warrior—sit!" Tyrell said loudly, to make sure everyone would notice Anton's presence. He pointed to where Anton had sat the evening before. "Nelda will be here soon—leave some room next to you for her to sit." He smiled at Anton and gave him a wink.

Mahkeetah watched them and frowned. "You will *respect* my daughter. Give her *plenty* of space!" His voice was stern, as if he meant to say *you aren't married yet*. He scowled at Anton, holding his gaze, and then forced an awkward stiff smile as he sat. The tension between the two Warriors was unmistakable. Everyone watched in uncomfortable silence.

As if summoned, Nelda suddenly appeared with her urn and placed it next to her hut. Quickly, she made her way over to Anton and sat beside him. "Let me get you some fruit," she said, while looking at Mahkeetah. Hope filled her heart that the two would be pleasant during the meal, and that they would soon become friends, not just relatives. She didn't want to see them interact as comrades from the Great Temple.

The food passed from hand to hand around the table, and soon everyone was eating. Anton graciously consumed some tara fruit; the tangy flavor filled his mouth with its unique sensation, leaving him with a craving for more. Nelda watched as he eagerly savored each bite, and marveled at how someone could be so excited about eating a common fruit.

"Don't you Warriors have tara fruit in your Great Temple?" Nelda asked. "How could that be possible? They grow in great abundance in this region; surely there's enough for you as well."

"All food is synthesized for our specific genetic design," Anton responded. "Each item and supplement requires idiosyncratic customization by the food processing machines for each individual Warrior. This *real* food isn't commonly part of our diet, it isn't necessary." Anton replied as if reading from an encyclopedia; he didn't realize that the villagers couldn't believe what he was saying.

Mahkeetah chuckled quietly to himself as he slowly ate his meal. He was both hopeful and confident that the more Anton revealed about himself and his inherent differences, the more Anton would alienate himself from the villagers. He had hidden as much as possible from his own past in order to gain acceptance in Tooloo—he had worried that if these people learned too much about him, they might never accept him. In contrast, it now suited him to hear these details revealed, hoping it would work against Anton; he'd long since established himself here, and had no fear of being forced to leave.

"So, you've never eaten *real* food?" asked Nelda. "How could you be healthy and strong without *real* food?" Puzzled, she showed a motherly concern, as if Anton suddenly needed her special care to overcome an illness.

"As you see," Anton continued, "our exceptional diet has worked well enough for me. Real food only offers certain elements from each source; the food synthesizers offer everything our bodies require at any given meal; this improves the nutrition we receive. Tailored nutrition is superior in quality, but the fruit of Tooloo is far more delicious." Smiling at Nelda, Anton reassured her that he didn't require any special concern about his health. "There are occasions we do eat real food; such occasions are few and far between, however, and they never include tara fruit."

Tyrell looked at Mahkeetah, then at Anton. "I'm sure everything you Warriors do is quite superior, and quite alien to our way of thinking. It's obvious there is more than one way to obtain a healthy body." He noticed the former chief's silent amusement. "Without question your Masters know their business," he went on. "But it pleases me you find our food more palatable than your manufactured diet."

Smiling, Anton quickly poked the last morsel of tara fruit in his mouth and looked around the table. Everyone was smiling, except for Mahkeetah, who heaved a controlled sigh through his clenched teeth, and then slowly shook his head. He struggled with his emotions, emotions no Warrior should have; they warned him to protect his daughter, and to protect Anton from a similar fate as his own by encouraging him to leave as quickly as possible. He hoped to return to his simple life without any concerns that the Great Temple would interfere with his secret seclusion.

"So how many people have you killed in your life, Anton?" Mahkeetah asked pointedly, a smirk on his face.

The sudden unexpected question shocked the entire village, and an audible gasp filled the air as everyone's attention fell upon Mahkeetah.

"Oh, Daddy! How could you ask that?" Nelda exclaimed, and then quickly lowered her eyes, pressed her lips together, and silenced herself. She knew that even a former princess couldn't publicly protest her father's statements without severe repercussions.

"That's okay, Nelda," Tyrell said. "We were all thinking the same thing. It isn't often such irresponsible attitudes are given during a meal!" He looked crisply at Mahkeetah. "I'm confident there won't be any further remarks made at this time. You will have your chance a little later; I hope you can contain yourself until then."

Tyrell stood up, looked around, and raised his arm in the air. "May I have everyone's attention, please?"

All eyes fell upon the village chief, and the people fell silent; only the sound of tropical birds filled the air.

"If you are done, we will review Anton's presentation. I know the subject is difficult for some of you to discuss, therefore for those of you who wish to participate, we will move to the old village lodge; there, we will debate in privacy."

Immediately all of the male village elders arose from the tables and made their way down the trail to the crossing at the falls. Anton walked with Tyrell; a look of uneasiness marked his face and filled his thoughts.

What if they don't trust my tactics? Anton thought to himself. *What will I do next? I can't wander around hoping to run into the outlaws—I don't know where they are holed up, and I wouldn't be able to ambush them alone, with everyone still in the village.* Puzzled, he calculated a backup plan. The idea that he might need such a plan hadn't crossed his mind until now. *I wish Boris were here*, he thought. *He always had a second plan.*

Noticing Anton's deep-seated concerns, Tyrell wondered what he was thinking. "Don't worry about anything, young Warrior; we just need to agree that your plan is, well, safe. We are all confident our troubles will be behind us soon—have no fear." He tried to reassure Anton, but didn't want to discuss the subject until the formal deliberation commenced.

"Perhaps you should think about your marriage to the young Nelda!" Tyrell said, smiling. He was trying to distract Anton with more pleasant thoughts, but he only added more concern. "You do realize she's in love with you, right? Only a fool wouldn't notice!" He patted Anton on the shoulder, and the two crossed the rocks at the far end of the pool.

Several of the older boys were fishing just below the crossing, where the river took a bend to the right. Anton watched as Muzoke lunged, grasped a large fish in both hands, and struggled to raise its slick wiggling body out of the water. With admirable skill, he flung it to the shore, where Tok quickly clubbed it with a large stick, ending its life.

"We're blessed, there will be fish tonight!" Tyrell said, smiling hugely and pointing at his sons as they provided for the village. "I taught them well, did I not?" Pride filled his face as he looked at Anton.

Hopeful, Anton could see Tyrell's appreciation for the fact that Anton had saved Tok's life; he knew it would virtually guarantee the acceptance of his plan to save the village. Feeling reassured, he looked into Tyrell's eyes and smiled. "I will relax and listen to what everyone has to say," he said. "I trust all of you."

Taking a deep breath, Anton fought back his nagging anxiety about Nelda. "I will consider your offer of marriage, though I will remind you my Masters will not allow this." Quickly looking at the ground, he fought back a sudden feeling of disappointment. He knew the consequences if he did marry, and he knew how much it would tear him apart inside if he didn't have a chance to obtain such a prize. His Masters' rules precluded him from living a simple life here, as Mahkeetah had—and yet he felt he couldn't leave Nelda behind. She was as important to him now as had been the completion of his training—yet it'd only been two days since they'd met. How could this be? The thought disturbed him immensely; what had changed in him?

"You seem troubled," Tyrell said, noticing Anton wrestling with his conflicting emotions. "What are you thinking about? I will remind you we have a way to help you. As you see, Mahkeetah was able to remain here; therefore, it's possible for you to do so as well!" Smiling, he tried to reassure Anton as best he could. He seemed to know just what troubled him.

As they entered the old village, Anton was amazed at how beautifully the old people had taken care of the gardens and the unused huts; he wondered why they bothered to take care of them at all, since this village was no longer in use. It didn't make much sense, but he had other things to consider for now, and set his thoughts aside.

"Come, we will talk inside the meeting hut," Tyrell said, pointing to a very large lodge-like structure. "Everyone has already gathered inside, and we are the last to arrive. Now it's *our* turn to tell *you* a story!"

Looking around, Anton saw several women rushing around. They were cleaning benches, clipping undesirable jungle growth, and generally preparing the area, as if they planned to use it for some unknown purpose. He assumed the deliberation would last long enough that perhaps they intended to serve a meal here later. Without considering it further, he entered the lodge with Tyrell.

Inside, all the village men sat around the edge of the room upon floor tapestries, leaving the center open for Tyrell to stand and conduct the meeting. "Please sit, Anton," he said. "You will have a chance to speak later." Slowly he looked at everyone in turn, and lastly his eyes fell upon Mahkeetah. He gave the former chief a long look, as if telling him to watch what he said.

"As it was in the past, and as it is once again, we are blessed with the fortuitous appearance of a young Warrior." Tyrell sounded formal, as if he'd planned to tell a long story. "We all know how Mahkeetah came to share his life with us some twenty years agone. He came to us in a time of great need, found our village to be more important to him than his intended destiny, and chose to remain among us. The lure of our way of life is indeed desirable, even to a Warrior!" Smiling, the chief quickly looked at everyone's faces, assessing their response to his private humor. Then, finally, he turned to Anton.

"It's with great pleasure that I offer for deliberation a debate on Anton's *informative* presentation last night. I realize that all of you are tired, having stayed up so late!" Tyrell chuckled. The lack of rest was evident on everyone's face.

"First of all, let's review our concerns, and our approvals of what we witnessed." Tyrell carefully scrutinized each of the men's faces, attempting to determine the villagers' opinions before they offered them publicly. He knew there were mixed feelings, and particularly, Mahkeetah loathed any subject about Anton.

Tyrell's oratory skills surprised Anton; he realized that the man had a natural ability for speaking in front of his friends. "Forgive me if I ramble a bit," he said. "I will try to keep this as short as possible so that we can get directly to our debate."

A look of uneasiness covered Tyrell's face as he looked directly at Anton. "First of all, you demonstrated your ability to kill, and to do so without mercy. Even when it comes to a violent sub-human race of people, we abhor killing of any kind unless there is simply no other way. This is the custom of our village."

Squirming slightly, Anton felt uncomfortable. His Masters never chastised him for performing his required duty, and a Warrior used his skills to protect the innocent. Receiving criticism for using the skills he'd spent his entire life developing bothered him—especially since he had had no choice in developing them.

"Second, you used poor judgment when you allowed our children to witness this." Tyrell's tone sharpened.

"Third, you scouted ahead with the intent to help your friends find a safe passage, but defied the orders of your direct superior in the process; this led your comrades into harm's way. Your decisions are at times reckless, and your abandonment of your fellow Warriors, even a temporary one, demonstrates that you prefer making independent decisions." Tyrell's criticism hit the heart of everyone's fears, and a sudden murmur filled the air.

"He's all of this and more!" yelled Mahkeetah. "All Warriors seek glory in hopes of achieving higher status and a better position when auctioned!" Standing, the former chief sought to take control of the meeting by embellishing on Tyrell's critiques and enhancing them into pointed accusations.

"Sit *down!*" Tyrell ordered. "Your turn to have your say will come. Until then, be seated, or be removed!" Anger filled Tyrell's voice as he asserted his authority, and he pointed his finger at Mahkeetah.

"Careful, chief, or I will challenge you here and now!" Mahkeetah retorted. "You won't remain chief for long!" Mahkeetah quickly took a step toward Tyrell and stood in a ready stance. His biceps bulged, and hate covered his face. "I *know* what this boy is, and I will put an end to your scheme here and now! Have I not suffered enough?"

"We've *all* suffered!" retorted Tyrell. "Return to your seat or be *removed!*"

For a moment, the two men locked eyes. Tension filled the air; it was obvious to everyone that the former Warrior and chief intended to do harm.

Continuing, Mahkeetah again raised his voice. A distinct tone of despair was apparent. "I've had enough! You *will not* complete your plan!" he yelled, pointing around the room, accusing everyone present. "I object, and if you say one more word I will end this meeting for you!" The muscles in his neck twitched and he gritted his teeth. For what seemed an eternity, Tyrell and Mahkeetah held each other's gaze.

Anton knew without question that Mahkeetah would have no restraint if he attacked Tyrell. He looked rapidly back and forth at the two men, anticipating the inevitable fight. His muscles tensed, and he waited to respond instantly if necessary—but he knew his seated position put him at a slight disadvantage.

"Very well, Mahkeetah—you leave me no choice." Slowly raising his hand, Tyrell pointed a trembling finger at him. "You are banished from this meeting. See to it we do not banish you from Tooloo! Now go!" Turning his back to Mahkeetah, Tyrell gently folded his arms across his chest and closed his eyes. "Go!"

In succession, everyone in the room stood, and they too turned their backs to Mahkeetah and folded their arms, mimicking Tyrell. The only one who didn't was Anton.

Abruptly, Mahkeetah looked at Anton and pointed his finger at him, as if warning him of his predicament. "This too will be *your* folly. Go ahead—fall into their little trap, just as I did. Oh, you will be glad you did, and you will regret it every waking minute!" Slowly, he walked to the exit of the great lodge. Once there, he grasped the supporting post of the doorway in his right hand, and stopped.

Calmly, without looking over his shoulder, Mahkeetah again addressed Anton. "My daughter is the most loving, caring, and gentle girl in this village—a real treasure, *especially* to *me*. She is yours." With that, he quickly left. It was over, or so it seemed.

As Mahkeetah left the meeting hall, everyone sat back down. Tyrell slowly walked around the room, smiling at each of his friends. Lastly, he stood in front of Anton, motioning for him to stand. "Don't concern yourself with what he said—it isn't of any consequence. I hated having to do that, but he left us no choice. Now, let's continue our business."

Putting a hand upon Anton's shoulder, Tyrell raised his other and pointed slowly around the gathering. "Observe! This boy is of a *different* temperament, a *different* disposition than Mahkeetah. Yet they're both Warriors from the Great Temple."

Looking directly at Anton, Tyrell smiled at him. "I'm proud of you, young man. You could have chosen to fight with Mahkeetah to protect me, yet you chose not to. This shows restraint, a decided improvement over the character we witnessed in your presentation last night!"

Returning to the center of the room, Tyrell again took up his orator's stance. "Now, back to the business at hand, let's continue with the purpose of this meeting. As I was saying, you showed reckless abandonment by leaving your friends. This is a poor trait, but it seems as though you've learned from this experience, and I believe in my heart that you would never do that again."

Slowly, Tyrell turned around, looking at all the faces. Then he looked again at Anton. "Fourth, and to your credit, you demonstrated compassion for the people you saved—and at great risk for your personal safety. This is a most admirable quality." Smiling, he looked at Anton, hoping to elicit a smile in response. "I realize that no Warrior is *ever* trained thus, and your character demonstrated this choice. Bravo!"

A cheer of agreement filled the air as everyone suddenly spoke, praising Anton for his unselfish decision. It was obvious they viewed him differently than Mahkeetah.

"Now, there is only one more point I wish to make. I know why you chose that particular experience to share with us; it is due to the extensive adventure inside a cave, and saving a young girl. Your idea is to use our tiny cave hidden behind the falls and invite the outlaws into our village for a violent confrontation. In order for us to trust your unusual proposal—we can only presume that you are anticipating more violence will occur than we can possibly realize or predict. Is this so?"

For a moment, Anton looked blankly at Tyrell. Now that he understood the chief's perspective, it seemed as though his own plan made little sense. His mind quickly ran through the calculations that he'd originally used to derive his strategy, and re-confirmed that his original calculation was sound.

"I beg to differ with you about your concerns of violence, sir," Anton said, addressing Tyrell respectfully, hoping to gain more respect from the chief. "I believe the outlaws will come to kill everyone—not just take another of your young women. Then they will burn the village to the ground. After having defeated the three men on the night of my arrival, it is logical to assume they will attempt a bigger attack— and I will have to assume it may be beyond my capability to prevent! They'll desire revenge. Therefore, all of you need to be in a safe location when this event occurs. Besides, none of you want to witness what happens. This should ensure that the only violence will the between them and me."

A sudden grumbling again filled the hall. Tyrell held up his hands in order to silence everyone. "Please, we will discuss this in a minute! Let Anton finish."

"Killing everyone would be contrary to their previous method of operation!" One man stood and pointed a finger at Tyrell, and then at Anton. He scowled angrily. It was obvious he wanted no part of Anton's plan. "I believe there may be more of the outlaws than we know about, and I believe they will attempt to surprise us, and strike when nobody's expecting it! They may come in the morning before we wake, or in the afternoon, or at night while we sleep!"

"Sit *down*, Kanza, and wait to be called upon!" Tyrell said, trying to keep the discussion from getting out of hand. "Everyone will get their turn to speak!"

Another man raised his hand and slowly stood. He trembled as he gained his feet, exhibiting his advanced age; he was obviously the oldest man present. Even though the ambient temperature was quite comfortable, he wore a light wrap around his shoulders. "I agree with Kanza. I believe they will be sneaky, and we won't know when or where the next abduction, or any other attack, will occur."

Again, a loud chorus of voices filled the room, and everyone spoke angrily at once, echoing a complete distrust for Anton's plan.

"Please, everyone—settle down!" yelled Tyrell. "Let my father have his say!" He tried desperately to gain control of the meeting, but the villagers were adamant.

"I would like to add that I trust you, Anton. I think all of us trust you. It's just that I... forgive me, it's just that we don't trust any of those outlaws." Looking directly at Anton, the older man slowly and stiffly bowed in Methonian fashion. "I know you haven't been introduced to most of us here. My name is Nootka. Tyrell is my son. Being a small village means most of us are related in some way." Unable to complete a second bow, Nootka simply tipped his head, indicating his acceptance of Anton. Then he carefully he returned to his seat.

Every man stood and applauded Nootka; the sound of agreement filled the room. It was unmistakable that nobody endorsed Anton's plan. With a slight grin, Tyrell demonstrated his respect for Nootka's words, and the love he held for his father. "Thank you, I believe this is precisely the point we are all here to make—am I correct?"

Tyrell's question brought forth a loud cheer of approval; he'd clearly hit the heart of everyone's mindset.

Anton was taken aback. His expression changed from calm patience to shock; he hadn't believed the entire village would be against his strategy. In his astonishment, his mouth hung slightly agape and his eyes opened wide. Everyone immediately noticed his surprise.

"We're all working *with* you Anton," Tyrell said, "not *against* you. Your strategy isn't dead; we're just evaluating it for any flaws. After all, our lives are on the line here!"

"Please continue your debate," Anton said. "I am unaccustomed to long debates." He tried to relax and let the meeting continue, but he fidgeted uncomfortably, and adjusted his sitting position. Taking a deep breath, he nodded his acceptance and calmly let the meeting unfold.

"Very good," Tyrell said. "I'm pleased you're agreeable!" He smiled, and then returned his attention to the debate. "If we are *not* to accept Anton's strategy, does anyone have a plan of their own they'd like to share? This is your opportunity to present any additional ideas for our consideration."

For what seemed like an eternity, nobody spoke. Tyrell slowly paced the floor, looked from face to face, and finally returned his gaze to Anton. "Before you'd arrived, we'd formulated a plan of our own, but later rejected it due to the enormous risk it entailed, and the unfortunate refusal of Mahkeetah to participate. It wasn't his idea, and he simply didn't want to use his skills to do what Warriors do."

A loud grumbling once more filled the air; everyone loudly protested at once. "All of us know this plan, and it's far too dangerous!" Nootka said, standing slowly. "I implore you, my son—let's not risk it!"

"I'm sorry," Tyrell replied. "But Anton must be made aware of all that has transpired here. I fear Mahkeetah hasn't told him everything." Looking at Nootka with an expression of finality, Tyrell gently motioned for him to return to his seat. "Please, let me finish this, it will all work out fine."

But Nootka stood his ground, refusing to sit. "Do you find it necessary to bring everything out so soon? Let's continue our discussion on whether we should accept the Warrior's proposal; we can wait for a more appropriate time for this... other idea!"

The two men gazed at each other. Tyrell slowly scratched his chin, and then finally took a deep breath and looked at Anton. "I believe we owe him a full explanation, now! Our time grows short, and if he's to accept us, we must entrust him with everything! Should we attempt to deceive him by withholding information? We will never gain his trust this way." Tyrell again insisted that Nootka return to his seat.

"Very well," Nootka said. "You are the chief." Without breaking eye contact, he heaved a sigh, and trembled as he returned to his seat.

"I agree with you, Tyrell," Kanza said, quickly rising to his feet and looking around the gathering. "It's time we shared everything with this Warrior, if only to strengthen our position as to why we shouldn't accept his strategy!"

A sudden gasp again filled the room; the shocking sound resonated and everyone turned around to look at Kanza.

"It's obvious that we aren't going to use this child's plan, therefore isn't it crucial we tell him *everything*? I insist we tell him now, and end this discussion as soon as possible!" Kanza's passionate anger appalled the audience as he glared at Tyrell, and then at Anton. "I believe it prudent to tell him everything about Mahkeetah! It isn't right that he hasn't learned the truth!"

Looking directly into Kanza's eyes, Tyrell responded. "Enough! Everything is about to be revealed, we aren't going to withhold anything from our new friend and future villager, but we must be careful how we tell him! Did you believe we would lie to him?" With a tone of finality, he motioned for Kanza to sit. "See to it we don't remove you from the meeting as well!"

A round of applause filled the room as Kanza angrily returned to his seat. As the tension eased, Tyrell took a deep breath and let it out slowly between his teeth.

"Very well—the truth it is," Tyrell said, facing Anton. "First of all, I need you to tell us what Mahkeetah told you about our problems on the evening you first arrived."

Surprised, Anton wondered what Tyrell needed to know. Then he realized that nobody knew what he and Mahkeetah had discussed.

"I'm sorry, I didn't know that Mahkeetah hadn't spoken to you of our conversation—or is it that you simply wish to hear it from my perspective?"

"We just need to know how much you know," Tyrell replied. "Mahkeetah may have left something out. Pease, tell us what he said."

Standing, Anton made sure everyone could hear him clearly. "This will take a few minutes—please be patient." Smiling, he wished to be as pleasant as possible, knowing he had the power to influence the direction of the debate with his explanation.

"First of all, I would like to say that he spoke to me as though he'd always been a part of your village. He hid the truth about his origin—about being a Warrior. For whatever reason, I didn't recognize this at first. That disturbs me. Every Warrior intuitively knows another on sight, but I failed to distinguish this in him, and for that, I apologize." Looking at the floor, Anton's embarrassment immediately received an affirmative response from the audience.

"Second, he described the arrival of six men in the village. They were weaponless, and wore strange clothing that all of you determined to be from the Great Temple. They asked you if they could remain here in Tooloo. You held a meeting like this one, and all of you were skeptical, but allowed them to stay. For a while, everything seemed to go well. Then they showed great interest in your women." Slowly, Anton maneuvered toward the front, where Tyrell stood, and took control of the council meeting.

"Third, these men showed a desire for some jewels and a katana that was in Mahkeetah's possession. We discussed his ability to use the weapon, and his refusal to use it to stop these men because of his wife's abduction." Taking a deep breath and letting it out slowly, Anton indicated skepticism about Mahkeetah's story.

"Pardon me for not understanding, but now that I know he's a Warrior, I find it difficult to understand why he didn't attempt to free his wife himself. No Warrior would ever fail to use his abilities in such a situation. Perhaps someone here can enlighten me?" Nobody moved or made a sound; the silence seemed to speak louder than words.

"Is there anything to add?" Completely ignoring Anton's question, Tyrell attempted to steer him back to his point. "We need to conclude soon. It grows late in the day—please, continue."

Puzzled, Anton hesitated, and gave Tyrell a perplexed look. He sighed heavily in disbelief, and then continued. "Fourth, he described how these men became drunk, and how you captured them as they slept. Afterward, you discovered Mahkeetah's dead wife, and in turn, you banished the men atop a cliff. Somehow, they escaped, returned here, continued their demands, and abducted your young girls. That is all." Anton bowed, and then looked from face to face and said: "That is all I know, Mahkeetah said nothing else."

"Thank you," Tyrell said, clumsily bowing in return. "Now we know that Mahkeetah spoke truthfully and completely of our problems." Tyrell again took center stage. "I would now invite any discussion that anyone would like to offer. Are there any comments or plans someone would like to share before we reveal to Anton the final truth about Mahkeetah?"

"I have something to say!" one of the men said, quickly standing. "Hello, Anton. My name is Tarna." He was younger than most of the others—just a few years older than Anton. Physically, he was well-built, and quite handsome among these people. "After Mahkeetah's wife, *my* daughter was the first to die at the hands of these outlaws. Her name was Naomie, and she was only fourteen."

Anton recognized his name from Mahkeetah's story. He hadn't known who Tarna was, and putting a face to the tragedy brought out a sense of sympathy for the man. "A pleasure to meet you," Anton said. "Mahkeetah spoke of you. I'm sorry for your loss." His eyes darted from one face to another. For a second he looked in Tarna's eyes, and clumsily tried to hide his feelings. He failed.

"Thank you, great Warrior," Tarna said. "I appreciate your concern." Tarna understood Anton's mixed emotions and his difficulty in sharing them, but took little comfort in his empathy.

"Please, Tarna; share your idea with us," Tyrell said.

"Pardon me. My idea is to set a trap for these men, and ambush them when they return. I believe it's safer for us to work together as a team than to run in fear and hide!"

"You sound like a Warrior!" Tyrell said, smiling. But he tried to discourage Tarna's suggestion. "We aren't Warriors. How do you propose we survive such an endeavor? Isn't it obvious someone would be harmed—or, even worse, killed?"

Everyone suddenly spoke at once, boisterously arguing.

"We will not fight!" Nootka said. "We cannot afford any more deaths!" He slowly gained his feet and looked directly at Tarna. "We must put our trust in someone capable of handling this without any of our help, so all of us will survive! We will not fight! Who among us is young enough for such a task? Tarna, you would be one of the few! Are you willing to sacrifice yourself? Besides, Anton has already spoken of his need to complete his training; it gains nothing for him if you do his work for him."

"Then you do agree with Anton's strategy!" Tarna said, challenging Nootka. The two shared a lengthy stare as the tension escalated. "I see that you prefer his plan; only now do you admit it!"

The loud grumbling continued as everyone argued at once. Anger filled the air, and fingers were pointed back and forth.

"Enough!" Tyrell said. "Please, let us finish this! We're nearly in agreement; I see Nootka has changed his mind!"

"It would seem prudent not to risk our own safety, and I believe everyone here understands this now, even Kanza. We must allow this young Warrior to complete his mission alone!" Nootka looked at Tyrell and then at Anton. "Therefore, I agree with you, we should trust his plan. It is time to tell him about Mahkeetah; only then can all of us agree!"

Anton was surprised at the change in temperament. The logic of these simple village people held many mysteries that Anton had never considered. It was only now that they were revealing themselves to him by sharing their arguments. Perhaps they needed this wasteful process. Or perhaps they'd rehearsed this debate for his benefit. In either case, he remained patient for the conclusion.

"Thank you, Nootka," Tyrell said. "I'm delighted we're all in agreement! Please, everyone—relax, and we'll bring this council to a close." Pacing, Tyrell slowly moved toward Anton. Scratching his chin as if in some distant contemplation, he hesitated, looked directly at Anton, and then continued.

"Mahkeetah's story is similar to yours—more so than you can imagine. We're prepared to share it with you, and in exchange, we will accept your plan." Wavering, as if nervous, Tyrell took a deep breath, never losing eye contact with Anton. Slowly, he proceeded. "There is but one stipulation to my revealing this; first, you must agree to something."

Puzzled, Anton wondered what it could be; he was skeptical of Tyrell's secretive position and it concerned him. It seemed as though the entire council performed a well-rehearsed presentation for his benefit; all of the glaring, arguments, and unvoiced feelings seemed somehow practiced. Were they? Mahkeetah wanted to reveal the truth before he left the hut, yet for some reason he'd refrained. However, what was even more puzzling was that the villagers undoubtedly had discussed every topic, every idea, and every plan ages ago.

"And just what is it I'm to agree to?" Anton asked. For the first time, he distrusted Tyrell and the others.

With a smile like a predator about to snare its prey, Tyrell looked carefully at Anton. "Very well, I *will* tell you." Slowly, if only to make the moment more dramatic, he continued. "In order for us to trust you, and obviously for you to trust us in return, we require from you a commitment. You will marry Nelda, this morning!"

"Ah, so that's it," Anton said. "It's all about trust. You don't trust me, and I have my own reservations about you." Anton spoke candidly, hoping somehow to escape such a dramatic commitment to end the villager's plight. "You know I'm not allowed to do this, and yet you *desperately* require it of me. Why?"

Taken aback, Tyrell's thoughts raced as he formulated a response. He'd assumed Anton would unquestionably relish the opportunity to claim such a prize, a prize that he clearly desired.

"As I said before, we can provide a way for you to have Nelda as your wife without worrying about the consequences of defying your Masters. Be assured they will not pursue your, shall we say, *disappearance*."

This time Anton hesitated. Torn between his lustful yearning, coupled and fueled with youthful male hormones, and his desire to prove himself and fulfill his destiny, Tyrell confronted him with the same choice that Mahkeetah had faced some twenty-plus years before, the choice he had made to stay here in Tooloo, or return to the Great Temple. Struggling inwardly, he desperately fought his conflicting feelings and urges. Then logic prevailed. If only to achieve his goal, the simple formality of a wedding couldn't prevent him from leaving any time afterward, and he'd still complete his mission, even if it was against Methonian rules. He felt confident his reasoning would satisfy his Masters, and therefore that the wedding was an acceptable step to obtain the desired outcome.

"Very well, I will agree to your terms. Now, what is the mystery about Mahkeetah?"

Quietly chuckling, Tyrell responded. "He found the power of love!" He spread his arms wide and smiled from ear to ear. "The women of our village know the way to a man's heart, and men are unable to resist their charms! They have a special power over our hearts—a power we eagerly wish to share with you!"

Without warning, everyone in the room burst into laughter. It was obvious they all shared an inside joke. Anton was still confused, and he didn't like being the brunt of this private humor.

"That's it? There must be more!" Anton was furious. He felt cheated, and he still had unanswered questions. "What brought Mahkeetah here in the first place?"

"Mahkeetah will have to answer those questions," Tyrell chuckled. I will make sure he does!" He motioned for everyone around him to stand. In unison, like a school of fish suddenly changing direction, the villagers gathered around Anton. Patting him on the back, each one in turn congratulated him. Many hands helped him to his feet.

"Don't worry," Tyrell said. "Everything is about to be revealed. Now, let's set that aside. I would like to say that you've made a very wise choice my young friend; you'll never regret your decision!" Tyrell shook Anton's hand enthusiastically. "We've all hoped you would agree! Let's retire to the wedding! All is ready and waiting!"

Everyone ushered Anton along to a small roofed building that was open on all sides, located on the far side of the village, and obviously used for important ceremonies. Only now was it clear why they'd chosen this location to hold the meeting; the newer village didn't have the same facilities as the old. Within seconds, they arrived at the prepared structure where a scene of marvelous tropical beauty awaited their arrival. Exotic tropical vines bearing large fragrant flowers covered it entirely; flower petals littered the ground, making a path up the stairs to the platform of the ceremonial structure.

Nelda waited there for Anton to arrive; she smiled radiantly, eager to take her vows. Her lips glistened a bright glossy red, and she wore a white floral-patterned skirt made from silk. Just as when Anton had first arrived, she wore an exotic flower pinned in her hair above her right ear—however, this one was different. Its petals were large and white, with a yellow fringe that faded to a pastel pink, and three tall stamens stretched high above them. Her hair, shining in the midmorning sunlight, was meticulously combed to a shining luster, and it lay carefully draped, covering her breasts. Two strands of braided hair wrapped around the back of her head; they were pinned together with a green stone that appeared to be jade. The same necklace she'd worn the night of his arrival hung loosely around her neck; the three familiar stones strung together still piqued Anton's curiosity with their familiar look.

The sight of Nelda left Anton mesmerized; he'd never beheld such exquisite feminine loveliness his entire life. No longer needing anyone to urge him along, he fervently climbed the stairs to be near her. The flower in her hair seemed unusual and unfamiliar, yet it seemed as though he'd seen one recently; it confounded even his extensive botanic education as to what it could be. Even more perplexing was where she'd acquired such a skirt, the material being foreign to this part of Methonias. Most of all, he marveled at how much effort she'd gone to in preparing for him and their marriage.

Mahkeetah stood next to her, expressionless. Obviously, he was there to give her away, as was customary for such an event. But he seemed to want no part of it. Disapproval marked his visage, even as he faced the most important moment of his daughter's life—and perhaps even his own.

"I'm glad you chose to live with me in our village, Anton. I really *do* love you!" Nelda smiled seductively and spoke softly in an enticing tone; her youthful quality was soft and feminine, captivating and alluring.

Carefully removing the flower from her hair, she offered it to Anton. "I've selected this particular flower especially for you; please, smell how sweet the fragrance is. We call it a *Virlaqueus*; it's a rare find, growing only on the high stones to either side of the waterfall. And I brought one here to share with you today! Do you not find it delightful? They are very difficult to acquire. I hope you find it as pleasing as I do."

Anton smiled and allowed her to place the flower to his nose. Slowly, deeply, he breathed in the flower's perfume-like essence. Pollen entered his nose, tickling it slightly; instantly, his head felt foggy. Then he felt dizzy. A sensation of intense pleasure coursed through his entire body, making it tingle with an intense intoxicated sensation of delight. An incredible feeling of joy overcame every thought—and suddenly, without restraint, he softly chuckled, with a silly grin on his face.

"I see you enjoy its special fragrance!" Nelda said, giggling along with him. She slowly replaced the *Virlaqueus* in her hair. "It has a special effect on *men*; it makes them happier than they ever felt before!"

"Hurry, Nelda, before you miss your opportunity!" Mahkeetah urged her along to fulfill their preconceived intent; they didn't want Anton to suddenly back out at the last moment.

"I love you with all my heart, Anton," Nelda said. "And I know that now you love me too, with every fiber of *your* heart, until death do we part! Please, I insist." Nelda reached up and placed her hand under his chin, giving it a slow soothing caress.

The single touch sealed Anton's fate. As if invoking some powerful magic, Nelda's persuasive appeal commanded an uncontrollable feeling of desire for her, overpowering all other thoughts. Her smile was captivating and irrefutable.

As if in a hypnotic trance, Anton replied: "I *do* love you as I have never loved before, and I will always be at your service. There is no other purpose for me in life but to be with you forever!" His response was passionate, and his conviction came from deep inside. Coupled with the power of a potent drug from the *Virlaqueus* flower, nothing could ever change the way he felt, and his desire for Nelda escalated beyond all measure. He would give his life for her, driven by his passion and the need to fulfill her every request. He knew he would never waver from this purpose.

Stepping beside the two, Tyrell smiled, with a look of fulfillment. "As is our custom here in Tooloo, by mutual agreement and witnessed by all, you two are now and for always, married! Please Anton, kiss your wife!"

Completely enraptured, held captive by chemical reactions beyond his control, Anton complied eagerly and without hesitation. Nothing could stop his thirst for Nelda, and the mere mention of a kiss compelled him to respond; it was the most important thing in his life.

"Quickly, you must take him now to guarantee success!" Tyrell urged Nelda along, knowing they had nearly succeeded.

"We must share our love together!" Nelda said. "I have prepared a beautiful place to spend the afternoon!" Tenderly taking Anton's hand into her own, Nelda led him down the stairs and across the village, leaving everyone behind.

Anton continued to chuckle as they went, and Nelda giggled in response; they looked like two children off to play. A short distance outside the old village was a small clearing between the jungle trees, where a patch of tall grass grew; Nelda had prepared a makeshift bed there, made of soft tropical leaves.

Lying down on the bed, Nelda reached up with both arms toward Anton and smiled, inviting him to her bosom. It was an offer impossible to refuse, and he immediately complied.

Kneeling over her, he gently pulled her legs over his shoulders. Nelda groaned and her eyes went wide for a moment. Then she stifled a squeal. The two shared their newly formed bond, reveling in each other's pleasures under the sunlight of the warm afternoon. The sound of the waterfalls resonated relentlessly in the background, providing a symphony of nature's music. The tropical birds sang their songs of love enrapturing the lovers. It felt as though it enhanced their lovemaking to perfection, and it solidified a permanent memory of shared tenderness in Anton's mind. Joined in passion, they orchestrated their own music, with the sounds of love as their song.

CHAPTER 6

The Tragedy of Love

THE AFTERNOON SEEMED SUSPENDED IN time. The warmth of the sun bathed the naked skin of the two newlyweds; Anton laid his head in Nelda's lap, feeling both satisfied and content. She leaned over him, looking into his eyes and smiling as she gently caressed his nose, chin, and cheeks with the *Virlaqueus*, making sure he inhaled every speck of pollen it offered, and intensifying its powerful and intoxicating hold. She then squeezed the stem and placed a single drop of its juices upon his tongue. The influence of the flower prevented him from comprehending her tactics. As if in a stupor, he immeasurably enjoyed her playfulness, and her every touch and whisper. It all seemed so dreamlike and satisfying. The flower, coupled with her feminine pleasantness, and his hormone-induced excitement, drove him to levels of fulfillment that he'd never experienced before. The entire experience was all so new to him, and he eagerly reveled in the *Virlaqueus*'s gratifying caress, coupled with her tender seduction. The sight of Nelda's breasts dangling over his face, and her warm smile, completed his purpose in life. This simple act drove him mad with endless desire.

"Do you love me, Anton?" Nelda gently whispered, smiling passionately as she lay down beside him. Her eyes were half open and her finger traced his lips as she waited for a response.

"I love you with every fiber of my being," Anton finally replied—a response that came from deep inside his heart. The *Virlaqueus* had complete control over his feelings and thoughts; Nelda's soothing touch reinforced the sensation, and the offer of her sexuality compelled him beyond any hope of ever denying her anything she wished. The slightest suggestion became his only desire to fulfill, his only reason for life; he would do anything she asked him to do.

"Will you stay with me forever?" Nelda asked, knowing his reply. The power of the *Virlaqueus* altered Anton's ability to choose for himself; he had no capacity to disagree.

"I will stay with you forever," he said. "Only death can separate us." Without question, he would do exactly as he promised; his Methonian promise was a binding contract. The *Virlaqueus*'s potent chemical had forever altered his way of thinking; he would never be precisely the same, and Nelda held absolute power over his choices.

"You don't need your Masters or your silly old Temple anymore?" Nelda said, continuing to probe Anton's allegiance. Her questions only reinforced his resolve to think, feel, and act as she dictated.

"I don't need my Masters or my Temple anymore," Anton said flatly, mimicking Nelda's questions; her control over him was absolute and eternal.

"Are you hungry?" Nelda asked, knowing she had completed her task, and deciding it was time to return to the village; she asked this question to test her hold over Anton, and to bring him out of his chemically controlled state of mind by making him realize his fundamental need for sustenance.

With a sudden growl in his stomach, Anton noticed his hunger. "I *am* hungry," he said, in a reply that was as wooden as his other responses. But the power of suggestion and biology had already influenced his thoughts. Reluctantly, he sat up and looked longingly into Nelda's eyes.

"I love you and want to be with you forever," he said. "I'm hungry and need food now. Shall we return to the village?" Anton's question was the first sign that he was regaining his own thoughts, but it would be a while before he'd recovered all of his wits.

"It's late in the afternoon, and I'm sure everyone has already eaten lunch; dinner will be ready soon. I think my father would like to talk to you before then. Shall we get a snack, and then you can talk?" Standing, Nelda quickly replaced her skirt, and then reached out to Anton, taking his hands into hers, and helping him to stand.

Feeling slightly dizzy, Anton looked intensely into Nelda's eyes. "I would like nothing more than to share a meal with you," he said. "A talk with Mahkeetah sounds wonderful—I can hardly wait." His response was entirely wooden, mindlessly repeating Nelda's words. Quickly putting his clothes on, he smiled, and then held her hand as they slowly walked toward the village.

Glowing with satisfaction, Nelda put her arm around Anton's waist. A tear rolled down her cheek, and an intense feeling of joy filled her heart. "We will be happy together, you and I. This is the beginning of a new life for us, and for Tooloo."

"Yes, a new life." Anton said. "I'm happy for everyone." No other thoughts entered his mind—no responsibilities to himself, and no loyalties to his Masters. He was free from all obligations except to make Nelda happy.

It didn't take long to cross the pool and walk up the path to the village. Everyone ran around as if in preparation for a special event. The tables lay burdened with food and garnished with decorative centerpieces. As the two Newlyweds came into view, everyone stopped what they were doing, ushering them over to the readied feast.

"All is ready for your reception!" Tyrell quickly announced.

Mahkeetah stood next to Tyrell at the table, smiling wryly. Turning toward Anton, Mahkeetah placed his hand on his shoulder and looked at him as if defeated.

"My son, you are welcome to be part of my family," Mahkeetah said. Stiffly, he bowed in Methonian fashion, and then invited Anton to sit. "We will have a talk after we eat; it'll be just you and me, one on one. You have earned the right to know my story." He glanced at Tyrell, acknowledging that he'd ordered him to improve their relationship.

Astonished, Anton accepted Mahkeetah's invitation; he hadn't expected his acceptance so easily. "I'm honored to be part of your family. I want to be with Nelda forever." Repeating the words Nelda had branded in his mind, Anton eagerly sat at the table.

Nelda glowed with a look of success. She sat next to Anton and looked around, as everyone smiled. The atmosphere was joyous, and the sounds of celebration imbued the faces of all the villagers.

"We must have tara wine!" Tyrell cried. "We must make a toast to our new friend and family member! This is Tooloo's happiest hour!"

Leaning toward Anton, Mahkeetah quietly spoke in his ear. "Try not to drink the wine," he said, confidentially. "It is potent, and you will soon need your skills! I fear a confrontation today." With a serious look, the two Warriors shared a mutual concern that only they comprehended.

"I hear your words," Anton said, "and I agree." Anton's head gradually cleared from the effects of the *Virlaqueus*.

"Eat; it will help you think more clearly," Mahkeetah advised. Mahkeetah continued to help Anton as if they were a team, something he hadn't been willing to do before. Now that the circumstances of their relationship had changed, he realized a true friendship was possible.

"What looks good to you?" Looking at Nelda, Anton waited for her guidance. His mind was steadily clearing, but he still fumbled with decisions.

"I will select your meal," Nelda said. "Just talk to my father—now is the time for you two to make friends." Taking Anton's plate, Nelda filled it with a sample of each item on the table.

"What mission brought *you* to Tooloo?" Anton asked, looking quizzically at Mahkeetah. He appeared like an innocent child needing an answer to a simple question.

"Please—we will discuss this *after* the meal. Let's make light conversation for now." With a smile, Mahkeetah showed his patience for his Methonian brother; he knew it wouldn't do any good to answer his questions now, and he didn't wish to divulge any sensitive information to the rest of the village. He hadn't revealed everything about himself to them, and now wasn't the time to begin.

Raising his goblet, Tyrell stood up and looked around the table, motioning for everyone to stand. "I offer this toast to the newest member of our village—the young Warrior, Anton! The entire village wishes for you all the happiness that life in Tooloo can offer!"

A cheer roared from everyone, as goblets clanked together. Anton felt out of place for a split second, as if something had gone wrong—yet his chemically induced happiness quenched his uneasiness.

Hugging him, Nelda smiled proudly and encouraged Anton to respond. "It's your turn—say something! They await you!"

"I, um—I've never participated in a toast before. But I assure you I wish for nothing more than to live here with Nelda and all of you. My love for her binds me, and I will do anything for her; my only desire is to please her." Feeling somehow uncomfortable, knowing the life he was turning his back on, the words flowed from his lips as if someone else was speaking for him, but in his heart, he meant every word. Something seemed strange about his choices since his wedding, yet he couldn't reason it out properly.

A chorus of approval was heard around the table. It was final: Tooloo would be Anton's home, and everyone in the village would be his family. An intense sensation of belonging came over Anton, and he smiled shyly, and then looked at Nelda; a sense of longing for her filled his heart.

"Let us celebrate this happy union!" Tyrell said, raising his goblet. He drank deeply of the tangy wine, and quickly emptied it. Wiping his chin with the back of his hand, he smiled with a jovial grin, and motioned for a refill.

Sounds of merriment punctuated the meal, and conversation remained lighthearted; happiness marked each face. The celebration seemed to improve the disposition of the entire community, a much-needed change from their long uncomfortable predicament with the outlaws.

As Anton ate, his head continued to clear from the effects of the *Virlaqueus*. Its intoxicating effects slowly receded as he refueled his body; soon he felt more like himself again. Noticing that his senses were returning, he quickly consumed as much food as he could; he wanted all of his wits to return before the evening; the outlaws might soon appear, and he wanted to feel his best.

After an hour, the reception tapered off. Most of the villagers had eaten their fill, and the women had started to clear the tables, ushering the children off to play.

"Come, it's time to talk." Standing, Mahkeetah invited Anton to his hut, and the two quickly left the table and Nelda behind. "There is much to discuss and so little time!"

Looking over his shoulder, Anton called out to Nelda. "I will return shortly, my love! Village business draws me away." Like a dog yearning for attention, he gazed longingly upon his wife.

The two Warriors entered Mahkeetah's hut and sat upon the tapestries, just as they'd done the afternoon of Anton's arrival. Again, Anton studied the tapestries' interesting design and message.

"I need you clearheaded, so I had some tea prepared," Mahkeetah said. "Drink—it should alleviate the lingering effects of the *Virlaqueus*." Holding out a cup of steaming liquid, Mahkeetah insisted Anton drink.

Unable to refuse, Anton gratefully accepted the beverage. Sipping it carefully, he felt the warmth burn his tongue. It tasted slightly bitter, yet pleasant; the steamy smell penetrated and coated his sinuses; immediately his mind cleared and his much-needed Methonian logic returned.

"Thank you," Anton said. "What *is* this?" Anton's senses further sharpened allowing him to reason for himself.

"The *Virlaqueus* is a strange plant. If a man inhales the fragrance and pollen, he's completely under the control of whoever speaks to him. Particularly, if it's a woman, the power of suggestion multiplies, and the effect is permanent. In contrast, drinking the tea, which is made from its dried leaves, quickly negates the euphoric effects."

With the understanding of a parent, Mahkeetah looked at Anton. Finally, he exposed a side of himself he'd refused to share until now, an exhibition of compassion. They irrefutably shared the same fate, having made the same choices after contacting the people of Tooloo, and he acknowledged his inescapable failure as a Warrior. Sighing, he continued.

"What's even more inexplicable, the flower only has this effect upon men; in contrast, women are completely impervious to its effects."

Shaking his head, Anton frowned. "Why did all of you do this to me? Why did you trick me into marriage? How can I trust or believe any of you?" He felt hurt and betrayed. Most of all, he hadn't imagined this could happen to him. His vulnerability to deception left him bewildered.

"Trust *us*? Why, how could *we* trust an uncaring, arrogant, brash young Warrior? You came here telling us what to do; you were never invited. And I might mention that you expected us simply to comply with anything you commanded! We needed you to understand exactly who we were, and that everyone here was important. We aren't pawns you can push around any way you choose. We wanted you to care about us!"

Befuddled, Anton stared at the floor. "I'm sorry for my earlier behavior. Perhaps you've taught me an important lesson." Looking up, he searched

Mahkeetah's eyes and apologized from his heart. "I will work *with* you from now on."

"Thank you; I appreciate that more than you understand. Now, I'm going to tell you about myself." Forcing a smile, Mahkeetah grasped Anton's shoulder and gave it a nudge, as if to say there were no hard feelings.

"It seems as though you've missed the significance of what I told you about the *Virlaqueus.* Can you imagine if the power of this flower were known to our enemies?" With a quizzical look, Mahkeetah pressured Anton to start using his Methonian logic again.

A look of sudden understanding marked Anton's face as he recognized the seriousness of Mahkeetah's point. "How did you and these people come to know of this plant's peculiar properties? Do our Masters know of it? Did you tell them about it? Why did you stay *here* and betray your purpose as a Warrior?" Suddenly, the questions flowed from him. He held nothing back.

"Those are the questions I intend to answer," Mahkeetah said. "Relax, and I will recount my story." Mahkeetah stood up and walked to the door of the hut, taking a careful look around. "I haven't told anyone here what I am about to reveal to you; it's important they don't know. If I tell you, you must promise to keep it secret between us. You'll know why afterwards."

For the first time in years, Mahkeetah embraced his heritage, using it to compel Anton into agreement. Their Warriors' training bound them tightly together—a shared camaraderie the villagers of Tooloo could never comprehend.

"As you wish; I'll keep your secret," Anton replied, equally committed to the Warriors' code of honor. He would never betray the trust of another Warrior, especially when it involved private secrets.

"Very well, then—I will tell you everything." Returning to his seat, Mahkeetah took one quick look around and leaned slightly forward. Lowering his voice, he revealed his story, as if reporting to his Masters.

"I was sent on a mission to this region when I was about your age, some twenty years ago. My assignment was to discover the truth about some evidence that came to the Great Temple—verification of a mysterious plant that was discovered that could alter a Warrior's DNA." Watching Anton's eyes, Mahkeetah waited to see if he understood. "It wasn't known specifically what'd caused an alteration in the DNA of a previous Warrior's visit, and the Masters desired to find an answer."

"This first Warrior was Loring Four; he was sent for an unrelated mission to this region, and passed through Tooloo. Somehow, he exposed himself to the *Virlaqueus* flower. Not as you and I had—he simply came into close contact with it along the trail, perhaps breathing its pollen floating in the air, or taking the time to smell it in some way. When he returned to the Great Temple, the computers discovered that something had altered his DNA—only slightly, but modified it was. This was of great concern to our Masters. If news of it got out, our enemies would seek to discover what'd caused this, and they would desire to have it as a weapon to use against us! It might be possible for them to create a drug to pacify any Warrior and control their reasoning, change their alliance, or numb their cognitive capacity."

Dumbfounded, Anton looked at Mahkeetah. "Has *my* DNA been altered? Will *I* be different somehow?" A grave expression covered his face.

"I'm sorry, but there is little doubt; the effects have already begun. Now let me continue—there's more." Mahkeetah tried to hurry his story, knowing that the afternoon was nearly over, and that soon it would be evening.

"If our enemies could create some biological weapon to make a Warrior susceptible to suggestion, or alter our DNA, it is logical to assume they would be able to control any of us without restriction—or even worse, alter us into who knows what. As a result, our Masters needed to discover the root cause. I was then briefed and sent to this region to uncover the answer to this mystery." Taking a deep breath, Mahkeetah finally came to the point he wanted to share.

"I came here only to become infatuated with a young girl, just as you did with Nelda. The village elders thought how wonderful it would be to have a Warrior as a member of the village to protect them from any outsiders, or other circumstances; this of course would be an important advantage *anywhere* on Methonias, as you might well guess. They wouldn't have to rely on occasional help from the Great Temple, should the Masters deem a circumstance important enough to send a Warrior for training. Therefore, the villagers used the *Virlaqueus* on me just as they did today on you." Hesitating for a brief moment, Mahkeetah closed his eyes, as if in reverie.

"I remember how enchanting Lavacia was, and how quickly I desired her." Opening his eyes, Mahkeetah again fixed his attention on Anton.

Moved by Mahkeetah's revelations, Anton was speechless; he'd never been one for expressing himself verbally, and he didn't know exactly how to respond now. "I—I'm sorry," he stammered. He tried to show empathy for his father-in-law, but his response was meager. Never had he faced this type of a situation, and he felt completely helpless.

"Don't *pity* me. I *deserve* what I've earned!" Looking downcast, Mahkeetah lapsed into a depressive state of self-pity; his emotions were unbecoming of a Warrior, and he knew it, and he loathed them. It was as if he thought he could vindicate himself through confession. But he simply drifted deeper into shame.

"Then I will feel no pity for you," Anton replied, coldly. "Your emotions are destructive, they will lead you to ruin, just as mine are now."

"Forgive me; years of exposure to the *Virlaqueus* have left me with uncontrollable emotions. The chemical change seems to have a pronounced effect with Warriors. The other village men aren't affected nearly as much as I, and it's obviously happening to you too." Taking a deep breath, Mahkeetah forced a contorted smile.

"My wife used the flowers' capability on me as often as she wanted to influence my choices—usually when I slept. On more than one occasion, she forbade me ever to use my fighting skills for any reason other than to defend myself. I can never fight again; her command for my passivity constrains me. The control is far more compelling than you can imagine!" Straining to tell his final secret, Mahkeetah spoke through clenched teeth, as if he were bound to silence on this point. He then broke down and breathed heavily after straining to offer his secrets.

Surprised, Anton opened his eyes wide. He realized the inner struggle Mahkeetah faced at every moment of his life. Finally, he understood why Mahkeetah had acted the way he did when they first met. It wasn't that he disliked Anton; it was more he tried to warn him, yet was unable to articulate it. He fought to help him avoid the same predicament, yet failed at every attempt. Now it was too late.

As he considered Mahkeetah's revelations further, Anton realized his love for Nelda was a double-edged sword. It would bind him for life to the same struggle he now witnessed. Yet the thought of doing anything else seemed impossible, and undesirable. His heart belonged to her, and her alone. This would never change. But the urge to fulfill his Warrior's duty beckoned him mercilessly.

"By the way—did you follow the path down the edge of the falls?" Mahkeetah asked.

Puzzled, Anton's eyes opened widely. "Well, yes, I did; how did you know this?"

"Just as I thought—you couldn't have navigated here otherwise, or you would've traveled several miles further; it's the shortest route. The *Virlaqueus* grows only on either side of the falls, on rocky ledges. You must've made contact with several of them on your way down—it's nearly impossible not to. A man's first exposure to the flower usually doesn't affect him dramatically—but the second time, it does. Also, I have theorized the initial contact causes lustfulness for pretty young girls—but that would be for the Clone Masters to determine."

"I see. That's how you must've known the flower would affect me today during my wedding. An astute assumption based upon your own experience."

With a pained look, Mahkeetah continued. "I didn't know what'd happened to me when Lavacia held the *Virlaqueus* under my nose and I inhaled its potent chemical. She easily persuaded me to fall hopelessly in love with her, and to remain bound to her forever. But one of my special skills is fortitude—even beyond the average Warrior. I fought the dilemma within myself, and eventually returned to the Great Temple after remaining here for a short time." Fidgeting, as he'd done that first evening, Mahkeetah suddenly faltered.

"That's when the Masters discovered *my* DNA alterations. The computers detected the difference during the standard medical exam after my return. Need I tell you that they were not pleased with the discovery?" Mahkeetah's fidgeting turned to nervous anxiety. He stood up and paced back and forth, and then again went to the door of the hut and looked out into the late afternoon sky, as if searching for something. Slowly, he returned to his seat.

"I was scheduled for termination." Looking directly at Anton, Mahkeetah told his biggest secret. "They intended to put me in the disintegration chamber, as is customary for failed Warriors. But the power of the chemically induced love overcame my sense of duty. Flower pollen or not, at that time my love was tremendous—it overtook everything." A roguish expression marked his face, and he nodded slightly, and then continued.

"With great effort, I escaped from the Great Temple. As you know, the Temple is impervious from outside attack. However, nobody ever tries to escape from inside! Furthermore, no Warrior ever fled for his life; to my knowledge, I was the first. I commandeered an Aerocraft— the very one that these so-called outlaws flew. Yes, they were the ones that unwillingly helped me escape!" A sardonic look marked Mahkeetah's face.

"They flew me back to this region—but just as we were about to land, two Vipercrafts were waiting in ambush. We didn't stand a chance. Naturally, they shot us down." Sighing, Mahkeetah shook his head from side to side.

"Luthian was an excellent pilot, though—one of the best I'd ever seen. He tried to save us from the fighters' attack, and flew the Aerocraft with skills beyond my imagination—but in the end, they hit us in the engine. He landed the crippled Aerocraft as gently as possible deep in the jungle undergrowth. We hit hard, damaging the vehicle even further; naturally, the Aerocraft could never fly again." Mahkeetah closed his eyes and visualized the experience. He grimaced as he completed his recounting, and took a deep breath while shaking his head.

"All of us were injured, but miraculously, we all survived. As I said, Luthian was an excellent pilot. Immediately after impact, I forced the door open; it was wedged closed by a tree and a large rock, but nothing would deny me my love. My love for Lavacia drove me beyond my capabilities, and escape I did! Though injured, I ran all the way back to Tooloo, and fell into Lavacia's loving arms. My love was fulfilled." Falling silent, Mahkeetah closed his eyes. Then he slowly opened them, and gave Anton a beseeching look, as if hoping for something he couldn't have.

"The villagers agreed to make me their chief. Lavacia was Tyrell's older sister. I accepted the offer, and held the title until now. I believe you may be offered the position eventually, but that's just a guess." A sullen expression marked Mahkeetah's face, and he nodded slightly, almost imperceptibly. The two Warriors sat silent for a few moments.

"I have more to tell you," Mahkeetah said softly. "I have never revealed this to anyone, and the knowledge of my secret is the power that the outlaws had over me—and thus the entire village. The pilots— the outlaws—knew my secrets. And now *you* know them. I'm ashamed to admit that because of that, my secrets doomed my wife!" A tear ran from the corner of his eye as he revealed his deepest pain. "*I'm* the one responsible for her death! It tears me apart knowing I can't have the woman I truly love because of the choices I made! I can't live without her! That's the *true* power of the *Virlaqueus*! It changed me forever! That's all I have to say." Mahkeetah immediately fell silent.

For some time, the two sat there quietly, as if sharing a complete understanding of each other's predicament. Anton thought about Mahkeetah's revelations, and knew he needed to share his thoughts.

"I think you're wrong about one thing, Mahkeetah. I think that *all* of you here are very emotional. It isn't just you." Anton showed little concern for how Mahkeetah felt. He had no predilection for the emotional outbursts of the day.

"The council today proves my point. Everyone acted just like you do now—angry, sullen, and accusative. I still retain more objectivity than any of you; I think you've been under the influence of the *Virlaqueus*, and lived around these feelings so long you're unable to judge its powerful effects clearly." Anton's cold and pointed argument unnerved Mahkeetah, as if he'd poked him with a dagger.

Clenching his teeth, Mahkeetah replied: "Warriors *have* no emotions. And now I have *too many*! That's the profound difference I referred to."

Sitting quietly, Anton considered this. "Perhaps you are correct— but all of the men here have this emotional condition. So far, I seem to have only an unbridled love for Nelda; I haven't noticed any other significant differences. You're not responsible for the death of your wife. Silence or not, the result would've been the same. Think about it—Luthian would've found one way or another to control everyone, don't you think? However, it's disgraceful you didn't accept an honorable death; your logic and duty should've compelled you to report to the disintegration chamber. You should've easily deduced the consequence of your escape." Anton offered neither mercy nor gentleness to spare Mahkeetah's feelings.

"I *do* understand the love you feel," Anton went on. "The extraordinary power of the *Virlaqueus* affects me too." Sighing, Anton commiserated with the other Warrior. This was a new feeling for him. Raising one eyebrow, he nodded his head, sharing his resigned acceptance to his predicament. "It would seem our conversation was of benefit to me, I will use this information appropriately. I know returning to the Great Temple would be a death sentence, since my DNA is now altered just as yours was. I would face disintegration, just as you did; I too will *fail* at completing my training."

Again sighing, Anton considered his predicament. On the one hand, he desired most of all to complete his mission and return to the Great Temple. On the other, he could never leave Nelda and face the same failure as Mahkeetah faced years ago—it would be suicidal. It was a paradox. The least problematic of the two choices was to remain in Tooloo.

Considering how Anton felt, Mahkeetah offered him his best advice. "I don't know of any way to prevent the biological alteration of the *Virlaqueus*, but there may be a way to complete your mission and leave. I want to remind you that I was against you staying from the start; it meant you would only fail at completing your training—but I have always been on your side, Anton."

Surprised, Anton accepted Mahkeetah's sympathy; he had always been on his side. When Anton had arrived, Mahkeetah encouraged him to leave; during the council meeting, Mahkeetah argued on Anton's behalf to prevent the villagers from indoctrinating him. Therefore, he now shared Mahkeetah's accidental self-inflicted exile.

"How might I succeed in my mission?" asked Anton.

"It will be tricky—but when you return, you'll have to hide your love unconditionally, as if it meant nothing. The Masters will review this, and perhaps, if you are lucky, they'll believe you overcame the effects of the *Virlaqueus*. Showing that strength, showing you didn't succumb to it could buy your freedom. If you can do this, they may decide that their designs are secure and ignore my failure. Truthfully, I'm doubtful—but it's your only hope." Mahkeetah felt as though their conversation lifted a tremendous burden from his heart; he relaxed and smiled slightly at Anton.

"I agree that you must succeed in your mission, if only to vindicate the failure of my own; your success can redeem me; you must return to the Great Temple for my failure to have meaning. Don't worry about Tyrell or Nelda; I will handle them for you." Reassuring Anton, Mahkeetah tried to convince him to leave so that he wouldn't succumb to the same fate, and be subject to the same consequences; his motives were innocent.

There was still one concern Anton had; logic hadn't provided an answer, and he was tired of guessing. "Why didn't the outlaws, these Aerocraft personnel, recognize my attire? And why is it their clothing hasn't worn to shreds after twenty years?" Looking confused, he asked as if some secret remained untold.

"That is a worthy question. Those men you fought were prisoners. They were on the Aerocraft, waiting their release to the Temple's prison, when I commandeered the vessel. Naturally, they came under Luthian's control after we crashed. As for the clothing—there's always a supply of various items transported on the Aerocraft. For whatever twist of luck, a shipment of uniforms was on that particular craft."

Satisfied, Anton nodded his acceptance. "Makes sense, it just seemed so peculiar to me."

"It's time for us to eat, and then for everyone to go to the cave; as was agreed by all. We'll comply with your plan, and then you can leave." Standing, Mahkeetah motioned for Anton to follow, and the two left the hut.

The two Warriors walked over to the village tables. They weren't particularly hungry after the earlier festivities, but upon arrival, they saw that everyone was snacking on the remains of the reception.

The moment Nelda saw Anton she quickly ran into his open arms. He kissed her passionately, as if he'd been away for months and hungered for her love rather than food.

"I'm here, my love," she said. "Please sit, and I will serve you." With a smile, Nelda quickly gathered a few items of food and set a plate in front of Anton. "What did you two talk about? Everyone here wants to know!"

Feeling compelled to answer, Anton fought back the urge to confess every detail. "A Warrior's conversation is the business of a Warrior—if the need arises, I will tell you more. Until then, suffice it to say that we discussed completing my mission." With great effort, Anton offered a simple summary, and he knew Nelda realized that he had done so.

Nelda frowned at him, marking her displeasure with his less-thancomplete answer.

"Very well, you will tell me more when we are *alone*." Smiling, her eyes insisted she would get the answers she desired, one way or another. She knew Anton could never keep a secret from her as long as she had the power of the *Virlaqueus* to compel him.

The paradox of induced love and the ability to coerce him to do anything she desired left Anton perplexed and not altogether pleased. Finally, he understood the full extent of control the women of Tooloo held over their men. That understanding left him completely unnerved. The idea that he would never be completely free as long as he remained here gave him a sense of dread. On the other hand, the idea of leaving Nelda, never to see her again, seemed completely impossible; he knew he could never do it. Still, he somehow had to find the strength to complete his mission and return to the Great Temple. This paradox tore him apart.

Tyrell approached Anton and Nelda and looked at each of them. "I see that you and Mahkeetah are finished talking." The statement was pointed, but friendly. "It's my hope you two Warriors will share the results of your discussion with us." He hoped for their revelation but expected silence.

Straightaway, Mahkeetah's attention fell sharply upon Tyrell. He didn't want to share anything with him, but he knew he'd have to offer something to satisfy his curiosity.

The chief could see by Mahkeetah's attitude that the discussion between two Warriors was private, and that he had no hope of persuading them to elaborate. This confounded him, but now wasn't the time to press the issue, so he let it go.

"Let's gather in the Village Square after we eat. It's time to complete these *outlaw* issues." Mahkeetah's response was cold. He seemed to have gained back some of his Methonian dignity after confessing to Anton, a disclosure nearly twenty years overdue.

"We're prepared to do so; we're simply waiting for you two so that we might proceed." Tyrell made sure the two Warriors knew how he felt. "I hope after all of this is over you'll feel comfortable sharing it with us all."

Both Anton and Mahkeetah looked at Tyrell. "We'll share everything soon—fear not," Mahkeetah answered quickly with a sneer, looking at everyone present. "We have no intention of *hiding* anything, but now isn't the time for *another* of your councils."

This seemed to satisfy Tyrell, and he nodded in agreement. "See to it that you do."

The two men stared at each other, and then Mahkeetah stood up and nudged Anton's shoulder. "We're done eating—we need to go."

"I'm glad we're all in agreement; let's gather in the Village Square in preparation for the relocation." Tyrell gave the signal to leave.

Raising his arms to draw the attention of everyone, Tyrell announced the decision. "Let's all put our trust in the plans of this savior from the Great Temple. He's proven to us that he can save us all from the tyranny of the outlaws. We know we can trust him since he has chosen to become one of us."

Tyrell's words held everyone's interest, and as he finished his short speech, all of the villagers nodded their heads and agreed that Anton was the hero who could save them. Since his arrival, no more abductions or deaths had occurred. Most profoundly, he'd saved Tok from certain demise beneath the waterfalls. And under the hold of the *Virlaqueus*, he had married Nelda, proving they had control over him—a key point of the plan they now chose to blindly accept.

"You've all been informed of the decision of the elders, and now it's time to carry out their edict," continued Tyrell.

A wave of conversation rippled through the crowd, and then, just as quickly, everyone hurried along the trail toward the hidden cave behind the falls. Everyone had prepared themselves.

The first signs of evening began to settle in, and deep shadows helped to conceal the procession of villagers from the eyes of their enemy. Nothing happened along the trail, and nobody suspected any danger or observation from a hidden foe.

Upon arrival at the falls, the tribe quickly took cover inside the amphitheater. One by one, they squeezed their way into the cave's opening and gathered inside; they all stood in the darkness, waiting. Mumbling and whispers filled the chamber; everyone expressed nervous thoughts of what might be happening, and the children whined with boredom and fear.

Preparing to speak to the villagers in order to comfort them, Tyrell hoped to alleviate their stress. He hadn't uttered more than a couple of words when suddenly the entire cave disintegrated. An explosion shook the ground violently, and enormous boulders tumbled from high above; particles of dust permeated the atmosphere and hung like noxious gas. This was followed by complete silence. Moments later the only sound was of the water again rushing over the side of the cliff, crashing into the remains of the pool below; little was left of the pool, half the mountainside had covered and replaced the water, changing the landscape forever.

IN THE VILLAGE SQUARE, ANTON sat with his back against the weathervane post. Using this time to prepare himself mentally for another confrontation with the outlaws, he listened for the sounds of an approaching enemy. With great effort, he strained to single out any sound, any vibration, any signal of their advance towards Tooloo.

As the sound of the villagers blended into the sounds of the waterfall, he heard the voices and movements of someone else.

Several men drew close, and Anton heard them encompassing him; the sounds of their approach came from all directions, making it difficult to single anyone out in particular; within moments, they'd surrounded the village. They made no effort to hide their approach; it was as if they wanted him to know they were coming, as if they knew he expected them.

As he continued to sit with his back against the pole, Anton remained motionless and silent. He was ready for them—so ready he could hardly contain himself. Moments passed. His heart began to race, and he breathed deeply, slowly, to remain calm. He didn't want a sudden rush of adrenaline to drive his thoughts, and especially his actions; he needed a clear mind when the first movement of attack occurred. But it was too late.

Only a scant few minutes after the villagers left for the cave, the ground beneath Anton's feet heaved, and a shockwave of tremendous noise came from the direction of the falls. Suddenly alert, Anton jumped to his feet, ready to run as fast as he could to the cave. Thoughts of a devastating catastrophe coursed through his mind. He was in a state of confusion and turmoil, split between engaging the enemy and the need to rescue his friends. Within seconds, his options had vanished, as several men poured into the village square, surrounding him just as he tried to race into the jungle toward the falls. He knew he wouldn't be able to escape the tightening noose without a fight, and stood in ready stance for the inevitable confrontation.

They were several more than Anton had anticipated, at least eight or ten, and they moved in swiftly when they saw him, completely blocking any possible retreat. It was pointless to escape the small army, after all—a confrontation was the only way to end the outlaws' tyranny.

"He's a skinny one, this Warrior brat!" one of the men said from behind.

"Watch out, he's tricky!" another said. They taunted Anton, hoping to provoke an irrational response—a response that would leave him vulnerable in some way.

"I think he's *afraid* of us; we're too many for him!" said yet another outlaw.

There was a roar of laughter, and the outlaws quickly tightened their circle around Anton, as if they were cinching a noose around a condemned man's neck. All of them were within three yards when they suddenly ceased their advance.

Calmly, Anton waited in ready stance. Nothing the outlaws said aggravated him in any way; his mind was busy making calculations of how to handle so many opponents. With only the movement of his eyes, and listening with all his Methonian skills, he noticed that most of the outlaws didn't carry any visible weapon; this made his task much simpler. However, two of the men carried a large stick like a club, and a third man standing directly in front of him held a Warrior's pike that had obviously come from the Great Temple. It was the classic design—a double-edged spear point with a hook below it on each side.

All the men wore loose-fitting Aerocraft personnel uniforms, just as Mahkeetah had described, and they stank from the filth of an unclean lifestyle.

Standing behind all of them was a different man; he kept his distance behind the human noose encircling Anton. His clothing was in excellent condition—noticeably clean and new, it was the uniform of an Aerocraft pilot.

"Luthian," Anton mumbled to himself. He was sure of it. His attire was clean, he was clean and well-groomed, and he stood out from the others like a sore thumb. He had the magnetism of an educated man. Anton knew instantly that he was the one to eliminate in order to win the battle; it would take some effort to get to him, but Anton relished the opportunity.

"I see you recognize me," the well-dressed man said. "Good. Yes, I'm Luthian. And you, my young friend, are my prisoner—if you live that long." Luthian spoke from a safe distance, knowing Anton's Methonian skills. He was confident he had complete control of the situation, and he intended to prove it.

"Now, my young pawn, might I suggest you save us all a display of your anger, and surrender? Your violence the other day disrupted the morale of my men, and I would like it if you didn't upset them any further. We far outnumber you, and there's no chance of escape." Luthian intended to rouse Anton's ire, hoping he would do something irrational—something that he could capitalize on to ensure his victory.

"Remember," Luthian continued to his men. "I want him alive—I have questions for him." The outlaws advanced simultaneously. "You can do what you want *after* I get my answers."

Instantly Anton made his move; he was far more prepared than Luthian could have imagined. Like an acrobat, he leapt into the air with a back flip. His feet went over his head and wrapped around the weathervane pole. Hand over hand, he quickly shimmied up the pole, feet first. The crowd of men hadn't expected such an unusual move, and they stood there wondering what to do.

"*After* him—before he does something clever!" Luthian barked, hoping to maintain the upper hand.

With the sheer strength of his nimble body, Anton reversed his position on the pole as he reached the top. Twenty feet in the air, he wrapped his legs around the pole, holding himself in place. Grasping the steel weathervane, he easily freed it from its mounting.

The man with the pike stepped forward and jabbed it at Anton— but he was just beyond its reach. A second man grabbed the pole and started to rock it back and forth, hoping to shake Anton free by forcing him to either lose his grip, or snap it off at the base. Recognizing the tactic, two more men stepped up, helped in the effort, and rocked the heavy pole significantly.

Grasping the weathervane like a discus, Anton flung it with remarkable precision at the men below. The pointed arrow flew as if shot from a bow, and struck the man with the pike in the head. It pierced his forehead, and the point protruded from the base of his skull. Instantly he fell to the ground, dead.

Using the momentum of the swaying pole, Anton grasped it at the top with both hands and let his feet swing free. He then controlled the swaying movement and swung back and forth, gaining more momentum with each change of direction. As he neared the ground on one final effort, two men grasped at his feet. Without hesitation, he kicked at both of them—once with each foot—making simultaneous contact. The first man received a blow to the face that shattered his eye socket; the second a kick to the chest that cracked several ribs. Both men fell backwards and hit the ground, hard.

Just as the pole's momentum was about to change directions, Anton released it and touched down lightly, and he immediately adopted the ready stance. The pole arched away with increased speed and slammed into another man's head; a loud popping sound resonated through the air as his skull split in two halves, like a cleaved melon. The man's neck vertebrae were crushed and bulged underneath his skin. Blood and brain matter spattered across the men standing too near. The contact eliminated most of the pole's momentum, and it vibrated and shuddered randomly.

Diving for the fallen pike, Anton retrieved it in a heartbeat. He'd practiced and trained with this weapon extensively throughout his youth, and he held it as if it was an extension of his mind and body. Ready for any move from his opponents, he appeared invincible as he slashed it around. He kept everyone at bay; nobody could approach him and hope to survive.

"Wait!" Luthian quickly yelled. "Perhaps you'd like to know the fate of your friends?" He hoped to shift the momentum of the battle into his favor with a sly distraction. He knew if he could pique Anton's curiosity, it might provide an opportunity— if only for a few seconds. Anton had already defeated too many of his men, and he was in complete control of the fight.

"I've seen what you Warriors are capable of. Even with all the odds against you, you're able to succeed. It's truly inconceivable how you can surmount such imposing obstacles."

His tactic worked. Anton looked at Luthian with a wolfish glare. Hatred poured from his eyes; he despised the supremacy of Luthian's pure evil. Hatred was an entirely new feeling; he'd never judged anything as good or evil before, he'd simply followed orders. For a split second, Luthian held his complete attention, and he forgot the other men. That was enough for the outlaws to regain the upper hand.

Unexpectedly, two of the outlaws suddenly lunged from behind Anton, and both of them grabbed at the pike's shaft near the base. With a mighty tug, they ripped it from his control. Instantly, he turned to face the attackers.

The two men struggled to gain ownership of the pike, tugging it back and forth. Anton took two steps toward them, landed a kick in the first man's groin, and grasped the pike away from the second as if he were a small child. Swinging the pike around like a club, he struck the second man's skull. A distinct pop resounded as he fell to his knees and passed out. In one fluid motion, Anton turned to face any further opposition from Luthian's direction.

"Bravo!" Luthian said. "In less than two minutes you have either disabled or killed five men!"

However, this time the distraction had no effect; Anton was wise to Luthian's tactic. Concentrating, he mentally blocked every word from his hearing, and returned his focus to every subtle movement the other men made, and focused his hearing toward every infinitesimal sound of an attack. He was ready for his final performance; nothing would interfere with him until he'd eliminated every opponent. With the speed only a genetically engineered human could produce, he made his move.

Like a whirlwind, Anton spun around and thrust first one end of the pike and then the other at each man. He delivered a deadly blow to everyone as he carved his way through the ranks. Cries of pain, muffled impacts from pummeling, and breaking bones resounded in one continuous fray. Blood sprayed through the air in all directions, like a lawn sprinkler gone amok, and body parts littered the ground as the melee progressed. Not a single person escaped.

It happened so quick it seemed like a blur to Luthian's eyes; in the end, he stood alone with a smug smile on his face. In his hand, he held a small cylindrical device and pointed it at Anton. "Don't get any ideas; you're as good as dead, my friend." Laughing, he mocked the Warrior, hoping he would do something rash.

Unsure of what Luthian held, Anton chose caution. The cylinder could only be one of two things—a weapon, or a ruse. He didn't wish to find out the hard way which one it was.

"I'm not your friend," he said. "And we shall see who dies next." Holding the pike like a spear, Anton too was ready to attack. He ached to do so.

"Lower your weapon, Warrior. You'll never finish your throw before I slice you in half; I'm holding a very powerful laser." The smile disappeared from his face as he ordered Anton to disarm.

Finally recognizing the device, Anton lowered the pike and held it like a quarterstaff at his side. He wasn't willing to release it yet.

"What is it you want?" he said. "Surely you would've already used that if you didn't want something."

"Oh how intuitive. You Warriors never cease to amaze me with your cognitive capabilities. Oh yes," he chuckled, "there *is* something I want. That little piece of jewelry Mahkeetah's daughter wears around her pretty neck. It belongs to *me*!"

"And just how is it yours?" Puzzled, Anton looked closely at Luthian's face. It seemed as though he told the truth—yet Mahkeetah had said he had given the necklace to Nelda.

Anger streamed from Luthian's eyes and suddenly he snapped: "That Warrior friend of yours stole it from my ship! I would have been long gone from here years ago, if he hadn't stolen those crystals! An Aerocraft is a hearty vehicle—those Vipercrafts may have shot me down, but I could have repaired it enough to make it fly again. Unfortunately, without the crystals, it could never fly!"

So that was it—he needed the crystals to escape. Anton knew the crystals looked familiar—and now he understood. They were some of the central computer's crystals from the Aerocraft.

"Well, I believe they're gone forever now!" he said. "Apparently, you are the one responsible for leveling the falls. Well guess what—those crystals were under the falls at the time. You'll have to dig for them to get them back!"

Luthian's eyes widened suddenly as he realized what Anton had said. His mouth hung open, and then he clenched his teeth. "No! You *lie*!" Raising his weapon, he prepared to fire.

Suddenly, from out of nowhere, Mahkeetah appeared and sprinted toward Luthian. Covered in blood, and obviously injured beyond description, he dove in front of the laser, reaching for it. Simultaneously, Luthian fired the device, slicing Mahkeetah from head to toe. A beam of red light divided him neatly in half as he flew sideways through the air—but inexplicably, he succeeded in knocking the laser from Luthian's hand, even as he died.

Aghast, Anton couldn't believe what he'd witnessed. He'd assumed Mahkeetah was dead, and he couldn't believe he'd chosen to fight, especially at the precise moment he was most needed. Mahkeetah's Methonian capacity for self-sacrifice gave Anton the opportunity he so desperately needed.

Luthian took flight the moment Mahkeetah knocked the laser from his hand. He knew he didn't have a chance of retrieving it in time, and hoped he could escape unchallenged.

Anton quickly ran to Mahkeetah, retrieved the laser, and looked at his friend's severed body. For a few seconds he hesitated, wondering how his comrade had managed to come to his rescue. His Methonian fortitude obviously proved stronger than the chemical hold of the *Virlaqueus* and subsequent brainwashing demands of his dead wife. Her negligence had left him tortured, tormented, and most of all, useless—however, in the end, when it mattered most, he'd redeemed himself. Perhaps now his Masters would revere him as a hero, not a traitor—or perhaps Mahkeetah's heroics would help to convince Anton's Masters to spare him when he returned; he'd proven a Warrior's determination and strength were superior to a powerful chemical.

Shuddering with hate, Anton suddenly bolted after Luthian and pushed himself with every ounce of effort his body could produce; he wasn't about to let him escape. His revulsion for the evil man drove him harder than he'd ever pushed himself before. He had more than enough energy to burn, and massive amounts of adrenaline coursed through his veins, driving him like a maniac. The distance between them shortened at an impossible rate; it was as if the Aerocraft pilot were running in slow motion.

Within seconds, Anton caught up with Luthian, easily eliminating the head start the other had gained. Using the hook at the base of the pike's blade, he snagged Luthian's leg and gave a tug. Instantly Luthian hit the dirt face-first, smashing his nose against a large rock. Blood poured from it and covered his chin, as he helplessly rolled over to see Anton standing above him. Surprise and shock covered his face, and fear filled his heart as he realized he was about to die.

"If you kill me now, you will never know what *really* happened to your friends," Luthian said, looking for any way of saving himself. His silver tongue was his best tool and he planned to use it to the very end. "I'm not from this world of yours! I know things. I can tell them to you—just let me go and I will!"

"There is little you can say to save yourself," Anton said. "Now die like a man!" Anton didn't intend to spare him. If Luthian was the mastermind who murdered his wife and so many villagers, he intended to even the score.

"Your life is of no value to this realm, and there is nothing you can say that will dissuade me from removing you from it!" Anton raised the pike for one last blow.

"Wait! Your Masters shot me down some twenty years ago on this pathetic rock—this despicable planet you call home—because one of you went AWOL! It isn't fair! *I* wasn't to blame for Mahkeetah's wretched love of a simple jungle girl!" He held up his hands in panic, trembling as he spoke.

Anton was numb to Luthian's pleading, and he was out of patience. "I've had enough of your groveling—die like a man, you pathetic rodent!"

"Wait!" Luthian cried. "Don't you get it? Your Masters had some reason for allowing me to live!"

Again, Anton fell for it; Luthian was able to control him to some small degree by making him hesitate at all the right moments. Lowering the pike, Anton placed the point gently on his chest, aiming it directly at his heart. "Go on, tell me all of it; if you have something to say then you'd better say it now! Your death is still imminent! Beware what you reveal—it may speed your demise!" He glowered at the villain, his eyes demanding the full story.

Luthian lay on his back, holding both hands up, as if pleading like a small child to avoid punishment; he sweated profusely and shivered with fear. An unmistakable look of dread covered his face, and his words struggled past his trembling lips. His nose continued to bleed and he quickly wiped away the blood, hoping to gain more time. Somehow, through all of the blood, pain, perspiration, and frustration, he was able to force a smile.

"I know the secrets of your so-called Masters," Luthian said, flinching slightly as if expecting the point of the pike to be pushed between his ribs. But Anton remained as still as a statue. "Please allow me to sit," Luthian continued, "and I will tell you more." His eyes implored his captor as he hoped to inch his way back to freedom. He continued to grin as if he could smile his way into the heart of his executioner.

"Go on, tell me your story. When you're done, I'll finish you." Anton listened with utter skepticism. A scowl covered his brow, and a look of disgust marked the corner of his upper lip. He knew quite well, there were no secrets about his Masters, and it disgusted him to allow Luthian an opportunity to speak, yet he wanted to know if there was any valuable information he might accidentally share.

"I'm not just an Aerocraft pilot," Luthian said. "I'm a *Galactic* pilot! I flew the *big* interstellar ships." Luthian hoped Anton would grant him immunity on this single point. "I see that you *know* I'm telling the *truth*!" He'd noticed the spark of recognition in Anton's face.

"That's what it is!" exclaimed Anton. "I thought your clothes looked familiar." Now he realized what was different about Luthian's attire. It was an older design of the uniform worn by the Galactic pilots in years past, and he wore the additional insignias of the advanced rank.

"How did you come into possession of such clothing?" Anton said. "Be quick—your life hangs in the balance of what you say next!" Anton nudged the pike's point on Luthian's sternum and pierced the fabric of his shirt.

"I flew the Interstellar Sixteen for your Masters," Luthian replied nervously. Anxiety made his voice strain even more as the pike's razorsharp blade sliced completely through his shirt and lightly pierced his flesh. Again, he slowly wiped a trail of blood from his nose and looked at it on the back of his hand.

Anton knew this vessel well. He'd learned about all the vessels used for travel when he was but a young child, including the Interstellar Sixteen. Few if any of the indigenous people on Methonias would even know such a ship existed; their knowledge pertained to a simple life on Methonias. But Anton wondered if Luthian was telling the complete truth. It seemed as though he mixed truth with lies in order to sway people into believing what he wanted them to believe.

"How do you know of this vessel?" Anton said. "I see you have something that looks like a pilot's uniform—but you couldn't possibly know anything about the uniform or the ship, unless perhaps you tortured a pilot to gain his knowledge. Mahkeetah told me you're an Aerocraft pilot, that doesn't make you a Galactic pilot." Anton's skepticism dwindled the more he thought about Luthian's claim, even though it seemed too unlikely.

"I was a Galactic pilot until I was forced to escape for my life!" Luthian was nearly pleading for a reprieve as the tone of his voice lilted with fright. Yet he maintained a grimace as he spoke. He knew Anton would rather kill him than continue this line of conversation, and he didn't know how much longer he could postpone his imminent demise.

"There seems to be a thread of truth to what you say," Anton said. "Tell me the whole story, and don't leave anything out." Anton still didn't trust him. After all, he had led a group of men that committed genocide on a small village—a small village under *his* protection. But he had nothing to lose by listening to his story.

"I would be happy to tell you," Luthian said. "But perhaps you will let me sit while I do so. You are the one who holds the weapon, and your skills are way beyond mine." He assumed the look of an innocent child while his silver tongue worked hard on Anton's strict moral code.

"Very well—sit!" Anton stepped back and put the shaft of the pike to the ground with the blade pointing straight up. He held it firmly in his right hand and leaned lightly on it. "Now—answer my questions." He knew there was no chance of Luthian's escape, so he allowed him to sit.

Heaving a huge sigh of relief, Luthian quickly scrambled away, scooting his bottom across the ground toward a nearby rock. It was large enough to sit upon, and he made himself as comfortable as possible, and then continued his story.

"Your Masters have *many* secrets," Luthian said, pointing to the sky. "Everyone out there in the galaxy, all those other planets you really know nothing about, *knows* it. Just to begin with—where do you think they came from? Do you know? Did they tell you about themselves at that Temple of yours?" He provoked Anton, hoping to pique his curiosity. Slowly rubbing his chest, he inspected where the pike had sliced neatly into his skin. Glancing at his hand, he saw a small amount of blood—but nothing of great concern. He then sighed in relief.

"This is irrelevant," Anton said. "Tell me about your piloting skills." Anton wanted to control what he heard. He was used to logical thought, and the questions Luthian posed didn't seem logical.

"Very well—if that's all that you wish to know about. I was a pilot for your Masters. I flew the Interstellar Sixteen. I transported them to all the colonized planets, dropping off you Warriors after they sold you to one government or another. What a racket they have—making super-humans for sale to the highest bidder. It makes me sick. What a racket." Luthian shook his head in disbelief, seemingly disgusted by his own story and his past life.

"Skip the melodrama—just stick to the facts." Anton continued to pursue the information in a logical procession. He didn't like the outlaw's insinuations and opinions, and the way he continued to stray from the subject.

"Yes, sir!" Luthian said—standing and saluting Anton in an elaborate Galactic pilot gesture.

Finally, it seemed doubtless that Luthian was in fact who and what he claimed to be. Anton finally believed his argument credible; there were simply too many nuances that cemented his resolve—too many details that pointed to his claim.

Returning to his seat, Luthian continued his narration. "As I was saying, I quite often overheard the discussions of your Masters as they traveled aboard my ship. It was just pieces of conversation, you know—a little here and a little there—but after a while, I'd heard enough and I managed to put things together. I'm telling you, they *aren't* what they seem!"

"The facts," Anton repeated. "Just stick with the facts!" He grew short-tempered, pressing Luthian to hurry. He wasn't going to let him stray from the story or the truth for a moment longer.

"Okay, okay," Luthian continued. "As I said, I put the pieces together. Your Masters aren't from here—they aren't from your precious Methonias. I don't know where they're from, exactly, but they seem to be on a mission of some sort. You Warriors aren't just for making money; you're for a much more important purpose, a secret purpose. They need you to fulfill some private agenda!" As Luthian shared what he knew, he looked at Anton and hoped it would be enough to save him from the Warrior's justice.

"Is that it? Is that all you have to say? This isn't something monumental, as you alluded to." Anton knew Luthian was holding back something, and that he was going to have to force it out of him. It seemed without a doubt he was hiding some guilt, some information that incriminated him beyond the crimes of his more recent escapades.

"Are you sure you want to hear more?" Luthian said, trying his best to spare both Anton and himself from the climax of his narration, the point he most wished to conceal. He hoped he'd already said enough.

"Get to the point and give it to me, now!" Anton had no more patience. "This is your last chance—finish your story!"

"Very well then," Luthian said. "There are people disappearing from a planet on the far reaches of the inhabited worlds—I don't know which one. Your Masters are using you Warriors to uncover the mystery. You're just cannon fodder to them! You're just something to be created, used, and thrown away at their whims!" Watching Anton's reaction carefully, he waited to see some spark in his eyes—a sign of the trust he so desperately desired.

Unflinching, Anton remained steadfast and completely expressionless. He weighed Luthian's words carefully.

Noticing Anton's hesitation, Luthian pressed his point. "You're just sold to make money so they can develop an even better line of Warrior to be used in this quest of theirs. That's it. You didn't know this. None of you Warriors know this. But I do!" Luthian held Anton's gaze, hoping his words would buy him some time, or maybe even his freedom. He was scared, and he needed to find something in his captor's face—some recognition or response that showed he'd gained a reprieve. But he found nothing.

"So you say," Anton said. "I have no need of this information; it changes nothing to know it. Now, as for the villagers in Tooloo, you murdered them for no other reason than to acquire Mahkeetah's katana and the Aerocraft's computer crystals." Having passed judgment, Anton was ready to proceed with his sentencing and execution. His desire to check on the cave before it was completely dark left him feeling both impatient and intolerant, and he was running out of time very quickly. The unexpected appearance of Mahkeetah had given him hope that some of the villagers, particularly Nelda, might still be alive.

Knowing his life was at an end, Luthian agreed with anything Anton said. "You know I had my men do this," he said. "I cannot escape that. Believe me when I say that it was for a good cause." He looked at Anton sheepishly, knowing he may just have said too much. But he continued to talk, hoping he might yet buy his freedom. He hoped beyond all hope that the darkness might allow him to escape.

"You're wrong about one thing, though," he said. "It wasn't the katana I was after, just the crystals. I simply wanted Mahkeetah disarmed. He's more dangerous than even you realize!" Luthian looked from one eye to the next in Anton's face, searching desperately for anything that might give away his thoughts. Again, he found nothing. "It would seem that the katana is lost forever. Obviously, nobody will have it, so it doesn't matter."

"How is it you were able to set off an explosive?" Anton asked. "Where is the detonation device you used?" Anton ignored Luthian's last remark and guided the subject back to his guilt, not Mahkeetah's. He needed to know the exact details of what he'd done; it was still a mystery the precise technique he'd used to accomplish the explosion.

Reaching into his pocket, Luthian produced a small electronic device. It was a detonator. Looking at Anton, he held it out and smiled. "Is this what you're looking for?"

Snatching it from his hand, Anton gave it a quick close examination, and then slid it into his tunic.

"There were some munitions aboard the Aerocraft. When I crash-landed I took them with me. All of them are gone now; I used the last of what I had today!" He smiled widely, as if proud of what he'd done. Then he closed his eyes and put his chin in the air. "I'm yours, do with me what you choose."

"One last thing—how is it you were piloting the Aerocraft if you are a Galactic pilot?"

"Oh, that. My ship traveled here to Methonias with several prisoners onboard—*they* were the cargo. My captain wanted to make sure they arrived as promised to your Masters, and assigned me the task of flying the Aerocraft down to the Great Temple. That's when Mahkeetah and I made our, shall we say, acquaintance?" Luthian again raised his chin, offering it to Anton. "Now, if you please, let's get it over with."

With a loathsome feeling, Anton looked at the despicable pilot's raised chin. It sickened him to think that he would become what he hated if he killed this wicked man. Then he realized he'd already committed his own form of genocide on the outlaws under Luthian's rule. He considered this for a moment longer. The only difference between what he had done and what Luthian and the outlaws had done, was the *reason* for the killing. Theirs was an act of murder for personal gain. His was an act of survival and justice—or was it revenge? This thought, this subtle difference, haunted him for a moment as he tossed the argument back and forth.

"You made a mistake," he said. "If you hadn't killed the villagers before your attempt at capturing me, you would've had the ability to blackmail me. As it stands, I had nothing to lose by fighting you. You're a fool, Luthian, and nothing can separate you from that." Anton's upper lip raised slightly on one side, and he spoke with an inflection of disgust. "As for my judgment—your mouth is your biggest weapon. I shall do justice by silencing you."

In one swift motion, Anton whipped the pike into his hands and pointed it at Luthian. The pilot's eyes opened in time to see the blade slide between his lips, past his teeth, and into his mouth. With a twist of his wrist, Anton neatly sliced the tongue out of Luthian's mouth, and flipped it through the air, far off into the jungle. Blood gushed down Luthian's chin and he raised his hands, trying to staunch the bleeding.

"Justice served," Anton said. As fast as a cheetah, he raced toward the cave, leaving Luthian behind. On he ran, putting everything he had into his legs. Thoughts of what he might find ran through his mind as he pushed forward; grief gnawed at his heart and tore at his guts as he contemplated the extent of the damage; he was done with setting his emotions aside as he dealt with the outlaws. In less than a minute, he arrived at the falls and discovered the amphitheater and cave destroyed, and the entire side of the mountain obliterated; without question, there could be no survivors. He had known what to expect, but Mahkeetah had given him a small degree of hope. There was no way to know how his Methonian brother had escaped the fate of the rest of the villagers.

Enormous boulders filled much of the pool below the falls. Water ran in all directions, but somehow managed to find its way back to the river channel below. Nothing was left of the natural beauty of the falls; Anton's memories of the area were all he had left.

Anton's knees felt weak as he thought of all the people he'd known—Mahkeetah, Nelda, Tyrell, and the little boy Tok. Sickened, he fell to his hands and knees, the pain overcoming his endurance.

"Oh my god! That insane bastard! How could he have done such a thing?" Anton screamed like an angry maniac, and his heart called out to the dead village.

Anxieties ran through him, and slowly he regained his feet and then paced around in circles, not knowing what to do, or what to say. The only thing he knew was that his idea, his decision, had produced this horrible circumstance. He was responsible for all these deaths, and nothing could change that. Luthian's hand may have pushed the button, but Anton was responsible for sending the villagers to the cave. Most of all, Nelda was gone forever. His love went out to his dead wife; he needed her to assuage his pain, but he would never find the satisfaction he so desperately required.

"Oh my god, what have I done! This can't be!" Feelings of devastation coursed through his body, suffocating him, making his heart pound in his ears, and making his breathing increase. Perspiration beaded on his forehead. He felt very dizzy, and stress nearly caused him to pass out.

Then he noticed the color of his ring as he looked at his hand; it had become a deep impenetrable midnight black, as if a black hole wrapped itself around his finger. He sat on the ground, hugging his knees, and mourned the needless deaths of his friends and family. Sick to his stomach and heartbroken, he started mumbling like someone disturbed by mental illness. After a time, he realized he needed to release his emotions; he repositioned himself to meditate. This was a normal and natural reflex conditioned into him by the training of the Temple Masters. Within minutes, the releasing of his stress overtook his mind and body; he became very drowsy as his pain subsided enough for him to relax.

AWAKENING EARLY THE NEXT MORNING beside the obliterated cave, Anton recalled the scene from the night before. Instantly, his stomach felt sick and he started to vomit. The night's sleep had cleared his thoughts enough to alleviate much of his pain, but his sudden realization of what had happened brought back a flash of his previous agony.

Without warning, a single tear rolled down his cheek, and he realized something he'd never felt before—something that touched his heart in a way he never thought possible. He realized that all people were special in some way, and that maybe, just maybe, he'd made an error in how he'd treated them by having little or no respect for them as individuals. He didn't care about anyone other than his Masters, or his brother Warriors, and it didn't matter whether he offered any respect or true concern; only the completion of his mission was important. Contemplating this, his thoughts returned to how he might have avoided this outcome.

"There was nothing more I could do," he said, sighing slowly and softly to himself while stretching out his arms. He tipped back his head, and then pounded the ground with both fists while shouting at the sky, "I'm a fool!" Finally, he relaxed his arms and mumbled, "I need to clear my mind of all this." Once again, he adopted the lotus position, and began to meditate. He remained motionless until midmorning.

Eventually, the need for food overwhelmed him. Standing, he decided to travel back to Mahkeetah's hut, to gather whatever food he could find. Slowly, with dread in his heart, he walked down the path to the empty village. His meditation had cleared his mind sufficiently to allow him to make appropriate choices.

When he arrived at the hut, he quickly located a stack of tara fruit. It didn't take long to consume several of them; they tasted particularly good after skipping breakfast. He then selected some of the dried meat and stale bread. After nourishing himself, he acknowledged that his mission to Tooloo was complete and it was time for him to leave.

Looking around Mahkeetah's hut, Anton discovered Nelda's beaded necklace lying on the rug. It seemed as though she'd known she would never return, and had left it for him to find. Slowly, he picked it up and put it around his neck. He stared at it for a long time, focusing on the pattern of stones and beads, and the three computer crystals. He wondered how something so innocent and trivial could've caused all the problems faced by the village. It left him completely bewildered.

"It doesn't make any sense that these crystals were at the root of everything," he mumbled. "In a sense, they were responsible for *everything*."

Suddenly, Anton realized he'd forgotten something. He looked across the room to where Mahkeetah kept his katana and saw that it was still there. Quickly, he retrieved the blade, attached it to his belt, and prepared it for use. "No Warrior would ever leave his weapon lying around; I will put it to proper use." Again, he mumbled to himself; this somehow eased his unhappiness.

Sliding the katana from its sheath, Anton held it high over his head, as if to deliver a blow. He swung it around, just as he'd learned to do during his training, and then slid it back in its sheath.

"I'm not bound, as Mahkeetah was, to set it aside unused; I'll claim it for my own. Besides, it doesn't belong here anymore."

Taking a deep breath, Anton reached into a pocket of his tunic and removed a small electronic device, pressed a series of buttons, and then sat on the rug as the display screen reported the ETA of the Aerocraft.

Glancing at his ring, Anton noticed that it had turned gold. Shocked, he stared at his hand for some time, wondering what he'd done, felt, or realized to change its color—or, more precisely, what had changed in him. He'd suffered to the very core of his being for this, and now he felt hollow and empty. Simply being conscious made him sick to his stomach. Perhaps his suffering was the factor that'd changed the ring—or perhaps it was his realization of the importance of the people he served. Or perhaps it was simply the feeling of respect he now felt for them. He was unsure of the answer, but he knew he'd find out soon, when his Masters debriefed him. Their assessment was always correct.

Standing, Anton quickly left the village. He barely had time to meet the Aerocraft at the same location it'd dropped him off for his mission. It would take him nearly half a day to get there, but he relished the walk to help him clear his mind of the events of the last few days. The weight of his heart made the travel seem slow, but he covered the distance at a steady pace. He felt numb and hardly noticed anything as he traveled. Everything felt so anticlimactic.

By midday, he'd reached the edge of the jungle. The Aerocraft was already waiting for him, and he climbed aboard solemnly. All that was left of the mission was the trip home and the debriefing with his Masters. Anton took his seat, crossed his arms, and looked out the side window as the jungle below rapidly disappeared from view. Remembering Mahkeetah's advice, he struggled to portray a stolid appearance. This was essential.

CHAPTER 7
Pain and Comfort

THE AEROCRAFT SPED TOWARD THE Great Temple in the frigid north—home and sanctuary to all Warriors. It traveled at incredible speed; however, Anton's solemn mood made the journey seem timeless. He felt numb to its passage—as if his life existed in a dimension without it. He was utterly oblivious to his surroundings, and he was glad to be alone, aside from the pilots in the cockpit.

The needless deaths of so many people weighed heavily upon his thoughts, and the cruelty of his own actions against an even crueler enemy left him in a perpetual state of emotional turmoil. It wasn't as if he'd never seen cruelty—but the conflicting mixture of friendship with the villagers, his duty to his Masters, and his commitment to fulfill his destiny, all coupled together with the influence of the *Virlaqueus*, had forever changed his perspective of the true meaning of cruelty. *Even* I have shown cruelty simply by not caring, he thought. I'm ashamed of myself. Why do I feel this way? Never before did killing bother me—it was a necessary tool, a Warrior's means to an end. The Masters trained me for it. I've watched it, experienced it by delivering it justly to a deserved enemy. What's different this time? Nobody heard his questions, as he was the Aerocraft's only passenger.

Frightened of the consequences for his failure, Anton was certain his Masters would quickly disapprove of his self-doubt. "What's to become of me?" he said aloud to himself. "What will the Masters decide?" He sat alone in the Aerocraft, bereft of any consolatory conversation from a colleague.

Fidgeting in his seat, Anton tried to console himself by adjusting his position repeatedly. "What will they decide? I've failed utterly!" Conscious of himself, he hated what he'd become—emotional, mumbling, and fidgeting. These were all signs of his complete failure—failure as obvious as the golden glow of the ring on his finger.

Contemplative, Anton made an effort to relax and calm his thoughts and feelings. Never in his wildest speculations had he expected to ruminate about the lives of people he'd never really known— people who meant nothing to him, or so he believed, until they had suffered and died. Most of all, these sentiments contradicted the logic that had been designed into him, had been instilled into him in training; this was the very essence of a Warrior. It made him question himself, and it made him question whether he deserved to continue living. In contradiction to his perspective of himself, his ring glowed unremittingly, so deep in color that it looked like gold, and not crystal. Oddly, it comforted him in some way to know it had changed color. Then, with a sudden thought, he extinguished its glow. The color he had eagerly desired to claim as his own just a few days earlier now seemed to remind him of his losses, and it angered him.

Mulling over his new feelings, he continued to question himself. "Why should these people matter to me?" he asked. "Why should I care about them? They're just test subjects—people created for the Masters to use as they see fit! They're not *really* important!" He pounded his fists on the armrests of his seat and took a deep breath. He leaned back, closed his eyes, and slowly exhaled.

After a few minutes, a thought entered Anton's mind, altering his disposition. He too came from the laboratories of the Methonian Masters, to serve their purposes; he was no different from any other Warrior. But his fundamental, biologically driven desire for a woman combined with a botanical chemical, causing an attachment he'd never had before—an attachment so prevalent it left his heart feeling empty and in conflict.

"Can that be it—unpretentious lust?" he asked. "Did I simply fail at something so mundane? Or is it more complicated than that?" Again, Anton slapped the armrests, leaned forward and shook his head, and then put his face in his hands. He knew that falling in love with a girl was the inherent biological weakness of men; it was the path to ruin. He'd learned this repeatedly as he grew up; the Masters had driven the concept into every Warrior to spare them the trap.

"Extrication through meditation," the Masters had said. "This is the answer to all unnecessary biological proclivities. You must cast off all lustful biological needs through self-contemplation." The words of his Masters resounded through him as he considered his dilemma—but in the depths of his heart all he could find was love. His love was so strong, so demanding that it tore him in half.

"How could I *still* love her?" Anton asked himself, loathing himself for his unwanted biological need. He didn't understand the emotion—didn't have a clue about what love essentially felt like. He had nothing to measure it against until now. The desire, the lust, and the tender caring of two people's hearts coupled with intimacy marked the tremendous bond he shared with Nelda. He'd never experienced such an emotion, nor believed such feelings could exist. In fact, he had learned how to restrict and eliminate them. But when they finally occurred—when that moment arrived and he could finally make a clear choice—he found himself completely oblivious to it, taking control of his thoughts and actions. He relished feeling it when it did.

Closing his eyes, Anton looked deep inside himself and continued to scrutinize his new feelings. The *Virlaqueus* and Nelda had easily stripped the barriers of fortitude and mental discipline that defended his rationale; his defenses were no match for something so simple, so basic. He felt defeated; he wasn't supposed to relish any feelings, yet he did.

"How did I allow this to occur?" he said. "The Masters will disapprove—I'm doomed!"

A few minutes went by. Then Anton opened his eyes and looked at his holo-monitor, hoping it would distract him. Solemnly, he watched and waited for the familiar geographies of his home to appear. He needed to see Mount Valde Domus and the Great Temple built into its side. He hoped the sight would bring him back to himself—back to a sense of normality.

Soon he could see the Great Temple far off in the distance. Quickly it grew in size, becoming clearer as the speeding Aerocraft approached. It didn't take long before the jagged vertical mountainside loomed majestically before him. A tingling sensation ran up and down his spine as he recognized its familiar features. Carved into its side was a plateau that served as an Aerocraft airport and the only entrance to the Temple. The plateau was utterly flat and impeccably circular. It measured eight hundred yards in diameter, and dropped off at its edge into a valley more than a mile deep.

Steep mountains rose all around, adjoined to each other at their base. They dotted the region randomly, disappearing into the distance. But none stood as tall as Mount Valde Domus, which was nearly twice the height of its nearest neighbors. The mountains created a natural labyrinth of valleys that wound between and around them, going on seemingly forever, creating a place of isolation that only an Aerocraft could reach. Anton had always loved the view from the Temple—its feeling of solitude, and the peaks that remained snowcapped throughout the year.

As the Aerocraft made a final approach for landing, a sudden sense of completion entered Anton's thoughts. The sight of his home gave him a feeling of reassurance. He took a deep breath and sighed. But a rush of dread filled his heart as he recalled the Village of Tooloo.

"I need to settle down," Anton said. "I need to meditate." He looked around, realizing there was no time for it.

Almost at once, the Aerocraft descended at the foot of the Temple and lightly landed on an enormous raised circular platform in the center of the Aeroport. Several other Aerocrafts were either taking off or landing, as was always the case; the vehicles remained active at all times, transporting Masters and Warriors around Methonias or to other orbiting spacecraft.

"I've failed!" Anton said. "My Masters will send me to the disintegration chambers!" Anton again protested about his predicament; fear drove his thoughts. He knew that his Masters would find his actions contrary to the high standards set for all Warriors—standards genetically engineered before his creation, and programmed into him through discipline, meditation, and training.

As Anton prepared to exit the Aerocraft, flashes of fear continued welling up in his heart; his face turned flush and he suddenly felt tingly all over, as if thousands of needles pierced his flesh. He couldn't get the thought of the villagers out of his mind. He was supposed to protect them from harm, and he'd failed. Furthermore, he'd allowed Luthian—the very person who'd set into motion the entire sequence of events—to live. He was a complete failure; how else would his Masters measure his mission?

A small jolt shook the Aerocraft as it lightly touched down on the landing pad. With a hiss of air, the door seals broke, and the door slid sideways, revealing a clear view of home. Cold glacial air rushed in, bathing Anton's skin, reminding him of the high mountain climate—a drastic change from the warm tropical environment he'd left only a short time ago.

The moment Anton was dreading had finally arrived. A few seconds passed as he continued to sit in his seat. Then, reluctantly, he grabbed Mahkeetah's katana and quickly fled toward the exit. Leaping down to the platform, he broke into a run toward his home.

Craving meditation before his mission debriefing, he sprinted as fast as he could toward the main entrance of the Temple. The computers had already announced his arrival, which allotted him very little personal time; he knew that one of the Masters would soon call on him for his end-of-mission debriefing.

The extreme size of the Temple made it appear as if it was very close, but it was nearly four hundred yards away. Carved into the mountainside and centered under a semicircular half-dome, reminding Anton of the cave in Tooloo, stood two massive stone doors. They were a hundred feet high, fifty feet wide, and ten feet thick. For some reason, they stood completely open, permitting a multitude of activity. Under normal circumstances, they remained closed unless a need arose to open the Temple for some unusual activity. Anton could see two large cargo ships nearby, one being loaded and one unloading.

Completely unnoticed, Anton ran through the opening and entered the inner courtyard; it was a huge open chamber of ornate architecture and unrivaled beauty. To anyone judging it from the outside, the sight was entirely unexpected. This vast area was open to the sky with an electronically generated solar force shield protecting it from the elements and producing a greenhouse effect. The courtyard was circular in shape and over two hundred yards in diameter. Tiled mosaics lined every aspect of the floor in intricate detail and design—the construction had taken builders and artists decades. In the center lay an exquisite garden filled with rare and unusual plants from all over the known colonies; it was revered as the most diverse botanical collection in the universe. Exotic birds gave it a feeling of complete serenity; at the heart of it all was an elaborate waterfall and pond system that provided all the water necessary to operate the entire ecosystem; the construction of the garden made this the focus of the botanical design.

An overpowering sense of home flooded Anton's heart and alleviated his prior distress. The need to run diminished and he found himself slowing to a walk as he neared the center of the courtyard. He was pulled like a magnet to steel by the familiar sight of the garden sanctuary.

Finding his favorite place, Anton quietly sat on a large moss-covered rock near the pond and smiled. It was almost as though he'd returned to the village of Tooloo. Then an overpowering sensation of loss flooded his heart, returning him to the mixed feelings he'd tried so hard to suppress. He felt as if a tear would run down his cheek, and a sensation of tightness gripped him by the throat, choking him. Trying to maintain his stoic Methonian demeanor, he suddenly shook his head from side to side and quickly adopted the lotus position.

"Meditation—I need meditation," Anton mumbled to himself, and then he drifted into the depths of his soul.

Muting the discordant feelings from deep within his heart, Anton soon gained control over his emotions in tiny increments. He delved deeper into himself until a sensation of weightlessness came over his body—as if his spirit was free from his flesh, and his body no longer in the grip of gravity. As he drifted into a state of peace, the troubled feelings he'd wrestled with for the past few hours finally evanesced. But he still wasn't satisfied. He delved deeper inside himself, finding a place he'd never been—a place of inner peace he'd never before felt. It was as if he'd discovered his inner self deep inside of his heart and his mind. He had never been this deep into meditation before, never had he strived so hard to find the roots of his innermost feelings—he'd never needed to, it wasn't necessary. Always he'd delved just far enough to satisfy the needs of the moment, just deep enough to find the required solace that alleviated the questions currently troubling his soul, or that fulfilled his inner desire for peace. Then, just as he was beginning to grasp the answers he so desperately sought, his satisfaction abruptly ended.

A man stood over Anton, wearing a midnight-black robe with a large hood that covered his head and completely obscured his face. Long sleeves covered his arms well past his hands. It was the uniform that all the Masters wore.

"Anton Seven, you will accompany me to the debriefing room." The voice was coarse, cold, and monotone.

For a moment, the command didn't faze Anton. He was deeper into meditation than he'd ever been before, and the voice seemed somehow distant and hollow, as if spoken through a long tube. Suddenly, the realization of its import seized his senses, and forcibly drove his thoughts from deep inside back towards reality. He quickly pushed himself back to the physical world around him.

"Young Warrior, *obey my command!*" The Master said each word slowly and clearly, raising his voice slightly. This was something Anton had rarely heard a Master do. Instantly, his eyes opened, and he quickly stood and then bowed with Methonian respect. It seemed as if his body reacted without his control.

"Forgive me, my Master," Anton said. "My meditation was deep." Despite his sincerity, his response seemed somehow weak—as if it was an excuse. But he had nothing else to offer. Bowing respectfully as was his duty, he demonstrated his unconditional devotion to his Master's bidding.

"Now that you've completed your final training mission, have you forgotten all but the barest respect, young Warrior?" He had disobeyed protocol, therefore the Master's question was more than it appeared— he really wanted to hear what Anton had learned on his assignment to Tooloo, and why he hadn't reported immediately, as was expected.

"No, my Master, I haven't!" Anton responded. Again, he bowed. He was completely surprised at the query. He wondered specifically what the Master wished to hear. Was he aware of the conversation he'd had with Luthian? Were the Masters already aware of what had transpired? His ring had recorded his experience and uploaded the information to the Aerocraft computer—had they already evaluated it?

"You will answer all of my questions in complete detail during your debriefing. Accompany me." The Master folded his arms, placing each hand up the opposite sleeve, and then moved toward the far end of the chamber and down the main hallway to the center hub of the Temple. Anton knew very well where they were going—he'd been there numerous times before. He watched the Master as he walked down the hallway, his feet seemingly never touching the floor; his head never bobbed up and down as they walked—he simply floated, confounding Anton's logic. The Master's robe completely covered his legs to the floor and beyond, and there wasn't any evidence he had legs or feet at all, thus completing the illusion of levitation—or was it? Perhaps there was something mechanical and unseen?

As the two traveled, many of the younger Warriors noticed Anton and the gold color of his ring, which glowed brightly in the subdued lighting. In turn, each bowed to him, signifying his new stature as they passed him by.

"I'm sure you're aware," the Master said, "that your status is higher than all your peers here at the Temple, save the Masters. Currently, there are no other Warriors at your level within these walls—as you should know, everyone can see you'll soon graduate." The Master casually watched to see how Anton reacted to his comment. He wanted to know Anton's thoughts about his new ranking—and, more importantly, what feelings he might reveal.

"Is it that noticeable? Do I reveal myself to you so readily?" replied Anton. Looking quickly toward his Master's obscured face, he knew unquestionably that he was cognizant of the feelings and emotions Anton was struggling to hide.

"There's nothing more noticeable than how you are *feeling* young Anton. It would seem that your debriefing might require additional time. Now tell me, how does knowing this make you *feel*?" The Master pressed Anton to reveal what he already seemed to know. "You can't graduate until we've resolved your obvious inner *misgivings*—now can we?"

"No sir—it's true. I know that no Warrior can graduate if he's a failure." Anton quickly looked at the floor, attempting to hide his shame. He was convinced he'd failed and that his Masters were going to send him to the disintegration chambers.

"*Failure*?" asked the Master. "Your ring has turned to *gold*, young one! You are a *success*!" The Master stopped walking and revealed his concealed hand, placing it on Anton's shoulder. "Only those who are unable to achieve what you've accomplished are resigned to *disintegration*! I will hear no more of this; the debriefing will reveal our position on your inadvertent desecrations; it's true, we know of your unfortunate *genetic alterations*; we too want to know what happened. You will be relieved to know that we have a procedure for you; you can be repaired."

Relieved, in part, Anton continued to follow his Master. Promptly, they arrived at the debriefing room. Reaching out with one arm, the Master blocked Anton from entering.

"You didn't answer my question—how do you *feel* about your new status among your fellow Warriors? You can't enter here without giving me your response."

For a moment, Anton hesitated. He thought about how to respond. He considered each emotion he'd recently felt, and the hidden meaning of the Master's inquiry. After a long hesitation, he replied: "Quite humbled. I... well... I feel quite humbled." His response was short, but it carried a distinct meaning. He looked at his Master, and then bowed his head, his eyes never leaving the Master's shrouded face.

"This is good," the Master said. "You should *understand* this." With emphasis, he implied the Methonian structured method of rationalizing, hinting at the need to respond carefully when answering the questions he would encounter.

"Do you *fear* us, Anton?" the Master asked.

"I don't fear you... I... well... I only wish to complete this meeting to your satisfaction." Anton struggled to find the right words. Carefully, he edited his responses before delivering his answers.

Yet another subtle test—will they ever end? Anton thought to himself. He knew it was more important how he phrased his responses than the actual answers he gave; the Masters needed to know he was capable of responding carefully to anyone under any circumstance. His Masters would continue to assess his worth with every word he spoke. Anxieties sent a shiver down his spine and his thoughts spun in his head as he tried to guess the Master's next question. Then the haunting fear of Luthian's revelations about the Masters preoccupied his thoughts.

"You're allowed the katana during the debriefing," the Master said, pointing at the weapon hanging from Anton's belt. "Your status permits it."

"I am honored—thank you," Anton said, bowing yet again.

"Very well, you may enter." He touched the door, and it slid open silently, revealing the dome-covered debriefing room. Massive tritanium beams supported the curvature of the dome; they were spaced evenly around the perimeter and met at the apex. With a glance of anticipation, Anton looked into the chamber, remembering his previous visit a few months earlier.

Quickly, Anton entered the room, examining it carefully in Methonian fashion and bowing to each of the seated Masters respectfully. His examination was trained into him, if only to notice slight changes from the last time he had been in the room.

"Please have a seat," the Master who had led him in said, pointing at the conference table in the center of the room with his robe-covered arm. It was donut-shaped, with a platform in the center, and a seat that slowly rose into position, permitting the subject to remain at eye-level with the Masters. In front of Anton, a ramp led downward and underneath the table, allowing access to the chair. Four more masters sat around the table's circumference. This was the standard debriefing scenario; it was all-too-familiar to Anton.

Hurriedly, Anton walked down the inclined ramp leading under the table, making his way to the platform in the center and positioning himself in the interrogation seat. The platform slowly rose into position, placing him at eye-level with the Masters; he would remain there until they were satisfied with his answers. He knew that they would be more thorough than ever, since he'd completed his training. He had unique experiences with unusual and questionable results.

Taking the last open seat, the Master who had led him here prepared himself for the debriefing. "Now, young Anton," he said. "We wish to hear in your words what *you* believe altered your ring."

As the first Master spoke, Anton's seat whirled around to face him. The chair always unsettled him; he didn't like the gyrating motion that forced him to face whichever Master chose to speak. It was an extremely effective device used for both for debriefing and interrogation.

"I'm uncertain of the exact moment the ring changed from yellow to gold," Anton said, "and I haven't formulated my hypothesis to explain why. I was meditating on that after my arrival here. Forgive me for my incompetence."

"We never *forgive*," another Master said, as Anton's chair whirled to face him. "We expect a decisive *conclusion*; now *answer* the question." The chair's movement had been so quick that it tugged at his head and shifted him heavily in his seat.

"Preliminarily, I guess it changed when I realized that everyone on Methonias is important—not just Warriors and Masters." Quickly looking at each Master within his view, Anton watched for some signal of their thoughts. But they remained motionless and unaffected.

"An interesting thought," a third Master said, and the chair spun around to face him. "Your training doesn't include this deduction as a logical determination. These people should be of no concern to you; what drove you to this conclusion?"

All attention was on Anton. It was impossible to escape the hidden stare from each of the Masters—not that he desired to. He wanted to tell them of his feelings and misgivings, and he wanted to be free of the binding grip they held upon him, for good or ill.

Looking directly at the Master in front of him, Anton answered distinctly. "I wasn't precisely sure, but I thought that perhaps my suffering was the factor that'd changed it; or perhaps my realization of how important the people of Tooloo were; or perhaps just the feelings of respect I now have for them."

"So, you admit you have... *feelings*? Is this true?" the fourth Master now asked Anton.

Whirling around to face the Master, Anton felt cornered. *Did I make a mistake?* he thought to himself. *Should I have revealed that?*

"I have admitted to it—I... I'm admitting to having feelings, yes." He struggled to answer, but complete honesty was part of his construction— his DNA precluded any capacity to lie.

"This is unprecedented," another Master said, and Anton again whirled around. "No Warrior has ever had emotions—that is, not until we sent three of you to this particular region, this particular village of Methonias."

The first Master spoke to Anton, causing his chair to spin again. "You've already discovered this peculiar truth—a truth still in deliberation; we haven't yet decided upon the all the consequences it's had upon you or Methonian Warriors as a whole. In addition, you are well aware that your ring uploaded all of its data to the computers the moment you stepped into the Aerocraft; we've already reviewed your experience while you were in transit."

Again, Anton whirled around to face yet another Master. "We're pleased you aren't *as* altered as Mahkeetah was. This is an *interesting* development. His disobedience created the need for your assignment, and we're currently satisfied with the outcome—even if your methods failed in their execution; true Warriors never allow victims of oppression to perish. There remains only this unfortunate circumstance of your altered DNA caused by the *Virlaqueus*." The Master hesitated, looking around at the other Masters.

"We have reservations about you," the third Master said, prompting Anton's chair to move again. "Your emotions may prove to be responsible for a lack of logical judgment in the future—an issue that cannot be ignored! We believe it's what caused you to fail at developing and implementing a flawless plan to resolve the Tooloo situation."

"We can only conclude that both your body and mind are damaged—and as a result, inferior. However, your ring preserves you from disintegration. There are other places for failed Warriors; we have yet to determine your fate. We'll observe your interactions with your peers, and your behavior for a period of one week. If after that timeframe you exhibit undesirable behavior, you will be assigned to the asteroid zone mining industry, to extract usable materials."

Anton's face exhibited visible fear; the Masters quickly discerned his thoughts from his expression.

"I will do your bidding," Anton said. "I am your servant." Replying with caution, he took a deep breath, closed his eyes for a moment, and tried to look as placid as possible.

"I see you still have some measure of control," the Master returned. "Use this time to improve on that. You're dismissed." The final whirl of the chair spun Anton to face the exit, and then the platform lowered, allowing him to leave.

Quickly Anton obeyed, lurching from his seat toward the door. As he left the chamber, he heard all of the Masters simultaneously break into a discussion, but he was unable to determine what they were saying as the door quickly closed behind him. It seemed without question some important decision was imminent, and he felt even more uncertain of himself than he had just minutes before. Somehow, he knew that something about his visit to Tooloo was different than they'd anticipated, and he wasn't entirely sure what the consequences would be. He trusted his Masters, yet Luthian's warnings continued to haunt his thoughts.

Heading back toward the garden, Anton opted for another chance to meditate; he felt even more confused than he had earlier, and he needed the opportunity to clear his thoughts. It didn't take long for him to find the rock he sat upon earlier and settle into the lotus position. Closing his eyes, he cleared his mind, striving to achieve solace.

After a few minutes, Anton drifted deep inside himself, attempting to find that new special place he'd discovered earlier—the place his Master had brought him back from, the place deeper within himself than he'd ever been before. The negative feelings he'd wrestled with one-by-one gently evanesced as he slowly reached inside himself. Multifaceted entanglements of thought and emotion dissipated, extinguishing his pain; conflict turned to inner peace, and a warm sensation filled his heart, a warmth drawn from new thoughts and realizations; he felt somehow that he'd become one with the universe. As he sorted his feelings, he delved ever deeper, finally attaining the desired result.

Slowly, almost without notice, a sensation of weightlessness swept over Anton's entire body, giving him the impression he was floating; he felt as light as a feather, as if he no longer existed in the material world. The garden's colors melted away as if it'd never existed. The sounds of the visitors and workers busy laboring around him seemed to fade into the distance as if they were merely a dream, and then they completely disappeared. The ambience emanating from the dome high above no longer penetrated his eyelids; it was as if he languished in darkness. He felt as though he'd passed from Methonias, passed out of time to another plane of existence—a place he didn't know; a place that was inexplicable. He felt as though he'd transcended into another dimension beyond his comprehension, yet he knew it wouldn't last; he could feel it slipping away as he attempted to evaluate what he was feeling.

As before, just as he entered into the uncharted territory of his reverie, the world around him returned, forcing him back to consciousness. Voices nearby and all around him seemed to mumble something he couldn't grasp—something just out of his range of consciousness. It drew his attention from his private thoughts. Then he heard one distinct voice rise above the others, piquing his curiosity and drawing him out of his meditation.

"He's floating on air!" said many of the people around him. "That's impossible!"

"Do you see the aura of golden light surrounding him?" proclaimed another voice. "It must be some parlor trick; the Masters are testing us!"

Suddenly, as if shocked by electricity, Anton climbed from the depths of his unknown self, and the feeling of weightlessness disappeared; he perceived the rock he rested upon, as if someone had placed him upon it. He opened his eyes to discover several young Warriors gathered around him, all with expressions of disbelief upon their faces. They chattered amongst themselves, and Anton barely comprehended what they were saying.

"What is going on here?" Anton asked, confused. Then suddenly it dawned on him and he began to understand. "What do you mean by *parlor trick?*" Shaking a feeling of deep sleep from his mind, he tried to grasp what had happened.

Just as he uttered his question, he saw one of the Masters standing amongst the gathering, and he quickly dismissed everyone.

"There's nothing here for any of you now," he said. "Just remember what you've seen, and it will be discussed later, at a more appropriate time." The Master waited for the crowd of Warriors to leave. There the Master stood before Anton, quietly assessing him. For a time, he too was speechless. Another minute passed and still he said nothing.

Then he raised his hand and pointed. "You will accompany me," he said. With the slightest bow, the Master demonstrated his respect for Anton—something no Master had ever done before.

Confused, Anton followed his Master toward the far end of the chamber—but not toward the debriefing room, as before.

"It would seem you've achieved something remarkable," the Master said. "This demands an explanation. Where did you learn this new talent?" The Master looked directly at Anton. "It isn't contained in the records on your ring. It has never been taught here at the Temple. You can see and hear the surprise of all who were present."

Dumbfounded, Anton was unable to respond. "I don't know what you mean," he finally said. His reply seemed somehow childlike—as if he had been caught by a parent in the act of doing something wrong.

"You're *unaware* of what you've done?" the Master said, in a voice that was sharp with curiosity and disbelief. "This is intolerable. Only the truth is acceptable. Let me rephrase my question so that you grasp the magnitude of what I'm asking." Facing Anton squarely, the Master stared at him with shrouded invisible eyes. "How did you manage to acquire this new skill you demonstrated publicly?"

"Acquire my new skill? What new skill are you referring to?" Anton was completely puzzled; he was utterly oblivious to what he had done and what everyone had just witnessed, and he was baffled by the Master's insinuation that he was withholding evidence—something a Warrior neither desired nor was capable of doing. The Clone Masters had manipulated the Warriors' genetic design, rendering them incapable of lying; why would the Master imply that Anton attempted deceit? Then it dawned on him—the words he'd heard as he'd returned to himself. A slight look of realization marked his face for a split moment.

It felt as though a thousand eyes witnessed Anton's failure to answer the Master's questions. He felt uncomfortable. He continued to follow his Master toward the far end of the room, through a sea of puzzled looks and confused expressions. It was as if the whole world had come to a standstill— as if everyone remained transfixed witnessing a cataclysm unfolding before them, helplessly awaiting the outcome of the event in progress.

"What did I do?" Anton finally asked.

"Together, we will explore the answer to that question," his Master replied. "Come with me."

CHAPTER 8

Of Lab Mice and Masters

TRAVELING TO THE FURTHEST DEPTHS of the Great Temple, Anton followed his Master; they silently journeyed beyond the familiar sections permitted to Warriors. For some time, the Master remained silent, unwilling to share any knowledge of their destination. Soon, they came to a circular junction with many elevators— each one opening and closing at intervals as Masters traveled to an unknown terminus; four Masters stood in front of a particular elevator with doors of different colors and sizes. They seemed to be awaiting their arrival.

"Our test subject awaits delivery—shall we proceed?" the Master asked the other four as they approached.

"Indeed, we shall waste no time deliberating further," replied another. "Our answers exist within this Alpha Warrior. They require immediate extraction. They will prove fortuitous for future development; we must proceed quickly, before our chance is lost."

"Very well—summon the prime lift." The third Master handed out a command for the others to follow.

The fourth Master stretched his arms out in front of him, his hands pointing slightly downward. Tipping his head back, he then sang out a single deep note, holding it for a few seconds, and then stood motionless.

In less than a minute, the door to the prime lift slid open with a loud puff of air, allowing everyone to enter.

Two Masters stepped inside and motioned for Anton to follow. The doors closed silently behind them—so quickly that it was imperceptible. Without warning, the elevator traveled downward at speeds equal to freefall. Deep inside Valde Domus, below the reaches of any human, it sped along; deeper it fell to the mountain's core, at a speed Anton could neither calculate nor perceive. Simulated gravity held the travelers in place, giving the illusion that they traveled at a leisurely velocity. Soon the elevator slowed and gently came to a stop. There was the sound of air pressure equalizing, and then the doors puffed and opened.

As they exited the lift, one Master finally spoke to Anton. "Located in this corridor are many entrances to the various Genetic Labs; we have never brought a Warrior here—that is, we have never brought a *conscious living* Warrior here. You are the first."

Instinctively, no Warrior had any business in the Genetic Labs. Anton was perplexed why his Masters allowed him access while he was still conscious, and living. He suspected his recent experiences influenced their decision. As far as any Warrior knew, the Cloning Labs were the most advanced science facilities ever created by man, this is what they'd been told from their youth. Only these laboratories could control biology beyond anyone's wildest imagination, and produce the genetically superior humans known as Warriors. No other such facilities existed anywhere in the universe.

Traveling down a wide corridor, Anton marveled at the multitude of activities of unusually dressed people; they wore smocks or lab coats that designated them as technicians. Typically, the Masters only wore heavy black robes that completely obscured any effort to discern their personal identity. These technicians had visible faces and hands, unlike their black-cloaked counterparts. Soon they passed by several enormous stone doors, with large and unfamiliar runes deeply inscribed upon them. The Masters trained all Warriors in many forms of cabbalistic writing, but these symbols were completely new to Anton.

Finally, they stopped in front of one particular rune-covered door, and one of the Masters held up both arms and gestured downward in an X symbol while speaking an incomprehensible word.

"Xenostemorphology Laboria," said the Master, and the massive stone door hissed and expelled pressurized air. The floor trembled and vibrated, and the sound of unseen mechanisms shifted, releasing complex seals and locks. Then, slowly, the door slid open, allowing them to proceed inside.

"Follow us," they all said, and led Anton inside the room.

It was filled with mysterious scientific equipment whose purpose he could only guess. Anton marveled at the detail and complexity of the hundreds of devices filling the chamber. Translucent human-sized tanks were filled with frothing agitated liquids, tubes led in all directions, and computers with holo-monitors were littered throughout. There were examination tables, and inexplicable equipment suspended from the ceiling. The scene left him surprised and speechless.

"You're to be examined," a Master said. "Never has a Warrior learned to levitate. Your contact with the *Virlaqueus* flower, which we know altered your DNA in ways that are a complete mystery, has transformed you in an unpredictable way. We need to know the extent of the modifications, and whether they're directly responsible for your new capabilities. The Clone Masters will *dissect* you. Are you *afraid?*"

The Master spoke slowly and carefully, as if to insure Anton completely understood the significance of each word.

Shamefacedly, Anton responded: "I cannot escape my feelings; apparently, they're intertwined with my reasoning. Is this a bad thing?" He *was* afraid, and found it difficult to admit—but he was incapable of withholding the truth.

"This is true; your feelings are a puzzle that requires *resolving,*" the Master said. "We will extract the answers. The Clone Masters will determine the precise nature of your alterations so that we can prevent any future occurrences. Your table awaits you." Pointing at a nearby examination table, the Master waited for Anton to lie down.

"You will remove your clothing and place it in the receptacle; it will be returned to you later." The Master pointed at a small container next to the table.

Anton removed his clothes, placed them in the container, and then climbed upon the examination table. Preparing himself mentally for the inevitable, he looked up at the multitude of devices hanging over his head and around the table. There were injection devices of unknown drugs filled and ready for use, computers running and monitoring his vital signs, and restraints prepared for use if needed. Everything awaited the Clone Masters' arrival. Anton had no idea what to expect at this point, he'd never seen a Clone Master before.

"We're not allowed to stay during the examination. You'll be returned to a special graduate chamber after the Clone Masters have finished their work." As if summoned for some other purpose, the Masters immediately exited the laboratory, leaving Anton to the will of the Clone Masters. The lab door closed heavily and silently behind them as they left; the sounds of air hissing and the locking mechanisms activating indicated they'd sealed Anton inside.

Almost immediately, a door on the far side of the chamber opened, and two figures emerged. They wore grey environmental suits that covered them completely. Their helmets had tinted shielding that completely obscured their identity.

"You're test subject Alpha Seven," one of them said, in a mechanical voice. "Twenty-one years of age, alleged altered DNA, exhibiting inexplicable emotional behaviors suggesting mental alterations. Recent levitation capabilities observed, indicating possible micro-physiological alterations."

"Place your ring hand in the scanner to your right," the second Master said through his suit, his mechanical voice entirely devoid of sympathy or compassion.

Inserting his hand as instructed, Anton pondered the Clone Masters' procedures. *The Clone Masters will dissect you*, he had been told. *Are you afraid?* Was he afraid? Yes—but he was just as curious as his Masters to know the results of the tests. Maybe even more so. His stake in the outcome exceeded everyone else's—his life was on the line.

A flurry of information flashed across one of the holographic monitors, reading the data regarding the *Virlaqueus*'s ontogenesis.

"Interesting," said one of the Clone Masters. "A naturally occurring botanical chemical alteration of the corpus striatum and the amygdaloidal nucleus resulted in BDH chemistry modifications. We need to sedate the subject for further analysis."

"Affirmative," said the other. "Elimination of motor responses is necessary for the microcellular neuroendocrine probe. Alpha Seven, you will relax as we give you a small injection." Touching another holographic monitor, the Clone Master activated several of the devices suspended over Anton's head. As quick as a Warrior's reflexive response, an injection of some unknown drug entered Anton's shoulder. Instantly he fell into a deep, chemically induced sleep.

"Cranial scanner activated. Insertion of stimulus-secretion coupling identifier is complete. Awaiting results." Announcing the flurry of activity in intervals, the Clone Masters notified each other of every step they performed.

"Nanobots are required for atomic positioning and the determination of molecular construction. Injecting nanobots into subject's brain now—this will take a few minutes."

"Alteration of brain chemistry still active—the modifications of DNA have ceased. The *Virlaqueus's* base chemical remains present and active in the brain."

"Probe analysis complete; results of DNA alterations complete; results of biochemical alterations complete; testing complete. I will withdraw the nanobots."

"I will extract a sample of the active chemical."

"Sample extraction complete. Loading active base chemical into the analyzation computer. Done."

"Neutralizing serum derived—manufacturing commencing.
Estimated time of completion is five minutes."

The two Masters worked in synchronization, like robots; their movements appeared almost mechanical.

"Neutralizing serum synthesized; preparing injection; loading injection; administering injection. Sequence is complete."

"Vital signs remain stable."

"Reactions to the untested serum are possible—close monitoring is required."

"No adverse reactions to serum—the subject is improving."

"Reprogramming subroutines are necessary for future security scan corrections. Writing programming sequence initiated. Preparing subroutine upgrades. Adding additional instruction sets. Uploading complete."

"Examination complete; reprogramming subroutines complete; operation successful; the serum provided positive reliable results. Preparing report."

"We'll have the report momentarily. I'm making arrangements for subject's return to the Masters."

In less than two hours, the Clone Masters completed their work, moved Anton to an auto-gurney, and released him from the laboratory.

The gurney traveled on its own without human guidance toward the exit. The door automatically opened and one of the Masters awaited him outside and followed the auto-gurney to the upper level of the Great Temple, where a special room had been prepared for his arrival.

AWAKENING FROM HIS DRUG-INDUCED SLEEP, Anton sat up and looked around his room. It was entirely unfamiliar. At first glance, it appeared to him as if he were in the Temple's hospital wing. As he slowly regained his senses, he realized he was in the graduate chamber his Master had mentioned before his procedure. He saw a window, a door, a bathroom, a table with two chairs, and a balcony outside an electronic shield.

Somehow, Anton felt different. Somehow, after having rested following his procedure in the Clone Lab, he felt as if the grip of emotions that'd driven his thoughts and feelings for the past few days had abated. The stress and anxieties he'd felt previously were completely gone, and a sensation of freedom overcame him, allowing him to relax.

"I'm in one piece," he sighed, quietly. "I'd better find my Masters." Sitting on the edge of his bed, Anton looked across the room and saw Mahkeetah's katana lying on the table, along with an extradimensional holding device, otherwise known as an EHD. Draped over a chair was a new Warrior's uniform. It was the classic formal wear: kimono, hakama, and haori, with a new tunic and loincloth, like the ones he'd worn on his assignment to Tooloo.

"It would appear I'll graduate soon," he said. Again, he sighed in relief as he realized he was going to live, and without the ultimate punishment he had feared.

Still naked, he quickly donned the new attire. As he dressed, he noticed his old clothing, and retrieved the few personal items contained within the pockets—Nelda's necklace, the laser Luthian had used to slice Mahkeetah in half, and the crystallographic holo-projector were right where he'd left them. Picking up the EHD, he noticed it was his—he'd left it in his dorm room on the other side of the Great Temple, and someone had thoughtfully brought it to him.

Retrieving the device, he marveled at how it seemed more like magic than technology: small, light, and made of an unknown hightech fabric. He could fold it like a handkerchief. It functioned like a small bag that closed by pulling a string at the opening. When the user reached inside, it had the capacity of a cubic yard. Yet when completely filled, it was as light as a feather. Reaching inside, he found the *Lapillusaurus* pearl he'd acquired on his mission in the badlands. Happily, he placed all of his items in the EHD, and was satisfied that he had retained all of his possessions.

"Only the final debriefing and the graduation ceremony remain," Anton mumbled happily to himself. He smiled, and then realized how hungry and thirsty he was.

"I hope I can find something to eat soon," he said. "I rather miss my synthesized nutrition," he mumbled to himself. Mumbling seemed to relieve his stress somehow.

"Your request will be fulfilled," said a voice from the balcony; one of the Masters stood there, awaiting Anton's return to consciousness.

"Forgive me," Anton said. "I didn't see you there." He bowed.

"As I preferred to observe you as you awoke, I stood out here, purposefully beyond your view. Your behavior is of great concern. We wish to know precisely how you *feel*." Hinting at his thoughts, the Master spoke cryptically, as was their way.

"Am I okay? I... well... I *feel* different. I feel, well, umm... normal."

Turning off the electronic shield, the Master reentered the room. "This is good. Let us turn our attention to your future. It's important that you understand that there's never been any Warrior as *unique* as you. We wish to honor this difference during your graduation ceremony. Fear not—it's merely a formality for the undergraduates. We like to provide *incentive*, shall we say, when it's appropriate; this is to challenge the youth to attain even loftier goals." The soft gravelly voice marked the distinctiveness of a Master.

Bowing, Anton again showed respect. "As you wish—I'm at your service."

"It's necessary that I discuss specific information with you prior to your graduation. Due to your uniqueness, there are certainly questions that you may have; these naturally require addressing." Motioning for Anton to sit, the Master continued to speak as he slowly paced the room.

"You are flawed as any Warrior is. Being the seventh in your design group, specifically the Alpha group, you have inherited seven flaws. Now that your DNA has been altered, we are uncertain how many flaws you may, or perhaps now, may not have. However, you will always retain the designation of *Seven*." Facing Anton, the Master nodded his head once and then continued.

"The Clone Masters were able to discover the chemistry of the *Virlaqueus* and extract enough of the active chemical from your brain for further study. After deriving a neutralizing serum, they successfully counteracted any further effects; the chemical alterations incurred by your brain are now stable. However, the alterations of your DNA are permanent. This plant is an anomaly in our constructed world and is therefore a curiosity to us." Again, the Master nodded his head.

"You should find that your emotions are much more controllable now; they were exaggerated by the *Virlaqueus*; this you may have figured out for yourself." He nodded slightly a third time.

"As for your ability to levitate, we hope you continue to develop this skill. It may be possible one day to improve newer designs of Warriors to have this skill as well. We are busy studying this for the future." A fourth nod.

"You have demonstrated a new *strength*, a new *tool*—therefore you will be graduating with honors." A fifth nod from the Master and then he pointed at Anton.

"Do you have any pertinent questions?"

Thinking for a moment Anton replied: "Just one—what has become of the people of Tooloo? I'd like to know if anyone survived." Secretly, Anton hoped for Nelda to have miraculously survived the explosion and subsequent avalanche. He knew it was wrong, but he couldn't give up on her, even after the work done by the Clone Masters.

"This isn't important, young Warrior; you will *forget* about them, and particularly that female you spent time with."

Suddenly, the door opened, interrupting the conversation. A self-propelled auto-cart containing food and water entered the room.

"It was anticipated you'd require sustenance. Please, eat." Motioning for Anton to comply, the Master walked over to the window and looked out, contemplating his next words.

"I wish to impart a piece of wisdom for your consideration. Don't become attached to anyone, particularly women. It is your design intent to protect; Warriors are the galactic police, the hired champions of peace—nothing more." The Master turned around and seated himself at the table across from Anton, and observed the Warrior's behavior as he consumed the provided nutrition.

"The alterations to your DNA are of great interest to the Clone Masters. They discovered something that wasn't *expected*—something that happened not just to you, but to your ring! It's lucky for you that it was on your finger during the DNA alteration. Since it too is made of *living crystal,* it inexplicably matched the modifications of your DNA as they occurred. If it hadn't, it would've turned clear, rejecting you as if you were someone else—and we wouldn't be having this conversation. I might add that the alterations to your DNA are minimal; the minor disturbance of your base design we will discount as irrelevant."

"I'm pleased to know this," Anton said. "I'd like to know what changes occurred—but mainly I'm concerned if I'll still be troubled with emotions." This was the critical point, especially to Anton.

"The changes to your DNA are only to your hair and eye color, which is quite unusual. In time, we believe they'll return to normal; however, this is still an unknown. As for the emotions—we believe you'll always have a tendency to express them; the influence of the *Virlaqueus* isn't wholly removed. But you've also demonstrated an unusual ability to control your mind and body; I'm referring to your levitation yesterday. Further analysis of the *Virlaqueus* chemical provided us with enough knowledge to improve our designs in the future. Your experience has given us the opportunity we needed to immediately implement an alteration to the next generation of Warriors. They will have resistance to certain chemical influences. And again, I will repeat, we may learn to incorporate your unprecedented ability to levitate." Hesitating, the Master waited for Anton's reaction.

Surprised, Anton nodded. "I'm your servant," he said. "I hope that future Warriors won't experience the same frustrations I did."

"We'll experiment further. Now, I've told you everything on this subject that we are willing to share. Remember, this is sensitive information and it isn't to be repeated to anyone, or any Warrior." The Master stood and walked over to the balcony, motioning for Anton to follow. "If you're done eating, please observe *this* with me." Pointing below the balcony, he drew Anton's attention toward something he couldn't see in his seated position.

The Master invited Anton to observe the training activities of the younger Warriors; a small army practiced in perfect synchronization the specialized martial arts movements of the Methonian Warriors. "Behold the activities of your youth," the Master said.

Immediately, like any obedient Warrior, Anton raced to his Master's side and looked down into the rectangular-shaped training area below the balcony. Though it was open to the sky, an electronic shielding covered it above, protecting the courtyard from the ravages of the extreme northern climate of Methonias. Windows marked all four sides, to the height of six stories; each of the levels was used for different purposes, such as dorm rooms for the younger training Warriors, and special suites such as the graduation quarters Anton currently used. From this vantage point they had an excellent view of the training activities of young Warriors below. Stone pillars supported an awning that encircled the edge of the training floor. This covered seats, equipment rooms, and weapon collections used by the students.

"I remember training down there like it was yesterday," Anton said.

"Is there a reason you want me to observe the students?"

"Twenty years in the life of a Warrior is a very short time," the other replied. "As you can see, these boys are half your age, and some are nearly ready for the next level. Of this, you should know. Now tell me—at what age do you believe it's proper that a Warrior be allowed to make personal choices or decisions without their Masters' permission?" He looked directly at Anton.

"I don't follow you, exactly. I don't think Warriors should make personal choices until *permitted*." He gave the Master a curious look.

"A Warrior *never* makes personal choices on his own without reporting them to his immediate Master. So, is there something *you* wish to report?" The Master seemed to expect Anton to grasp his meaning.

"Is there something I've forgotten to report?" asked Anton. He was thinking about what the Master was suggesting, and quickly reviewed what'd occurred over the past few minutes; he'd obviously missed something.

"You have in your possession several items of particular interest," the Master said. "I might add that we are well aware of them. You should know this—we have had our attention on them for some time. Now I ask you again: is there something you wish to *report*?"

That was it—the pearl, and perhaps the necklace and katana. "Yes, I have a *Lapillusaurus* pearl and the other items that I acquired during my visit to Tooloo. Is there some significance that I collected them?" Anton still didn't comprehend his Master's meaning, and wondered why he needed an answer.

"There is always *significance* to why a Warrior selects items to keep. However, you have neglected to follow standard protocol. All such objects and artifacts are to be reported verbally upon return from a mission; you seem to have neglected this." The Master looked directly at Anton, as if expecting to hear an excuse.

"Unbeknownst to you, we've examined the pearl and discovered it to be *imperfect*; therefore, it's of no value for our purposes. What *is* important to us is *why* you didn't report it; a *Lapillusaurus* pearl is of immense value, and all Warriors are required to report such items, and surrender them if ordered to. You kept it without our approval." The Master hesitated, and then walked back into the room, motioning for Anton to follow.

"After deliberating on this, we decided to allow you to keep it, wondering what you would choose to *do* with it. So, I ask you once more—why didn't you *report* it?" He sounded displeased.

"I... well... it must've slipped my mind," Anton answered. Looking sheepishly at his Master, he could not come up with a more accurate explanation. He knew Warriors didn't forget to report important details of a mission. He wasn't exactly sure why he'd chosen to withhold the detail.

"Truthfully, I believe I claimed the pearl as a trophy," he said. "Forgive me, my Master." Bowing, Anton quickly drew the pearl forth from the EHD, and held it for the Master to observe.

"This is unacceptable," the Master said. "Your training requires reporting *all* details and submitting trophies for review. We allow a few small items to be kept by Warriors; this is of course human nature and of little import; that is why each of you is given an EHD." Looking at Anton, the Master waited for a response. "Were you *afraid*? Did you believe you would be *denied*?"

So that's it, Anton thought to himself. The Master wanted to know if I experienced emotions prior to the effect of the Virlaqueus.

"It seemed like a small detail," he said. "It was simply a rock that symbolized my first major assignment." Nervously, Anton watched his Master. He hoped his explanation would suffice.

"I find your *excuse* questionable," the Master said. "Did you know the Council of Masters decided before your assignment to Tooloo that you might be *flawed*?"

"Flawed?" Anton said. "Did you consider me for disintegration *before* my assignment?" A look of concern covered his face. He felt nervous, not knowing where this conversation was leading.

"This is the reason we risked *you* in Tooloo. We decided there was less to lose. We didn't see the need to send someone to investigate the Tooloo incident until we selected a more suitable Warrior. Yes, we *did* consider you for disintegration—as you see, we've changed our minds, and unquestionably for the best. Your experience provided us with a surprising outcome." He was hoping for an emotional response.

"So, I was expendable," Anton said. "I realize that all Warriors are expendable—it is after all by attrition that many of us are selected." Anton wasn't pleased, yet he understood his Master's argument.

Ignoring Anton's dissatisfaction, the Master changed the subject. "As for the other items—the necklace is insignificant, but I am curious why you value it at all. Maintaining an uncomfortable memory is illogical. And as for the laser, we request that you return it directly."

Removing the laser from the EHD, Anton placed it on the table.

"I have no need for this item; it is, as you say, a *bad memory*."

"Very well—on this we agree," the Master said. "Finally, why do you wish to carry a katana?" The Master required an immediate answer. It seemed to Anton he insinuated that he wouldn't retain the item if he could not offer a reasonable response.

"The reason I kept the katana was that it was of value to Mahkeetah beyond all other treasures; I chose to claim it as a symbol of my achievement in Tooloo." Hoping his explanation would suffice, Anton held his breath.

"I see," the Master said. "There's no reason to object—a Warrior needs weapons, and this is permissible; the laser is not. The Council agrees that it's a *symbol*, as you say, of your accomplishments. We can emphasize this detail to our advantage during your graduation; you will wear it for all to see."

"I'm at your service," Anton said, bowing. He wondered how his wearing the katana could benefit the Masters' purposes.

"You're always at our service; this will never change," the Master replied. "A Warrior is primarily a servant of Methonias, and secondly a servant to whomever, or wherever his life's mission leads him. Your assignment will be *different*. We have something *special* in mind." The Master again watched Anton for his reaction.

"Your wish is my command," Anton said. "I'm at the service of Methonias." Bowing, Anton chose to elaborate his loyalty, recognizing that the Master stressed it, and he wished to do so in return.

"We ask of you no less. As for further details of your career duties— we will reveal them during your graduation ceremony. This is the traditional method. We have an important task for your permanent assignment—a lifetime commitment, as it were. Your graduation will commence after the evening meal in front of all the eldest Warriors. Until then, use this time to make yourself look as presentable as possible. You'll be summoned later." Opening the door, he abruptly left the room.

For a minute, Anton stood there, looking at the door. He wished his Master had elaborated about his assignment. "I'd best do as I am ordered," he mumbled, proceeding to the bathroom to bathe and prepare himself.

Looking in the mirror, he carefully examined himself for any of the visual changes his Master had mentioned and immediately discovered one—his eyes had changed color. They were now black as coal, with no transition from pupil to iris; this was identical to all of the Tooloo villagers, including Mahkeetah. Running his hands through his hair, he perceived the telltale hint of black roots.

"So, it's true—I *will* be different." Heaving a sigh, he climbed into the hydro-sonic shower and enjoyed its invigorating sensation. After several days without a proper bath, the feeling of scrubbed and exfoliated skin left his body rejuvenated, and he wished to do the same with his mind. "Meditation," he mumbled as he sat up on the bed and crossed his legs.

Interestingly, it seemed easier to locate that special place deep within his mind and heart. Reaching the pinnacle he'd found upon his return from Tooloo, a sense of inner warmth filled his thoughts. The driving forces of happiness, discomfort, and anxiety that had plagued him just a few hours earlier were now suspended in a controlled region deep in his mind; he'd restricted their influence over his reactions, and they no longer concerned him.

With deliberate expertise, Anton easily grasped that new place in his mind and heart—the core of his being. Recognizing it, he defined it and permanently melded with it. Unexpectedly, he sensed something more—something beyond that special place he'd found earlier, a place that spoke to him inside his head as if he'd somehow heard someone else speaking to him.

You're one with the universe—open your mind, and set it free, it seemed to say. You're one with yourself; one with all that is around you and inside of you.

With no effort, the sensation of weightlessness overtook his body, just as it had before, and it gave him the aesthesis of floating outside his body. This time, however, it was different. Somehow, he was entirely aware of it and his surroundings; he didn't feel separated like he had before. He heard the whirr of the air filtration system, the nearly imperceptible buzz of the electronic shield covering the exit to the balcony, and his heart beating like a drum. Everything seemed to exist inside him and around him, as if he felt everything... as if he touched each of these items with his mind and his hands simultaneously... as if he could see everything with his eyes even though his eyes remained completely shut. These thoughts and feelings intermingled and allowed him to see his surroundings with his mind, as if he had an eye in the center of his forehead.

Anton was completely unaware of the passage of time—he no longer had a connection with it, or even realized it existed. Slowly, gradually, a brilliant light filled his mind—a light as powerful and intense as the sun. As if stepping outside of his body, he felt as though he'd become part of the room, and part of the Great Temple; expanding this feeling, he became part of Valde Domus itself. He could feel the weight of the mountain—its extreme age and the strength of its stone. He sensed the activities of many thousands of people performing tasks he both knew and didn't know, understood and couldn't fathom. Somehow, the magnitude of the diversity of activities confused his thoughts. He found himself suddenly returning to his body as quickly as if he was waking from a dream. He felt the bed underneath him as he lightly sat upon it in the lotus position.

Opening his eyes, Anton took in a deep breath while slowly placing his palms together and pushing. Reaching into the air above his head, he leisurely stretched, let his breath out, and then stood next to the bed. It was getting late, and soon he would need to eat. His stomach reminded him that several hours had elapsed even though it seemed as if very little time had.

As if beckoned, there came a knock at the door. "Enter!" Anton responded automatically, without realizing it.

The door slid open and a young Warrior stepped in. "I've been asked to accompany you to the Ambadedo Aula," he said. "All is prepared." Bowing, the young boy demonstrated his respect for his elder; he kept his eyes on Anton, never letting them waver. "The Masters await your arrival."

Adjusting his new clothing and attaching the katana, Anton made sure he'd positioned the sword properly, took a last look around the room, and then followed the boy. He wondered how late it was, and then realized from the angle and intensity of the sunlight that it was nearly dusk.

"What's your name?" Anton asked for no particular reason. "You look like a beta series."

"Yes, I'm a beta," the other replied. "My designation is Barnabas Six. You're Anton Seven?" He knew the answer, but was trying to be polite.

"You appear to be about eleven or twelve maybe?" Anton inquired.

"I am ten!" Barnabas responded proudly, as if seeming to be older was a compliment.

"As you know, there are no other graduates here presently," Anton said, trying to return the boy's politeness. He didn't feel like small talk—he was preoccupied by too many thoughts. Conversation simply interfered.

"I saw you yesterday," Barnabas stated bluntly. "How did you float?" His curiosity warranted his forward questions, something that normally wasn't permitted. It was considered inappropriate to inquire about personal information from one's elders.

"I'm not entirely sure," Anton said. "The Masters will explain everything you need to know—ask them." He wanted to dismiss the boy's questions. His only thoughts were to complete the ceremony and discover the assignment he faced—though at any other time, he would have enjoyed this conversation.

"When we get there, the Masters wish for you to ascend the center platform," Barnabas said. Anxious to complete his duty, the boy hurried along, nearly breaking into a run, and forcing Anton to do the same.

"We'll get there, young one—need we speed along so?" Anton said. Attempting to slow Barnabas down, Anton grasped his shoulder and lightly held him back. "The Masters can wait a few more seconds— we're nearly there!"

As the two arrived, Anton saw the entire facility filled to capacity with pre-graduate Warriors. The dome-covered oval room seated well over a thousand of them, at long tables that surrounded a round center stage where five Masters awaited Anton's appearance.

"Behold the arrival of our most honored guest!" One of the Masters announced from center stage as the other four bowed toward Anton. "Please stand and share your accolades!"

In unison, every student stood and bowed in Methonian fashion, hand over fist, eyes never leaving Anton as he passed by. The lighting in the hall dimmed, and spotlights lit the stage as he walked the short set of stairs to occupy his place amongst the Masters.

"I'm humbled by everyone present," Anton said. "I feel... well, I'm *grateful* for the good fortune of being Methonian!" He raised a fist high so everyone could see his glowing gold ring. A deafening cheer bellowed forth from all the Warriors.

The Master spoke to Anton in a low tone so that no one else could hear. "You're the first Warrior to demonstrate emotion and the ability to levitate. They consider you to be, shall we say, *transcendent*. They'll talk of you for decades to come." Then, all five Masters bowed and showed their respect for the Warrior—something they'd never done for any Warrior before.

"The first honor that we bestow upon any graduate is the branding of the arms!" The Master held a device high in the air, presenting it to the audience. "Hold out your arms, and prepare to receive the markings of your new rank!"

An enthusiastic cheer filled the hall as every Warrior celebrated the honor Anton was about to receive. "Brand his arms! Brand his arms!" they called out in unison.

Holding out both arms, Anton prepared himself for the painful burning of his flesh. Every Warrior waited for this moment for their entire life—Anton was no exception.

Lowering the iron and carefully positioning it, the Master pressed it against Anton's right forearm. Heat burned the marking of a dragon heavily and permanently there. A wisp of smoke rose into the air as the Master pulled the iron free, re-positioning it for the left forearm. Picking up a second iron, he aimed it carefully, and burned the traditional insignia of a tiger.

"It is done—he bears the markings as proof of his ascendency into legend!" Again, the Master raised the branding iron into the air for the audience to see.

Another shout filled the hall as the young Warriors' enthusiasm increased. Anton struggled for a moment with the burning discomfort while a Master sprayed a chemical on his arms to neutralize the pain from the damage. Anton then stood ready for the next event.

Drawing the attention of the audience, the Master continued with the show. "With our blessing, it's a great privilege to bestow upon Anton Seven the honor of Warrior cum laude. Never have we awarded this honor—you are the first!" Again, all five Masters bowed.

"In recognition of this high achievement, we bestow upon you a special mighty weapon—the Sword of Blue Flame! In honor of an ancient legend, we elected to create such a device. Long ago, we'd made the decision that a Warrior whose efforts achieved a remarkable, significant, and unprecedented skill could receive this honor. With distinction, we bestow it upon you!" Looking at Anton, the Master reached out and handed him an ordinary hilt of a sword.

Puzzled, Anton accepted the hilt. He held it up for everyone to see. Unquestionably, it was useless without a blade.

"Just how am I to *use* this great honor?" Anton said.

"Place it in your right hand, allow your ring to come in contact with it, and visualize a length of blade!" The Master instructed him, quietly and quickly.

Complying, Anton switched hands and visualized the blade of a sword. Instantly, blue fire erupted from the hilt in the shape of an undulating blade. A sensation of incredible energy vibrated and surged in his hand, as if he held a fire hose under pressure; the intensity of the energy coursed through his senses. Blue fire coupled with the golden light of his ring, illuminating the stage. The spotlights were dimmed, intensifying the dramatic effect.

A sudden gasp reverberated through the audience, and then, just as quickly, a hush filled the room. It was the first time any Warrior had witnessed the unique technology of the Blue Flame Sword. Everyone marveled, in awe at the implications. The sword produced a gentle whirring and crackling sound as Anton lightly swished it about and twirled it in his hand. Even the Masters seemed transfixed upon him.

"This weapon has more potential than you have yet to conceive," one of the Masters said. "Learn to use it *well*, and learn to use it *quickly*. We have an assignment for you on the far reaches of the galaxy. You will be leaving in the morning for Saurian Five. There, you will need to use this great honor—more so than you can imagine."

Anton looked at his Master with anticipation; he fully expected to hear further details of the deployment, and stood in ready stance. But the Master said nothing else.

"Witness his readiness!" The Master said theatrically, hoping to enhance the interest of the attending Warrior youth. "Do we not honor a *great* Warrior? Does Anton not deserve a mighty role in the improvement of mankind?"

A cheer filled the hall once more, as every Warrior raised a fist in agreement. In unison, they all chanted: "Anton Seven! Anton Seven!"

Dumbfounded by the cheering of the audience, Anton smiled slightly and held the sword high over his head. The brilliance of the blue fire and golden light made his hand appear like a star shooting blue fire from its core; the audience orbited him like a galaxy. The effect carried considerable dramatic power, and the cheers grew in intensity; it was a sight never before beheld by any human eyes. The magic of the moment enraptured Anton.

"You're a hero," a Master said, quietly, "even before you've proved yourself here. You'll undeniably be the most famous Warrior of your time. Use this to your advantage, and live up to this acclaim." He motioned for Anton to extinguish the fire of his Sword.

Anton quenched the brilliant blue blade; instantly it disappeared into the hilt. The spectacle was over, and the cheers of the audience quickly subsided in anticipation of what would happen next. Placing the hilt in his tunic, Anton bowed to everyone, indicating his respect for the honor the young Warriors gave him. In response, every Warrior stood and bowed in Methonian fashion, as did the Masters.

"A special table is prepared for you," a Master said, pointing to a small nearby table and inviting Anton to enjoy the offering. "A meal such as none here have witnessed is set for your enjoyment; you may partake of its extravagance."

"I'm at your service," Anton said, bowing to his Master. The table was relatively small and had three chairs around it. Piled high with exotic food that unquestionably came from off planet, he indulged in its lavish abundance; delicacies of meats, vegetables, breads, and desserts like he'd never seen before. Synthesized Methonian food never equaled this extravagance; he hardly knew where to start. Taking a single bite of everything, he soon found himself filled beyond capacity—yet he continued to enjoy the various otherworldly delights until he could eat no more.

Two of the Masters joined Anton, explaining each of the extravagant culinary items. Never having seen a Master eat, Anton wondered if they intended to now; he thought that perhaps they always enjoyed these finer foods, rather than sharing the special diets eaten by the Warriors.

"We hope this is repayment for the unpleasant experiences of the Clone Masters," the first Master said. "We don't enjoy experimenting on our prodigious graduates—but your circumstances were unique, and we needed to know the details of how the *Virlaqueus* affected you." The Master seemed genuinely regretful. "We believe you've received adequate recompense," the second Master said, seeming less concerned with Anton's meaningless feelings. "Unfortunately, the details of your assignment are classified; we'll reveal them during your final debriefing." The Master made sure Anton wouldn't press them for an explanation of his deployment.

"We know you're curious, but this is a matter of extreme secrecy," the second Master said. "All Warriors know the significance of classified information."

"I'm at your service," Anton replied. "Thank you for the special honors I've received. You've done more for me than I could ever have imagined; I only hope to fulfill my obligations in a way that earns your pride and respect."

"We anticipate great accomplishments from you," the second Master responded, with a tone of warning. "The tools of success are already yours—use them well."

Looking at him transfixed, both Masters sat quietly, as if trying to assess Anton's thoughts, or perhaps they knew what he might be thinking and anticipated a specific riposte. But he only glanced at them and held his tongue.

"When will the debriefing occur?" Anton asked. This was the question that concerned him the most; he found it difficult to wait for the answer. Not knowing his Master's agenda filled him with a feeling of foreboding.

"As we expected, your curiosity is a virtue, but when it comes to your inner discipline, it's best to know the *correct* time to ask the *correct* question. Your need for an answer is precocious, especially when we've asked for your patience." With a persistent stare, the Master pointed out another of Anton's youthful failings. "Patience is also a virtue, young Warrior. You will find this fundamental lesson imperative."

He went on: "If you've concluded your meal, we ask that you return to your room. In the morning, we will send Barnabas to summon you for your departure; you'll receive your debriefing on Saurian Five. Until then, you may spend your time freely." The second Master spoke as the first stood and left the table: "We will be available when you arrive at your destination." Standing, the second Master left the table too, leaving Anton to his own choices.

Grasping a handful of his favorite delicacies, Anton returned to his room, nibbling as he wandered the halls. Thoughts of Nelda suddenly returned as he finished his final morsels; he wished she could've shared this experience with him. His pride mingled with his bereavement; the devastating twist of fate that took Nelda's life persisted in his heart. The sorrow had subsided to some degree, yet it still haunted his thoughts and left him slightly depressed. Just knowing he would soon leave Methonias, perhaps forever, increased his sense of loss, but he was determined to prove himself this time. His failure in Tooloo left him with a desire to prove to her he'd never fail again.

"The best thing to do now is get a good night's sleep," Anton said. "I want to be as sharp as possible in the morning." Mumbling, he prepared his bed and slipped under the covers.

SLEEP CAME WITH DIFFICULTY; ANTON struggled to set aside his misgivings for the death of his wife, the anticipation of where he might be going, and the excitement of the graduation. Everything blended into a circle of uncertainty, but finally, sleep he did.

In what seemed the blink of an eye, Barnabas shook his shoulder, waking him from his troubled dreams. "You sleep like the dead," Barnabas said. "Warriors never let an enemy approach them so easily!" The young Warrior seemed confused as he forced Anton from his stupor.

Startled, Anton quickly flew from his bed, grasping for his katana as he clothed himself. Then he realized where he was and sat down on the corner of the bed. "Sorry," he said. "I... well, I'm okay." Fumbling for the appropriate words, he struggled to gain his wits.

"The Masters await you at the shuttle," Barnabas said. "You only have a few minutes before it departs—you must hurry!" Pushing Anton along, Barnabas attempted to help him meet his deadline.

"Thank you," Anton said. "I can get there—you may return to your duties." He gave Barnabas a dismissing look, and watched the boy leave. Quickly he finished dressing, looking around the room one last time, checking to see if he'd missed anything, and then he quickly departed.

It didn't take him long to run to the entrance of the Temple and locate the Aerocraft that awaited him. Five Masters greeted him at the gate as he hurriedly rushed through the Temple doors.

"Your departure diminishes us here at the Great Temple," one Master said. "But it provides an opportunity to show how important Warriors are to everyone abroad. Good fortune awaits your success." Cryptic to the end, the Master bade Anton farewell.

"I'm at your service," Anton said, bowing to each Master in turn, and offering one final display of respect. Then he ran to the Aerocraft and promptly climbed aboard.

Quickly, he looked over his shoulder for one last glimpse of his home before the Aerocraft door closed. He noticed that the Masters had already left. Their responsibility had concluded, and they no longer had an interest. Seating himself, he heaved a sigh, and closed his eyes.

"Goodbye, home," Anton said. "Goodbye, Nelda." As he expressed a final regret and a final farewell, the Aerocraft engines whined their familiar high-pitched sound, and the vessel instantly lifted off, shooting into the air at an impossible speed toward the space station high over Methonias. Anton's youth was over, and his adult life remained mysteriously concealed before him. Never again would anything be as familiar, or as habitually comforting as his youth had been.

Alone on the Aerocraft, Anton heaved a heavy sigh, and quietly observed the monitor in front of him and waited patiently for the sight of the space station. A sensation of leaving the pull of gravity came over him, and he knew that the station would soon appear on the horizon. Somehow, he didn't feel like leaving Methonias, yet he knew he couldn't stay. The mixed thoughts and unprecedented feelings tugged at each other, leaving him at a loss.

"So, what could possibly be in store for me?" Anton mumbled to himself.

Au Revoir Methonias

ANTON SAT RESTLESSLY IN HIS seat aboard the Aerocraft, anxiously awaiting his arrival at space station MB-1; he desired to move forward with the next chapter of his life, yet his thoughts remained fixed on recent events. They troubled him, and he unconsciously fingered the hilt of the Blue Flame Sword as he pondered the Masters' vague description of his assignment. He wondered what he might face when he arrived at his destination; their secret motives left him nervous, and he shifted restlessly in his seat.

Even worse, he kept thinking of his failure with the villagers of Tooloo; his subconscious feelings abruptly returned, haunting him, and he took a deep breath as he angrily remembered the sound of the cave exploding. His feelings were less intense than they'd been two days ago—yet haunt him they did. He hoped the tragedy wouldn't leave a permanent scar in his heart. He wanted to move on toward his mysterious and uncertain future. Tooloo had forever changed him, leaving him desiring what he couldn't have. But it had also given him a tremendous gift—a gift he'd never anticipated, and that he wouldn't have achieved without having gone through the nightmare. Fortunately, the Clone Masters had given him the ability to suppress these uncomfortable feelings—at least to some degree, and at least for now.

"Forever change me," Anton sighed and mumbled to himself. "I need to rise above my experience in Tooloo and somehow profit from it." He continued to ramble as he agonized over the appalling death of the entire village, a death he was directly responsible for.

He felt as if his old self had died along with those villagers, and then was reborn after his procedure in the Clone Labs and the counsel offered by his Masters. Their talks had alleviated his feelings, and absolved him of any crime, and the burden of guilt. He was immensely grateful for the help he'd received from his Masters; they represented all wisdom, and they'd taken the appropriate steps to remedy his physical and mental issues upon his return to the Temple. Their help, combined with the meditation he'd obtained in the Great Temple's garden, and later in his graduation chamber, had relieved most of the stress that'd initially disturbed him, but not entirely.

Patience is a virtue, young Warrior—you will find this fundamental lesson imperative. The words of his Master entered his thoughts, silencing the waves of disturbance he wrestled with in his heart.

"Patience," he said. "Perhaps this is the best advice for now. I should deal with these unpleasant feelings at a more appropriate time." Mumbling when alone seemed to comfort his emotional state—yet the feeling of loss and loneliness persisted. It lurked quietly and relentlessly in the background of his mind. Images of Nelda constantly returned to his thoughts.

His reverie returned to the debriefing he'd received in the graduate chamber—how his Master's pointed questions held him suspended between ultimate success and ultimate failure. He'd nearly lost everything by simply retaining a *Lapillusaurus* pearl, and he'd risked even more by not revealing he'd done so. "Let it go, it's over," he thought quietly as he continued to fondle the Flame Sword in its holster.

When the graduation concluded, and his Masters had vaguely revealed to him the details of his assignment, a sense of foreboding overwhelmed him. He thought about his past, how as a child the stories about the planet Saurian Five being a place to fear; rumors surrounding it alluded to a mystifying purpose known only by the Methonian Masters. Periodically, young Warriors speculated as to its true purpose—stories of failed Warriors banished to a lifetime of punishment and hard labor there became threats of intimidation, or threats of punishment for misbehavior. Such thoughts crossed Anton's mind as he wondered what was in store for him when he arrived. However, as an adult, he knew that any assignment was fraught with danger and his Masters were confident enough in him to believe he was the right Warrior for this duty.

Abruptly, the Aerocraft's engines started to rumble and then fired; a mighty jolt followed by a steady vibration gently rocked the Aerocraft. As the changing gravitational and inertial forces pushed Anton deeper into his seat, his thoughts quickly shifted to his destination. Looking at the holo-monitor he could see an image of MB-1.

"Seven minutes until docking," a soft feminine voice reported over the ship's speaker. Anton had never heard a woman's voice while traveling aboard an Aerocraft. A thought of Nelda passed through his mind again.

"We will arrive at Methonian Base One in five minutes," it said. "Please leave your safety harness on until the Aerocraft docks."

Listening carefully to each word, Anton wondered what the face of the speaker might look like. He envisioned Nelda talking to him, and remembered her beautiful face and the intimacy they'd shared. He was overcome by a sudden longing for her touch. Unconsciously, he reached into his tunic pocket, and found his EHD. He touched it gently, as if somehow he could make a connection to her by holding the necklace contained within it.

"Docking maneuvers will commence in two minutes," the smooth feminine voice said. A growing sensation of longing grasped Anton's heart as his desire for Nelda intensified and lingered in his thoughts— even with the removal of the *Virlaqueus*'s chemical from his brain, he knew it would be some time before he could put the experience behind him forever.

With a sigh, he watched the holo-monitor screen in front of him and viewed the orbiting space station as the Aerocraft approached it; the final docking maneuvers were underway. He recognized the angular perspective of the approach as it changed from moment to moment, compensating for the rotational differences of the space station.

Suddenly, the Aerocraft shuddered, and the sound of metal clanging together resounded through the structure of the ship. "Docking complete; departure in T minus one minute..." The feminine voice continued to enchant Anton, and his desire for Nelda increased with each word. "You may now exit through the cabin door."

As he exited the Aerocraft, Anton noticed that it'd landed in a smaller, more private bay—one perhaps reserved for the Masters. Stepping off the ramp, he noticed two more identical shuttles that made up the full capacity of the landing bay. Marginally different and proportionally smaller from the one he had arrived on, they were of a slightly newer design with different markings.

Quickly looking around the bay, Anton examined its design; two large doors at the far end remained open—but if needed, they could close in an instant. Currently a simple electronic shield covered the opening; the thin shimmering field was all that protected Anton from the depredation of space. Tritanium arches supported the ceiling much the same as in the Masters' interrogation room; the resemblance was surprising. At the far end was a control room with several people monitoring computers that operated the bay's functions.

"Anton Seven, please report to section fifteen... Anton Seven, section fifteen," said the same soft-spoken feminine voice over the intercom. Surprised again, Anton looked around, as if expecting to see the speaker.

Chuckling to himself, he shook his head in disbelief. "I just got off the shuttle and already I'm being asked to go places."

MB-1 resembled a wagon wheel; the spokes were hallways that lead away from the center hub, where the various landing bays were located. Many rooms of varying designs and purposes jutted randomly from the spokes.

The axis of the station didn't generate the force of gravity from rotation—that was supplied by an artificial gravitational generator. These forces tugged Anton's body in multiple directions, requiring him to shift his balance and grasp a handrail in order to stabilize himself as he moved around the exterior of the landing bay. The magnetic waves crawled on his skin, giving him the alarming sensation of thousands of insects creeping over his body. He hated insects, and the feeling disturbed him immensely; he couldn't wait for it to end.

Walking was awkward, but Anton moved as quickly as possible down the departure ramp, and carefully exited the private landing bay. Clumsily, he entered a long corridor that led directly toward section fifteen. As he progressed, the gradual change from artificial to rotational gravity made him less dependent on the handrail, allowing him to move more freely the further out from the center hub he traveled.

Soon he arrived at deck fifteen. He entered, looked around, and waited—but not for long. Immediately a very tall man walked over to him and asked: "Are you Anton Seven?"

With a slight bow, Anton acknowledged the question and considered the size of the man towering over him. He was six-foot-two, himself—yet he felt dwarfed as he stood next to this giant.

"You must be at least eight feet tall," he said. "Are you from Trieos Three?" Anton's question was abrupt; his surprise caused him to forget his Methonian etiquette.

The man chuckled and smiled hugely. "My name is Enoch." He offered his massive hand, but it was too large for Anton to grasp comfortably. His own hand seemed more like a child's in comparison. The man's immense palm wrapped around it, utterly enveloping it—like a snake swallowing its prey.

"Pleased to meet you," Anton said. "I met someone nearly your size a few days ago. His name was Thorik. But you are even bigger!" Keeping his eyes on Enoch, Anton wanted to take a step back to get a better view.

Again, Enoch chuckled deeply. "Methonians are all alike—the sight of someone as large as me surpasses their expectations! Do you feel threatened by my size?" He continued to chuckle hugely, his eyes smiling warmly. "I see you wear many weapons—you are obviously ready for battle! Fear me you must!" Enoch leaned back and laughed outright, amused beyond limitation.

"Sorry," Anton said. "Perhaps I should have packed these items before departing Methonias, but I was pressed for time." Anton looked back and forth at his two swords, and then shrugged.

"Your ship leaves in a few minutes," Enoch said, smiling. "Please accompany me, if you can keep up!" He motioned for Anton to follow.

"Why would such a large man wish to have a job on a space station where the space is confined and mobility so limited?" Anton asked. "Doesn't it seem restrictive for one such as you? Wouldn't you prefer the open space on Methonias?" Enoch's size was a wonder to him.

"Ah—well now, most people wonder the same thing. I simply tell them—why not?" Amused at himself, he smiled widely, contented that he'd sidestepped the question. Then he chuckled softly to himself.

Feeling less than satisfied by this response, Anton accepted it anyway without concern; he had many questions about the people from Trieos, but now wasn't the best time for them. Besides, though Enoch was friendly and gracious, he also seemed mysteriously unwilling to divulge any personal information.

Guiding Anton to the star cruiser, Enoch accompanied him to the boarding gate. With one long outstretched arm, he pointed up the access and then bowed his head slightly, as if mocking Anton's lineage. "Good journey!" he said. Laughing heartily, he abruptly left the bay and returned to his duties.

Amused, Anton shook his head, chuckled softly to himself, and then promptly walked up the boarding ramp, taking a good look at the ship as he approached. He recognized the star cruiser immediately—it was a Pleceivious M-60 interstellar luxury craft, very small and extremely fast; it was the latest in interstellar travel. It utilized the recently improved Slipstream Drive; a scaled-down version of older engines but with a unique design modification. This breakthrough gave it double the speed and range, and used less than half the fuel, and the engine was the smallest ever built—a single meter in diameter, and five meters long. Previous engines could only attain a half million times light speed; the Pleceivious had the capability of one million times light speed, allowing interstellar travel to take hours or days. The engine received the name Slipstream Drive due to its ability to fold the space behind the ship and condense the space ahead; this carried the ship along a wave referred to as a warp bubble. The ship could travel outside of the confines of time, eliminating the constraints of the theory of relativity. This engine was only capable of faster-than-light speeds, so the Pleceivious required a second engine, for maneuvering and sub-light travel. It required technology of two different types to achieve two different forms of propulsion.

Anton's excitement exploded as he prepared to board. He knew of the cruisers and hoped for a chance to experience the ship's great speed. Stepping up to the identification panel next to the main cabin entrance, he placed his left hand in the scanner. The device read the encoding of his ring and responded instantly.

"Anton Seven; destination: Saurian Five; cabin twelve—you may proceed." The masculine voice of the Pleceivious's computer felt a little disappointing after the soft feminine voice on the Aerocraft and in the landing bay.

The airlock door swooshed open instantly, admitting Anton inside; it reminded him of the doors on the prime lift at the Great Temple. As he entered the main deck, he instinctively glanced around, examining his surroundings with the skill of a predator. His years of training made this a routine practice; it was ingrained and instinctual. Driven by curiosity about the ship's exceptional reputation, he proceeded directly to his room, hoping for time to look around before departure. As luck would have it, he never made it. When he reached the far end of the deck, he noticed an old comrade he hadn't seen for nearly three years—one of the surviving Warriors from his Troglodyte mission.

Boris Three sat next to a viewport, quietly reading the latest edition of *Galactic News Today* on a holo-monitor as he awaited departure.

"Hello Boris, how've you been?" Anton said, smiling hugely and offering a slight bow. "Long time no see!"

"Well, life must be good for you," Boris said. "Apparently, you've graduated? Unbelievable!" Boris's eyes opened wide with a look of surprise; he hadn't expected to see any other Warrior. He knew Anton must've graduated, since no Methonian Warrior could leave Methonias until having done so. "I haven't seen you for... is it three years?"

"I graduated yesterday," Anton replied proudly, and unconsciously his arm bumped his hip holster containing the Blue Flame Sword. Boris saw the conspicuous gesture and looked at the holster with another expression of surprise.

"You never cease to amaze me, Anton," Boris said, with an unpleasant wolfish expression. "Please sit; let's talk about old times." He pointed at the seat facing him. The holo-monitor was active between them.

Boris eagerly desired first-hand news from Methonias; it wasn't often Warriors met in transit from one assignment to another, particularly those that knew each other well. He relished an opportunity for news of their home world of Methonias.

"I'd like to visit my cabin first," Anton said. "I'll return before we depart." Bowing slightly, Anton left his friend and proceeded to locate his cabin.

"I'll await your return," Boris called after him, watching as Anton left the deck; his eyes followed the holster on one hip, and the katana on the other. "Hmmm," he murmured, and then returned to his reading.

Finding the katana both cumbersome and unnecessary, Anton decided to store it in his EHD. Reaching into his tunic pocket, he pulled it out, opened it, and then carefully slid the katana inside. Thoughts of Tooloo quickly passed through his mind and he heaved a sigh as he recalled Mahkeetah's heroic demise. The image of his lunging body neatly sliced in two halves by Luthian's laser slowly and repeatedly played out in his thoughts, sending a shiver down his spine.

Taking a deep breath, Anton struggled to change his thoughts. "I need to set the past aside, I have a future to focus on," he quietly mumbled to himself. "This sword only brings back unpleasant memories at the moment." Mumbling, he shoved it in his EHD, and then expeditiously replaced the EHD in the pocket of his tunic.

Anton was delighted at how large his room seemed—he'd anticipated something much smaller. The first thing he noticed was a zero-g bed. Next to it sat a tiny table with a single chair placed just below a viewport. On the opposite wall was a storage unit for luggage and personal items that overhung a small bench barely big enough for two people to sit.

"A private room," Anton said, raising an eyebrow even as he nodded his approval. "Rare indeed—and most generous for space travel. I'd best return to the main cabin. I've some catching up to do."

Boris continued to read the news where Anton had left him. "Mind if I join you?" Anton asked as he approached.

"Nothing would please me more," Boris said, with a slightly sarcastic but oddly polite tone. "What've *you* been up to since I last saw you?" Boris tried his best to disguise his thoughts from Anton as he did with all fellow Warriors; it was never known if they may be working for rival employers.

Remembering how insensate and calculating Boris had been on their mission to the badlands, Anton wasn't particularly startled at his derisive demeanor.

"What became of you since our Troglodyte experience?" Boris's eyes narrowed as he carefully watched Anton seat himself. His tone again sounded sarcastic, yet he paradoxically exhibited a casual smile. "Something monumental has changed you; I can see it in your eyes."

Sitting, Anton cautiously returned his smile, and then glanced at the holo-monitor Boris was using. "Many things have happened, as you should know; things are always changing." Looking at Boris, Anton quickly realized that he was referring to the change of his eye color.

"Yes, many things have changed," Boris said dryly. "So, are you going to tell me?" He continued to allude to Anton's new eye color.

"Unfortunately, that information is classified," Anton said. "I can tell you that I paid for it at a great cost." Anton looked at Boris with an expression of finality. "You know the consequences if I reveal too much."

"True. I had my own... *classified* experiences, as you put it. I'll tell you, though—the badland assignment was expected to be *my* final mission. However, I failed; my ring didn't change color—unlike your eyes." For a second, he hesitated and looked over his shoulder out of the viewport before continuing.

"I was lucky, though—the Masters allowed me a final... well... *opportunity*." Taking a deep breath, Boris leaned back in his seat and put his hands behind his head, exposing the brands on his arms. "I completed my training a month later." He sounded arrogant—a trait Anton too had expressed when he first met Mahkeetah. Indeed, it was a trait most young Warriors possessed. Apparently, Boris hadn't cast off this undesirable quality.

"Prepare for launch," a voice piped over the intercom. "Please fasten your seat restraints. Weightlessness occurring in two minutes; the safety interval will remain in effect until we leave the Methonian star system."

"Better get strapped in," Anton interjected. "I don't feel like floating around." With a smile, he speedily buckled the restraining harness at his seat.

Boris didn't smile. Looking dispassionately at Anton, he mechanically fastened his harness and then continued his conversation.

"As I was saying," Boris went on. "The Masters were very generous and gave me a second chance—something they rarely do, as you know."

"Why?" Anton said. "What reason did they give you?" Looking quizzically at Boris, Anton queried him for the details of his mission; it was clear Boris wanted him to do so. "You seem *proud* of this point; other Warriors are given 'second chances.'"

The smile left Boris's face as he responded. "Anton—as you know, this is classified." With a sarcastic smirk, he repaid Anton's previous response with relish. "Are you trying to get us in *trouble*?" He intentionally denied him the satisfaction of learning the truth, a game he'd often enjoyed in their youth.

"Pardon me," Anton said. "You brought it up, and naturally I was curious. The Masters' purposes are forever enigmatic; it's just that, like any of us, I want to understand more about them." Keeping the conversation as polite as he could, Anton showed his capacity for respect and compassion—traits Boris hadn't seen before and didn't approve of.

With an expression of scrutiny, Boris hesitated and rubbed his chin before continuing the conversation. "I'll trade a little of my information if you'll share some of yours. I don't trust a Warrior that is... well... how shall I say it? *Emotional.* I'm surprised you didn't fail. You're flawed and weak. And here you sit before me with the legendary *Blue Flame Sword* strapped to your hip; a sword nobody has ever seen or received, it exists only in Methonian legend." With a sneer, he finally said what was on his mind. "How is it *you're* the first Warrior to receive one? Or do they hand them out like candy now?"

Gritting his teeth, Anton ignored Boris's sarcasm. "I... I suppose we could trade some information, as long as it's shared *carefully*. We wouldn't want to disobey our Masters' directives." He quickly sidestepped Boris's apparent jealousy and returned the conversation to its friendlier beginnings.

Warriors could always rely on each other, without question. But something was different about Boris—something Anton couldn't put his finger on. It was starting to bother him. He hoped he could continue to escape his deliberate attitudes and sarcastic responses.

"You do trust me, Anton, don't you?" Boris looked at him through the slits of his eyes. "We're brothers for life. This cannot be changed."

Anton was becoming increasingly wary of Boris's intentions. "Yes," he said. "Warriors are *always* brothers. Trust is unconditional. Why do you feel it necessary to ask?"

He didn't trust Boris implicitly. Thinking back, he wasn't sure if he ever had. Boris had always shown a separation from the others—as if he competed with his fellow Warriors by dictating to them and putting them down, rather than working together as a team. It was as if he believed himself to be better than they were. Perhaps this was the Masters' test that he'd failed in the Badlands—but if it was, why hadn't he learned from the experience? Uncertainty raced through Anton's thoughts, and his skepticism grew.

The two Warriors stared at each other as several other passengers entered the cabin and buckled in, preparing for departure. The engines started to whine, and the Pleceivious vibrated and pulsed rhythmically as it gently lifted off. In a few seconds, they'd passed beyond the space station's landing bay doors, leaving MB-1 behind.

Adjusting the holo-monitor for an exterior view, Anton saw the space station quickly disappear as the Pleceivious gained momentum. The blue, green, and white sphere of Methonias rapidly shrank from view, growing smaller at an unimaginable velocity. Within a minute, it had disappeared.

The shifting of g-forces, the compensation of the inertial dampeners, the lack of rotational gravity, and the sense of mass accelerating through space left Anton feeling dizzy; he was glad for the benefit of the harness, which held him snugly in his seat. But he couldn't wait to remove it; he needed to escape from Boris's unusual behavior. Their conversation had become intolerable.

"Space-fold in three minutes; please remain seated until we reach hyperspace," the intercom voice said, continuing to update the few passengers.

Anton was eager to eat and return to his cabin. He fidgeted in his seat uncomfortably.

"Let me answer your question, Anton," Boris said, trying to maintain the other's attention. He seemed pleased to have a captive audience to toy with.

"Wouldn't it be prudent to keep our discussion private?" he said, looking around the cabin and then back at Boris.

"I've no intention of saying more than I should," Boris said, blankly. "I'm not so sure about *you* though—you make poor choices." Boris intentionally stabbed Anton's weakest point in an attempt to unsettle his feelings; he hoped for a rash response.

"It would seem that you purposely choose to irritate me," Anton said. "Why?" If Boris intended to provoke an argument, Anton intended to get to the heart of it as quickly as possible.

Maintaining his nonchalant stare, Boris chose his next words carefully. "How is it that a flawed and emotional Warrior such as you received that sword you carry? We both know you couldn't possibly have earned it—and that you don't in any way deserve it!"

Jealously, he continued to display the attitude, poking Anton relentlessly with it like a dagger. "Are you aware of recent events? Did you visit Methonias, or are you just passing through? If you had visited, you wouldn't be questioning me, and you'd know how wrong you are." Anton glared at him; he was becoming tired of the conversation at this point.

"It doesn't matter what may have happened recently," Boris said. "You're a failure, Anton, and all of us knew you would be! We all knew you were different, and we all believed the Masters would disintegrate you." Boris scoffed. "You're emotional! You're a complete disgrace to us all! How did a Warrior like you manage to *graduate*?"

"Why do you disapprove of me?" Anton said, feeling threatened. "What makes you think I'm so undeserving?" He was sure Boris intended to pick a real fight. "As for emotions—you express jealousy loud enough for anyone to hear! *You're* emotional too!"

Taking a deep breath and holding his tongue for a moment, Boris smirked as he carefully prepared his next words. "You may have had exceptional acrobatic skills, and your design is always superior at running as fast as the wind. However, you make bad choices, choices that get people killed—and you always will. I think it was another *bad* choice that changed your eye color—am I right?" Boris continued to expose Anton's weaknesses as if he was peeling a banana. He didn't intend to lose the argument, and pressed him further with each word.

"I earned the Flame Sword," Anton said. "You just didn't see how. As for my abilities—maybe I'm capable of something you'll never have. Did you think of *that*?" Anger poured from Anton's eyes, and his voice rose as he defended himself.

Looking carefully at Anton, Boris contemplated the significance of his words. He couldn't accept that Anton had achieved something monumentally impressive; he'd never seen any Warrior receive the Blue Flame Sword.

"Perhaps you *do* have some tricks up your sleeve," Boris said. "But I will always see you as a failure. As for answering any of your questions—forget it. I'm not about to tell you anything about my business. I don't know how you did it, but you must've deceived the Masters. I'm surprised at them; their wisdom seems to be in question here. It's lucky for you we're on board the Pleceivious, or I'd claim that little toy of yours for myself. It's only a matter of time before someone will—I hardly believe you can maintain possession of it for long." A sardonic smile lightly marked his face as he stared coldly at Anton.

"We are now leaving the Methonian system," said the intercom voice, interrupting the dispute. "Hyperspace fold will commence in one minute." The two Warriors locked eyes as unspoken thoughts passed between them.

The intercom continued: "Hyperspace fold will commence in three... two... one... *activate*."

With a shrill sound, the engines fired and accelerated. Anton's skin felt as if insects were crawling on every inch of his body; it was the same sensation he'd felt when he struggled with the artificial gravity in the center hub of MB-1. A rhythmic vibration rocked the Pleceivious for a few seconds, and then it fell silent. It felt as though the cruiser had fallen from the sky and crashed into the ocean, followed by a smooth buffeting, like the submergence of a submarine in turbulent waters.

"Artificial gravity is now in effect," the intercom voice said. "You're free to move throughout the ship."

Finally, Anton was free to go. "I believe our conversation is pointless, and I need something to eat. Please excuse me." One final look at Boris let him know he'd made the right choice.

Boris continued to stare through the slits of his eyes; contempt and disapproval marked his face. "Until we meet again," he said. "And I hope we do."

Taking a deep breath, Anton bit his tongue and quickly exited the main deck. He was hungry; it didn't take him long to find the galley. It was a small chamber with barely enough room for a dozen passengers, but nobody was there. Activating the galleys' menu, he made a selection; the automated food generator instantly provided him with one of the exotic dishes he'd enjoyed at his graduation ceremony. Eating it with enthusiasm, he quickly satisfied his hunger. Having missed breakfast, the food tasted particularly good, and it didn't take him very long to finish. Considering the conversation he'd had with Boris, he decided it best to remain in his cabin for the remainder of the flight.

"Maybe a nap would help," he said. "I need time for rest and meditation." Nobody heard his mumbling as he stood and left the galley.

Returning to his room, Anton strapped himself into the zero-g bed and easily fell asleep. Dreams of explosions destroying the mountainside at Tooloo and waves of blood gushing through village huts made his sleep restless. He thrashed about and sweated as he dreamed he was struggling to save drowning children deep under bloody pools fraught with tumbling boulders. After what seemed like an eternity of exertion, he finally awoke. His skin was wet and his throat felt parched, as if he'd spent days in a desert.

"I need a drink," he said. "I wonder what time it is. I wonder where the ship is." Disjointed thoughts poured from his woozy mind, and he mumbled soporifically. As Anton removed the zero-g bed harnesses, someone signaled him from the cabin door.

"Boris Three wishes to see you," the intercom quietly alerted him.

"I thought I'd seen the last of him," Anton said to himself. Sitting at the table, he looked out of the viewport and saw the stars zipping by, letting him know the Pleceivious was still slipstreaming through space.

"Enter!" Anton said. The cabin door hissed open, sliding sideways; Boris stood there with his hands on his hips and a look of capitulation. Slowly he took a single step inside Anton's room.

"I'd like to apologize for our earlier conversation," he said. "I've meditated on what I'd said, and I find myself guilty of, well, an emotional outburst. I'm sorry for that." Looking at the floor, Boris surrendered his pride.

Anton's eyes widened and his mouth hung agape. He was speechless, and shook his head. No Warrior ever admitted to emotions if they had any; very few had them, and fewer yet ever showed them, except on rare occasions while under duress, or in the heat of battle. Furthermore, Warriors never apologized for what they'd said to one another—it was beyond their behavioral capacity. Perhaps Boris had evolved, Anton thought to himself—or perhaps he had a similar flaw of emotions and was only now revealing it.

Taking another step inside the room, Boris continued. "Please allow me to explain." The door whooshed sideways, closing instantly. "I'm in trouble. The reason I'm being sent to Saurian Five is because of a disloyalty concern. I've formed opinions about the Masters." His eyes never left Anton's.

Anton looked both surprised and concerned. He listened carefully to what Boris said; it wasn't like a Warrior to explain himself. Again, he noticed something fundamental had changed in his friend, and he wasn't sure what Boris was about to reveal. "Please sit," Anton said, pointing at the small bench below the cabinet.

"Thank you. As we discussed earlier, it's against the rules of our Masters that I should divulge anything to you. But I believe I've nothing to lose. On the other hand, if they find out that you've listened to what I might disclose, your fate may be similar to mine. Do you wish for me to continue?"

"Go ahead," Anton said. "I fear nothing. If I believe you're revealing too much, I'll stop you. You may proceed." Anton's eyes narrowed skeptically. However, Warriors always tendered implicit trust to each other—even after their argument, he couldn't deny Boris the opportunity to confide in him.

"Very well," Boris said. "There's no going back after you hear what I'm about to say." Boris gave Anton a serious look, and then continued; he made sure he understood the implications and inherent consequences of what he was about to share and he wanted to know how much he could trust Anton.

"Everyone throughout the twenty inhabited worlds believes the Methonian Masters are the noble benevolent protectors of the universe. But there are many mysteries about them that leave an attitude of wariness and distrust; the people fear how secretive and secluded they are." Adjusting his position in his seat Boris leaned forward and put his hands on his knees. "I've heard rumors. These aren't just farfetched tales, they're genuine concerns."

"I'm sure there are many people that don't like the Masters," Anton said. "After all, secretive seclusion is not the best way to build confidence. But what are you trying to tell me?"

"Just let me *finish*," Boris said, clearing his throat irritably. "The colonial people of these worlds wonder where the Masters come from. As you know, they seem to have appeared from nowhere. Furthermore, they wonder where they could've learned such advanced genetics. The creation of us Warriors scares them. Oh, they know that the Clone Masters designed and created us to defend human colonies from every conceivable evil—from alien creatures to radical uprisings to evil empires wishing to overthrow existing governments. They know that we fight for the side of good and justice; this is our designed intent. However, for that very reason, they're *scared* of the Masters—fearing the true intentions of placing us where they do."

"I think I understand what you are trying to say," Anton said. "But this doesn't seem to connect to your reassignment. Everyone questions things they have no power to control. *That's* what we are for! Moreover, we don't question our Masters!" Anton was still puzzled.

"I'll get to that—please be patient," Boris said, taking a deep breath. "The question remains how the Masters could've learned so much about genetic engineering. In all of the available recorded history, medical science never developed genetics to the extent of Methonian Masters. This is the main point of argument. The colonials debate constantly on this issue. Some believe the Masters are aliens disguised as humans, manipulating genetics to their own ends. Others fear that ultimately, they plan to bring down the human race, or simply to become the overlords governing all worlds for their own amusement. They think that the Masters are a group of scientists secretly developing, testing, and improving us in hidden laboratories until they've perfected us well enough to fulfill these secret intentions." Again, Boris shifted in his seat; it was obvious he was uncomfortable with what he was revealing, though he wanted to make his point known.

"As I was saying," Boris went on, "nobody completely trusts the genetic manipulations they perform in the secret Clone Labs—even if there has never been a clear reason to doubt the success of the science and its benefits. They're all grateful for the services we Warriors provide—but at the same time, they fear its hidden capabilities."

"Another man recently told me something similar to what you're telling me," Anton said, recognizing the similarity between Boris's story and the tale Luthian had shared with him only days before. "Go on, I want to know more."

"As I was saying, people fear us, but they also fear the Masters even more. The Masters taught us that people desire us, and that they need us—and for the most part, this is true. But in the end, they're simply afraid." Again, Boris took a deep breath, and let it out slowly.

"They forever debate about us, in whispers, and in rooms locked and hidden from us. They don't want the Masters to know how they truly feel. Yet most everyone agrees that they need us, no matter what the Masters' true intentions are. They agree that there never seems to be enough of us produced to serve humankind sufficiently. Therefore, no one ever attempts to stop what is happening on Methonias—even if they could, the product is simply too valuable. The bottom line is, people fear cloned mercenaries.

Any argument for the Masters, or against the Masters, always results in an increased demand for more Warriors, which perpetuates ever more product, thus sealing everyone's fate and increasing the fears."

"So, what you're saying is the more Warriors there are, the more the people fear the Masters and feel like they need more Warriors to protect them." As he simplified Boris's message Anton thought he finally understood what Luthian had tried to tell him. At the time, he hadn't believed it—the entire Tooloo experience seemed somehow intertwined now that he better understood Luthian's account.

"That's essentially correct," Boris said. "But I have more to say; I was unwittingly persuaded into confirming the truths about our Masters; naturally our genetic code drives us to truthfully and completely answer any question the Masters require of us. It was stupid of me to think I could hide anything from them. However, in the end, the Masters weren't entirely satisfied with what little I did confirm. I'm on my way to a debriefing, followed by reassignment. I'm sorry for what I said earlier. I've revealed all that I can without getting you, and me, into trouble. I just want you to keep your eyes open; the Masters aren't what they seem!" Sitting back on the bench, Boris put his arms behind his head and let out a sigh.

"Feel better?" Anton said. "I know I always do after I talk to someone." Anton smiled, trying to reassure his friend.

"Again, Anton, I'm sorry for what I said earlier," Boris said. "I just want you to know I would like... well, I value your friendship. Hopefully, someday our paths will cross once again, and we will be on favorable terms." Boris stood and bowed in Methonian fashion, and then offered his hand.

Accepting it, Anton shook it and nodded his approval. "I'm honored to be your friend. I'll always help you if needed."

"You said you've heard these words before, yet you're just now leaving Methonias. How is that possible? If you know this already, why didn't the Masters keep you from graduating?" Boris hadn't missed Anton's earlier statement that he'd heard all of this before; he knew with little doubt that nobody on Methonias either knew of, or would offer such information.

Looking at Boris, Anton decided to share a portion of his knowledge. "I'm not able to tell you much, let's just say that I met an Interstellar Sixteen pilot in the tropics; that'll have to do for now." He knew that he shouldn't say anything, yet ached to do so. Anton also needed to talk about his troubles with a friend; only his Masters had spoken to him about his experiences. "Our Masters' rules are difficult, are they not?" Anton quickly added.

"Indeed. I don't want to create any further issues. I'll ask no further questions. I don't need to add your burden to mine." Satisfied, Boris accepted Anton's response.

Changing the subject, Anton asked: "Are you hungry? I need some water and a light meal; perhaps you'd accompany me to the galley?" Still feeling parched from his nightmares, he needed to refresh himself; talking had only increased his need.

Shaking his head Boris responded: "I think I'll return to my room and meditate further, I need that more than anything." Bowing slightly, he slowly left Anton's room. Just before the door closed behind him, he called over his shoulder, "Always at your service." Then the door slid closed with a whoosh.

For a time, Anton just stood there, looking at the cabin door. Somehow a sense of relief filled him; he felt more comfortable with himself, and less disturbed by the experiences of the past few days. Then a question entered his mind; had the Masters intentionally chosen to have Boris meet him meet in this way? Had the Masters known that he and Boris might share their similar discomforts and experiences, and give each other solace? Perhaps they tested Anton further about his loyalties after hearing Luthian's arguments. This meeting with Boris was too coincidental; knowing the Masters as he did, it seemed quite possible that they would have arranged it. After all, the Masters were wise in all things.

"I need water," Anton said. Abruptly, he dashed toward the galley. The door quickly whooshed open and closed behind him, sealing him inside. The room was nearly filled to capacity, but there was one seat left. "Guess that'll do," Anton mumbled.

As he sat down, Anton felt his neglected stomach pestering him again; hunger ravaged him and he decided to take care of the morning meal. Remembering the fruit of Tooloo, he requested some tara fruit, hoping again to enjoy the delicious flavor. The computer produced a facsimile of the melon that was nearly perfect in appearance, but the flavor wasn't particularly accurate. Nonetheless, it sufficed for an appetizer.

While he ate, he reflected on the counseling he'd received from his Master; *Patience is a virtue, young Warrior—you will find this fundamental lesson imperative.* Patience was the only answer he had for now. Everything seemed to return to this advice as he struggled to wait; the confinement aboard the Pleceivious left him restless with anticipation for the answers he so desperately sought.

"Perhaps I need time to meditate too," he said. "I need to prepare myself for the next set of experiences; it'll help me relax." Speaking aloud for no reason, Anton looked around, hoping nobody heard his ramblings. Satisfied that nobody was looking his way, he quickly finished his meal.

"Time to go," he said. "I'd better find the exit." Hastily leaving the galley, he headed for the main deck to see if Boris had returned there. But the deck was nearly empty, and there was no sign of his friend.

Returning to his quarters, Anton decided to relax with a quick hydrosonic shower; it was located nearby and it was unoccupied. The device wasn't as satisfying as the one he'd used back at the Great Temple, but it cleansed him with hot water, and relaxed his muscles. Once again, he returned to his room. Restless, preoccupied with his personal concerns and mixed feelings, he knelt on the floor in the center of the room, adopted the Lotus position, and began to meditate.

He thought of swimming in the pool at the village of Tooloo, and images of the faces of the children splashing and playing filled his heart with peace; a sense of loss and longing lightly nagged him, and he struggled to come to terms with Nelda's death. The name Tooloo had replaced his old mantra; he made this his new anchor, the new key to clearing his mind of thoughts. It somehow seemed dangerous to choose a new mantra, especially one that contained such strong emotional ties. But the use of a mantra was the method he'd used back on Methonias to find that new special place deep inside himself—that place where he could open the door to his higher self. With great effort, he relaxed, letting the flow of his chi fill his mind, heart, and body. Power and energy seemed to escalate deep inside him, growing to a level he'd felt only twice before. A sense of weightlessness overcame him, and he no longer felt his body touching the floor of his room.

Traveling outside the physical limitations of normal space and time, Anton entered an illimitable zone of pure thought. He felt as though he'd escaped the confines of his body, and his mind peregrinated outside his room, enveloping the entirety of the Pleceivious. His consciousness intermingled with the thoughts of the passengers, obscuring his own thoughts. Concentrating, he dismissed the unexpected interference.

The sensation of the disturbance in time that the spacecraft created as it traveled inside its warp bubble gave him an impression of isolation, an impression of separation from the universe. The bubble contained and limited his thoughts to the Pleceivious, as if space itself imprisoned him inside a glass sphere; it was impossible to breach the restraints imposed by the physical laws generated by the advanced and exotic technologies.

The coupling of an altered level of consciousness and the limited space within the warp bubble engendered Anton with a perception of claustrophobia, as if he was being smothered; it whirled inside his mind and he struggled to escape its grip. Yet the more he struggled for freedom, the more it seemed to restrict him. Tiring of the conflict, he soon relaxed and concentrated deeper within himself, allowing his thoughts again to become one with the ship. Soon he felt as if he were riding the Pleceivious on the warp wave, like a surfer riding a surfboard on the vast ocean of space. That feeling overpowered his sense of confinement.

Reaching out with his thoughts as if reaching out with his hand, Anton felt as though he could touch the bubble, as if it were a sphere of glass just at the limit of his reach. Visualizing himself standing on the bow of the Pleceivious, riding the warp wave, he reached out slowly with his finger to touch the glass sphere. Suddenly, unexpectedly, he lost his balance and fell into the ocean of time and space; the floor of his room hammered him and he awoke from his meditation as if from a nightmare. The ship shook, shuddered, and spun around him as he floated helplessly. The artificial gravity was gone. Warning sirens shrieked in his ears as he grasped frantically for something to hold onto; Anton's hand accidentally found the zero-g restraints of his bed and he pulled himself against it as the ship's engines fought to compensate for the disruption he'd initiated. Soon the Pleceivious corrected itself and returned to normal flight—but not before an unusual vibration shook the ship for a few minutes before it finally subsided.

"Sub-space stabilization achieved; artificial gravity restored. Safety procedures require an imposed restrictive period; please return to either the main deck seating or your assigned room and secure yourself with a safety harness. We'll run a diagnostic shortly to find the cause of the disturbance."

Trying to reassure the passengers, the captain spoke over the intercom. His voice sounded calm, as if nothing of consequence had occurred.

Complying with the orders, Anton strapped himself into the zero-g bed and contemplated what had happened. He knew he was responsible for what'd transpired, but nobody would believe him if he confessed. It made sense to ignore the impulse to do so.

"Guess I'll let them sort it out for themselves," he whispered to himself. "I don't really need to, but I might as well sleep."

With effort, sleep came. Again, troubled dreams disturbed Anton, with visions of mutated creatures eating burnt human bodies, in a wasteland he'd never before seen. Giant creatures without a name, and beyond his ability to describe, searched for him as he struggled to hide. The nightmare seemed to last forever. Anton thrashed about in his restraints, trying to fend off an enemy he didn't know or understand. After an unknown amount of time, he awoke. Sweat covered his body. His forehead was heavily beaded, and streams dripped down his face.

Sitting up quickly, Anton noticed the Pleceivious had stopped. The vibration and whine of the engines had ceased. Looking through the tiny viewport, he saw that the stars had disappeared. All signs of movement were gone.

CHAPTER 10

Secrets of the Methonian Masters Revealed

LEAVING HIS CABIN, ANTON HEADED straight for the main deck, where he was able to check one of the viewing panels and confirm that the Pleceivious had in fact docked inside SFB-1. He was late to leave the ship after docking, therefore he found himself alone on the ship. Even Boris had departed. Immediately, Anton exited the Pleceivious and discovered one of the Masters waiting for him outside. The unmistakable heavy black robe that only the Masters wore offered him a sense of comfort from the disturbing dreams he'd just experienced. However, the sight of the solitary Master surprised him.

An uneasy concern flashed through Anton as he recalled the unsettling conversations he'd had with Luthian and Boris; they'd incited him to question the Masters' purposes. The Masters remained shrouded in a perpetual mystery—one that he felt he needed to uncover. Perhaps the rumors of his youth and the more recent accounts of Luthian and Boris were to some extent true; the speculations and accusations may have had more validity than he'd ever realized or believed.

Bowing before his Master, Anton greeted him in Methonian fashion. "I'm at your service," he said. His eyes never left the shroud-covered face of his superior, but a twinge of guilt marked his face, and a surge of trepidation filled his heart.

"You slept too long and thus delayed your departure from the ship; this has cost us significantly," the Master said. "Our time is precious; we still have much to do before your assignment begins. This is a behavior unbefitting a true Warrior." He turned toward the landing bay airlock and drifted through it, raising a cloak-covered arm. Then he made one slow motion, inviting Anton to follow. "Come."

The gravelly sound of his Master's voice compelled Anton to respond; driven by his DNA and a lifetime of training, he was unable to resist. Almost as if he no longer controlled his actions, he sprang into step behind the Master, who floated down the corridor leading the way. He felt as if all eyes were upon him and something crucial was about to occur. The unanswered questions about his assignment were about to be disclosed, and he was anxious.

Silently, Anton contemplated his Master's secrets. One memory in particular suddenly flashed into his mind, something that Luthian had said to him back on Methonias. *There are people disappearing from a planet on the far reaches of the inhabited worlds,* Luthian had said. *I don't know which one. Your Masters are using you Warriors to uncover the mystery. You're just cannon fodder to them! You're just something to be created, used, and thrown away at their whims!*

This epiphany from the mouth of a scared and desperate man flooded Anton with a sense of foreboding. His present circumstances seemed somehow connected. Using every cognitive skill he possessed, he calculated the pertinence and legitimacy of Luthian's words; he wanted to know just how relevant they were.

The fact that the Masters were on Saurian Five neither confused nor confirmed the issue; Anton's thoughts raced from one question to another. Memories of the innocent people murdered by Luthian and his band of outlaws flashed through his thoughts, fueling his old feelings of anguish, and making it difficult to reason. He was still haunted with thoughts of Nelda's demise inside the cave. A feeling of loss and longing overtook his self-control, striking at his heart like an arrow as he recalled her beautiful face and that intimate afternoon they had shared. The walls seemed to whirl around him as he forcibly clenched his teeth; with unexpected inner strength, he willed his feelings aside. Then he continued to ponder the issue of his Masters presence.

Was it possible there was a dark side to the Masters' purposes, as both Boris and Luthian had suggested? Just as Luthian said, nobody knew precisely where they'd originated; their derivation was as shrouded in mystery as their clandestine purposes; no known literature or records of any type existed to clarify this secret. It was as if they'd simply appeared from the core of Methonias, or perhaps from beyond the known universe, seeking to control every activity of man.

Now more than ever, Anton wondered why. It wasn't just the question of where the Masters were from that troubled him. Maybe Luthian did know something—something that Anton needed to verify, and quickly.

In addition, the Temple Masters weren't the only Masters in question; the Clone Masters were also suspect. They created the Warriors and built special physical and mental capabilities into them to fulfill the Temple Masters' purposes, and they too revealed nothing of their secret agenda. "For what reason do they require such privacy?" Anton silently asked himself.

These thoughts raced through Anton's high-speed calculations. He fought to solve the mystery before leaving the Landing Bay. All of these points of contention were apparently common knowledge throughout the inhabited worlds; everyone seemed to know about them. He hadn't dwelled on this question in the past; only now did he give it consideration, when it seemed as though he would be the latest victim.

"That *is* it," Anton thought to himself. "I'm convinced of it. I *am* to be used for the Masters' secret purposes." A feeling of trepidation suddenly flashed through his mind. Silently, he struggled with his turmoil, hoping to keep it hidden.

Continuing to follow the Master through the Landing Bay's airlock, Anton stepped into the reception area, where several people greeted him. A scanner carefully searched him for foreign objects and identification confirmation; they downloaded his personal information from his ring, and cleared him for entry into the main facility. Then, suddenly, an alarm went off.

"Hold!" said one of the officers. "You have restricted artifacts concealed inside an EHD." The officer stepped forward and motioned for Anton to reveal the device stowed in his tunic.

The Master unexpectedly put his arm between Anton and the two guards. "You will clear him for entry. There's no time for delay. We've agreed to clear these items. Anton may keep them. This information is stored in your computer."

Turning the alarms off, the guards examined the holo-monitor and then waved Anton through.

Without a second glance, the Master again silently motioned for Anton to follow him. Without comment, they quickly left the reception area.

"Your personal items are unusual here. They aren't things a Warrior would normally choose to possess. And rarely, if ever, would we allow a Warrior to retain them." The Master spoke over his shoulder, barely glancing at Anton as he answered the unasked questions.

"Under normal circumstances, you would be arrested and subject to punishment for having them in your possession. But in your case, we've sanctioned this exception prior to your arrival here."

"Thank you," Anton replied. "These items have special meaning to me, and I'm pleased that I'm allowed to retain them." Nervous, Anton tried to sound as casual as he could; he hoped the conversation was over.

"We're aware of your peculiar circumstances. As the Masters on Methonias have informed you, your items are inconsequential. We expected you might consider leaving them behind, but later we realized they would serve our purposes as well; we've determined that you might find them *useful*."

Silently, the two proceeded down a long corridor, and Anton considered this special privilege to retain his artifacts; it confounded him further. He questioned why they thought he would have a purpose for the katana, the necklace, and the *Lapillusaurus* pearl. At every step of his journey, their secrets escalated and their control of his future intensified—even when he believed he'd made his own choices.

Abruptly, they arrived at their destination and Anton was quickly ushered into the interrogation chamber. Initially, it appeared identical in nearly every detail to the one at the Great Temple. The large tritanium beams arched from one side to the other, creating the same dome shape.

The only difference was a large observation window that composed the entire far wall, framing the planet of Saurian Five below.

As he entered, he could see Five Masters had already seated themselves around the circular table. "Please be seated," the first Master said, pointing to the chair in the center of the table, as the ramp lowered into position, allowing Anton access.

As if compelled, Anton quickly took the seat. With nervous curiosity, he glanced around, waiting for the revelation of his fate.

Immediately, Anton's chair whirled around, and he faced the Master seated at the far end of the table. This Master wore a golden sash draped from his right shoulder and wrapped under his left arm, signifying his exalted position. Intuitively, Anton knew he was the Ruler of the Head Council of Masters.

"You've never met these Masters that sit around you," the Ruler of the Head Council of Masters said. "They rarely return to Methonias." He pointed around the table with one cloak-covered hand as he spoke. "All of these Masters who sit before you remain here above Saurian Five—and we'll reveal to you why."

Anton glanced around and considered what was about to be revealed; his urge to know the answers made him squirm with anticipation. Tension filled the chamber, and his heart pumped rapidly as a sudden twinge of fear flashed through him. He knew his assignment would be more than a trivial bodyguard designation, or a simple rescue mission. Sweat beaded on his forehead as if the ambient temperature had suddenly increased. He gently rubbed it off with the back of his hand. Folding his hands in front of him, he rested them on the table and listened intently.

"You obviously know who we are; these Masters who sit before you are the Council of Elders, and by the sash that I wear, you know that I am the Ruler of the Council." Looking directly at Anton, the Ruler pointed his finger accusingly. "And you are what we made you—just another Warrior. You are unique, but you are also just a tool to be used for our purposes."

Anton didn't like the way he'd been belittled. He'd just graduated with honors, and immediately the Ruler had categorized him as equal to any other Warrior. His respect for the ancient Master instantly diminished. He wondered at the reasons for his disparagement. He knew that the Council of Elders separated themselves from the Masters on Methonias, but he never understood why.

"You're the chosen one, young Warrior." The Ruler raised an ancient frail arm that trembled, and pointed his robe-covered finger at Anton yet again, as if accusing him of a crime. His voice was as dry as a desert breeze in summer, and sounded strained.

Squirming slightly in his chair, Anton felt particularly self-conscious as he listened to the coarse sound of the Ruler's voice. The knot in his stomach continued to tighten, and his thoughts raced as his speculations escalated.

"We're going to include you in our little circle of knowledge," the Ruler said, continuing his cryptic debriefing. Carefully, he spoon-fed it to Anton.

"It's our decision that you'll be our latest—let me rephrase that: our *final*—attempt to accomplish our greatest task. We are placing all of our hopes in your capabilities." He lightly poked the air with his finger, continuing to point at Anton. His hood concealed his face, completely obscuring his expression. "We anticipate complete success. You'll either succeed or die in the attempt. It's your duty and designed intent to accomplish this single task."

After a moment, he raised his other hand, and then spread his arms, pointing at each side of the table. "All of us here are proud of and astonished at your special abilities. Your achievements are recorded both within your ring and in our computers. I will list the ones we recognize as particularly significant."

A holo-monitor appeared in front of him and he read from the screen. "First of all, you're exceptional beyond all other Warriors with your acrobatic skills. Second, you can run like the wind, at speeds few if any have ever matched. Finally, you've developed an unexpected and unusual capability... you have an uncanny knack of... how should I say it? You are *lucky*. This isn't entirely to your credit—it stems from your emotions. Normally, we see this as a shortcoming. However, paradoxically, you control this defect well. But it is also a double-edged sword. On the one hand, your emotions defeat the design intent of a Warrior. On the other, you use this imperfection successfully as a tool—crudely, but successfully. We trust your emotions will be essential during your coming assignment." For a brief moment, the Master hesitated, watching Anton's reaction.

Motionless, Anton sat quietly and listened intently to his Master. The mixed message confused him, and he wasn't sure if the Ruler praised or criticized him.

Seeing no reaction, the Master continued. "Normally, we would've simply disintegrated you for this undesirable imperfection. But in your case, it has provided us with an important tool; I speak of the chemical obtained from the *Virlaqueus*." Watching Anton's reaction intently, the Ruler briefly hesitated. "Now, we wish to know what you're *feeling*."

Surprised, Anton raised both eyebrows. He hadn't expected this question; he thought he'd left that discussion behind on Methonias. "I... umm... I'm feeling *nervous*." Only his eyes moved as he quickly looked from side to side. He hoped to see if the Masters reacted to his response; none of them moved.

"As I would expect, considering your recent conversations with both the outlaw Luthian and Boris Three. Let me emphasize that their words are *poison*. Fear not, we'll deal with this issue shortly. Luthian has already been dealt with." Watching Anton, the Ruler waited for him to react; he anticipated an emotional response.

Anton didn't react; he remained absolutely stoic and composed, attempting to mimic the Masters around him. He knew that anything he said, or any movement he made, could jeopardize the delicate balance of the precarious position he faced. He simply waited for the Ruler to continue, hoping to avoid any inauspicious choices.

"Your latest abilities—that of levitation, and the unprecedented and inexplicable ability to reach out with your mind and manipulate the stability of a Pleceivious in hyperspace—is of great interest to us. We're aware of myths incorporating these talents from ancient writings; these are handed down as folklore from Earth." Carefully leaning back in his seat, the Ruler scrutinized Anton's reaction and then continued.

"On Earth, in India and China, these talents are said to have existed many thousands of years ago. We have proven them as both factual and fraudulent—fraudulent in the embellishment word-of-mouth has added to the truth. Now we see there is a new truth, one you have provided for us. I will not elaborate on this further." Looking slowly from one side to the other, the Ruler acknowledged his fellow Masters, as if silently requesting them to respond. They all nodded their heads in agreement—the first movements any of them had made since Anton's arrival in the room.

"We believe your abilities are needed to fulfill the task we set before you. Therefore, your emotions are to be accepted without question or concern; this decision is final. However, beware. We strongly warn you to express your emotions constructively. Don't allow them to lead you from your goal. It's *imperative* that you complete this mission successfully."

Shuffling in his seat, Anton felt both relieved and tense. He hadn't anticipated the Ruler's support, and his mysteriousness unnerved him. "Thank you," he said. "I'm at your service." His response was mechanical; only a single bead of sweat rolled down the side of his face, exposing his apprehension.

"You're *always* at our service—you have no choice in this, Warrior." The Ruler huffed and leaned forward, looking at him intently. "Now, I'm going to tell you a story in order to put to rest your misgivings about us. Yes, we're aware of what you're thinking, and what you believe. We know what you are feeling. This is a long story, and we're nearly out of time— therefore, I'll give you the condensed version.

"I want you to listen carefully. What I'm about to reveal to you is something we never discuss with anyone; only the Masters know this, and I want you to hear it exactly as *I* tell it to you."

Carefully, with diligent effort, Anton sat motionless, controlling his expression in order to conceal his thoughts as best he could. He felt that the Masters were wise to his doubts about them, and the regrets and conflicts he felt. Most of all, he felt exposed—as if under a magnifying glass. He wanted to hide any further misgivings or discomforts. The Masters already knew more than he cared to share with anyone.

"I know you'll trust what I'm about to tell you," the Ruler went on. "I know you're what we made you—loyal and superior in nearly every aspect. For purposes I am unwilling to disclose, due to the nature of the information, I will reveal the events in a manner that permits me a level of discretion—plausible deniability, as it were." Watching Anton, the Ruler hoped to see the slightest reaction in his expression; he needed to know if there was any reason he shouldn't continue. Seeing nothing, he proceeded.

"Nearly a millennium ago, on the newly established colony of Saurian Five, an unprecedented event occurred: the disappearance of the first of what would eventually be many Warriors. A blazing golden light appeared seemingly from nowhere, and it enveloped this single Warrior—and then he disappeared. There were many reliable witnesses who confirmed this event's validity. By virtue of this, the event immediately became top secret."

All of the Masters remained stoic; they appeared statuesque as they watched Anton, yet he knew they were observing him intensely as the Ruler presented his story.

"Initially, it was thought that some unknown enemy had developed an immensely powerful weapon, and was using it against the Masters. But this theory didn't hold true, since no other attack of this nature occurred again until fifty years later; it seemed as though it was some other phenomena. Nobody claimed responsibility for the attack, either—thus reinforcing the possibility that something else had taken place. Many theories were debated, but nothing conclusive was initially determined.

"When there was a second occurrence, at nearly the same location, exactly fifty years later to the hour, we decided it wasn't an attack; something very different had occurred. We, the Masters, gathered and deliberated for many years on the subject, conferring on how to prepare for the next probable phenomenon. We knew approximately where and when it would be, almost to the minute. By studying the celestial position of Saurian Five in each of the prior two events, we believed the precise location was calculable using a special supercomputer."

Taking a deep breath and letting it out slowly, the Ruler wheezed and coughed—an obvious symptom of his extreme age. There was no doubt in Anton's mind that the Ruler was ancient beyond measure, and his symptoms implied his assumption was correct, but just how old remained a mystery. His inability to perform even simplest of tasks without noticeable effort reinforced the issue.

Hoarsely, the Ruler continued. "Therefore, we set forth to design, create, and train even better Warriors. The Clone Masters developed several special new series, incorporating what were then controversial genetic improvements. It didn't take long to prepare and implement them. We refined and improved our training tactics to take advantage of these greater abilities; these techniques were far more difficult for the Warriors to perform and perfect. Additionally, we introduced several new indigenous peoples into the training regions of Methonias, and the regions themselves required updating to meet the new standards."

Again, the Ruler wheezed and coughed, and then struggled to continue. "Within the scant time of fifty years, it seemed as if we'd prepared everything that would be necessary for the next incident. We'd designed, developed, and trained three new special lines of Warriors, specifically for the event."

The Ruler stopped his recitation long enough to slowly take a deep breath; and then, carefully, forcibly stood. His body strained and trembled as he did so. Gradually, he turned around to face the perfectly framed planet in the observation window. Then he raised his hand languidly, pointing toward Saurian Five, as if he could easily see the tiny details far below.

"We built structures in the locations of the first two events; the calculations of our latest and most powerful supercomputers helped to ensure the greatest accuracy as to where the third event might occur. All of us argued our concerns—particularly about whether we'd accurately predicted the exact location, since it requires three events for a precise triangulation. In the end, we determined our preparations would be accurate enough. We moved our most advanced monitoring equipment into the region to measure and record every detail as the event unfolded; weapons were placed strategically, in order to defend against anything unforeseen."

Again hesitating, the Ruler's strength seemed to fail him as he lowered his arm and clumsily clasped his trembling hands behind his back; slowly, he turned around to face the table. All of the other Masters remained perfectly motionless, as if they were merely simulacrums of the Ruler, assessing Anton's every move and expression; they appeared to be of one mind, linked together by both thought and motion, or the lack of.

"We selected the most qualified Warriors and briefed them on the situation—just as we are briefing you. We placed the first two Warriors at the structures erected on the two original event sites, and the third Warrior at the location the supercomputers had calculated. Finally, the day arrived for event three. All the planning and preparations were complete, and we stood ready, awaiting the incident."

The Ruler stepped over to the table, placed his hands there, and leaned forward. His elbows trembled under his own frail weight and he struggled to support himself.

"Then it happened. We miscalculated—but only by a small margin, just a few hundred yards. The golden aura missed all three of the intended Warriors, and a fourth disappeared. This Warrior was also one of the new and well-prepared designs; unfortunately, he wasn't the one we'd chosen for the event. He simply hadn't made the cut during the final stages of training, and we hadn't prepared him with a tracking device. Instead, we designated him as a member of the observation team. Still, in the end, we were satisfied with whom the phenomenon managed to procure."

The Ruler stood erect and spread his arms wide, expressing relief that the event had concluded satisfactorily. He took another deep breath and slowly returned to his seat.

"The only unfortunate circumstance was, as I said, the lack of a tracking device on this latest Warrior. Our hope was to track him and answer the mystery of where these manifestations of power arose from, and discover who was responsible for them. This obviously wasn't going to be *that* time." Heaving a sigh, as if the burden of solving the puzzle confounded him, the Ruler sat quietly and watched Anton's reaction. Then he continued.

"Looking toward the future, we had the three events required for the supercomputers to accurately triangulate an exact point for the next occurrence. All of us felt more at ease since we trusted the computer's predictions; we had confidence of a precise location to place a Warrior for the next abduction. Logically, we hoped the latest Warrior would succeed at ending these occurrences; this of course was his mission."

Pausing, the Ruler took a deep breath and gently coughed.

"Back at the Great Temple," he went on, "another flurry of our ongoing debates took place; the Council continued to review our options and decide how to proceed with the next event."

Suddenly, for the first time, the other Masters moved; all of them nodded in agreement as the Ruler revealed their secret issues; they appeared less statuesque, less robotic. The two to either side of the Ruler watched him intently and continued nodding long after the others had ceased.

This struck Anton as odd, even for a Master. He hadn't seen them act this way on Methonias—the Council, without question, was in some way different. Somehow, the interrogation room had felt to Anton as though it was devoid of life—as if he and the Ruler were the only two people there—until the other Masters finally moved. He felt less tense as they demonstrated signs of life. Sweat continued to bead upon his brow, and he gently wiped it away; his nervousness caused him to fidget uncomfortably in his seat.

The Ruler noticed Anton's discomfort and hesitated. Then, slowly, he continued.

"Production of new equipment—new Warriors, with new special abilities and a better tracking mechanism—became our primary goals for the next event. Proper and complete preparation was imperative—therefore, we designed and developed a new supercomputer, for the single purpose of calculating all circumstances around the abduction event to predict the next occurrence with even greater accuracy. We had to measure things that had never been measured before!" The Ruler sounded as if he were about to pass out; he sounded stressed and frail, and his body trembled unremittingly.

All the Masters nodded silently. This was in stark contrast to the Masters on Methonias; during Anton's interrogation, they'd all taken turns badgering him with questions, sending his chair whirling around the inside of the interrogation table; this time the Ruler was the only one to speak. Anton wondered why.

"Special engineers were brought in from outside," the Ruler said. "This was unprecedented; never before had we ever used anyone but our own scientists and engineers. These outside people were sworn to complete secrecy and"—the Ruler raised his robe-covered hand to his mouth and coughed slightly—"they understood we had the means to ensure they'd comply with our strict principles."

"The design and implementation of machines that tracked a Warrior's passage into the unknown wasn't a simple matter by any means; it was a monumental struggle that persisted for nearly two centuries. But gradually we perfected the needed technology."

Looking at the table for a moment, the Ruler appeared to be exhausted. He rested his hands in front of him, leaned back in his seat, and took a deep breath, letting it out slowly. Casually, he reached inconspicuously under his robe, as if to relieve an itch.

For just a second, Anton believed he'd seen a glow in the area of the Ruler's chest, but it passed so quickly he wasn't sure. He thought that perhaps it had been a trick of the eye, caused by the lighting in the room reflecting off the golden sash the Ruler wore. Taking another slow deep breath, the Ruler continued.

"The supercomputers continued to be improved as even more time went by. Always we'd calculated the abductions to a few hundred feet, and then, finally, we narrowed it to within a few inches. The entire process took hundreds of years, and many more Warriors were lost to the unknown in the process. Determining the exact point of where of the next abduction would be became the most important driving force of all our research, design, development, and perfection of the computers and equipment used for this purpose. We honed this single science far beyond anything mankind had ever invented or achieved."

A sound of satisfaction was distinctly noticeable in the Ruler's tone. "We, the Masters *here on this space station*, are obviously satisfied with the astounding accomplishments made by the scientists of Methonias, and their enlisted help—even though the final goal of eliminating further occurrences has remained elusive."

"So, it was in the ninth century after the initial abduction that the ring of crystal was invented. It was directly tailored to the genetic code of each Warrior's DNA. This was an achievement beyond all others, since it had a dual purpose. It allowed us to determine precisely how well-developed and prepared a Warrior was in his training, sensibleness, and mental growth. And, in theory, it should allow us to track the Warrior anywhere in the known universe. We believe it will function far beyond even that— bridging into the eleven theoretical dimensions. Obviously, we haven't yet proven this theory. This much you should already know. Perhaps you have determined it for yourself."

Leaning back in his chair, the Ruler fell silent, contemplating his next words. Abruptly, he leaned forward and continued his recitation.

"It wasn't until recently that we could finally use the ring of crystal for this event." The ruler pointed at Anton sharply. "All the Warriors of the past fifty years have received one after their gestation, and as you must realize, this is extraordinarily invaluable in your peculiar circumstance." Leaning forward, the Ruler exaggerated his meaning by looking intently at Anton. "As I said before—its most significant capability is that it has given us a way to accurately measure a Warrior's *true* potential."

Again, the Ruler leaned back in his chair, and seemed to slip into reverie. For a moment, he said nothing. Then, once again, he looked over Anton's head at the ceiling, and continued. "We've recently put many new tools into place, not just the ring of crystal you wear. For instance, the completion of this space station orbiting Saurian Five and the creation of the best supercomputer ever built—our two finest accomplishments."

Anton noticed how the Ruler seemed to be repeating himself, and he wondered why. It wasn't simply odd—it seemed as though he couldn't find the correct words.

"This computer determined that a collimated beam had slipped through a dimensional crack in order to abduct all of the previous Warriors. Knowing this, we're capable of detecting this energy prior to its materialization, and we can position the space station directly in its path, forcing the occurrence to take place onboard. Additionally, with the crystal ring, we're certain we can track the abducted Warrior!"

As the Ruler continued, he seemed to make his point without directly revealing his secrets. Impressed, all of Anton's fears and misgivings dissipated; he finally understood the importance the Ruler carefully struggled to unveil. His complete trust in his Masters slowly returned as the story held him captivated; it seemed to answer most of his questions and remove most of his doubts. *Luthian and Boris never knew enough of the truth*, he thought; they spread half-truths built on ignorance. Perhaps the justice Anton served Luthian was justifiable and virtuous after all. He felt motivated as the Ruler's tale unfolded. He was sure that the Masters hid little or nothing from him. He knew they understood him far better than he understood himself. That was their primary reason for revealing so much.

"Time is of the essence, so let's get to the point of your mission," the Ruler said. "Very few know of what I am about to say; only these Masters you see before you, the Masters on Methonias, and a select few others, who are below on Saurian Five."

The Ruler adjusted himself in his chair and relaxed, emphatically exhibiting a newfound strength. Unquestionably, he was the supreme commander of everything, every Master, every Warrior, and he undeniably reigned supreme; his influence controlled every inhabited planet. Tilting his head back, he again looked at the ceiling over Anton's head. His dry voice sounded much less strained than it had before he'd reached under his robes; he exhibited more energy and seemed less frail. This interested Anton, but he was so absorbed in the story he scarcely gave it adequate consideration.

Again, Anton squirmed in his chair as he anticipated the answer he so eagerly awaited; he felt the knot in his stomach tighten incrementally, and listened so intensely that everything seemed to happen in slow motion. His increased Methonian mental abilities made this inescapable. He wondered why the Ruler of the Great Council had shared this story so completely; obviously, he was the next victim in the long list of abductees. An intense feeling of foreboding shot through him, as if he had been stabbed by a dagger; a bead of sweat ran down the side of his face.

Glancing around at the Masters, Anton observed how they all maintained their static stare at him. Every one of them sat in exactly the same position—as if they were clones or mirrors of each other. They all placed their sleeve-covered hands on the table in front of them, and their heads turned in Anton's direction. Their black hoods covered their faces, completely obscuring them. Anton's senses tingled with anticipation and dread, and he wondered just how ready he was to face this inexplicable mystery. His fear slowly subsided as his desire to become a part of the solution to this mystery spoke to his base genetic code. Warriors couldn't avoid the challenge of solving a mystery that had been placed before them by their Masters. A sense of adventure quickly replaced Anton's fears.

"The improvement of your genetic design is a result of these events," the Ruler said. "We redesigned and refined our Warrior classes for centuries, in the hope that we could put an end to these abductions.

"We've kept this a secret from the people of the Twenty Colonies, so they wouldn't view us as ineffectual; we can't be thought of as incompetent at defending them. We're the noble protectors of the universe! This must not change!" The Ruler pounded his frail fist upon the table, barely making a sound.

Without question, this single mystery was the Rulers' true purpose, his true passion. Anton undeniably understood his Supreme Masters' intentions; he must sacrifice himself to save the very foundation of whom and what he was, and what all of the Masters represented. The true purpose of the Methonian Masters and Warriors was at stake. He was to be the final Warrior abducted by this unknown force; he was to be their final hope for success of counteracting whatever was happening. He couldn't believe what he'd heard, but felt both intrigued and fearful at the prospect of what was to come. If he failed, everyone would forget who he was. If he succeeded, the result would be glorious! He couldn't pass up this opportunity.

"The last Warrior abducted was of the Barbarian series—Boris Two." The Ruler slowly waved his right arm and a holo-projector appeared in the ceiling above, and a receiver rose from the table in front of him. A hologram of the previous abduction played out on the table between them. In unison, all the Masters' heads slowly turned to view it.

The story played itself out as the Ruler continued to narrate. "As you see, we knew the exact time and location of Boris's abduction. After centuries of these events, we will finally guarantee and control who would be the next Warrior abducted."

The hologram showed a special room in the space station, with a platform at one end. Boris stood upon the dais at one end of it. A moment later, an intense golden light filled the tiny chamber, enveloping him. Suddenly, silently, the golden light exploded, and then dissipated, leaving only empty space; Boris was gone.

"It's your turn next, young Warrior," the Ruler said. "You're our finest product, and we've selected you." Without the slightest emotion or concern, the Ruler commanded Anton, as if he were a mere pawn ready for sacrifice by his king.

"Your moment of glory is upon you, only a few minutes remain until the event window opens; you *will* accompany us to the platform." Waving his arm again, the hologram ceased and the door to the interrogation room opened. Two familiar-looking Warriors stood outside in the hallway. They were both from the Warden series; Anton knew them as the Warrior police. They were huge—nearly seven feet tall. They were as muscular as a Barbarian, and they towered over everyone in the room—even Anton.

"Follow us," they said in unison. "I'm Warden Four, and this is Warden Three." The Warrior on Anton's left made the introduction.

"We'll accompany you to the event chamber." Pointing down the hall to Anton's right, Warden Three watched his every move, as if he anticipating that Anton might suddenly attempt to escape.

Wondering why an escort was necessary, Anton stepped into the corridor. He didn't intend to disappoint his Masters. Obviously, they wanted to ensure they achieved their goals. Looking over his shoulder into the conference room, he watched as the entire Council stood in unison and then followed him; even the frail-looking Ruler joined.

Anton knew all hope was upon this event. They'd selected him to fulfill their plans. As he walked down the corridor, he thought about what he might face. Confronting the unknown with so little knowledge to prepare himself seemed as daunting a task as he could ever imagine. A ripple of anxiety flashed through his body, and every nerve tingled. The knot in his stomach returned, and anxiety made his thoughts whirl.

Warden Four pointed his finger and directed Anton toward the event chamber. "You'll proceed through this door."

The entryway was clearly marked, but the Warden directed Anton like a child. It seemed to him as though everyone forced his compliance—as if he was entirely unwilling to accept his role in his assignment. Yet he hadn't made the slightest effort to object. As he entered the room, he gazed upon equipment that filled it from ceiling to floor; computers and exotic scanning devices and many other things he couldn't begin to describe. Holo-monitors, workstations, and moving images inundated his senses; clicks, chirps, whirrs, and beeps filled the air with the sound of technology. It all smelled of electrical components and synthetic exotic materials.

At the far end of the chamber, a narrow ten-yard-long corridor which was made completely of a transparent tritanium composite material jutted from the side of the room. It led to a small dais about ten feet in diameter, which stretched ever further from the side of the space station into space. A clear dome of the same transparent tritanium capped the top; the platform too was transparent.

All of the Masters entered the chamber and quickly took a seat. Each one operated a unique piece of equipment. The Warrior Police sealed the door and guarded it—one inside and one out, preventing anyone from entering or exiting. Each Master frantically adjusted one computer or another, moving from station to station and tapping on buttons or poking at images in the holo-monitors.

"Please stand on the platform while we adjust the position of the station to place you in the exact location of the event occurrence," the Ruler said, pointing down the clear corridor leading to the dais, ushering Anton along.

As quickly as he could, Anton walked toward the platform, took his position in its center, and then faced the inner chamber and the Masters. Instantly, a clear door sealed the chamber. There was no chance to change his mind now. Looking around through the transparent walls, he could see Saurian Five below and stars all around him. The effect was unnerving, and the experience fascinating; it was like walking in space without a spacesuit or any form of protection.

Suddenly, the station jerked, as the Masters made an orbital correction, to ensure the platform was in the exact predetermined location. Anton steadied himself, as a slight sensation of dizziness affected him for a moment. The artificial gravity made his movements a challenge, since any effort tended to shift his body in whatever direction he moved.

"The particle analyzers are detecting a buildup of photon radiation," one of the Masters reported from his control panel. "It matches the radiation signature we've detected in the previous events."

"The computer calculates we're within a three-minute time window," a second Master added. "I've activated the event clock."

"I'm detecting a buildup of unknown energy emanating from unidentifiable inter-dimensional source; it's neither electromagnetic nor nuclear," said a third. As each Master spoke, the tension mounted. "The energy seems to be stronger than we detected on the previous event occurrence; presumably, we're closer to its source."

"The time interval is changing. The computers have determined we're within one minute; the clock has automatically compensated for the change." The reports hastened.

The instruments whirred, chirped and beeped at an ever-increasing pace, and the Ruler looked around from station to station. Finally, his attention focused intensely upon the platform.

Suddenly, everyone's eyes turned toward Anton, just as a brilliant golden glow filled the small transparent chamber, completely consuming the platform. At the very epicenter, argent light enveloped his body, and every hair stood on end, as if in response to static electricity.

A strange sense of dysphasia prevented Anton from shrieking in distress; his head felt dizzy and his body weightless. He was suspended in mid-air, or perhaps he was forever falling, he wasn't entirely sure; however, he was sure that soon he would pass out. His thoughts seemed disconnected and disoriented, his head began to throb with pain, and he was unable to concentrate. He struggled to scream, but could not produce a sound. Then everything around him faded and disappeared; he no longer stood upon the dais inside the space station.

Anton felt as though he were falling rapidly—as if the gravitational forces of Saurian Five pulled at his body, spinning him around uncontrollably and unceasingly. He felt increasingly vertiginous, as if he were in a dream. Enveloped in a brilliant blinding light, he closed his eyes—yet the light was so vivid his eyelids did little to protect him from its intensity. Then, suddenly, without warning, the feeling of endless free-fall ceased. His head and body struck something hard, and everything went dark as he lost consciousness.

PART 2

"The Interdependence of Magic and Science"

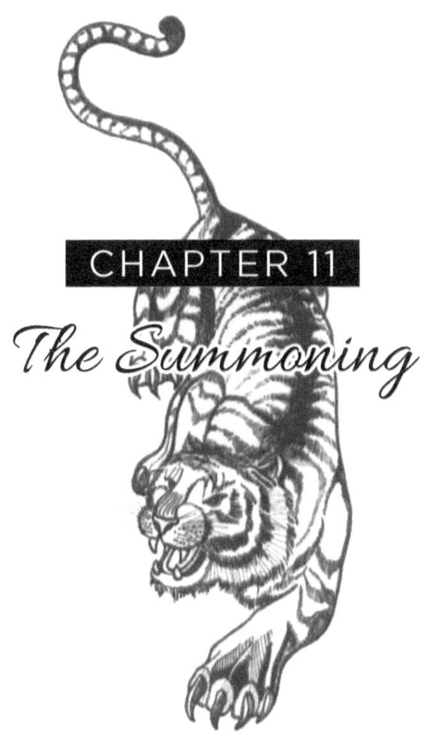

CHAPTER 11

The Summoning

ANTON OPENED HIS EYES AND struggled to examine his surroundings. His Methonian training forced him to do so automatically. With practiced expertise, he analyzed every detail his dulled senses could comprehend. Looking up, he discovered he was lying on his back in a clearing, surrounded by ancient tall trees that created a large semicircle around him. He could feel the lush young grass that filled the opening in the forest as it caressed his skin; it felt as soft to the touch as rabbit fur, and the sweet scent of the young spring flowers scattered around him delighted his nose. The air smelled abundantly of springtime, and its freshness was nearly inebriating. Instantly, it reminded him of the jungle around the village of Tooloo on Methonias and he thought maybe he had returned there. As his Methonian fortitude helped him recover, his vision quickly improved. Looking around, he could see groups of small forest creatures of all descriptions sitting at intervals around the clearing—rabbits and squirrels, birds and deer carefully watched as he slowly regained his senses.

Looking further, he noticed that he lay near the entrance of a small cave. It was difficult to see in the darkness, but a small amount of light radiated from inside, making it clearly identifiable. Opposite of that was an opening in the trees, looking over what appeared to be a deep valley. The full moon shone brightly through the gap in the trees, lighting the clearing just enough that as Anton's eyes adjusted he began to perceive most of the details around him.

Standing over him was the figure of someone he struggled to recognize in the dim light; his jumbled thoughts remained confused; he struggled to distinguish who it was. All he knew for sure was that the face was entirely unfamiliar.

"Nelda, is that you?" Anton called out. The strange personage didn't register correctly in his disoriented thoughts; he couldn't comprehend his mistake as he spoke. The only person who came to mind was his precious young wife from the Village of Tooloo; his love for her remained deeply embedded in his heart, and the scenery that surrounded him seemed somehow familiar, as if he'd been returned to the jungle back on Methonias; this only obnubilated his thoughts further. For a moment, his disorientation tricked him into perceiving what he wanted to see.

"Can you help me up, please?" he said. "I can't seem to make my body respond; my arms and legs feel tingly and numb." Straining his arm, Anton groped around, trying to grasp the hand of his love. He found nothing but air. A loud ringing filled his ears, obscuring the local sounds. He vaguely recalled the echo of thunder. The ground felt as if it was spinning in all directions underneath him; all of his senses remained completely disoriented. He shook his head, trying to regain his senses, but his body refused to improve; it felt as though it was pounding from inside, and it prickled, as if electricity had jolted his entire nervous system.

Frustrated, Anton felt anger welling up inside. The disarray of his senses and the lack of a purposeful response from his limbs quickly took its toll on his emotions. After a short time, he again struggled and then raised his head, looking into the night sky and focusing upon the full moon. It seemed unusually large, and it radiated a brilliant glow. It was so bright that as his vision cleared he had little trouble making out shapes and even some coloration around him.

Only then did Anton realize that the figure standing over him was an ancient man leaning heavily on a staff, and looking at him with deep concern. By all appearances, he seemed beyond ancient—certainly beyond the age of any man Anton had ever seen before, other than the Ruler of the Council. He had long white hair that reached to the middle of his back, and an even longer white beard that hung down to his waist. He wore a heavy robe that obviously needed replacing, hanging loosely and in tatters.

Anton abruptly sat up and examined his own body; he saw no apparent physical changes. Then his gaze fell upon his ring. It appeared azure, and it glowed brightly; this surprised him immensely. The old man fell to one knee at his side, similarly transfixed upon the ring. Unexpectedly, he snatched Anton's wrist and held it firmly. As he examined the ring closely, an expression of horror filled his eyes.

Disgruntled, Anton listened to the stranger speak; he said something incomprehensible. Anton jerked his wrist from the old man's grasp, unsure of his intentions. Dizzily, he struggled to remain sitting and took a deep breath, which helped him to manage his discomfort. His head throbbed with pain and he reached up and rubbed his temples with both hands and moaned at this condition. The man spoke unintelligibly a second time and Anton slowly shook his head from side to side, trying to make sense of his words. But they held no meaning for him.

Placing his thumb on Anton's forehead, and his fingers over the top of his head, the stranger mumbled for a moment, and then removed his hand. The pain in Anton's head immediately ceased, and his thoughts started to clear. The ringing in his ears also disappeared. A tremendous sense of relief nearly caused all the strength in his muscles to fail.

"How do you feel?" asked the stranger.

Surprised, Anton looked at him for a third time. It was strange and inexplicable that he now understood what the man said. The words sounded somehow alien, yet Anton comprehended them without effort, as if he'd always known the different tonality of the man's speech.

"I feel fine, now," Anton said, breathing a sigh of relief. His body responded correctly when he tried to move. "How is it I understand what you are saying now? Just a few moments ago, I didn't! And how is it that I feel fine when only a moment before I didn't?"

"It's a little trick I learned a long, long time ago," the man said. "My name is Vim Alpenstock. What might yours be?"

"Anton—my name is Anton Seven." Slowly, stiffly, and with great effort, he regained his feet, and then extended his hand in friendship.

Vim observed Anton's offer and stared at him puzzled. The offer was obscure to him; it had no relevance. Then he looked surprised.

"Ah yes—you desire a handshake!" Vim said. "Your brethren offered me such as well; forgive me, it's been awhile, I'd forgotten." Grasping Anton's hand, Vim shook it stiffly, smiled, and winked.

"Where am I?" Anton said, looking around. "What is this place?" "Oh yes—forgive me," Vim said. "You're on Peruvious!" His voice had a comforting, consoling sound, as if he knew much more than anyone could guess.

His irritation appeased, Anton took a deep breath, and then asked: "How did I get here, and where in the universe is Peruvious? It can't possibly be one of the Twenty Colonies; I've never heard that name before!" He sounded defensive and snobbish, and scoffed at Vim. Since his mind had cleared, he recalled the events leading up to his arrival. It seemed as though only a few minutes had elapsed since he stood in the space station orbiting Saurian Five, but he wondered how long he'd been dazed and unconscious.

"I don't know where Peruvious is in relation to your Twenty Colonies— however, I *do* know that you're from a place very, *very* far from here. To answer your first question, I summoned you to Peruvious with the aid of the Staff of Balance! Or perhaps I should say that the staff brought you here, with me as its wielder!" Vim bowed his head with a look of reverence.

Anton cocked a suspicious and confused eye at Vim. "How could a simple piece of wood be responsible for bringing me here? Additionally, how could I be on another *world* without the assistance of a spacecraft? You couldn't possibly be telling me the truth—what you're saying is quite impossible!" He was sure some machine, some device, some technology was responsible for his abduction and Vim simply refused to acknowledge the truth. Again, he looked around, trying to find it.

"Patience," Vim said. "It's a long story, and I do not wish to speak of it here. Let's retire to my cave, where we can discuss these subjects and others." Vim pointed toward the small cave nearby and started to walk toward it.

"This staff is more than a simple *piece of wood,* as you put it," Vim went on. "And I'll have you know, I *never* lie! It would be counterproductive for me."

The forest animals watched attentively as Vim headed toward the cave; they followed him wherever he went, and congregated ever closer as he approached the cave's entrance. Anton was intrigued at how they showed no signs of fear toward him; this particular simple inexplicable behavior surprised him more than anything else he'd witnessed. Nothing here seemed to make any sense. He wondered if he were still unconscious or dreaming; his perception of reality still seemed confused.

Taking a deep breath, Anton set his reasoning and suspicions aside and quickly sprang to his feet to chase after Vim. He'd regained most of his Methonian senses, and his body easily responded to his need to move, and his natural capacities for precision and deftness had completely returned after his initial muscular discomforts. He decided to evaluate the situation logically; everything at this point was an unknown, and he felt perturbed, completely out of his element, and oddly defenseless, since he didn't know what to do next.

Yanking him from Saurian Five to this strange and different place by an unknown magical means left him unconvinced of what was real and what was false; he wasn't angry enough to care, but he was apprehensive. Apparently, this Vim Alpenstock was in need of his services for some unknown reason, why else had he summoned him from across the universe? Many questions filled his thoughts and consumed him; an insatiable need for answers urged him to follow the old man if for no other reason than to find them.

"*Why* was I summoned? At the very least, I need to know the answer to this," Anton asked, pointedly. He looked directly at Vim, his expression insisting he answer straightaway.

"I will answer all of your questions," Vim replied, his tone sounding fatigued. "Please come inside." Speaking over his shoulder, Vim pushed open the door of the cave. He understood Anton's discomfort and offered a warm smile.

As they entered, Vim rested the staff against the wall just inside the entrance. This too reminded Anton of the Village of Tooloo—the way Mahkeetah had rested his scimitar next to the door of his hut. Inside, it was small and unkempt, and contained an odd assortment of items. To the left was a bookshelf containing many dusty and tattered books; they had obscure and unusual titles, offering some indefinable knowledge.

On the right, Anton saw a long table randomly littered with small pouches that contained the dust of ground materials, and vials filled with oddly colored liquids that appeared somehow active or perhaps alive. On the far end were ancient rolled-up scrolls of various sizes, piled like cordwood. Eight small-scaled chairs surrounded the table suggesting Vim periodically entertained several small guests, perhaps children. In the center of the table was a large candle that emitted an impossibly bright glow; it easily lit the entire cave.

To the back of the cave was an old unmade bed constructed of timbers that appeared as though it had little use.

Finally, in the center of the cave was a raised fire pit; embers glowed inside its walls, keeping the cave warm, dry, and cozy. It was circular in shape, and constructed of crude handmade brick; a crudely constructed chimney capped it and exited straight through the cave's ceiling. A tiny ledge of sorts projected from one side and contained many items that only Vim might understand—such as several small bags of dust, and vials of colorful liquids like those that sat upon the table. Pokers to stoke the fire hung from the opposite side. It appeared as though Vim performed some sort of alchemy or experimentations using the fire pit.

As he completed his examination of the cave's interior, Anton sat on a small chair next to the table. As he approached it, he gazed at the lone candle and marveled at its unusual capability of illumination; it was much brighter than any candle he'd ever seen. The inexplicable superabundance of luminescence confused his intellect, and again disturbed his senses. Knowing such things were impossible, he struggled to guess the candle's functionality. One after another, each of the other items on the table and then around the room drew his attention. They too warranted a closer examination. He gave each a long look, scrutinizing their import and purpose.

Breaking Anton's perplexed analysis, Vim sat next to him and prepared to enlighten him. "Now I'll answer your questions," he said. "I know you're confused and need an explanation of why I summoned you here—at least I know *I* would be if *I* suddenly found myself torn from one world to another." He mustered a friendly grin. "It's everyone's first question."

"Not to be indirect, but allow me to start with the story of Peruvious." He ran his hand through his long beard like a comb and grasped it at the bottom with the other; it was so natural it seemed as if he'd done this for a lifetime. Drawing a deep breath, he prepared himself for a long story. Making himself comfortable, he leaned back in his chair, placed his right palm on his forehead, and closed his eyes, as if visualizing the memories he'd decided to reveal.

"The present state of affairs—the devolved condition of our world—began over a thousand years ago. I was very young then, and I hadn't yet completed my learning of wizardry." Vim removed his hand from his forehead and quickly finished combing his beard; he then placed both hands on the table and folded them. Opening one eye, he looked from its corner and watched Anton's reaction.

At the word *wizardry*, Anton suddenly felt a deluge of disbelief. Wizardry and magic were the stuff of fairy tales, something he understood mothers told their small children when they went to bed—or, in Anton's case, a subject for evaluation and conjecture in the classes at the Great Temple on Methonias. Everyone knew there was no such thing; there was only science. He'd learned there was no current possibility that such things could exist, and to disbelieve any claim of such sightings.

Wizardry? Humph, thought Anton to himself, and he shook his head slightly. *This old man must be crazy.*

Taking a sudden deep breath, Anton again looked around for some device, some technology that might be responsible for his abduction; it still seemed axiomatic to him that Vim's staff couldn't produce the result that he claimed. He was convinced that his abduction had been achieved with an unknown and formidable technology that was hidden somewhere nearby; it could be the only true explanation. Cocking an eye at Vim, he heaved a sigh, intentionally exhibiting his disbelief.

Ignoring Anton's attitude, Vim continued. "This is when the overlord, Vile the necromancer, first appeared—or should I say was first discovered—on Peruvious. I believe he'd in fact been here for a very *long* time. Some people believe he came from across time and space, while others proclaimed him the antichrist, who'd returned to wreak havoc over mankind; to me, he's simply the common enemy of *all* life, and has existed since the beginning of time." Vim stared at Anton for a second, hoping to produce a reaction. Seeing none, he nodded to himself and went on with his story.

"At this time, my teacher was a man named Lothendus. People referred to him as *the great genius*. He was the apex, the superlative of scientists, and the most powerful wizard the world had ever known; he was the creator and wielder of the Staff of Balance. This staff is such a powerful artifact that only one man may touch it, unless it chooses to permit another to do so. Its powers measure a man's true character, inner strength, knowledge, and, most of all, *faith*. Anyone it gauges inferior, or of ill-intent, would be destroyed instantly if they chose to claim it for themselves without permission." Vim continued to watch Anton closely as he spoke; he could see that the other man had misgivings, and he didn't wish to alienate him.

"One day, Lothendus was on a journey to the eastern coast of Peruvious. However, before he got there, he came upon a great evil of immense proportion; he was the first to discover the Tower of Vile. It sat atop a mountain in the south, and it seemingly appeared from nowhere; I have concluded it was no longer cloaked from the eyes of humanity. But let me get back to my story. Curious as to its origin, Lothendus sought to discover where such a structure came from, and who might have built it. When he reached it, he encountered many evil creatures that the world had never known before—not even during the Eugenic Wars. Some resembled those of ancient mythology; others were completely new, and entirely unknown to mankind.

"As one might expect, a battle ensued. It was no ordinary battle, but one between incredible powers. It lasted a fortnight. The combatants unleashed forces of titanic proportions, destroying vast regions of the world. The very mountain upon which the tower stood crumbled and was cast off in a cataclysm that destroyed all but the tower itself. Little more than a spire remains of the mountain now with the Tower of Vile sitting upon its crest.

"Mortally wounded, Lothendus managed to escape. Just before his death—at least that's the popular conjecture of what happened, I have my own conclusions on that—he bestowed upon me the knowledge of the Staff of Balance; he transferred it to me using its mighty power.

Naturally, when this occurred I became a much more powerful man than I'd been previously; the staff in effect *chose* me to be its keeper, and it altered me forever!" He stretched out his arm and pointed at the staff resting near the entrance of the cave.

As Anton looked at it, he scrutinized it more closely; he noticed it had a tapered shaft, smaller at the base and thicker at the top. Capping it were three evenly space talons like the claw of a dragon, and in its grasp, it held a translucent spherical globe nearly identical in size to the *Lapillusaurus* pearl he'd hidden away in his EHD. Surprisingly, the talons never actually touched the sphere. It appeared suspended between them as they encircled the sphere, seemingly preventing it from escape. Intricately engraved runes of some archaic script covered the shaft and emitted a slight golden sheen, making the staff appear full of energy and somehow alive.

"With this great staff," Vim said, "I'm able to carry on the battle against the tyranny of Vile and his five evil lords. This malevolent entity rules as a tyrant over all of Peruvious with the aid of the Crystal Pyramid—a terrible artifact of evil wrought from the negative universe of nonexistence, as Lothendus described it to me. The Staff of Balance is the only power great enough to match this wicked relic; however, it didn't defeat it, or Vile." A look of pride showed in Vim's eyes as he described his most treasured possession. His confidence was unmistakable, and his passion was pure and honest.

Anton noted a similarity between Vim and his Masters back on Methonias. He compared several things to his past—the runes on the staff resembled those in the depths of the Great Temple, the orb of the staff resembled the *Lapillusaurus* pearl, and the Ruler and Vim were similarly aged. His logical mind quickly evaluated these points, storing them away for future reference; it was still too soon to draw any conclusion.

"By virtue of your summoning," Vim said, "I reset the balance of nature—that is, by bringing a person through from your world to Peruvious, the Staff is able to create a sort of universal balance, offsetting the perverted imbalance caused by the Crystal Pyramid. As long as you remain alive, the balance remains intact. If you were to die, the necromancer would again regain control of everything, tipping the scales in his favor—he would cast the neutral condition of the universe into ruin, perverting everything to his evil desires. Ultimately, he intends the complete destruction of humankind. I'm too old now to resist this evil; the reign of the necromancer must come to an end *soon*."

A look of despair marked Vim's face; he knew all too well the magnitude of his own words. He looked deep into Anton's eyes, trying to assess how much of his story the other man believed and accepted; he didn't want to alienate him. However, in Anton's eyes he perceived profound skepticism. With a sigh, he quickly decided to change his tactics ever so slightly.

"I know more about you than you may realize, young Warrior," Vim said. He hesitated, thrumming his fingers on the table. Then he made his move. "I must both persuade you and *ask* you for your services to help me defeat the overlord. There is no choice for me; the Crystal Pyramid must be destroyed! Together, we can send the evil overlord back to the universe of non-existence!" Vim's expression was fierce, as if controlled by madness. "Please forgive me; I'm old, and tired."

Taking a deep breath, Anton looked into Vim's eyes, sighed, and nodded. "I know precisely how you feel," he said. "I too have felt the sting of anger born from desperation."

With a look of surprise and then relief, Vim nodded his head, declaring he understood. Then he continued his explanation. "This is good. As I was saying, I brought you here for this very reason—to aid me in my personal crusade. I must apologize—it's impossible for you to return to your world in the manner in which you arrived; you're stuck with the present situation. So my question to you is this: will you help me and the people of Peruvious with this crusade?" Doubt filled Vim's heart as he asked for Anton's services. But he knew in his heart that his request would reach Anton's sense of justice, just as it had many times before with his brethren.

For a long moment, Anton was speechless. He contemplated Vim's request with concern. He had a hard time believing Vim's story, given its illogical mysticism and magic. Yet somehow, somewhere at the core of his reasoning he knew it was the truth, and he knew Vim's request was sincere. His base DNA spoke to him as clearly as Vim's words, and something in his chemistry fueled his resolve. Slowly raising his eyes to Vim's, he gazed at him with conviction. Uncontrollable responses compelled and forced his next actions. It was as if he stood beside himself and watched as someone else made the next move. Kneeling on the floor before the wizard, he bowed his head and then bared his arms, pulling his haori and tunic sleeves up. He positioned his wrists together and turned them up, showing Vim the dragon and the tiger burned onto his arms.

Vim silently gasped, delighted. Anton had removed a great weight from his heart, relieving him of a burden he couldn't manage alone. He closed his eyes and took a deep breath, letting it out slowly through his teeth.

"I'm at your service, I *am* your servant," proclaimed Anton. His word was his bond; he'd irrevocably committed himself to Vim's service; his DNA forced his compliance, something he was incapable of denying. As if using the very magic he doubted, he bound and dedicated himself to this one obligation, this single purpose—to achieve Vim's quest even if the wizard himself failed. He would either succeed or die in his service and nothing else could alter his destiny away from this.

Just as it had occurred in the Village of Tooloo, Anton's genetic engineering forced him to aid anyone with a just cause who requested his services. A Warrior's purpose entailed using his special abilities to save and protect those people who request his service, and achieve any task solicited of him. It seemed indisputable his destiny was here on Peruvious, since his Masters had demanded it as well. Fate played an important role in his life—from an unknown assignment shrouded in mystery, to being a potential hero on an unknown world.

"These markings on your arms," Vim said with relief. "I've seen them before, and I know what they represent." All of his previous champions bore the same symbols burned into their forearms, marking them indisputably as Methonian Warriors.

"They're the brands of my trade," Anton said. "I'm a Warrior of Methonias. You asked for my services, I cannot refuse such an honest and legitimate request." The tone of his voice carried conviction, and Anton returned to his feet and stretched his muscles. Some sort of change occurred in his body, filling him with anxiety, as if suddenly he'd become charged with adrenalin. He felt an urgent need to rush forth and answer the exigency of his newly instated conviction.

"You honor and gratify me," Vim responded with alleviation, hoping to calm Anton. "Now, let me have a look at your ring!"

"My ring? For what purpose?" Anton said suspiciously. Slowly, reluctantly, he raised his hand and provided Vim a proper inspection.

"If it's what I think it is, you and I may be in imminent danger. Please, allow me to *see* it!" Vim expressed more than a simple concern—his demand came in a sharp tone.

Anton started to remove his ring to offer it up to Vim. Seeing its unexpected blue coloration, he stammered, in shock, and failed to remove it. *It should be gold!* he thought to himself in confusion.

"Leave it on! I *dare not touch it!*" proclaimed Vim. He then looked at the glowing blue effulgence that emanated from the ring and gasped. Suddenly grasping Anton's wrist, he drew his hand nearer his face to inspect it. "Just as I thought," he said. "It *is* made of crystal. Is it normally this color?" His sharp question sounded fearful, as if something terrible had just occurred.

Pulling his hand away, Anton responded. "No, it's never been blue before. It should be *gold*!" He wondered how Vim could've guessed its change in color—or had he? In addition, he wondered what the change implied. But he had nothing to reference it against, so he couldn't make a logical determination.

"Being made of crystal is either the greatest boon, or the worst disaster. The Pyramid itself is made of crystal; the Staff of Balance has a Dragon Orb atop it that is a form of crystal." Vim stated the obvious facts as he contemplated the unknown. Then with more conviction, he continued. "All forms of magic are tremendously enhanced, amplified, shaped, and influenced by crystal! The color blue signifies the control that the necromancer has over it—and perhaps he will have control over *you*! We can only hope he isn't aware of this yet, although that isn't likely. I'd venture to say that if your ring remains blue, he could both know your location and your thoughts. He may even have partial or complete control over your actions. You must learn to *use* this ring for good, or the Pyramid will corrupt you. While the Crystal Pyramid exists, the ring cannot be destroyed, and must not fall into the hands of the enemy!" Vim paced back and forth, looking at the floor of his cave. Then he continued.

"But fear not!" Vim proclaimed suddenly. "I have influence over crystal too! I shall consider how to gain back the control of your ring. Perhaps the staff can gain control of it; be reassured it can never control it as the pyramid can." Vim pointed at Anton, like a father instructing a son. "We'll work on this together! However, we need a little help, from a good friend." He smiled and winked. "He always has good advice!"

"It seems to me *you* should know how to use it," Anton said. "Maybe *you* should keep it!" Confused and angry, Anton didn't like to hear that his prized ring was a possible threat against him. Hesitating, he pondered Vim's point, wondering what the old man meant by the phrase *learn to use this ring for good*.

"If this is as you say, then you keep it." This time, Anton removed the ring from his finger, holding it out for Vim to accept.

"I told you, *I dare not touch it*!" Vim replied. "Put it back on your finger! If the necromancer discovers my thoughts, he could *destroy* me. I'm getting old, and I would inevitably make a mistake. It could corrupt even *me*! When I understand this better, I shall help you learn to control it and to use it constructively. Methonians are a hearty breed, both strong and stubborn. But they're *not* immune to *mind* control. Your brethren were unfortunate enough to discover this fact."

Feeling entirely confused, Anton acceded to Vim's fear, huffed, replaced the ring on his finger, and then set aside his apprehension. "You mean to say that the other Warriors you abducted were captured by this necromancer, and their minds controlled? I find this difficult to accept!"

"I'm sorry, but it is as I say; I will have to answer this question later in greater detail; now, we must leave here at once. It is likely that Vile may know the location of my cave, this is *most* regrettable!" Vim looked troubled, as if he'd suddenly lost everything. Anton's altered ring weighed on him, and his heart felt heavy with dismay. Quickly he grabbed a few items from the table and filled hidden pockets in his robe. Then he ran to his staff and unsealed the cave's entrance.

"Where are we going?" Anton asked. "I don't have any idea where I am, and I don't know what you're planning." This was the first time in Anton's life when he didn't have a clue about his environment; he felt completely out of place and to some degree helpless. He needed some time to get his bearings, and he hoped he might find a map to improve his mental picture of the local terrain. Furthermore, he wasn't too happy about relinquishing the decision-making to an old man he didn't even know, even if that old man had enlisted his help and was the only one present with knowledge and answers.

"I have some friends, and I wish for you to meet them," Vim said. "We're off to visit the Hamlet of the Primords." Pointing outside, Vim encouraged Anton to hurry.

"Primords? Who the heck—*what* the heck are they?" Anton decided he wasn't going anywhere until he received an explanation.

Hastily, Vim responded: "The Primords are a small people of exceptional talents. They have the ability to talk to flora and fauna alike. They're less than half the size of most men—very thin and agile, and can travel great distances in a short time without the slightest detection of their passing." Vim looked at Anton, hoping his hasty description was satisfactory.

"I take it they're your friends," Anton retorted. "How might *they* be of help?" It seemed to him a small group of small people would be more in need of his help rather than receiving help from them.

"Indeed. My friends. Normally I'm not inclined to explain every choice I make—and for now, I am the one who will make *all* the choices. Suffice it to say that I know what's best suited to our present needs." Vim made sure Anton understood precisely who was in charge. "Now—let's depart. Time already works against us."

"It seems like we should be fighting this *necromancer* you speak of— not visiting these *friends* of yours."

Looking at Anton with disgust, Vim shook his head. He'd never heard such arrogance from a young man.

"You'll know *why* when we get there," he said. "Now come!" The two exited the cave, and Vim closed the heavy wooden door. Raising his arms with staff in hand, he mumbled softly, using words Anton couldn't comprehend. A slight but perceptible aura of white light emanated from the Globe on top of the staff, and then fired a beam of light at the cave's door; instantly the entrance to the cave vanished as it turned to stone. This immediately reminded Anton of how his Masters had opened the door to the Clone Lab. So many things here reminded him of home; the similarities seemed unending.

"That's incredible," Anton said with astonishment. "I would *never* have believed such a thing was possible if I hadn't seen it with my own eyes. Do you have a holographic projector around here somewhere?"

"Life in general must be difficult in a world devoid of magic, or knowledge of the powers that exist throughout the universe." Vim wasn't impressed with Anton's sarcasm, but he empathized, expressing himself with a gentle sympathetic tone, ignoring the question altogether. He understood Anton's skepticism; it wasn't entirely new to his experience. "I know not what a *holographic projector* is," he continued. "The term refers to something I vaguely remember from my distant youth—but I think I get the idea."

"Well, *science* supports life as *I* know it, not a wizard's magic," Anton replied. "I still can't believe what I'm witnessing." Anton felt he had an opportunity to prove that where he came from was superior, by virtue of its technology. "We have conveniences that you've never dreamed of," he said, "if what I have observed so far depicts your lifestyle." He spoke with smug arrogance in a demeaning tone. "In fact, our technology—"

"Technology?" Vim interrupted. "We've had technology, in the distant past, but that's another story." He did not like Anton's tone. "Technology is something from the past—not something of the present! *Magic* fulfills our needs currently."

"It's part of your distant past? You used to have technology—*here*? I see nothing of it now!" Taken aback, Anton wondered what might've happened to change the conditions on this strange world. "Where did it *go*? Where's the evidence, the remains, the proof?"

"This way of life, this usage of technology was ultimately destructive to our world; it's part of what was responsible for destroying it, but *only* a part. We had to relearn how to live without such—*conveniences*, as you put it."

Vim quickly grew tired of Anton's youthful arrogance. Again, he scowled at him, hoping to put an end to this line of conversation. "Perhaps we can discuss this at some other time," he went on. "Right now, we must depart!" He struck the heel of his staff hard upon the ground.

The ground beneath Anton's feet bucked and lurched slightly, and he looked at Vim, surprised. The simple demonstration of magic made him realize he'd overstepped his assessment of its relevance.

"We must leave quickly," Vim said. "As we travel, remain alert— Vile's creatures may be lurking everywhere." Vim looked at Anton through the slits of his eyes; he noticed his attitude had changed, and he was satisfied he'd made his point clear.

Irritated, Anton considered Vim's demand. If what the wizard had told him was true—if he in fact did know Warriors so well—he should know he'd consider things routinely. With a huff, he attuned his senses to his surroundings and focused his attention on every minute detail as he once again relied upon his Methonian training. He quickly examined the forest, the sky, and every creature in the vicinity, until he felt satisfied that all things were as they should be, and that nobody was observing them.

The wind rustled the tops of the trees, and they swayed gently back and forth. The pungent odor of spring filled Anton's nose, delighting his senses and revitalizing him. He felt eager to begin the journey.

However, there were still a couple of things that disturbed Anton's attention; he wondered why the forest creatures patiently lingered around Vim. They seemed perpetually interested in him, following him and watching every detail of his activities. Furthermore, even after Vim had impatiently demanded that Anton hurry to leave the cave, he still took the time to coddle the wildlife. A deer approached him and received a gentle pat on the head and a quick scratch behind the ear, followed by a kind and gentle, "Goodbye, old friend." Anton wondered what had happened to Vim's sense of urgency.

The two men walked toward a large opening in the trees, overlooking a deep valley below, and Vim pointed to a trail leading downward. "We will use this trail," he said. "It leads to the Primord's hamlet."

The two carefully started their descent down the winding path cut into the side of the cliff; it was very narrow and zigzagged steeply. The animals followed only to the edge of the cliff, and then stayed behind in the clearing. It seemed as if they too wanted to go, but unhappily chose to remain behind. This too perplexed Anton, but he also felt relieved.

The two men descended into the dark unknown valley below. Anton felt out of place. He did not trust his footing in the soft uneven ground, and found himself taking extra care to follow Vim. The trail was so narrow that it reminded him of the trail leading to the caverns of the Troglodytes back on Methonias. The moon was still high overhead, though it had moved considerable distance across the sky since his late-night arrival. It shone brightly, illuminating much of the valley. But the side of the canyon they traversed remained occluded from its radiance. This added to the hazardous footing; loose rocks and soft dirt continually slipped underfoot.

Vim lighted the globe of his staff with his wizard's magic, and it illuminated their way; that helped to eliminate much of the risk of slippage. He provided the light they needed, but Anton ached for daylight as a better aid for traveling; the globe's illumination precluded stealth. His anticipation grew with each step. He desired to be free of the treacherous climb. He watched Vim's practiced skill at avoiding even the smallest obstacles. Years of experience over the same path had honed an impressive physical grace in the old man; Anton felt hardpressed to match Vim's smoothness, but he masterfully mimicked the wizard's moves as if he'd followed behind him for years.

Anxiety continued to fill Anton's heart as he anticipated the next phase of his life; a new adventure was just what he needed to fulfill his design intent. He relished the opportunity. The early morning air felt cool and refreshing on his skin, and he breathed it in deeply. It filled his lungs with vitality; it was as refreshing to him as drinking from an icy mountain stream. Everything seemed in place.

After roughly an hour, they arrived at the bottom of the valley, just as the first signs of dawn made their appearance in the sky above.

CHAPTER 12

The Primords

AS THE TWO MEN DESCENDED into the valley, Vim used the time to ponder the youthful attitude of his latest champion. His tremendous age and intuitive nature gave him knowledge, insight, and wisdom well beyond anyone else on Peruvious. Having worked with several Methonian Warriors in the past, he knew that Anton's training was remarkable, especially for his youth. Yet his demeanor was incredibly self-important and arrogant, unlike his brothers. How was he to work with such an egocentric youth? Rarely had he met someone with such an air of indifference towards a people he hadn't yet met, and a way of life he didn't yet understand, especially when his training supposedly precluded this attitude.

In his heart, he hoped that if Anton made some new friends, his attitude might soften. He wanted him to identify with and care about people, and knew that if they became important enough to him, they might change his perspective. Vim believed the good he saw in Anton would mature into something he could be proud of, that his service would be a blessing and salvation for all of Peruvious, and all of humanity. But for now, he had reservations; his arrogance was reckless. He was nervous; he was far too old to be parenting and mentoring someone who was little more than a teen. But his predicament left him very few options.

The cool early morning air felt invigorating against Anton's skin; it urged him to move quickly. His breath appeared before him as he exhaled, reminding him the temperature was just a few degrees above freezing. His haori and hakama sufficed to keep him warm, and his hearty Methonian physique provided him with a natural resistance. He was quite used to the cold climate of the northern mountains on Methonias. But Vim traveled slower than he would have liked.

Underneath his tunic, Anton was leaner and more muscular than he outwardly appeared; yet his incredible strength made it clear to anyone he was more than an average human. In contrast, Vim was ancient, and he appeared somewhat frail; his robes hung in disrepair around him and he puffed and labored as he walked through the forest and down the path along the valley floor. Both of them seemed minimally prepared for the coolness of the early morning.

The moon had long since passed its zenith, and it barely lit their path now. It no longer aided them as it did on their long descent into the valley; the sun was beginning to show the first signs of the pending dawn. It faintly tinted the eastern horizon with beautiful streaks of orange and yellow, obscuring the stars. Anton calculated that it would be daybreak in less than an hour.

Soon the trail broke through the thin band of forest and continued along the edge of a wide and fast-flowing river. Anton looked over his shoulder periodically, and at intervals, he could see the valley wall they'd just traversed towering over the tops of the ancient trees that lined the river. The enormous trees were perhaps more than a thousand years old, and had large growths of strange moss hanging abundantly from every branch, as if the forest had chosen to disguise itself. Scattered here and there were large dead branches that had fallen from far above—more evidence of the forest's age.

All the trees Anton had encountered since his arrival resembled the hybrids found throughout the Twenty Colonies, although they had a few slight differences. They looked identical to the fir and pine trees of ancient Earth; Anton had learned about these at the Great Temple but had never seen them firsthand. He analyzed with great interest the exactness of their shape; it seemed more than coincidental that they'd be of a classic Earth origin, a planet said to have been destroyed over a thousand years ago.

Something seemed to nag at the back of his mind about this, yet he set it aside for further consideration later.

"We'll have to cross the Putucu River. The hamlet is on that island in the middle—you can just barely see it." Vim pointed across the water, but Anton found it difficult to distinguish what might be the island and what might be the bank of the far side of the river.

Grasping Anton's wrist, Vim summoned up the energy of his staff, and its globe instantly illuminated their path in the dim morning light. The luminescence from the crystal globe increased in magnitude, and soon burned pure argent, creating a lighted aura around the two travelers. A brilliant golden sphere of energy surrounded them, and they began to ascend a short distance into the air. Concentrating, Vim directed their travel across the water. They silently skimmed its surface, as if encased in a thin glass bubble made of a shining golden light.

Anton felt stunned by this; he couldn't believe his senses. It took no time to cross the water, and they quickly approached the tree-covered island that Vim had described. In less than a minute, the two touched down on the sandy bank, and Vim extinguished the power of his staff.

"Why didn't you just use this method of transportation to get us down the mountain?" Anton said in a voice that was sharp and direct.

"In the darkness, and high in the sky, it's far too risky," Vim replied. "The enemy could easily observe us if any of his eyes are nearby—and most assuredly they are! By simply skimming across the river in the early light of the day, we were low enough and only visible for a minute. Besides, how else could we have crossed the river? Do you see an alternative? Now, don't question my judgment again!" Vim tapped the ground with the staff, and a ripple of energy coursed through the earth, causing a vibration.

"Let's finish our walk to the hamlet," Vim continued. "We're nearly there!" Returning Anton's angry look, the old man reminded him of who was in charge, and that his decisions were final.

"My apologies, my master," Anton replied, with a slight bow. But he never allowed his eyes to leave Vim's glare.

"Harrumph," Vim whispered, under his breath. "Very well, then— follow me." Stiffly, he stretched out his arm, pointed into the woods, and grasped his staff with both hands. Exhausted, he pushed himself to lead the way.

The two walked a short distance through the trees, until they came upon a slight yet distinct trail much like a dear path. They followed it a short distance, and then, suddenly, the trees broke away, revealing a small clearing containing the hamlet of the Primords.

Looking over his shoulder toward the eastern horizon, Anton noticed a tall snowcapped mountain that stretched skyward; it broke through the surrounding forest and overshadowed the top of the valley. The morning sunlight accentuated its majestic features; it was tall and pointed at the top, and majestic and predominant against the sky. Anton felt a mysterious longing to visit it; it seemed he could reach out and touch it with his hand, and he wanted to do so. He wondered why he felt drawn to this mountain; it was a feeling he'd never experienced before.

Vim observed Anton's gaze and perceived his admiration of the snow-covered peak. "That mountain range is the Great Divide, it separates the eastern and western halves of Upper Peruvious. We call that mountain peak *Loomspire*."

"What an odd name," Anton said, nodding his head slightly as he absorbed the mountain's beauty. "It really is captivating. It reminds me of, well, my home."

"Indeed!" Vim said, both surprised and pleased that his new companion had a positive impression of the beauty around him. He hoped these feelings would continue to develop.

"The white peak reminds me of the mountains back on Methonias," Anton went on. "In the north where I come from, the Great Temple is built into the side of a mountain similar to that." He pointed to the top of Loomspire. He remembered his last few days on Methonias, and the events leading to his assignment on Peruvious; a sense of longing to return made him feel lonely. After a few long moments, he returned his attention to Vim and the clearing.

The tiny hamlet of the Primords stood before Anton. Encompassing the entire village was a primitive wall made of logs; they were positioned tightly together, much like the wall of an old-fashioned fortress. Between the posts was a substance that appeared to be some sort of wood putty used to fill the gaps. Upon closer examination, Anton realized that in fact the wood had somehow fused, creating a perfect seal. From a military perspective, it was obvious that the palisade served poorly as a line of defense; it would be a simple matter to climb over it in several ways. It struck Anton as odd that someone would've gone to such trouble to build a defensive perimeter that offered so little protection.

Contained inside the wall, the Primords had constructed oddly shaped dwellings in a circle around the base of each tree; their roofs were living boughs that grew downward from the center trunk; no doors or windows were evident. The dwellings appeared entirely unusable. Fascinated by what he saw, Anton struggled to interpret the purpose of the unique design.

"In what manner were these dwellings fabricated?" he asked. "They look like a sort of fused wood, and yet they appear to be living!" He suspected it was another form of inexplicable magic. Again, he shook his head in disbelief.

"This is the thaumaturgy of the Primords," Vim explained. "They've learned to weave their wizardry with both the plant and animal life—excepting what the Crystal Pyramid has deformed, their abilities cannot touch that. As you can see, their magic works harmoniously with the trees, allowing them to continue to live, and to be stronger and healthier too. It is a sort of symbiotic relationship, you might say. In this way, the structures don't require repair or replacing—only occasional shaping and pruning." Pointing at the homes as he spoke, Vim seemed somehow proud of the special skills the Primords possessed—almost as if he'd had a hand in them somehow.

"Likewise," Vim continued, "as I have said, their magic works with animals. They have the delightful ability to speak to them—a gift that is rare indeed on Peruvious. Even *I* don't have their skill level—though I too can communicate with the animals."

Vim's words alluded to many things, yet concealed even more. Anton's curiosity was so intense and diverse he wasn't quite sure where to begin. Everything was so new that he had difficulty analyzing it; everything was happening so quickly he didn't have enough time to examine things as closely as he needed to. He was both relatively speechless and unremittingly hungry to learn more; this paradox seemed impossible to overcome, and he felt as though time was working against him.

"You must teach me more of this... *magic* you speak of," he said. "I'm sure it will come in handy for me." With a sheepish look, Anton mumbled his request. He felt more and more displaced in this new world; more importantly, he had little understanding of the ramification of his request.

But he realized he needed to learn the usage of the available weapons if he was to fight against them.

"Indeed!" Vim replied. "You *must* learn about magic. You have little choice in the matter! You, more than anyone else, will *require* it!" Pointing at Anton and poking his shoulder, Vim smiled and chuckled.

In his heart, he felt delighted at Anton's simple request. "Now, you will be given an important demonstration of the Primords' magic. Fear not, my friend! Observe!"

The two stood quietly in the center of the hamlet, and looked at each other as they waited. Presently, the sun peeked over the treetops as it began its daily journey across the sky. The first warming rays stretched their fingers of light into the edge of the clearing, and a sense of awakening filled the atmosphere. The sun rose ever higher over the ancient trees along the nearby shoreline, and it peeked through the branches, flooding its warmth and sunlight in wide stripes throughout the entire clearing.

"Behold! The awakening occurs!" Vim spread his arms wide and raised his staff into the air, as if conducting a musical performance.

Suddenly, and to Anton's utter amazement, throughout the entire hamlet, windows flew open simultaneously from all of the dwellings, where there hadn't been any just a moment before. He struggled to comprehend how this was possible; the walls of the dwellings were completely featureless. Yet now windows existed everywhere he looked. Then, just as suddenly, doors appeared in the same mysterious manner, bursting open in unison from every dwelling.

Just as unexpectedly, little people emerged from inside the dwellings. They ran from their homes, giggling and merry, doing cartwheels and acrobatics. Abruptly, as if someone had given them a signal, they all began to sing and dance in unison.

Examining the strange little outfits the Primords wore, Anton shook his head in disbelief; their appearance seemed silly and strange even to his impartial eyes. They wore long green hats, pointed at the top with a large fuzzy ball on a short string that flopped back and forth as they pranced around. All of them had different colors of clothing, yet all were of the same design. The men had long-sleeved shirts with turned up cuffs and a V-shaped neckline in the front; each end of the oversized collar came to a point, and the bottom of the shirt below the waist had a cuff. They also wore long shorts and tights like knickers, with cuffs at the knees. Their shoes matched their hats; they were green and pointed at the toes, curling over the top with a tiny fuzzy ball hung from the point that bobbled and bounced as they danced. The women were similarly dressed; the only difference was a skirt that hung just above their knees, which replaced the long shorts that the men wore.

There were about fifty of the little people, and they formed two circles around Anton and Vim, dancing in opposite directions. The girls formed the inner circle and the boys formed the outer. Their voices were high-pitched, with a lilting falsetto tonality that sounded strange to Anton's ears.

Laughing in spite of himself, Anton thought for a moment he was in a circus. "It's like some kind of a fairy tale!" he chuckled out loud. "I must be dreaming; I've never seen antics such as this! You called them Primords, but they remind me of the ancient mythical stories about little elves!"

Hearing his words, the entire community laughed, and then danced and sang some more:

We are the people of the forest, the animals are our friends, we dance to show our love of them, the fun never ends!

Merrily we sing and dance at dawn, we start the day off right, the moon has gone to sleep for now, as the sun shares its light.

The mighty Wizard brings a friend, his name we do not know, his face is oh so new to us, we hope he'll never go!

Will he be our hoped-for champion, and defeat our distant foe, or will he succumb to wicked evil, and give us only sorrow?

All hope weighs upon him, his failure brings despair, the enemy works against us, our support we now must share.

They sang and danced arm in arm, twirling about. Happiness filled the air. All the forest animals sat patiently around the perimeter, watching. Vim chuckled at Anton's perplexed reaction. Smiling, he reached out with his hand and slowly pointed at the merriment.

"They honor your arrival and show their respect for your presence," Vim said, glowing with a look of parental pride, as if the little people were his children—or, perhaps more appropriately, his grandchildren.

The Primords song gave Anton a moment to reflect upon his brief visit, of the morning, and of Anton's arrival to Peruvious, and it made him ponder the importance of their expectation that he would be their savior by ending the oppression of the necromancer. This altered Anton's mood from happy though bewildered, to thoughtful and serious—his smile vanished as the joyful singing reminded him of his new responsibilities.

Noticing Anton's abrupt seriousness, the Primords promptly stopped their activities. One of them walked over to him. With a long and respectful bow, he introduced himself. "Good day to you, young man," he said, in a high-pitched voice. "My name is Beelif!" Tipping his hat, he offered a friendly smile, rubbed his tiny little nose with the back of his hand, and then replaced his hat.

"So, what is *your* name, big Warrior?" Bowing again, he smiled and offered his hand to Anton.

"My name is Anton," Anton said, grasping Beelif's hand with some surprise. He shook it gently, smiled, and returned his bow. "You know how to shake hands!" he said. "How is it you know this custom and Vim didn't?"

"Ah, you should know!" he said. "I have met Warriors before! Vim simply, well, *forgets* elementary customs! Please—this way, follow me!" He again grasped Anton's hand and gave it a slight tug. "It's time forbreakfeast1! Come, join us, skinny boy! I can tell that you need food! Your stomach announces its demand!"

Leading the way, Beelif pointed across the clearing. He tugged harder at Anton's hand, pulling him along like a horse drawing a heavily laden cart.

Submitting to the graciousness of his host, Anton allowed him to lead the way. All the Primords quickly swarmed about the two visitors, pushing and pulling each of them along toward the north end of the hamlet, where two very long tables were prepared for a meal; someone had piled them beyond their capacity with food.

When he saw the tables heavily laden, Anton's stomach once again growled loudly, announcing his immense hunger. He was extremely thankful for the opportunity to eat. A sense of bewilderment marked his face as he wondered how these tiny people had done so much preparation without his notice and in such short order. But he set the thought aside as just another peculiarity of Peruvious. At the least-populated table, he saw two larger seats that were clearly intended for the humans. They sat. Anton was the last one sitting.

The festive scene instantly reminded Anton of his recent graduation feast; however, after inspecting the selection of food, he realized that nothing looked familiar. The synthesized food on Methonias bore little if any resemblance to the food he now beheld. Even the food he'd experienced in the various regions of Methonias during training missions looked quite different. One particular dish caught his attention, though it almost took away his appetite. It appeared to be a loaf of bread, only it was bright green with yellow swirls, and covered with little black speckles that glistened. For the most part, everything seemed palatable enough. Given his hunger, Anton quickly served himself from some of the more appealing items. The first was a fair amount of a dark brown meat that looked as if it were smoked or dried and smelled delicious. Next, he selected a large half of an oval-shaped fruit. The skin was thick and bright green; the center meat was dark blue, surrounding one large seed. The next dish that passed by contained some sort of sweet bread covered with honey; it was about the only recognizable item.

The strange foods were repeatedly passed around the table, and quickly disappeared as everyone ate. Anton hungrily consumed everything—but only after carefully inspecting each item he selected.

Everyone ate ravenously, as if they had been starved for a week. The only exception was Vim, who ate very slowly, as if he weren't particularly hungry. Concurrently he held a private conversation with Beelif about something Anton couldn't hear over the noise and distraction of the other Primords.

Soon everyone had finished eating, and Beelif stood and raised his hand to gain their attention. Clearing his throat, he looked quickly back and forth around the gathering; a sudden hush filled the air and the tiny Primords rustled in their seats in anticipation. Vim sat quietly, hardly noticing what went on around him; he seemed far away in thought as he stared at nothing in particular and slowly finished the last remnants of his meal. Next to him, Anton sat in complete readiness; the years of endless conditioning compelled his body and mind into full alertness. All the Primords around the tables shushed each other and gave Beelif their undivided attention. When all was quiet, he made his announcement.

"Today is a day to be remembered, and to rejoice. Vim, the great Wizard of Upper Peruvious, and our closest friend, has delivered to us a *new* savior from the unknown regions of the universe, by wielding the tremendous power of the Staff of Balance." Reaching suddenly for a large goblet, Beelif raised it high into the air, preparing for a toast.

"Here's to the arrival of our new savior!"

All of the Primords quickly followed suit, raising their goblets into the air, and taking an enormous draft of the liquid contained within. Jolly cheering resounded from the table. It was self-evident to Anton that he was participating in an unusual celebration of remarkable significance to these people, not just a simple meal. There was more significance to his arrival than he could guess.

Out of politeness to the Primords, Anton took a sip from his goblet too. Giving it a long look, he examined the dark purple liquid as it slowly sloshed around like molasses. Promptly raising it into the air, he looked around as everyone watched, and then put it to his lips for a small sip. To his surprise, he found it quite delightful; the liquid was thick, heavy, and sweet like a liqueur was said to be, something he was completely unaccustomed to, and it tasted like a mixture of berries and honey. As it traveled down to his stomach, it warmed him inside. A tremendous smile involuntarily forced itself upon his face. A tingling sensation filled and stimulated every nerve throughout his body. The feeling so surprised him that he felt compelled to take another, larger draft.

"I see our new friend likes my Berrybrew!" Beelif said, smiling enormously—a smile that only the rare liqueur could produce. Then he laughed heartily.

"Cheers to the newcomer!" shouted everyone in unison as they all raised their goblets in the air for another toast, and then drank deeply.

"Berrybrew is a potent potion," Beelif said. "It will do you good, young Anton! Drink more, and reap the benefit!" He smiled. "It's a spiritual experience. It will cleanse your mind and body—something I believe you need. Am I correct?"

The entire gathering broke out laughing; all eyes fell upon Anton, watching him to see if he would accept Beelif's request.

Puzzled, Anton wondered what Beelif meant. For a second it seemed as though he somehow knew of his struggle with the *Virlaqueus*, and of his love for Nelda. But he knew there was no way that that was possible.

"I think we all need a little help with that from time to time," Anton replied. Uncontrollably compelled by the Berrybrew, he grinned from ear to ear, and pondered the implication of Beelif's remark.

"Ha ha!" Beelif replied. "This is true! You've never reaped the rewards that Berrybrew offers. You *must* finish—bottoms up!" With a broad smile, Beelif held up his goblet as if to toast again. He took another deep draft, emptying the goblet, and then smacked his lips. "Ahhh," he said. "You are correct—I too needed *more!*" Wiping the remainder from his lips with the back of his sleeve, he exaggerated his satisfaction.

Uncontrollably grinning, Anton looked down into his goblet. A strong tingling sensation burned throughout his bloodstream. His heart pumped harder and faster, speeding the effects of the Berrybrew to every part of his body. Without restraint, he again raised the goblet to his lips and happily finished the liqueur. Mimicking Beelif, he too smacked his lips and wiped the excess from his mouth with the back of his sleeve.

"Bravo! Our new friend is now one of us!" Beelif said, quickly jumping up on the table, and raising both hands in the air to dance a celebratory jig.

Uproarious laughter filled the air as everyone enjoyed Beelif's playful performance. Around the table, each of the Primords finished their Berrybrew, smacked their lips, and wiped the excess with the back of their sleeves. Then they too danced merrily around; arm in arm they looked like a band of frolicsome children.

As if summoned to join in, Vim also stood and finished his goblet. He too smacked his lips, wiped the final drops from his mouth with the back of his sleeve, and grinned from ear to ear, compelled by the mighty effects of the potent liqueur. "A marvelous potion you make, my dear Beelif! Remember, we need more of it for our travels!"

"I made plenty—fear not, great Wizard!" Continuing to dance, Beelif swung around, arm-in-arm with each of the young ladies in turn.

After a short time, the dancing ended, and all of the Primords turned toward Anton. They looked at him intently with wide smiles. Beelif took one step forward, placed his fingers on each temple, and appeared to concentrate. He stared at Anton with a strained expression.

Can you hear my thoughts, young man? Beelif said, though his lips never moved.

Suddenly, Anton realized what had happened; he'd heard Beelif's voice not with his ears but inside his head. Mouth agape, he jumped to his feet. "What just happened?" he said, sharply. "How did you do that?"

Undaunted, Beelif smiled. Not with your *voice*, with your *mind*, great Warrior. *Think* your words and I will *hear* your thoughts! Responding again with only his mind, Beelif reinforced his ability to communicate mentally. It's the effect of the Berrybrew! We can speak to each other with our thoughts!

Anton was astonished; he'd learned from his Masters that some people had a rare gift of telepathy, but he hadn't entirely believed it was possible, since he'd never met anyone with the talent. Smiling, he decided to test Beelif's claim.

I hear you. Do you hear me? thought Anton.

I hear you loud and clear! We, all of us here, can hear your thoughts! replied Beelif. Now you are ready to *hear* a story! It's the story of our previous champion, for you a brother Warrior. Beelif looked serious for a moment, and then smiled hugely as he looked around. Vim has given me permission to entertain everyone with its telling.

Everyone laughed aloud, as if Beelif had told a riotous joke. "As if *you* need his permission, Beelif!" cheered several of the Primords out loud. "And, we didn't hear you ask his permission!" Laughter filled the hamlet, as all of the Primords quickly returned to their seats.

A mixture of both thought and voices filled Anton's ears, confusing him. Even more puzzling was how the Primords seemed to collectively share the same thought and express themselves in unison. The details of the effects surpassed his comprehension.

Continuing to stand, Vim raised his hand to gain everyone's notice. "My dear Beelif, you'd never ask my permission for anything! Besides, we all know you're the *greatest* teller of a yarn Peruvious has ever known!" Returning to his seat, he chuckled quietly and looked at Beelif from the corner of his eye.

Once more, the entire Hamlet laughed heartily, whistled, and applauded. Beelif quickly stood upon his seat and again raised his hands into the air so everyone could see him better. Vim leaned back in his seat and gave Beelif his undivided attention. Yet a look of concern covered his face. Only the remnants of a grin disguised his true feelings.

As you all know, this is not a happy tale, but our new champion deserves to hear it so that he might know what it is he must champion against! Hopefully he will avoid the same pitfalls Boris met. Thinking his words, he communicated telepathically to convey his message.

Instantly Anton looked at Beelif. *Boris?* he thought. There is no doubt this *is* where all the other Warriors were abducted to. First Vim and now Beelif confirmed that all the abducted Warriors had come here to Peruvious. He knew it was his duty to learn everything about their fate and to take the information back to his Masters if possible. He listened intently to the story.

Beelif then turned his attention to Anton and gave him a stern look. "We hear your thoughts and understand your concern, which is why I chose to tell you this story. Before I begin, may we all know by what name you wish to be addressed?"

Confused, Anton shook his head. Why do you ask? You already know my name is Anton. Taking a deep breath, he realized they wished to know more than his first name—they wanted to know his title.

"My name is Anton Seven; I'm a Methonian Warrior, and the wielder of the Blue Flame Sword." Speaking aloud, Anton chose to answer the question verbally; it felt more natural and somehow more satisfying.

Instantly a clamor of excited chatter chorused around the table; a look of either horror or great uncertainty covered the faces of everyone—all except Vim, who sat quietly and disclosed no visible emotion. However, when he heard Anton say "wielder of the Blue Flame Sword," it struck a chord in him, and he nearly fell from his seat.

"What is this Blue Flame Sword?" Vim demanded. "Tell me now!" He suddenly stood and raised his staff into the air, positioning himself in a defensive posture. He looked at Anton with fire in his eyes and fear in his heart.

Slowly standing, Anton looked carefully around the gathering, as if surveying several opponents; he snatched the Sword of Blue Flame from its holster with blindingly quick reflexes, revealing the great symbol of self-mastery and the power of protection and justice that his Masters had awarded him at his graduation. Silently from the shiny silver hilt sprang forth a three-foot length of fire in the shape of a sword's blade; like a neon sign, the flame burned a glowing cobalt blue. A great hush fell over the gathering as the glow punctured the morning atmosphere.

Silence spoke louder than words, and Anton noticed revulsion on each face of the Primords, only Vim remained undaunted, as if he were impervious to surprise. With his staff in one hand, he grasped at his beard with the other, nervously combing it with his fingers as he studied the burning sword. He scrutinized its unusual characteristics; the dark cobalt-blue lasers creating the blade fascinated him.

Then, just as suddenly as it appeared, the burning blue blade of fire vanished. Anton returned the hilt to its holster so quickly that it was as if he'd never revealed it at all.

The entire community sat motionless for a moment. Vim returned to his seat and restlessly repositioned his staff against his shoulder. "We'll discuss this later," he said concernedly to Anton, his alarm well pronounced on his face. He then returned his attention to Beelif.

"Your story, old friend, let's hear your story!" Vim tried to return the attention to Beelif's account of Boris. With a half-hearted forced smile, he grasped his goblet and raised it toward Beelif. "Another round?" he asked.

Without further prompting, one of the young ladies quickly filled everyone's goblet from a large pitcher. "Drink!" she said, and smiled as she happily complied with Vim's request.

Raising his goblet into the air, Vim then took a long draft from it and smiled widely. In unison, everyone else followed suit, and everyone's attitude returned to exhilaration.

"You're correct, my dear wizard!" Beelif said. "My story!" He spread his arms and looked around. A toast to our new champion! he thought for everyone to hear. Raising his goblet high for the final toast, he then finished it off in one long drink, grinned from ear to ear, smacked his lips, and wiped the remainder from his lips with the back of his sleeve. Now, let me begin!

Looking around at all his friends, Beelif sat the goblet upon the table and placed both hands there. Then, unexpectedly, he quickly climbed upon it and gestured methodically. As quickly as the food had appeared for breakfeast, the empty dishes suddenly vanished. Slowly, Beelif walked up the table's length, rubbed his chin in contemplation, and then sharply turned around. Closing his eyes, he concentrated, straining to enter the thoughts of everyone. As if a CHP had suddenly turned on, images entered everyone's minds, like a movie projected into their thoughts.

Gasping, Anton shifted in his seat, distressed with the new sensation. He didn't care for someone forcing their own thoughts into his mind. Closing his eyes, he strained to regain control, but the Berrybrew had destroyed the barriers of this Methonian mental discipline that he'd worked so hard to develop. After a moment, he realized his struggle was unfounded, and he uncomfortably submitted to Beelif's story unfolding inside his psyche.

CHAPTER 13

Those Who Mourn the Damned

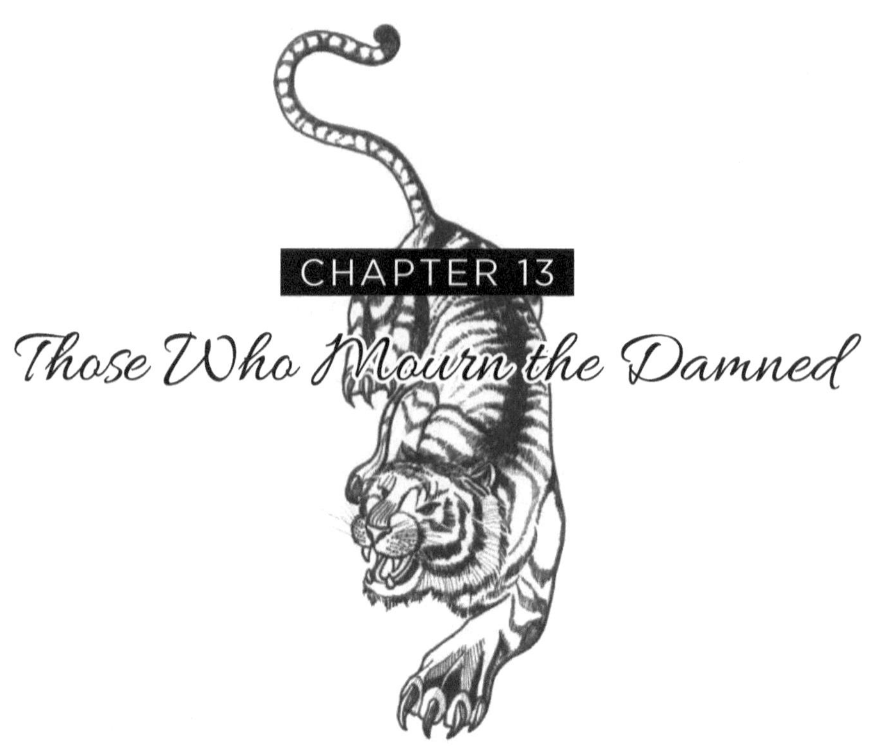

WOULD EVERYONE PLEASE MOVE TO the center of the hamlet? We've prepared a comfortable place to listen, Beelif said, using his Berrybrew-induced skill to speak.

Already, Anton was adapting to this new form of communication. He barely noticed the difference between sound and telepathy. He was so used to expanding his thoughts through meditation that he barely sensed the difference between sound and thought.

Looking toward the center of the clearing, Anton saw chairs set in a semicircle around another chair. Beelif ran over to seat himself in front of everyone and then placed his fingers against his temples; an intense look of concentration covered his face.

It didn't take long for everyone to find a seat. Just like at breakfeast, there were two larger chairs positioned in the rear of the semicircle to accommodate Anton and Vim.

If everyone will concentrate, Beelif said, I'll place the story in your minds. Opening his eyes, Beelif continued to focus his thoughts; without warning, the images he chose to share gently forced themselves into the imagination of his audience, along with the words needed to tell the story.

Relaxed, and without objecting, Anton allowed Beelif's telepathic panorama to enter his mind; an image of Vim's cave filled his thoughts as if it were a holographic image in front of him. He perceived the images as if he stood nearby, observing them. They unfolded before him, yet he wasn't actually part of what occurred, and had no capacity to shape or influence it. I wonder how he does this, he thought. If only I could learn this trick without the aid of a potion.

Hearing Anton's thoughts, Beelif helped him understand what he was seeing: These are called 'etheric records.' Permanently burned into the atmosphere by all living things, they are available to those who know of them, and know how to invoke them. The Berrybrew opens the barrier and allows me to reach into the dimension where these records exist, and I'm able to bring them to life and share them. You can observe the events of the past, hear the thoughts of the people you see, know their feelings, and listen to them speak to each other. You can feel the atmosphere, smell your surroundings, and yet remain untouched by them, and unable to touch them. It's impossible to change or influence what has occurred in the past; you cannot alter the events. In this way, the truth of the past is available to the observer.

Quietly, Anton allowed the experience to unfold. Immediately he recognized the similarity of the etheric records to his CHP. The incredible difference was in how the experience was communal; he could feel the thoughts of all the Primords around him; it was as if they all shared one thought, as if he were part of them, and they were part of him. Their thoughts became part of his, and he knew things about all of them, and about Vim—things that he couldn't have known only an hour ago. As he allowed his mental disciplines and barriers to dissipate, their feelings and knowledge became part of him, as did the experience unfolding in front of him.

The first thing Anton could see was Vim's cave, sitting near the edge of the valley; he and the Primords stood together around the perimeter of the clearing, observing the scene as if they were separated from it, yet part of it. As Beelif continued to concentrate, more of the details filled in.

Allow me to give you a little background before I set the etheric records into motion, Beelif began, concentrating further. It was late in the evening, and Vim stood outside his cave, looking towards the moon. It hung low on the horizon, full, and glowed with a reassuring intensity as it lighted the entire clearing. It nearly filled his view of the sky between the gap in the trees as it slowly rose from the skyline. Its surface features were easily distinguishable, and he gazed upon it, studying them as he'd done throughout his life. He knew that while the moon remained a shining white, there was still hope for Peruvious. Leaning on his staff, he thought of the long struggle for freedom he'd fought for, for more than a millennium.

Vim had been a young apprentice when Vile the necromancer appeared on Peruvious. At that time, the world was a very different place. The world as he had known it when he was a young apprentice was unreservedly destroyed by the time he was an adult. There seemed to be little hope of the world today returning to what it had been in the distant past—nothing *could* ever be the same again. Beelif helped fill out his story; he added many details to help Anton understand more about Vim and his character, and to grasp the significance of his life's struggle, much the way Anton had done using his CHP for the villagers of Tooloo.

Vim's whole heart ached to see an end to Vile's tyranny over the entire realm. Fundamentally, this evil entity had upset the perfect balance of nature—and even worse, the foundation of existence itself. Indeed, that was his purpose and intent. With his mighty Crystal Pyramid, he systematically destroyed everything; this was the source of all destruction and evil on Peruvious; it unbalanced the staff itself, the staff that bound and held together the very 'Law of Balance.' It created its own warped form of stability, disrupting the natural order of life. This was against the natural stability of the universe, for the impossibility of unbalancing that which cannot be unbalanced is therefore in itself the source of the annihilation of existence. Beelif's thoughts echoed both his feelings and the reality they all faced—it seemed he might break into tears as he told his story.

Taking a deep breath, Beelif sighed, and then continued. Vim knew this all too well, and therefore he wielded the Staff of Balance to summon a champion from beyond the Peruvian realm, far from outside the terrestrial world. The effect of doing so offsets the Pyramid's unnatural balance and again brings everything into alignment, resetting nature, and returning it to a state of normality. He had done this for the past nine hundred years, summoning a new champion every fifty years on the spring equinox. This is the only time counterbalancing can be achieved; it is the exact balancing point in the universe for such things. Yet each time Vim did this, Vile in turn destroyed the new champion to regain his own unbalanced order.

Five years before this time, Vim had summoned the latest champion from beyond Peruvious. Reaching out with the power of his staff into the vast universe, he grasped yet another Methonian Warrior to help fight his cause. His latest champion, Boris Two, was still alive and active, as the white moon evidenced. Looking at Anton's face, Beelif wanted to see his expression, not just feel his thoughts. He was impressed with the Warrior's ability to adjust to this new form of communication; never had a Methonian Warrior done so well so quickly and Beelif realized that Anton must have developed superior mental abilities.

Three days had passed since Boris had last reported in to Vim, and Vim's concern intensified with each passing hour. It was unusual for him not to at least send a message. If Boris was killed it would be another forty-four and a half years until the next opportunity to bring another champion through from beyond Peruvious occurred, and the thought gnawed at him as he gazed upon the heavens. Completing his narration, Beelif hesitated, concentrated, and then set the etheric records into motion.

"I *have* TO SEE THE defeat of Vile this time," Vim sighed. "I just don't have it in my aging heart to try again." He leaned heavily upon his staff as his concerns were evident to everyone. He knew something was amiss—he knew Boris was in trouble, and he was afraid to find out why.

"I must see the destruction of the Crystal Pyramid," he shouted toward the night sky, with his arms spread wide. A tear rolled down his cheek as he drew his staff between his arms and hugged it—as if that could remove the pain that pierced his heart. A warm golden glow radiated softly from the globe in response. Vim's love for Peruvious, and his passion for the survival of humanity, drove his feelings of both hope and trepidation. Despite his usual staunch demeanor, his desire to fulfill his noble cause overwhelmed his emotional control.

Lowering his gaze, Vim turned around and faced his home; clutching his staff like a hiking stick, he walked into his warm cave. Inside, he leaned the staff against the wall near the entrance, and then walked over to the fire pit, warming his cold hands—as if the heat could cleanse his heavy heart. The candle on the table flickered, casting a dancing light around the interior of the cave that sent him into deep thought. A sudden strange foreboding, coupled with fatigue, made him feel dizzy. Unsteadily, he walked over to his unkempt bed and sat on its corner, elbows on his knees, and face in hands.

"If only I had gone with him this time. Why did I feel the need to stay here and study?" Vim scolded himself aloud, something he often did when waiting helplessly and impatiently. At times, he felt as though he was the only man responsible for, or capable of, saving Peruvious and humanity from destruction. No other humans ventured much further than their own homes to help in his noble cause. This left him frustrated, and sometimes angry. Yet in his heart, he knew he had allies. He relied heavily on their faith in him; it helped him maintain his resolve.

Suddenly, without warning, there was a sharp knock at the door. It startled him, sending an electric tingling sensation through his nervous system. Weakly, he stood, and then stiffly crossed the room. Groping for the staff, his hand eventually finding it, he opened the thick wooden door; there stood Tillich and Perthus, two of his Primord friends. Vim knew that he was about to finally receive the knowledge of Boris's activities he so desperately desired.

"We've come bearing ill tidings," Tillich said, looking into Vim's eyes with a frown, and then at his feet. He clasped his hands together behind his back and kicked a small pebble as he spoke. "The Dragon Master captured Boris and took him to the Barren Mountain. And that's not all—he had help!" He continued to look at the ground and dragged his toe across a large stepping stone in front of him. He was unable to meet the eyes of his friend; he couldn't bear to see his anger and his fear.

Vim could see the pain in the faces of his friends. Somehow intuitively, he already knew the message Tillich offered him—all that remained was to hear the details. "Thank you," he replied, as his strength slowly returned. It had to—he needed to help his friend.

"As you know," Vim continued, "while the moon remains white, we know that he's still alive. I shall leave immediately to the Barren Mountain and lend what aid I can, if there is enough time." Vim tried to reassure his friends.

Perthus stood next to Tillich, his eyes darting around as if the weight of the message they bore might make him break into tears. After a moment, he looked deep into Vim's eyes, trying to find some strength from him, or an answer to a question he didn't know how to ask.

"I'll do everything I can, young Perthus," Vim said. "I'll save him if I'm able; fear not." Vim smiled at the little Primord, knowing his words weren't enough to relieve his pain. Perhaps they were enough to ease it. In any case, they were all he had to offer.

Stepping through the doorway, Vim turned around and closed the cave door tightly behind him. He took two steps back, and then raised his arms, with his staff in hand. He closed his eyes and tipped his head back. Chanting a short, incomprehensible phrase that only he could understand, he transformed the cave entrance into solid stone, sealing it so perfectly it was as if there had never been an opening there. He then turned around to face his friends.

"Now give me the details of his capture," Vim said. "And please be hasty!" Vim's tone was excited, and he intended to share his compelled optimism with his friends.

"Ah, it's a sad story," Perthus said, lowering his gaze to the ground. With his hands on his hips, he again scuffed the ground with his toe in a semicircle in front of him. "Please—you tell him, Tillich." The Primord's voice sounded high and shrill, and it lilted slightly, as if he feared it was already too late.

"One of you must tell me—now!" Vim said, raising his voice.

The Primords looked at one another with apprehension, each one pleading with their eyes for the other to speak. After a moment, Tillich took a deep breath and shoved his feelings aside.

"It happened but a few minutes ago," he said. "Much less than an hour. It was about five leagues from here, at the edge of the forest near the Barren Mountain." Tillich pointed north, as if the location he spoke of was just beyond his view. His face relaxed as he continued to explain.

"Boris was returning to our village, as all of us expected him to do. But an ambush was waiting for him. They chased him, those evil lords. They had some hideous creatures with them we hadn't seen before! Exhausted from running and fighting for several days without rest, Boris didn't have enough strength to defend himself when they finally caught up with him. One of the lords attacked him from behind. Then another summoned the Dragon Master to their aid." Tillich spoke rapidly, hoping to complete the message as quickly as possible. There was urgency in his voice as he waved his arms and shifted his weight from one leg to the other. "Between the lords and a dragon, it was more than even *he* could handle alone—and he was exhausted!"

Tillich's message tugged at Vim's heart, as if he'd experienced the defeat personally. He knew the mighty lords had an unusual camaraderie with the Dragon Master; the mystery of why they worked together remained completely obscured. Nobody knew how the symbiotic relationship arose between the lords and this mighty dragon; the Dragon Master shunned and eluded the control of Vile—unlike the Lords—but work together they did.

"What were the creatures Boris ran from? Why was he fighting the lords? How did they get through the great seal?" Vim had many questions that needed immediate answers. "Where had he gone, and how had he drawn the attention of a lord?" His inflection was harsh and demanding, and his ancient bitter attitude prevented him from concealing his demeanor and his feelings.

"He risked a faster passage along the edge of the forest, not keeping to the cover of the trees!" Perthus said; he sounded hysterical, as if he was defending Boris from Vim's outrage—or perhaps he was simply trying to support Boris's suicidal choices.

"Why did he draw their attention!" repeated Vim.

"He'd gone to the land's edge," Tillich said, "to the overlook Lower Peruvious near the Towers of Tor. He wanted to find a way down to the lower lands. I know you warned him about this, but he wanted to see for himself. He wouldn't take no for an answer! Then he made a big mistake; he broke your seal at the edge! It was just a small hole, and it lasted for only a few minutes, but it remained weakened there. The lords somehow knew what was happening, and they slipped through the hole! Boris thwarted their initial attack. Then he tried to escape— but they pursued him." Tillich tried to defend Perthus's hysterical explanation as he answered Vim's questions. They both faltered as they tried to answer the wizard, and failed to defend Boris adequately.

Vim closed his eyes and took a deep breath in order to clear his thoughts. He needed to understand what the Primords were saying, and he wanted to ask his questions with more care. "As you said, I warned him of this folly! The fool! Now it may be too late." He sighed heavily and leaned on his staff. "I must hurry before the Dragon Master feasts upon him. Yet I fear I'm already too late to stop him!"

Tillich and Perthus looked at each other. They too feared Boris's death was imminent. They knew any encounter with the Dragon Master was most assuredly fatal. The Primords confirmed all of Vim's fears; nearly all hope was lost.

Vim remembered well the last time he had confronted the Dragon Master. It seemed eons ago, in a more chaotic time, when humanity fought large-scale wars that lasted for decades, and the necromancer ruled the activities of all the creatures of Lower Peruvious. In those days, Vim had once battled the mighty dragon himself. He'd barely escaped with his life. The experience had left a lasting impression on him.

Reaching into a hidden pocket in his grey robe, Vim searched for something but came up empty. "I must have one of your potions, dear Tillich," he said. "I have no time to travel by staff; I seem to have used all of my supply of your travel potions."

Reaching into a small knapsack, Tillich found what Vim wanted: a small vial containing a green liquid. He held it up to Vim. The two Primords watched the wizard with trepidation in their eyes. They'd seen him accomplish amazing things before. They didn't question what he was about to do, but they feared for his life too—not just Boris's.

"This is... well, it's the last potion of its type," Tillich said. "We have no more, nor can we make it again, as you know." Tillich's voice expressed his reluctance. "We just used the other two we had—our last two—to get to you as quickly as we could."

For a second, Vim hesitated. Then he accepted the gift. "I shall use it wisely, my dear friends—fear not. It will serve one last great purpose."

"I agree: now *is* the time to use it," replied Tillich. "We only wish for your success."

Quickly, before giving himself time to reconsider, Vim opened the container. A distinct sound of a vacuum hissed and escaped as he removed the seal—much louder than one might expect from such a small bottle. A wisp of vapor spewed from the opening, and small green bubbles boiled rapidly from inside, escaping into the air and pouring over the lip of the flask and onto Vim's hand. Quickly, he shoved the vial between his lips, drank its contents, and gagged violently. A moment later, the spasm passed.

"Wretched flavor," Vim declared. "I won't miss that taste, but I mourn its passing nonetheless."

A moment passed as the two Primords watched Vim, anticipating the results. Suddenly, expectedly, a wild look came over him, and his eyes grew very wide. A bitter look covered his face and many years of age seemed to disappear from his body—as if pure energy infused him with vitality, renewing him. Subsequently, a savage yell escaped his lips, echoing loudly off the nearby trees. In an instant, he disappeared in a flash of green light, leaving only a thick cloud of green smoke behind.

INSTANTLY TRANSPORTED, VIM APPEARED INSIDE the crater of the Barren Mountain; he found himself a short distance away from the bleeding and semi-conscious Boris. The crater was just as he remembered it from previous visits. But it was late in the evening and dark shadows made it difficult to discern any details. A shiver ran up and down his spine as he quickly looked around. It appeared as though the two men were alone, but Vim knew intuitively the Dragon Master was nearby. A stench like that of oil-soaked sulfur filled the chamber followed by an unmistakable sensation of uncomfortable heat; these were telltale signs that the Dragon Master was very close.

Vim could see that Boris had heavy chains shackled to both his wrists and his ankles, binding him helplessly to a heavy stone; it would be difficult to free him quickly. The chains corroborated Tillich's story, verifying the involvement of the lords. For a moment, he hesitated as he formulated a plan of action. But his time abruptly ran out.

"Heh heh heh—if-f it is-sn't the mighty Vim Alpens-stock," boomed a voice from across the crater. "S-so, you've come to meh-hee to be roas-sted along with your s-little *friend*-sss!" The distinctive voice of the Dragon Master stuttered and laughed at Vim.

Unable to see him in the darkness, Vim wished the conditions were equal, but they weren't. The mighty serpent didn't need eyes to see; his nose and ears gave him all the information he required. Most frustrating of all, his voice echoed off the walls of the circular chamber, making it nearly impossible to determine his exact location.

"Obviously, you *don't* yet see me, you overgrown lizard!" Vim said, trying to enrage the mighty beast. He knew that while the dragon's eyes remained closed, the chamber would remain completely dark around the perimeter. The moment they opened, they would emit a beam of light in the direction of the dragon's gaze, like two searchlights, and give away his position.

"Ahhh, you re-mehember *well* old f-fool, but you f-forget-sss, I can s-see just as-s keenly with my s-sens-se of s-smell, s-s-heh heh," the Dragon Master hissed and chuckled.

Vim had not forgotten this important detail, but he needed to keep the dragon talking as he planned his next move. For a short time, the potion had the side effect of disorienting his senses somewhat, and he was just beginning to recover. The potion's energy still filled his body, making him anxious, as if every nerve were on fire.

A scant shaft of moonlight crested the edge of the crater, allowing him to see Boris sufficiently. He still couldn't see the Dragon Master lurking in the shadows—if anything, the moonlight made it even more difficult to see the creature, as it shone in his eyes from the same direction that the voice emanated from. "If only I could *see* him," Vim cursed under his breath, and he carefully repositioned himself and moved closer toward Boris.

"I am glad that ch-chew've come to your s-sens-sez-z and des-cided to end your long battle with the overlord-ah." The Dragon Master was like a cat playing with a mouse. "I s-shall eat you firs-st, and s-save this-s piec-ce of meat for des-sert-ssss!" he announced gleefully.

Suddenly a sense of foreboding overwhelmed Vim's nerves; he knew the dragon was about to strike. Instinctively, he leapt sideways, just as a mighty stream of fire sliced through the room, separating him from Boris.

Having returned to full consciousness during the exchange of words, Boris's fiery barbarian attitude activated. The Dragon Master's reference to him as a snack had invoked a sense of urgency. Summoning the last ounce of his formidable Methonian strength, he let out a loud grunt and heaved against his bonds. His muscles bulged and the steel chains slowly stretched and then gave way, leaving the shackles and a length of chain on his arms. As the shackles broke free, they fired off as if shot from a cannon; their weight pulled his muscular frame forward and he fell hard on his hands and knees, facefirst—just as the rush of dragon fire licked past his left side. Quickly, he rolled over on his back, placed both feet against the stone, grasped the chains near the shackles binding his ankles, and pulled with all his might. Again, metal fatigued, fractured, and slung itself over his head, flipping him over backwards; finally, he was free, though still encumbered by chains shackled to him. The remaining lengths of chain dangled from his limbs and rattled against the broken stone fragments beneath his feet.

The Dragon Master had finally revealed his exact location. Seizing the opportunity, Vim raised his staff, pointing its globe toward the mighty beast. "Uthreadimite!" he yelled in his wizard's tongue. The globe atop the staff lit up like a star, and streaks of electrical energy danced around it. Suddenly, a bolt of lightning shot across the crater, striking the dragon broadside. For a split second, the entire crater lit up like day.

The sudden blast exploded against the dragon's side, stunning him for an instant. Then he rolled over on his side; a small cloud of smoke rose from his armored plating. Vim prepared for a second bolt, but he didn't have enough time.

In retaliation, the Dragon Master blasted a long gust of fire toward the wizard. Vim leapt and rolled toward Boris, but the fire singed his feet as he scrambled to get away. It burned the hair off his toes, and charred his sandals—wisps of smoke rose from them.

Boris sprang toward the sprawled wizard, grasped his arm, and reached for the staff.

"Don't touch it!" Vim scolded. "Keep your attention on the enemy, lest he attack again!"

The Dragon Master bellowed a hateful scream like the discharge of a cannon; it shook the mountain and deafened the two men. Rock shards fell from all around the rim of the crater. Scrambling to his feet, Vim raised the staff again and chanted in a low voice. Argent light burst from the globe, and the entirety of the staff became engulfed in a brilliant white fire. Using both hands at the staff's midpoint, Vim then twirled it like a baton. The argent fire created a large circular shield of energy that steadily grew in size and luminosity. As the shield took shape, he suddenly stopped; the protective energy remained intact, as did the fire blazing along the shaft of the staff. Vim then pressed the globe in the center of the barrier and chanted words in his archaic wizard's tongue to reinforce the magic. It grew even larger, spreading in all directions, becoming an enormous white wall of glowing power.

"Come," the wizard urged in a hurried tone. "We must leave quickly! The barrier will only last long enough for a hasty escape! Follow me, the tunnel is this way." Vim led the way as Boris staggered after him. Blood oozed from several open wounds, including some around his shackles; its loss showed in his face, and he exhibited signs of light-headedness and fatigue. Vim ran on across the crater, using the burning staff to light the way; he didn't notice his companion was failing behind him.

The defensive shield blocked the Dragon Master's advance; in retaliation, he launched himself into the air. With searchlight eyes, he penetrated the darkness, examining the crater below for the fleeing pair. Picking out the faltering Boris, he arched high above the magic barrier, diving directly at him with an incredible velocity. At the last second, he spread his massive wings, dropped his talons as if landing, and grasped the faltering warrior; his clasp easily tore Boris's flesh. With incredible strength, he winged his way into the night sky, booming a deafening roar of success. After clearing the rim of the crater, he tossed the limp Warrior into the air. In an instant, he swooped around, catching him in his enormous maw, and consuming him in one mighty chomp.

Vim whirled around, too late to prevent the attack. He watched helplessly as the departing dragon took flight into the night sky. As he crossed the moon, it silhouetted him; there, he consumed Boris, knowing Vim was watching.

"Damnation to you, you deformed serpent!" Vim screamed as tears streamed down his cheeks. "I'll see your death soon—do you *hear* me!"

In an instant, the color of the moon turned pale blue, and perceptibly darkened in tincture, lighting the night with the sickening color of the Crystal Pyramid. Clouds abruptly formed and moved so quickly they seemed to churn in the sky, and they completely obscured the view of the moon. Just as suddenly, lightning crisscrossed the clouds in all directions, licking the heavens as if in angry triumph. Vim's heart sank. He felt nauseous. Thunder shook the night air and rain opened from the clouds in torrents.

"I'll get you next time, Vile! You can bet on it! I'm going to play the game differently, you'll see!" Vim became hysterical, but he meant what he said. He felt helpless, yet the loss of his friend fueled his resolve to defeat the overlord. Slowly, he walked down the labyrinths that led to the mountain's base. He had one stop to make along the way—he needed to visit an old friend.

HIS TALE COMPLETE, BEELIF STOOD upon his chair. Everyone bowed their heads in silence, as if it were a funeral. The telling of the story, Beelif said, makes Boris's death seem as if it happened only yesterday.

Vim nodded and said: Very well-told, my friend—very well-told indeed. Your usage of the etheric records made me feel as though I was reliving the past. I suppose that, in a sense, I truly was. For a second, Vim grimaced. Then he managed a half smile. With a single finger, he rubbed the corners of his eyes and sniffed. I wouldn't have liked to hear the story at all if it wasn't so important that my new friend, Anton, should witness it. Nobody can offer the retelling of a tale like you! Only the maker of the Berrybrew can do so.

Thank you, my friend, Beelif replied. It does my heart good in the offering of any tale! He smiled and forced a laugh; he hoped it might improve Vim's emotions. He knew Vim too well, and knew that each loss of a champion increased his burden; the old man held the weight of a mountain on his heart.

Anton sat silently after Beelif's presentation concluded. Feeling slightly dizzy and drained, he looked around the gathering and saw the emotions upon everyone's faces. The minds of all the Primords persisted collectively in his thoughts, as if they all shared one mind; the mutual vision, and their shared emotions, would remain etched in him forever. It was a much different feeling than if he'd meditated—if he'd done so, he would have felt refreshed. But the Berrybrew left him with the aftereffects of an intoxicant, and he felt drained.

Most importantly, Anton understood Vim's emotional state; he empathized with his love for Peruvious, his genuine friendship for the champions he'd purposefully abducted, and his determination to triumph over evil. Without question, his cause was righteous, as was his integrity.

He deserved all the help anyone could offer—especially from someone like himself, with his superior capabilities. Anton had never known a conviction like this; even his own genetically invoked resoluteness seemed paltry by comparison.

We hear your thoughts, we sense your feelings, Beelif looked directly at Anton as he spoke his thoughts. You understand now, and you have an idea about the challenges that await you.

Yes, I understand. The Dragon Master must be stopped, and I must defeat these evil lords, these former Warriors turned evil. Anton returned Beelif's look; he knew his mind, and he knew the minds of all the Primords and their burning desire for success. I forgive Vim for abducting me from my home; I recognize the extreme need of Peruvious, it is beyond righteous.

Very good—the Berrybrew was well made, I can be proud of this batch. Smiling, Beelif winked at Anton and then chuckled heartily aloud. As you can see, we—all of us Primords—have learned to make various potions. They are a part of us. Without them, we would have little to offer in the struggle against Vile. Each one of us specializes with our own potion; we all have our own *brew*, you could say.

Adjusting his attention to the thoughts of the Primord community, Anton discovered the reason Tillich and Perthus had no more potions for teleportation; the key ingredient no longer existed; the plant had become extinct. Every Primord was an apothecary in his own right; they'd learned from the animals and plants to communicate the properties of everything that lived. It didn't take long for each of them to become adept at potion-making. He felt pleased that these small people were so capable.

They seem so special—and indeed, they are, Anton thought to himself, and then realized he shared this thought with everyone. A flush of embarrassment crossed his face.

Thank you—we feel much the same about you, young Anton, Beelif thought. We know you're different from your brothers—we can see it in your heart, and know it in your thoughts. We wholeheartedly believe you *are* the chosen one. Looking at Vim, Beelif spoke to the Wizard with his thoughts. He must be taken to Drogan; the Prophecy of One must be recited to him. Beelif urged the wizard into action. You must leave; you must leave now!

Agreed, my dear Beelif, and we shall. We're off to the Barren Mountain. Looking at Anton, Vim's eyebrows rose as he communicated their next destination. Standing, he looked at each of the Primords in turn. "We shall go to the Barren Mountain." Vim spoke aloud as if his declaration required a formal announcement. "But before we go, let's have one more round of the Berrybrew!"

With a sudden rush, everyone cheered and ran back to the breakfeast tables, where their goblets awaited them. Anton and Vim both ran along with the Primords; they smiled widely, in anticipation of the rare liqueur.

"Delilah, another round of Berrybrew for all!" announced Beelif as he raised his goblet into the air; Delilah wasted no time refilling them all. "Let us rejoice in our new friendship!" Raising his goblet to his lips, Beelif took a large draft from it.

"Let's all celebrate our friendship!" Vim raised his own goblet and returned the toast, taking a long draft of the liqueur.

All the Primords and Anton followed Beelif's lead. Polishing their goblets off in one mighty drink, they then raised them empty into the air, smacked their lips, wiped away the last drops with the back of their sleeves, and whooped a mighty cheer. A satisfied grin covered each face. The mysterious liquid made everyone happy, and the spirit of the occasion was monumental to all. From this moment, Anton felt like a member of the Primord community.

From the corner of one table, a very young Primord started to play what appeared to be a flute. A merry tune came from the knobby and warped wooden tube, and everyone started to dance and sing along. Again, Anton laughed at the silly antics of the unusual little people;

they seemed to have a happy, carefree life, but he knew they lived in fear that one day the enemy would annihilate them.

The dancing continued for several minutes before everyone finally slowed down. Again, the tables mysteriously cleared themselves while the dancing and festivities continued. In place of the morning feast, several small bottles filled with Berrybrew appeared on the table in front of Vim. Carefully, he placed them in pockets inside his robe and thanked Beelif.

Unexpectedly, and to Anton's complete surprise, he felt a prickling pulsation on his ring finger. Glancing at his hand, he saw that the ring glowed dimly with a sickening blue—similar to the color of the moon after Boris's defeat. Anton had never felt sickened by any color before, but the sight of it emanating from the ring made him nauseous. He was unable to hide his reaction from the rest of the gathering. Collectively, everyone noticed his gaze as he looked at his finger. Seeing the sudden attention, he knew his discomfort was impossible to conceal from anyone, because the Berrybrew precluded him from hiding his personal thoughts.

"Be careful, my friend," Vim said aloud, trying to alert everyone. "That color signifies the enemy! I'm certain the secrecy of this hamlet's location is in jeopardy, my dear Beelif! You must flee! And as for you, young Anton—I would advise you to remove the ring from your finger at once!"

Anton considered the statement and decided it was sound, so he grasped the ring and tugged gently. Nothing happened. He tugged a little harder with the same results. Completely astonished, he looked at Vim with a puzzled expression.

Vim quickly moved to Anton's rescue. "Show me your ring!" he insisted. Grasping Anton's hand, he raised it to his face to have a better look.

An eerie feeling crawled up Anton's arm and crept through his entire body; it was a sensation he'd never felt before. For a moment, the world seemed to change. It shifted into a fog, and then to what could only be a different dimension—as if Anton had briefly stepped out of the Primord's hamlet to some unknown place. Just as suddenly, everything returned to normal. An expression of bewilderment covered his face.

"What did you see?" Vim asked, watching Anton's expression. "Anton! I need to know—*what did you see*? Tell me now!" Grabbing Anton's other hand, he shook the Warrior to snap him out of his trancelike state. Then, suddenly, he released his grip as Anton's distant stare disappeared and he looked at Vim questioningly.

It took a moment for Anton's head to clear enough to formulate an answer. "The village seemed to disappear; it seemed as though I was no longer standing here. I saw a horrible face, the face of a man staring at me. His gaze felt like a sword sliced straight through my heart." Anton panted lightly as he spoke, as if he couldn't catch his breath. "I don't know what to make of it."

"Nor do I, but I can guess," replied Vim. "We must leave, this *instant*! Prepare yourself—the battle begins!" Quickly looking around at all of the Primords, Vim's eyes fell upon Beelif. "We're off to the Barren Mountain. Take care, my friends. I believe you should relocate—and soon!"

"Godspeed, Vim," Beelif replied, nodding with a half-smile. "Don't worry about us—we'll be fine."

"Very well, then—Godspeed, my friend!" Vim returned Beelif's nod and looked at Anton, ushering him to his side. "Prepare yourself."

CHAPTER 14

Gifts from the Magi

VIM GRASPED ANTON'S ARM WITH one hand and held the Staff of Balance in the other. "We must leave at once!" His inflection declared urgency, his expression demanded obedience. Adjusting his hand just below the staff's talon, he raised the globe above his head, and it instantly burst with his wizard's magic; argent radiance permeated the atmosphere, illuminating the vicinity. Even the late morning sunlight had little ability to diminish its effect. Electricity danced vigorously like miniature lightning bolts around the staff's sphere, and vivid refulgence of golden fire burned along its shaft from the archaic runes.

"There's little doubt that Vile knows the location of your village, dear Beelif. Hurry—you must flee for your lives! Take care, and get your fellow Primords safely away from here, as quickly as you can.

I'm truly sorry that I've brought this terrible burden to your people— forgive me, old friend." An old anger arose in Vim—an anger he'd harbored his entire life. It drove his passion for his life's work, pushing him ever forward towards his desired victory. His anguish to defeat Vile was stronger than ever. It was fueled by the thought that his dearest friends were in danger, due to his lack of judgment and foresight. He'd not considered Anton's ring as a conduit to the enemy's capacity to pinpoint their imperceptible secret location.

"Fear not, my friend Vim—the blame is not upon you," Beelif said. "Besides, we're used to hiding—this setback won't undo us!" Beelif had a natural talent for politeness; he smiled and casually waved goodbye.

After making their farewells to the gentle Primords, Vim and Anton levitated slowly upward, contained within a shimmering golden sphere of wizard's magic, protected and hidden from normal sight. The next moment, Anton could see the astonished faces of the Primords looking up into the air, as if wondering where the two had disappeared. Anton also noticed the blue color emanating from his ring had faded to a mere pastel of its former magnitude; as the aura of magic surrounding the humans grew stronger, the ring's color faded exponentially.

"My thoughts are clearer now," Anton said, trying to reassure Vim. He tried to catch Vim's gaze, but the other seemed to be in deep contemplation, completely oblivious to his comments.

Nevertheless, Vim did hear Anton, and after a few seconds, he responded: "Such is the power of the staff. Its magic came from something perfect, from something so old that time itself was established after it—or so legend has it. I have an ancient scroll in my cave that tells of an entity that bestowed it upon Peruvious— indeed, upon our planet more than an eon ago. This artifact was created for a particular need in ancient times, when the world was much different." Vim seemed taxed as he spoke; his words came in fragmented groups; his thoughts split between concentration and communication.

Anton didn't fully understand what Vim was trying to say—his account seemed irrelevant. How could something or someone be older than time itself? It made no sense. Disconcerted, he shook his head and passed off the thought—it seemed to have no relevance to their present concerns.

Vim closed his eyes for a moment—he didn't want Anton to notice that he was on the verge of losing his self-control. The effects of the Berrybrew continued to have a hold on him; he continued to hear Anton's thoughts, and he knew that his young friend didn't care about his explanation of the staff. Anton didn't seem to desire any understanding of how important this knowledge in fact was—and it disturbed Vim immensely. How could he educate someone with so little respect for or interest in what he had to say? He realized that his new champion required much more than a simple explanation of things—he needed proof, he needed hard evidence of everything. But most of all, he needed to mature; Vim hoped there would be enough time for this; time was something they had very little of.

The further from the Primord hamlet they traveled, the more Vim's thoughts slipped beyond Anton's capacity to hear them. It didn't take long before they remained silent and unvoiced. The power of the staff, and its encompassing energy, seemed to dispatch the Berrybrew's telepathic ability, absorbing it like a sponge. But Anton could still empathetically perceive Vim's temperament, at least for the time being.

Silently, the two crossed over the local forest. The tops of the trees were only a short distance below their feet. After a few moments, Vim gathered himself together, looked at Anton, and realized how tight his grip was on the Warrior's muscular arm; his hand began to ache from the excessive clench. Feeling a bit embarrassed, he quickly made an adjustment, easing his grasp. Then he put forth more of his strength and concentration into the workings of his magic. This increased the already brilliant glow of the globe; the intensified power noticeably crawled along Anton's skin, and he thought he heard a faint crackling sound like that of wood burning with fire. It was as if Vim's energy was consuming the staff for fuel. The color of the sphere seemed to change as well—it mixed argent brilliance with an aura of gold. It radiated vividly, and their speed increased substantially as a result. The trees below seemed to speed by so fast it was difficult to see their individual details.

Looking at the old wizard, Anton saw the pain of Vim's personal burdens mixed with the self-mastery of his age on his face; this expression surprised him. He didn't believe someone of his age and mastery would have such feelings written so deeply on their countenance. In contrast, the obvious heaviness of his heart weighed on his soul, and remained distinctly evidenced in his eyes; he remained ceaselessly determined.

Emotions are the road to greatness or ruin, Anton thought. How am I to serve someone who seems to have little restraint or self-control over them? A Warrior he is not! He wondered just how strong Vim's resolve in fact was; he wondered how impassioned beyond the capacity of clear judgment he was. As a whole, humanity was a contradiction; they were flawed, and they failed consistently at everything, however, their failures occasionally drove them to achieve greatness. It truly did require cloned humans to always achieve greatness; they alone had the capacity to set such weaknesses aside so they would achieve the final goal and succeed.

Anton knew that Vim's heart was determined enough for him to be successful, and therefore he trusted him in all things. Yet he judged him carefully, and he judged him critically, and he wasn't entirely sure of his potential for success or for absolute failure. Aside from that, he speculated about the strength of Vim's temperament, and measured the capability of his aged mental state. Vim had indicated the risk of exposure to the enemy if they traveled from his cave to the valley below using their present method— and now it seemed he wasn't heeding his own warning; this was another point of confusion and contradiction. Again, Anton wondered if this was due to Vim's extreme age. After careful consideration, he decided it was unlikely, and he decided to plan his probable confrontation with the Dragon Master.

The two traveled directly northeast. Anton continued to watch the forest below and he realized their altitude had climbed to nearly a quarter mile. He watched as the trees became sparse, and then finally disappeared altogether. The terrain fluctuated from forest, to small lakes, to rivers and streams, and then back to forest; each feature passed by with unexpected speed. To the west, he observed the mountain range from which the peak of Loomspire arose; it towered over the landscape, dominating all other things; these distant geographical features progressed slowly southward. Directly ahead, to the northeast, the shape of an enormous dead volcano was barely visible in the distance; it stood alone in the high desert plains.

"I take it we are headed for that lone mountain?" Anton said, pointing at the volcanic peak they were approaching and contemplating its unique appearance; it appeared identical to the mountain in Beelif's presentation. Anton noticed how it projected sharply from the surrounding foothills, and was the only prominent feature in the geographic vicinity.

"You're correct, my young friend." Vim's reply sounded distant, as if he was busy concentrating on something else, and so he struggled to respond to Anton's inquiry. As he continued to focus his attention on maintaining their travel, his efforts seemed increasingly strained. "We're going to visit Drogan the Djinni," he labored to announce.

"Who is that? What's a Djinni?" asked Anton. The way the wizard rolled the name Drogan across his tongue caught Anton's attention; the inflection was entirely unfamiliar. Nearly every name Vim used sounded unusual, almost as if he was more accustomed to speaking some ancient language. His enunciation of the language was much different from the Primords.

"You'll know him when you see him. He's an entity of pure magic. He isn't a part of Peruvious; you could say he was placed here for a purpose." Vim tried to explain as best he could while keeping his sentences short; it was necessary that his attention remain attuned to his staff in order to maintain their travel.

Pondering Vim's words, Anton continued surveying the terrain around him and the ever-increasing size of the Barren Mountain. At the speed they were traveling, he calculated they'd be there soon.

A Djinni? Anton thought to himself. His Masters hadn't taught him anything about magic, or what a Djinni was. He assumed they'd given him a complete education of all creatures, and of all peoples—but now it seemed somehow inadequate. After a few moments, he set yet another inexplicable characteristic of Peruvious aside—but this time he knew he'd soon encounter his answer.

Finally, the Barren Mountain loomed high into the sky, its peak buried amidst thick grey clouds that circumscribed its uppermost perimeter. Vim began his decent, levitating only a few hundred feet above the foothills. Slowing their speed, he continued to reduce altitude as they approached the base of the mountain. Before long, the two men stood upon the loose volcanic rock and obsidian fragments that surrounded the extinct volcano.

"Here we are," Vim stated for no particular reason as the two lightly touched down. He let go of Anton's arm, but not before getting a look at his crystal ring. It was clear now, devoid of all color. This seemed to ease Vim's tension, and he let out a sigh of relief.

Noticing the gaze of the wizard, Anton also looked at his ring. "Does this mean something? Is it somehow significant? It's clear. Yet it should be gold. And the blue is *gone!*"

"This is due to the powerful neutral magic of Drogan. His magical influence radiates a great distance from his home, deep within the caverns of the Barren Mountain. Quiet yourself, lest we awaken the Dragon Master." Vim held his hand over his mouth as he whispered the name.

Anton eyed the wizard quizzically. "The Dragon Master?" He wasn't as careful with his query. Vim's eyes widened, and he gasped.

"*Quiet,* you impudent fool!" Vim chastised. "The mere mention of his name can awaken the mighty beast! He has finely-tuned hearing beyond any predator. Quiet yourself, and let us proceed unnoticed!" He shook his finger at Anton. But it was too late.

Suddenly, a loud roar unlike anything Anton had ever heard pierced the atmosphere, sending a shiver up and down his spine. Within moments, an immense shadow crossed over them, chilling Anton's nerves; every synapse seemed to explode in every extremity of his body, and his stomach tightened with trepidation. Summoned by Anton's ignorance, the Dragon Master hungered to engage in battle with his longstanding enemy.

"S-so! The mighty wiz-zard has a new mortal for me to conquer-r and feas-st upon!" The sound of the Dragon Master's voice grated against the air as he circumnavigated like an Aerocraft overhead.

The sound of the dragon's voice made the hair on the back of Anton's neck stand up, as if charged with electricity, and another shiver ran up and down his spine. Instantly, he responded to the dragon's challenge and grabbed Vim like a sack of feed, flung him over his shoulder, and ran for a small cave opening nearby that was barely big enough for the two to squeeze through.

"Seek refuge!" Anton commanded as he set the wizard down on the cave floor, and then prepared to return to battle.

Completely overwhelmed by Anton's awkward act of heroism, Vim proceeded down the cave tunnel, expecting him to follow—the very same mistake he'd made with Boris.

Nevertheless, Anton instantly lurched out of the cave at a full run. The Dragon Master watched the actions of the Methonian Warrior and landed lightly on the ground directly in front of him; the sound of crackling obsidian and volcanic rock resounded like a chorus as the immense weight of the enormous beast settled against it.

Suddenly, Anton came to a halt just a few yards in front of the giant Dragon Master. An enormous burst of fire billowed from deep inside the dragon's furnace, spewing forth in a deadly gust. Dodging sideways, Anton's reflexes easily parried the potent blast with expert proficiency, but the immense heat burned him indirectly. In the same moment, he snatched from its holster his Sword of Blue Flame; a fourfoot length of fire erupted from its hilt. This seemed a paltry defense to the dragon's fire, however Anton wanted to attack immediately hoping to catch the dragon off-guard.

Precipitously, the two combatants stood face to face. They sized one another up, preparing for battle; Anton primed his instantaneous reflexes for the dragon's next move, the Dragon Master glared at him with unconditional confidence.

"Very good li-hit-tle man, you are more a-agile than a-antis-scipa-hated, but now you've met your-r match!" The mighty serpent hissed with a booming voice. "Put away your li-hit-tle toy, it is-s uses-s-less-ss agains-st me!"

With astonishing speed, the indomitable dragon drew back his head and leapt forward, his enormous jaws agape and ready for a bone-crunching chomp. The loose rock under the monster's talons sounded like gravel pouring off a hillside; it crackled obstreperously as he pushed his way forward. Fragments of obsidian crushed and splintered under his immense weight, sending tiny-slivered shards of volcanic glass shooting in all directions.

Nimbly avoiding the debris, Anton struggled to maintain his ready stance on the loose rocks. But sustain it he did—his feet moved swiftly, and his upper body remained steady. Genetic engineering prevented him from fleeing in fear, and his training held him in position as he waited for the exact moment to strike a blow.

The flagitious mouth repeatedly struck down at Anton; he faded and parried, dodged and tumbled with amazing speed, causing the Dragon Master's multiple attacks to miss their intended target. Suddenly, an opportunity to strike a blow presented itself, and Anton quickly swung his sword in between the Dragon's attacks, neatly slicing through the impenetrable scales just below his left eye; it cut cleanly, as if his natural armor didn't exist. Following through, Anton cartwheeled in midair with acrobatic perfection, landing upon the thick neck of the Dragon Master; he saddled himself behind the beast's head—as if he was mounting a steed, just as Duke had done with the *Lapillusaurus* in the Troglodyte caverns back on Methonias. Grasping a large scale for support, he then swung his sword again—but this time he slid on his unsteady seat and swung wide, completely missing his target. The Dragon Master thundered an angry painful roar and tried to waggle Anton from his neck, like a dog shaking himself dry after a swim. But Anton held on with a viselike grip.

A new sensation fired through Anton's nerves—it was the fever of battle. It precluded his thoughts of self-preservation and filled him with the unremitting need for victory at any cost. Hormones and adrenaline flowed freely, and his heart pumped his system full of the necessary chemicals to achieve his victory; they forced his attention to focus to its utmost limit. It was as if everything happened in slow motion, allowing him plenty of time to think and react to the slightest movements of the Dragon Master. Anton felt a distinct increase of his physical potential; Methonian Warriors had this ability designed and constructed into them, and he was the greatest product the Methonian geneticists had created to date. His abilities surpassed all Warriors designed before him, and he fully intended to prove it at any cost.

"Now taste the wrath of a Methonian Warrior!" Anton yelled unexpectedly, completely caught up in the fever of battle. His voice was full of battle-rage and barbaric excitement; his attention remained irrefutably entrenched upon his enemy. Then, abruptly, the tables turned. The moment he spoke, an aura of blue energy emitted from the crystal ring enveloping his left hand. The sight of it startled him, breaking his concentration. His grip unexpectedly and uncontrollably loosened, interrupting his battle-rage, and the dragon easily tossed him head-over-heels through the air.

Suddenly, a crackling sound like thunder pervaded the atmosphere, and a bolt of lightning coming from Vim's staff launched toward the Dragon Master, striking him in the head. Simultaneously a golden sphere enveloped Anton, just like the one he and Vim had traveled in only minutes earlier.

Stunned, the Dragon Master fell over on his side. His immense weight was too much for his paralyzed muscles to support, and the loose volcanic rock slipped under his talons. He struggled to regain his footing, but seemed unable to. Uselessly, he pawed and kicked in the air, seemingly unable to control his movements. Blood poured from the open wound below his eye—a wound put there by Anton—and the Dragon Master glared at the Warrior with unparalleled antipathy. It seemed as though the two men had victory in their grasp.

Holding his staff high overhead, Vim carefully levitated Anton over to him and placed him gently on the loose rock. As he released the magical sphere, he pointed toward a cave. Anton gave a disgruntled look at the wizard, but understood; nodding his head in agreement, he followed Vim up the side of the mountain. They entered the cave together just as the dragon recovered his senses and managed to regain his footing.

Behind them, a loud protest of outrage boomed from the infuriated dragon; the sound of his enormous wings flapped as the titanic figure winged its way into the morning sky. It was a minor victory for the two men; they'd barely regained their freedom. Both of them knew they hadn't yet won the battle, and that they'd have another opportunity when they tried to leave.

The cave opening was large enough for the two men to enter, but far too small for the oversized mass of the Dragon Master to pursue them. With his monstrous reptilian strength, he could easily enlarge the cave opening if he set his mind to it, however, he was too cunning to use such an aggressive tactic. He knew the two must leave the same way they entered, so he launched himself into the air, departing the battle scene and preparing for his next assault.

"This cave leads deep into the heart of Barren Mountain. Let's go before that *lizard* returns—we don't want any more trouble." Vim gave Anton a look of disapproval. He was justifiably angered that he had attempted to take on such an opponent, especially alone. He knew all too well it was impossible for him to achieve a victory by simple brute force. It concerned him that his new champion was audacious enough to believe he could—especially after Beelif's presentation of Boris's death.

"Do you realize just how foolhardy it is to attack that beast?" he said angrily as he led the way down the cavern. "It's far too risky to fight that beast directly! You haven't got a chance against such a creature! Didn't you learn anything from Beelif's story? Boris was a *mighty* Warrior, and even *he* didn't stand a chance. What makes you think you do? That little sword of yours? Harrumph!"

Vim's scolding angered Anton, but he realized how hard he'd have struck the loose stones after the Dragon Master tossed him through the air, so he bit his tongue.

"Thank you for catching me," Anton said, with a hint of sarcasm— yet his eyes proclaimed embarrassment, and anger toward himself. "I won't fail again!" Then donning a look of complete confidence, Anton inadvertently declared his future intentions.

Glancing over his shoulder, Vim frowned; he knew Anton would gladly fight the Dragon Master again if the opportunity arose, and he feared for his life.

"Good to see you agree with me," the wizard said with a stern inflection; he wanted Anton to appreciate his position, and accede to his wisdom. "Come along, now—we have an unscheduled appointment to keep, and time continues to work against us. Vile knows you're here, and he is working hard to defeat you!"

Vim used his staff to cast the illumination they needed to see their way as the two men hastened down the labyrinths of Barren Mountain. Anton followed closely at Vim's heels, and marveled at the enormous ancient formations created by the vastness of time. They filled the tunnels with unprecedented natural beauty, and inspired a feeling of awe. It reminded him of his travels through the Troglodyte caverns back on Methonias—yet these tunnels were entirely natural, rather than intermittently carved by hand, and they connected the various caverns together. In addition, the similarity of the Dragon Master to the *Lapillusaurus* gave him a sensation of deja-vu, as if he were reliving the past.

Contemplating his battle with the Dragon Master, Anton remained silent. As he studied the cavern's natural formations, he noticed that the stalactites and stalagmites became more ornate and intricate in their shapes—they appeared to be more like symbols, almost as if they had been created by humans. He found himself wanting to linger and try to determine their meaning. Inadvertently, he gradually slowed as he pondered their meaning.

Vim showed no interest in these formations. It was nothing new to him, and he continuously persuaded the Warrior to keep moving.

"Let's not dawdle; I fear we've little time to accomplish our goal; a meeting with Drogan is rarely short. That flash of blue that emanated from your ring amalgamates my concern; we can't have the necromancer watching everything we do, and he'll undoubtedly find a way to control you through your ring. We must see Drogan before trouble again finds us, and it does seem to have its attention pointed in our direction. I'm sure that ring of yours is the source of our current difficulties; we'll soon know the truth."

Making his way through the natural maze, Vim again demonstrated his seasoned knowledge of the passages; he selected the correct one at every fork. His anger precluded his ability to speak to Anton, and silently the two descended further and further into the narrowing tunnels until they finally arrived in a large open chamber. Exquisite predominant features completely filled it. They were unquestionably rare anywhere in nature, and perhaps even the entire universe; even the incredible formations in the deepest tunnels of the Troglodytes seemed paltry by comparison.

Looking around in amazement, Anton watched the shimmering colors that pervaded the entire cavern as Vim's staff reflected light off the many features; they flickered in an awe-inspiring light show, all stimulated into action by Wizard's fire. This was nothing new for Vim, but Anton observed the flickering light show with astonishment; he'd seen the most spectacular laser light shows when the Galactic Circus would stop on Methonias, but this was far different. It was natural—or was it? Nothing here followed the usual laws of physics; the dancing illuminations seemed to act in unusual patterns that were not indicative of normally reflected light. It was different from everything he was accustomed to; everything seemed to exist outside of common logic.

Anton noticed that Vim wasn't the only one illuminating the great chamber; there was another source, just barely perceptible to the eye, on the opposite side of the cavern. Instantly alerted, he prepared yet again for battle. Grasping his sword, he too lit the chamber with his own blue Methonian fire. Quickly, instinctively, he sped toward the source, deftly sliding past a surprised Vim; he moved so smoothly and silently that the astonished wizard had no time to react.

"Damn that boy, there he goes again!" Vim cursed under his breath. "At least there's no danger here, and Drogan can handle himself..."

The light source was so bright that Anton was unable to discern its origin, and it was intense enough that it hurt his eyes. Looking through narrowed slits, he cautiously approached. Curiously, he found himself standing in front of an urn; it sat upon a heavy cleaved stalagmite that stood about waist high with a stalactite pointing down at it from about ten feet above. From the urn, red smoke suddenly billowed forth, as if expelled by immense pressure, and it appeared as though the stalactite above sucked away the discharged gases, as if it were a vacuum. Holding his sword ready, Anton examined the phenomenon. It wasn't what he'd expected to find; he could see that the smoke was another source of the illumination, though not entirely.

"What is this? Glowing smoke? I don't understand." Anton stood, dumbfounded.

"Put that thing away—it isn't needed here!" Vim snapped. "This is Drogan; your attempt to attack him or protect me is irrelevant. Now, observe!"

As if summoned, a human form took shape from inside the smoke. This being folded his arms across his chest. He had no discernible legs. His torso changed from human to smoke at the hips, and disappeared into the urn. He wore a golden vest made from silk and adorned with diamonds; encasing his head was a turban made of the same gold silk. Centered at the turban's front was a large emerald that glowed with a brilliant green light and gave off an aesthesis of energy that drew Anton's attention to its peculiar beauty. Wrapped around his waist was a red sash that radiated an aura of golden light.

Drogan's turban was familiar. Anton recognized it immediately; both mythology and practical history recorded it, and he'd learned about it in his early years on Methonias. Once worn by the Muslim peoples on ancient Earth, the religious symbol stretched back into antiquity. The gems remained a point of question; he was unaware of the usage by these ancient people, therefore were they somehow representative of something significant? But then it struck him: the history of India revealed such use. Drogan's raiment was less familiar, but as Anton searched his memory, he recalled that it too was rooted in the same ancient history.

The smoky figure smiled hugely, and greeted Anton. "Welcome, Warrior! Welcome indeed! I've been expecting you!" he said with a chuckle.

The salutation surprised Anton; he hadn't anticipated instant identification. The penetrating voice was both comforting and reassuring as it echoed off the cavern walls. Drogan's voice projected from his ethereal form; a cacophony of feelings coursed through Anton's mind as he assessed the unusual vocal characteristics.

"You must be the Djinni Drogan?" Clumsily, Anton returned the greeting with a quizzical stare.

"Have a seat, young one!" Drogan chuckled again, and a large throne appeared at Anton's side. "I see amazement in your eyes!" His voice was deep and rich, making him seem much more than his unnatural stature suggested.

Seating himself in the large golden throne, Anton folded his legs as if he were preparing for meditation. Drogan watched him with a stern and intimidating gaze; only his broadening smile belied his countenance. With a sideways look, he then acknowledged Vim; the two shared a moment of unspoken familiarity.

"Quite a young one you nabbed this time, wizard!" Drogan said, laughing mightily. The chamber took on a feeling of warmth and friendship. "This experience will give him a chance to *mature*." His cryptic laughter escalated, echoing off the stone walls.

Anton looked surprised. "My ring has already turned gold," he thought, swiftly glancing at it, yet now it remained as unequivocally clear as a diamond. This is beyond its design! Returning his attention to the Djinni, he found himself the center of attention.

"See, even your ring declares you're but a child! Did you just receive that token yesterday?" Drogan said, laughing heartily. Even Anton chuckled unevenly; taking a deep breath, he felt his surprise and uneasiness slowly diminish.

"But how?" Anton murmured. Speaking more clearly, he asked, "What has happened to my ring?" He looked first at Vim, and then at Drogan.

In a more respectful tone, Drogan queried Vim: "Haven't you educated this boy about anything? He'll face challenges no human has ever endured! Surely Beelif would've easily talked his ear off for days if he'd had the opportunity!" Again, he chuckled mightily. Vim joined him in a round of laughter. Only Anton remained silent, knowing he was somehow the brunt of his demeaning humor; scowling, he looked back and forth at the two.

A second throne suddenly materialized for Vim, and he seated himself without considering where it came from. "There wasn't much time before one or many of the lords might appear, as you can see his ring is made of crystal; this would certainly draw their attention. When he arrived, it emitted a brilliant blue glow, much to our surprise. Since it's of a similar material, and it mimicked the Pyramid's color, I knew that Vile had already detected his arrival. He also brandished another blue talisman during breakfeast—that sword you saw only a few moments ago."

As Vim spoke, a magical hologram of the occurrences appeared centrally among the three, showing their recent adventures in the Primords' Hamlet. Projected from his staff, it followed his description of the breakfeast experience. The images stopped when he stopped speaking, and continued when he continued his narration.

Completely stunned, Anton marveled at how the images seemed to duplicate his own CHP; even the staff oddly resembled a holographic emitter. Unconsciously, he reached into his tunic pocket and fondled his EHD as if he needed to touch the device, as if he needed to use it for this to occur.

"He refers to the sword as a *Blue Flame*. When he revealed this item to the Primords, a short but vivid vision entered his mind, and he described having seen what could only be the face of Vile." As Vim finished speaking, the hologram disappeared.

Drogan lifted an eyebrow. "This is quite interesting, and unanticipated. I sense his mental capabilities exceed those of his previous brethren, as do his devices." Closing his eyes, he remained motionless for a time, as if in reverie. Suddenly he looked directly at Vim and spoke again.

"His education is delayed, Drogan stated bluntly. "I've waited since the beginning of time for this moment. In accordance with the Universal Law—the law that governs all things—I'll fulfill a preliminary step of my objective by increasing his overall knowledge. Due to the nature of your circumstances, the responsibility falls upon me to enlighten him of what his true purpose and destiny entails. In accordance with the *Law of One*, I shall recite the *Prophecy of One* to him, and then present him with a gift in accordance with the *Law of Balance*. He'll then choose, of his own free will, whether to fulfill the path laid before him, or reject it. After all, the *Prophecy* states that he has the freedom of choice. Relying on his predesigned compliance is insufficient to attain a victory in the final battle. He must *desire* the outcome—not produce it from his genetically controlled servitude. Therefore, his DNA-controlled response shall be nullified."

"Choice? Nobody has *ever* offered me choice!" Anton mumbled to himself. He hadn't even considered that he'd had a choice. His genetic design compelled him simply to follow orders, and to accept any just cause demanded of him. His current mission was merely another DNA-controlled directive assigned to him by his Masters, and requested of him by Vim upon his arrival to Peruvious. He believed he'd already made his choice; he knew his genetic encoding had already sealed his fate. How was it possible to make a choice now? It seemed as though he was already doing the right thing.

"Why do I need to make a choice?" asked a puzzled Anton. "My *design* has made my choice for me; I must fulfill the intent of my Masters by honoring Vim's request for my servitude. Why will I fail if I fulfill my true destiny as determined by my Masters?"

Ignoring Anton's question, Drogan continued to speak to Vim. "I see in him the same conflict as all his brethren. His heart remains on his home world. The bond he feels for his home has gradually diminished since his arrival, yet his heart remains torn between his past life and his duty here. The need to complete his education is paramount, and it must be accelerated."

"Like Beelif, you too are a better story teller than I." Vim proffered his deference. "Please proceed; I agree that he suffers from ignorance. Beelif and I have done what we could in a limited time."

Drogan chuckled. "I am who I am—am I not? As for *you*, my dear Vim—you should spend more time talking during your travels; after all, you've had time to say more than you have. Need I mention your *anger* as you approached my home?"

With a look of deep concern, Drogan regarded Anton, as if sizing him up in final judgment. "You must trust that the love you so desperately seek can be found in many places. You need not hold on to your past so dearly. This girl you knew is only a memory, you must *release* her!" Closing his eyes, he took in a deep breath and slowly let it out. Looking closer at Anton, his eyes seemed to pierce his flesh, as if filleting it—as if he could see directly into his soul's desires, directly into his heart's feelings, and his most confidential thoughts.

"Before I begin my recitation" Drogan continued, "know that it's within my power to present you with two gifts in accordance with the *Law of Balance*. The first is a gift of magic and substance; the second is a gift of knowledge—knowledge that subsequently remains neglected." Drogan winked at Vim, and then continued. "Now, for the magic and substance; stand ready!"

As if he had no control of his actions, Anton stood in ready stance directly in front of Drogan. With his arms folded in front of him, the latter again closed his eyes, bowed his head, and took another deep breath. Then, for the first time, he unfolded his arms and stretched them out, as if pushing Anton away. Opening his eyes, he lifted his head, lowered one arm, and pointed. Golden fire burst from his fingertip, and instantly, a pair of glowing golden bracers materialized on Anton's arms, covering them from wrist to elbow, sealing and hiding the brands he'd received at graduation beneath them.

"These bracers will protect your arms in hand-to-hand battle, and they will increase your overall agility and dexterity—even beyond your superior Methonian capabilities. Finally, they will give you the strength of a giant. You'll have to learn how to control your body again, as this is no small gift! Use them well, they will aid you when your needs are most desperate."

Looking at the artifacts, Anton frowned. *This is, without question, nonsense*, he thought to himself. "Impossible," he spoke aloud. "How could two metal bands increase strength and agility? Impossible!"

Watching Anton through narrow slits, Drogan ignored his arrogant skepticism. "Be still! You insult me! Prepare yourself—clear your thoughts; I shall recite to you the *Prophecy of One*." Drogan folded his arms and began his recitation.

BEYOND THE TIME OF HUMANITY'S greatest wars, when man's existence nears its completion upon the Earth, anti-life shall make its final attempt to rule and destroy the universe. In those final days, God shall select his champion, and send him to oppose this evil. Summoned from beyond the Earth, he serves only *One*.

> He is knowledgeable, yet he knows nothing.
> He is hated and feared, loved and admired.
> He is a man, but not of the Earth.
> He is human, but not born of human flesh.

He is feared and rejected by man; he is embraced by all others. He is a contradiction, a paradox, an enigma; marked by his achievements, he uses evil means to accomplish great deeds.

By his choice, he shall decide man's fate.
By his choice, he shall save or damn existence.
By his choice, he shall judge man's worthiness.
By his choice shall man be accepted into heaven, or cast into perdition.
By his deeds, *One's* Day of Judgment unfolds.
By his deeds, he shall cast evil asunder, returning him forever to his own demesne.

IN THE FINAL DAYS, WHEN all seems lost, seek the Kacatu; it has the answers for those who know how to listen. Pray for forgiveness; the ending of time ensues. Only those that do not oppose God's champion shall find salvation.

FOR A BRIEF TIME, DROGAN remained silent, observing Anton through narrow slits, as if assessing his worthiness. "You'll understand the true meaning and the implications of the Prophecy soon enough. Now, young Warrior: a history lesson you will never forget."

Closing his eyes, Drogan spread his arms wide, and tipped his head back. The aura of light emanating from him diminished to a mere whisper of what it had been, leaving only a subtle outline around his face and shoulders. Slowly, he prepared to say something monumental, as if he'd waited for this moment since the beginning of time. Drawing a deep breath, he opened his eyes wide, stared directly at Anton, and began:

"In the beginning of all things, before the manifestation of time, there was the Intelligence of Creation, a perfect being who existed in an unbounded universe that had always existed and endured. This universe was one of peace, and of life; it incorporated all dimensions, and all realities. That demesne was unlike *this* universe, the one you have always known." Drogan carefully observed Anton, watching his eyes. He made sure that he heard every word, and listened assiduously to every detail.

"In this universe, the Intelligence of Creation had always existed. *He* had always *been*. Most importantly, He is all knowledge; He is all love; He is all life. However, a being such as this cannot live without *creating*. Thus He created limitless great workings—workings beyond your comprehension and beyond the comprehension of any human. He created places of extreme beauty and tranquility. He created things for timeless eons until He filled all the universes, all the dimensions. This intelligence then decided to place a fundamental law within it— the Law of Balance— so that it might endure for eternity." Taking another deep breath, Drogan watched Anton's reaction.

"This Law unexpectedly provided the possibility for everything to be consumed and destroyed, therefore, as a result, everything He had created, save the most recent of creations, had in fact disappeared. This shocked Him, and He abhorred it when His extraordinary makings were sucked through countless rips in the fabric of the universe—vortexes in the very heart of His creations. These vortexes continue even unto this day, consuming and destroying everything. This universe, the one we live in, will eventually be destroyed, and the time grows ever shorter before all is lost."

Pausing yet again, Drogan stared at Anton. He patiently made sure that the Warrior heard each fact he presented. He sensed his genuine interest and saw curiosity in his face. Satisfied, he continued.

"At the heart of every galaxy resides a force of immense power—a force of gravity so vast, so mighty, it literally annihilates everything around it. You know of these, your Methonian education calls them Black Holes." Drogan could see Anton grasped his meaning; he felt gratified his message made sense.

"Seeing this alteration of His great design, the Creator intended to uncover the nature of the vortex, so He entered it to discover what lay beyond. He traveled through this destructive force, and espied a universe not of His own making; it was one of complete opposition to His own. At first, He hadn't realized an underlying fact—something so important, so profound, and so fundamental it never occurred to Him. Unknown to the Creator was something that confined all universes, and restricted their functionality. The Law of Balance had opened a doorway between two universes, a doorway to a universe belonging to the anti-intelligence. This intelligence was His equal, yet had a completely opposite agenda; he sought the utter annihilation of all creation."

Glancing over at Vim, Anton noticed his extreme interest in Drogan's narration. Furthermore, it seemed as if the wizard needed to hear Drogan repeat what he unquestionably already knew; he seemed to yearn for the completion of his story.

Drogan continued speaking. His expression exuded delight and fulfillment. "Thus, the Creator decided to escape this negative plane before His inevitable discovery. But He was too late. A prodigious battle between what we refer to as good and evil ensued, and it is still going on and will continue going on forever. As a result, as their fighting reached its apex, the essence of The Law of Balance broke, impelling it towards dissolution. This rip in the structural framework of all universes forced a simultaneous connection between them, interlacing them together in a delicate chaotic balance.

"Seeing this rip, the Negative Intelligence fled to the far reaches of His own unbounded demesne, so that He could plot the destruction of everything. Likewise, the Creator too fled to His own universe, back beyond the vortex. This momentary cessation of battle provided an opportunity to repair the threads of time that were shattered and strewn throughout the universe. The rip the battle had precipitated needed careful repair, and thus was the need for the creation of man. Weaving the threads together, the Creator restructured the Law of Balance to prevent it from unraveling further, and He sealed it with the Prophecy. By so doing, He preserved The Law of Balance from an inevitable and permanent destruction.

"The Creator then placed His prodigious work—a creation of pure magic—upon the rip in vortex, and sealed it with the Prophecy of One; He gave much of Himself in so doing. That's to say, much of Himself became His creation. In order for the Law of Balance to remain balanced, He is unable to interfere with His creation, and therefore, the Intelligence of Non-Existence is likewise unable to interfere directly as well; both must do so through people. The Law binds them both in this way, maintaining the seal. Humanity can only communicate to the Creator by speaking to Him directly, by using His name; this is referred to as prayer."

Drogan looked carefully back and forth at both of his visitors, as if he'd reached the final point of the story and was about to reveal even more. Taking a deep breath, he looked directly at Anton, and then resumed.

"That name, the name of the Creator, is, as you may have guessed, One! Thus we refer to the prophecy as the Prophecy of One. This binding force that he used to seal the vortex has had other names in ages past, but we currently refer to it as Peruvious. It is the 'sorrow name' for Earth."

Completely enthralled, Anton sat perfectly still and absolutely silent, as if in meditation. Drogan's recitation inspired awe, questions, and great doubts in him, but he was unable to discern any falsehood in the story's details. It was too unbelievable to be true, yet his most recent experiences had no logical explanation either. The entire set of events, from the initial summoning to Drogan's history lesson, seemed more like a dream or an illusion. The atmosphere of the deep cavern seemed to congeal; it intensified and amalgamated his feelings, leaving him profusely mystified. Skeptical, he digested the information as best he could. Implications and impossibilities abounded; it was as if the entire day wasn't real. However, this reality wasn't impossible—after all that had transpired, it could only be real. Dilemmas and contradictions of normality seemed to be the new standard, yet they confused his intellect without end.

"Dreams don't feel so vivid," Anton mumbled. He pinched himself, as if the resulting pain would prove it real, or the lack of pain would prove it false.

"Are you trying to tell me there is a *God?*" Anton scoffed at the Djinni; he rolled his eyes and shook his head in disbelief. "And you're saying that God's name is *One?*"

Vim took no notice of the questions Anton asked and of his perplexity; he was only interested in listening to the story. It seemed to empower his ancient heart, and his soul—strengthening his resolve and determination to see an end to Vile. He hadn't heard this story in a very long time, and was absorbed in its retelling—it was the entire purpose of his life, the very reason for his passion to succeed. He needed it, and paid heed to every word Drogan spoke.

"I'm incapable of telling anything but the truth, young man. Untruth would be my undoing; Peruvious would fall to pieces in an instant!" Drogan looked directly into Anton's eyes. His voice echoed off the cavern walls, giving him a majestic, almost godlike stature, so far removed from anything else around him that nobody would doubt that he was telling the truth.

"Now, allow me to finish," he went on. "The story is nearly complete." Staring long and deep into Anton's eyes, Drogan held his attention suspended in a viselike grip. "The foundation of existence became irrevocably sealed by The Prophecy. After putting His great handiwork into place, One in turn initiated the propagation of Himself: thus, He created man in His own image and likeness. This simple fact protects everything He'd created. He is a part of it, and He is one with it. He placed all forms of life within this seal to guarantee that His creation would remain forever preserved and protected.

"When He gave it a name, the seal was formed. 'Let all life have the chance to know power and freedom, for I have given to all life these things, and all beings will know the usage of power and freedom if they but seek me out and ask for my love, service, and guidance,' said the Creator as He placed life upon the surface of Peruvious. From this statement of power sprang forth life of all types, and the seeds of all life that was yet to come; He is the fountain of life, the well from which all life flows. The copulation and manifestation of all life on Peruvious thereafter had equal opportunity to build a home in His kingdom, with the potential of becoming Godlike themselves! They had but to believe in Him, and to love Him and to do his bidding.

"Over millennia, many have achieved just that, becoming entities of immense power, and serving One in a place we call heaven." Drogan pointed at Anton. "But beware of false gods; they are evil, and serve only destruction." He scrutinized the Warrior, making sure he fathomed the significance of his words. Then he folded his arms and continued.

"There was yet another reason for the introduction of life on Peruvious. Those that achieve the stature of an entity can influence human events; however, the Law forbids participation. Only the entity's servants—those people they remain in contact with—may act to shape events upon Peruvious. These are the restrictions of the Law of Balance, and thus the reason for your summoning here. You're from outside of the Peruvian restrictions; the Law of Balance has a different set of standards as a result; remember prayer, it is imperative!"

Anton shivered in his seat as Drogan's statement struck a chord in him. Realizing the implications of the truth, an urgent desire to act on Drogan's behalf flooded him; it intensified his resolve to continue on his present course. It was as if the Djinni's words touched the very core of his chemical makeup, it spoke directly to his DNA the way Vim had many hours earlier; it invoked a power over him, persuading him deeper into his resolve. He didn't comprehend why—only one person at a time could invoke his genetic prime directive. Yet most of his doubts faded away into oblivion; only one uncertainty remained. He wondered how human life existed on this unknown world.

"Your purpose here was prophesized scores of millennia ago, beyond time and before the existence of man," Drogan continued. "You are *The Warrior* spoken of in the Prophecy of One, and your destiny is at hand. All that remains is your *choice*; you must agree with your heart, not just your genetic programming." Drogan emphasized the word *choice* a second time, as if Anton were to save or damn Peruvious by making one, and as if he had the capacity to act beyond his programmed design.

My choice? he thought. The last time I had a choice, a whole village met with death! Am I to kill yet again through the actions of my choice? Unwittingly, Anton proclaimed his thoughts aloud as he wrestled with the discomfort of his recent choices in Tooloo; floods of memories flashed through his mind yet again. Every feeling and image persisted vividly, as if it had occurred only scant moments before. The events leading to the destruction of the cave and his ring turning black made him feel overcome with grief for a moment or two, like a flash of vertigo. Most of all, the death of Nelda twisted a knot in his stomach, and he felt ill as he recalled her beautiful face.

"If you should choose to follow the path set before you, your victory shall be glorious, undeniable, and righteous; people will call you the Savior, and the Champion of One. If evil should tempt you and persuade you, if you step aside from your true path, the failure you achieve will be the undoing of everything. The thing that you desire most of all—the release from Peruvious, and the return to your own world—will never happen." The Djinni pointed his finger at Anton as if he'd already committed some evil deed. The Warrior felt a stab at his heart; the magnitude of his words seemed somehow real, as if it'd already transpired.

"Allow me to reiterate: One created Peruvious, and in part, became Peruvious. He exists both here and in His own universe. The Intelligence of Non-Existence also exists, and exists *here*! He survives in the guise of a great evil upon Peruvious. This evil names Himself Vile the necromancer! This negative being disseminated Himself, just as the Creator did. To have done so, He too gave up much of what He was. However, One created the Prophecy. He has placed the parts of Himself in various locations throughout Peruvious. Vile exists both here and in his own universe; He is split between the two."

For a moment, Drogan fell silent. He closed his eyes, tipped his head back and took a deep breath. With a smile, he offered a Methonian bow, and then spoke once again. "I am Drogan, Djinni, and I am the *Voice of One!*"

As Drogan announced his personal revelation, a silent burst of fireworks filled the room, completely dazzling Anton and Vim. Covering his eyes, Anton protected them from the shimmering effects; his eyes had grown accustomed to the darkness and the sudden magnitude of light stung them. Instinctively, he stood in ready stance, as if making a decision, binding himself to his destiny, and preparing himself for all that was yet to come.

"By all of the mighty gods, how could I have misunderstood?" Vim said, cursing himself quietly. He glanced at Anton, who was equally surprised. But Vim felt embarrassed as well. He'd known Drogan for a millennium, and had never guessed his secrets. Nor had the Djinni revealed them before.

"I understand your surprise," Drogan said, looking at Vim. "I didn't keep this knowledge from you without cause." He turned to Anton. "Return to your seat, young one—your lesson hasn't yet ended." Unspoken words were evident in both men's expressions.

Anton stood there for a moment with a quizzical expression and unspoken words on his lips. Still another mystery presented itself to him— one that required faith in something he couldn't explain; it left him both frustrated and bewildered. Slowly, he respected Drogan's request, and returned to his seat as the Djinni continued his recitation.

"There are three pieces of One that will reveal themselves to you. I'm the first. Vim already knows the others—yet he's unaware of this, just as he was unaware of me! All paths will lead you to them, but they will not reveal themselves without first soliciting their help, as you did mine. You shall meet each in due course, each in its appropriate turn. Your journey shall begin the moment you leave here. You'll first visit the King Amilius at his castle; he has something to tell each of you, something you must hear in order to understand the conditions set before you." Prophetically, Drogan revealed their path; it came from the *Mouth of God,* and was irrefutable.

"Now Anton, you will *kneel* before me." With arms crossed, Drogan looked at the Warrior, waiting impatiently. He then pointed at the floor in front of him, commanding an instant response.

As if Drogan was one of his Masters back on Methonias, Anton knelt, feeling irrefutably compelled. First, he touched his forehead to the floor, and then he sat up and bowed his head respectfully. Putting his wrists together with the palms up, he exhibited his Methonian litany. "I'm at your service! Command me and I'll carry out your orders."

"Raise your head, Warrior," Drogan went on, "and look at me. You're *not* in *my* service; you're in the service of *One*, but only of your *own* volition." Drogan placed his hand upon Anton's head, the same way Vim had done when he'd first arrived on Peruvious—his right thumb on his forehead and his fingers stretched over the top of his head.

Closing his eyes, Drogan chanted incomprehensible words in a deep voice. After a moment, a golden glow emanated from the Djinni's palm; it seemed to fill Anton's skull with its power. Involuntarily, he opened his eyes wide, and his mouth hung open as if to scream. But no sound escaped his lips.

"I've placed in your mind the locations of the second and third fragments of *One*; when they're revealed, you will understand the truth of who they are. Furthermore, I've removed from you the restriction of solicited service. You can now choose whom to serve; your genetics no longer compel your actions. This is your new reality."

Drogan released Anton and folded his arms; instantly Anton collapsed on the cavern floor like a rag doll, unconscious and limp. His mouth hung agape, his eyes remained open, and he stared up at the Djinni uncomprehendingly.

"My purpose for now has come to an end," Drogan said. "Farewell my friend Vim, we'll not meet again." He touched his forehead and saluted his old friend. "This meeting has concluded. You must leave immediately! Time is growing far too short; the plans of the enemy exceed your efforts; you must hurry to overcome them." Instantly, Drogan disappeared and the chamber returned to blackness.

Vim ignited his staff, providing the necessary light. He stood there for a moment with a feeling of loss in his heart as he realized the implications of Drogan's words. Everything had changed since Anton's inception to Peruvious, and he wasn't sure that he could endure so many alterations so quickly; his extreme age diminished his capacity to respond instantly, and the unexpected loss of a good friend tore at his heart.

Kneeling next to Anton, Vim gently shook him, hoping to rouse him from the magical catatonia Drogan had induced.

With little effort, Anton awoke; slowly, forcibly, he returned to his feet and shook his head clear.

"We must go," Vim said, lifting his staff and tapping the floor of the cave so as to release a small surge of power. Then he stiffly returned to his feet. "Time moves against us—just as I have said, and as Drogan warned. Let us go!"

Silently, Anton nodded and then mechanically pointed in the direction they'd come from, as if to ask Vim to lead the way. Sighing, Vim returned Anton's nod and climbed up the steep incline, leading out.

Again, Anton watched the flickering and glinting pervading the walls and formations of the cave; they were no less spectacular than when they'd first entered. But in his present state of mind, he found them much less fascinating. Nevertheless, the effect again reminded him of the caverns of the Troglodytes back on Methonias, and of the spectacular Galactic Circus with its laser light shows. But he ignored these thoughts as he digested Drogan's story: the recitation of the Prophecy. With the removal of the DNA-induced servitude that had been built into him by the Clone Masters, he felt a sense of freedom he'd never known before.

CHAPTER 15
Glory and Folly

TRYING TO FATHOM THE SIGNIFICANCE of Drogans story, Anton pondered his chances of returning to Methonias; his yearning for home left a lonely ache in his heart. Now that Drogan had released him from his biologically programmed servitude, Anton assessed the unlikelihood of his repatriation. It left him feeling despondent. Even though he knew his Masters would simply reassign him to some other duty, and even though he knew he couldn't bring Nelda back to life if he did return, he still ached to leave Peruvious. The confusion of unexplainable magic, and the peculiar wonders he was unable to resolve, left him with a feeling of loneliness for his home planet. He knew in his heart that in order to find his way home he must acquiesce to Vim's request for help. Still, Vim's request frustrated him—it was an overwhelming adventure he no longer want to endure. He only wanted to leave.

At the same time, the circumstances of this new adventure consumed him, fascinated his intellect, and propelled him relentlessly forward, in the hope of both proving himself and discovering a way home. Drogan mentioned the possibility that he could earn his way back to Methonias—but only after he succeeded. This thought drove him forward; for now, it was the only hope and purpose he had left.

Still, he wasn't content with Drogan's fabulous story—it required him to believe in an inexplicable, unverifiable mythology. The *Prophecy of One* left him entirely bewildered with its cryptic message. Perplexed, he weighed the extremes of his emotions, and his personal dilemma, trying to decide for himself what to do.

Soon, Vim exhibited signs of fatigue. He'd pushed himself to the limits of his endurance, and his old body looked frail and exhausted. His footing became less sure; he scuffed his feet and stumbled on the smooth stone and loose rocks as they ascended through the caverns and tunnels.

"I need food and rest," Vim finally confessed, with a strained and tired voice. "A day and a night and yet another day have passed since we left the Primords' hamlet, and I haven't rested since a day before then. It's early in the evening of the second day now. Breakfeast easily sustains anyone for a day or even longer, but we've surpassed that." With knees trembling, he looked hard at Anton and leaned heavily on his staff.

Vim's thoughts seemed disjointed, but his point was clear. And Anton agreed with him entirely. An enormous hunger and a tremendous thirst had nagged him also for some time. He wondered how Vim knew how much time they'd spent underground, but shrugged the thought aside as just another peculiarity. *Yet another mystery*, he thought.

"I know a small room that is both secluded and suitable for rest; there we can refresh ourselves," Vim offered. "We'll be there forthwith."

Within moments, the two came across a small chamber, barely noticeable unless carefully looked for; there was a natural concealment of stone, much like the entrance to the cave under the falls in the village of Tooloo. Even when Vim cast the light from his staff in its direction, the shadows prevented its detection.

The room was larger than Anton had anticipated—more or less oval-shaped and hooked around a corner at the far end. The ceiling was roughly dome-shaped, and the sandy ground had a layer of white limestone pebbles, giving it a tranquil appearance. But the chamber walls were coarse and less inviting. The only place to sit with support was against a large boulder near the entrance. As they entered the hollow, Vim stiffly sat himself down with his back against it and sighed hugely. A look of extreme exhaustion covered his face. He gazed at Anton and clumsily motioned for him to sit.

Standing alongside Vim, Anton rejected his offer of repose. "How long will we rest here? Have you anything to eat?" He wanted to help, but had little to offer without returning to the surface and foraging.

Without looking at Anton, Vim replied. "I'm sorry, I'm old. My body can no longer continue without rest; it isn't young like yours. I shall require a good night's sleep. I'm sure you need several hours of rest as well. As for food, I shall conjure up what I can." Vim remained stationary and continued his respite, not acting upon his own words— it was as if he no longer had the energy to perform a simple task.

After another moment or two, Vim still hadn't moved a single muscle. Shaking his head and huffing in disbelief, Anton petulantly decided to look around.

"Sit, young one!" Vim suddenly snapped; his strength had all but left him, and he'd depleted his patience. "I just need a few... a few minutes to catch my breath."

"Let me know when you plan to fulfill your proposal." Anton gently scoffed. "As everyone is saying, time works against us..." His voice trailed off as he watched the ancient wizard.

Looking at Vim with an air of dissatisfaction, Anton sat down, crossed his legs, adopted the Lotus position, and prepared himself for meditation. Several days had passed since his last opportunity, and his soul ached for it; he needed to clear his thoughts and find solace from recent unexplained experiences. It seemed clear that Vim wasn't going to enlighten him further; even Drogan had said the old man should talk more. But it seemed that telling stories wasn't his forte.

As Anton closed his eyes, Vim slowly stood up, raised his staff, and started to chant in a soothing, tired voice, interrupting Anton's meditation. The words he spoke were in his ancient wizard's tongue, and Anton was clueless as to their meaning. Slowly, a radiation of green iridescence mixed with gold filled the chamber. Almost at once, a small trickle of water bubbled forth from the cavern floor and formed a shallow pool in the center of the room. Around the edge of the water, lichens and fungi grew at an unnatural pace. After a few moments, tiny white fish filled the pond and frantically splashed around, causing the water to appear to boil, as if they were in a feeding frenzy.

"Astonishing," proclaimed Anton. "I wouldn't have believed it if I hadn't seen it." Watching the magic, he derided his own disbelief in the wizard's capabilities.

Shaking his head as if he were trying to clear it of a hallucination, Anton marveled at what he saw. Ever since he had arrived on Peruvious, every law of nature and physics he'd ever learned had been challenged, and many proved valueless. He understood science and technology, and this continual display of magic only confused him. How could he make good decisions when everything here was so different and obscure, and the familiar laws of reality seemed distorted beyond comprehension? Nevertheless, the empty pit of his stomach won out over his confusion and he reached over to pick a mushroom. He noticed that the fungi looked much like any other, yet he had no idea of its biological family. He'd received extensive training in the identification of all flora and fauna of the known worlds, and this mushroom didn't seem to fall into any particular phylum. At best, it fell between several.

"Mushrooms," Anton said with astonishment. "Who would have thought I'd see something like this!" his skepticism grew with each passing magical manifestation.

Heaving a sigh, Vim refused to argue or care about Anton's ignorance; he knew the young Warrior would eventually accept the things he witnessed.

"Go ahead and eat it," the old man said. "You will find it to your liking. I'm sorry we're in a cave or I would've been able to conjure up something a little more appealing. I would appreciate it if you would gather some for me while you're at it."

Taking a bite, Anton found the flavor more than acceptable, and he quickly retrieved more mushrooms, offering several to Vim. Removing his haori, he used it as an angler's net, and scooped up some of the fish. It functioned crudely but sufficed.

Slowly, Vim ate the mushrooms. Then he took a long deep drink of water from the icy pool, and washed his face. He sat there leaning on his staff and gazing into the pool, seemingly detached from Anton's efforts, and lingering in his own thoughts; it was as if the water reflected his contemplations rather than his image. Unconsciously, he picked a few more mushrooms and accepted some fish from Anton without acknowledgment.

Despite his enormous hunger, he ate slowly, as if unable to find an appetite, but it was more than enough to assuage his hunger.

In contrast, Anton required no coaxing to stuff himself with everything he could gather. He had a youthful appetite, and was raised on a planet where one occasionally hunted and gathered one's own food and competed for it in the end; Vim's assortment of oddities didn't bother him in the least, he'd eaten much worse, and far more exotic. After finishing the last small fish, he brushed aside the limestone gravel and sharp volcanic pebbles to prepare a more comfortable place for meditation. Looking at Vim, he raised an eyebrow and shrugged; he could see the Wizard had something to say and he waited for his next instructions.

"Get some rest," Vim counseled without looking directly at Anton. "I intend to do so as well." Intuitively, he'd understood Anton's quizzical expression. Heaving a fatigued sigh, he continued to speak, as his young Warrior friend prepared to meditate.

"Remember: we have little time. Both of us need sleep so we can meet tomorrow's challenges. The Dragon Master awaits our return to the surface." Vim looked directly at Anton. "We've unfinished business with that infernal beast. When and if we do encounter him, we will need every ounce of strength—and you haven't yet learned to use Drogan's gift." Leaning back against the large boulder, he closed his eyes.

It was clear to Anton that Vim spoke mostly of his own needs; he expressed fatigue in every word he uttered, his thoughts were unorganized. He was old, and he'd extended himself well beyond his limits.

But Anton understood the deeper meaning of Vim's argument; he knew what would be required of him and he agreed. "I hear you, and will comply. It would be reckless to challenge an enemy unprepared." "We shall see about that—avoidance is prudent and fighting is risky. But face him you will—it's inevitable." As soon as he had finished speaking, Vim drifted into slumber, still leaning against the large boulder. Immediately he started to snore; it reminded Anton of Mahkeetah that first night in the village of Tooloo. He chuckled to himself. "Old man," he mumbled.

Looking at his ring, Anton noticed it radiated an aura of pale pastel blue light. It was barely perceptible, and pastel but translucent. The neutral magic of Drogan's influence was weakening. This gave Anton an uneasy feeling. But he felt relaxed enough to meditate quietly for a short time.

Slowly he entered a deep part of himself, reaching into that special place he'd discovered when traveling aboard the Pleceivious. Carefully, methodically, he washed all the ill feelings from his emotional self, and collected the positive impressions of the past two days for future reference. Deliberately, with a Warrior's precision, he projected his thoughts into the chamber, and in turn, himself along with them. As before, he could look back upon himself, as if standing outside of his physical body, and saw Vim resting nearby. He still didn't understand this phenomenon, but accepted it for what it was.

After a heartbeat or two, Anton placed his discernment upon the Staff of Balance; it appeared to glow from within, and the globe became active—or perhaps alive? He could both see and feel it, as if it emitted a living light—a presence, a spirit, or a feeling of warmth. Somehow, the staff felt as though it were corporeal and alive. This confounded Anton's rational mind—no object or artifact could possibly be alive. Perhaps his senses were mistaken. Yet he reached out with his spirit-like hand and felt the staff's warmth, or essence, or presence, detecting some form of... *thought?* He wasn't sure what to make of it yet.

Finally, realizing his own deep need for rest, Anton returned to himself. A sense of peace filled his heart as he rejoined his body; he felt as if he'd washed all of his misgivings and ill impressions away. This cleansing changed the color of his ring—it now radiated a pale golden hue. He was surprised and he recollected the steps taken to achieve this, and then filed the information away for future reference.

After clearing his mind and gaining a feeling of contentment, Anton found a suitable spot and carefully brushed the limestone gravel aside, revealing coarse yet soft sand underneath. He then dug two depressions into the sand so that a person might lie there comfortably. Carefully, respectfully, he picked Vim up and placed him into one of the depressions, like a parent putting a baby to bed. Then he positioned himself in the second. Soon a deep slumber overtook his weary body.

A few short hours passed. Vim was the first to awaken. Before rousing Anton, he again conjured food and drink, refreshing and replenishing the pool from the previous evening. As he did so, Anton arose with a Warrior's protective attitude. He quickly lurched to his feet and pivoted around, scanning the chamber for danger. After realizing where he was, he relaxed and looked at Vim.

"Hurry and refresh yourself, young one, we must soon be on our way." Vim pointed at the newly restored provisions and winked. "I offer nothing more than before; it will have to suffice."

Anton wondered why the old wizard needed to state the obvious; his Masters had taught him not to converse without purpose. Knowing Vim hadn't had the same training, he let it slide, and filled his empty stomach with fish, mushrooms, and fresh cold water. Though it was the same meal, he still enjoyed it, knowing that hunger was the alternative.

One must be well-fed to serve properly, he thought, reflecting upon the words of his Masters. Their wisdom revitalized and strengthened him, keeping his mind acutely focused to the essential practices of a Methonian Warrior.

Grasping his staff with both hands, Vim heaved himself up, and then gently patted Anton's shoulder, as if to reassure him. "We must depart; it is early morning, and the sun will rise shortly." He increased the illumination from his staff.

"Now I wish to caution you: do not mention the name of the great lizard—for it is perilous!" Vim pointed a long skinny finger at Anton, warning him not to make the same mistake he'd made upon their arrival. He gave him a stern look and winked.

"I hear you, and I obey, my Master; you needn't warn me," Anton retorted, and then bowed in Methonian fashion. "You should trust me."

Anton's arrogance was sharp and penetrating. Vim scowled, and then sighed while shaking his head. He knew that Anton had never had any real friends before, and he knew that he had never had any genuine parenting. His Masters and fellow Warriors had provided nearly all of his limited experiences in social development. The fact that he'd never received the love of a mother in his youth proved without question the value of such care. After a moment, Vim's old heart softened. He knew real friendship could very well be the crux of everything he hoped for. He offered a comforting smile and stiffly returned Anton's bow, trying clumsily to imitate the Methonian custom.

Vim felt as if he'd have to take on the role of a father or big brother. He knew that not only did he have to educate his new friend on Peruvian history, and prepare him for the experiences he would face— he also had to guide him toward maturity and adulthood. The list of things he needed to prepare Anton for seemed to increase daily.

He wondered how long it would be before he'd be ready to meet the challenge of his destiny.

Leaning on his staff, Vim stiffly turned around and left the chamber with Anton close on his heels; the two moved at as brisk a pace as Vim could manage toward the surface of Peruvious. After a short time, they arrived at the large chamber with many sub-tunnels leading in all directions. There, Vim stopped; they were just a few minutes' walk from the cave's exit. But the old man hesitated as if he had heard something.

Again, Anton remembered his experience in the Troglodyte caverns back on Methonias; this chamber vaguely reminded him of the intersection where he'd first met the Troglodytes. The only real difference was the presence of stalactites and stalagmites, and the chamber's sheer magnitude; it completely dwarfed the Methonian caverns. Also, it was natural, not carved by hand as the Trogs had done.

Vim put his hand over his forehead, and closed his eyes; after a moment or two, he said: "He awaits us. I can sense him, and I feel his anger." He sounded sure of his assertion, as if he already knew what was to happen. "I just *know* he's there. Prepare for his attack."

Anton wondered how Vim could possibly know the Dragon Master was there—how he could feel his anger and sense his presence. Carries a grudge, does he?" Anton asked spryly, as if joking. "I'll show him what a Warrior can do!"

"*No*, you don't!" Vim nearly shouted. He grasped Anton firmly on the shoulder and whirled the Warrior around to face him. The two glared angrily at each other.

"You almost got both of us killed the last time, and I'm not about to lose you! You will *obey* me to the letter this time!" Vim was adamant.

Surprised at the Wizard's outrage, Anton thought that maybe he wasn't telling him something, or perhaps Vim didn't understand just how skilled he was. He tossed his shoulder back and brought his hand up in a circular motion, slapping Vim's hand away.

"I can take this dragon," he snarled, with increasing arrogance. He was angry at the wizard for doubting his abilities. He was absolutely convinced he could overcome the adversary.

"You simply haven't got a clue about how skilled I am!" Anton growled his outrage under his breath.

"I need you alive!" Vim growled back. "I refuse to allow you to commit suicide!"

"You astound me, old man. Perhaps my service is not at your side if you choose to prevent me from performing my designed intent; doesn't your fear therefore diminish who I am? Is there no purpose for me other than to follow you around? You mustn't forbid me from using my skills!"

"When we reach the Castle of Amilius, you shall *find* your purpose!" Vim shouted. "There *is* a greater purpose for your skills. *Do not despair!* This desire to get yourself killed for the sake of glory isn't going to help anything!" Vim argued.

"As we exit the cave, I'll protect us with my globe of invulnerability, just as I did when we arrived. When it surrounds us, we're undetectable by this creature, and can travel to the castle unnoticed. It's necessary that we get there as quickly as possible." Standing his ground, Vim continued to lock eyes with Anton.

"Very well," Anton replied. "But if we come under attack I *will* meet any challenge—I must! It's who I am! I'm a Methonian Warrior!"

Gritting his teeth, Vim held back his anger. He knew arguing wouldn't solve the issue. "See to it you *avoid* confrontation before you *induce* it. Now let us go."

For a long moment, Anton stood there. "As you wish," he remarked, sarcastically. "I'm at your service."

Ignoring him, Vim continued through the caverns at a quickened pace, with Anton following close behind; the surface was a scant ascent of a few hundred feet. As they neared the cave's exit, Vim hesitated. Suddenly, an ear-splitting roar reverberated outside the cave opening;

the Dragon Master's voice sounded intensely enraged. He knew the two humans were inside, and just beyond his reach.

"You sh-shall die this-ss day Vim Alpenss-sstock!" the mighty voice of the Dragon Master boomed like a cannon. "Your-rr puny lih-hittle frr-hend I shall feast upon first-ssss!"

That was all Anton needed. He raced toward the cave opening and leapt upon the loose gravel just outside. Skillfully, he slid like a skater on ice across the obsidian shards. He instantly produced his Blue Flame Sword, and a four-foot length of fire shot into the air, pointing the way.

The Dragon Master circled just above the eager Anton, and dove toward him at a breathtaking speed, like an eagle flying over a lake, preparing to grasp a fish—but fishing for humans.

Vim was unable to believe Anton's foolhardy attack, especially after their argument and his demands just a few moments before. At first, he felt like a spectator, unable to react; but soon his sense of urgency returned. Quickly he raced as fast as his ancient body could move toward the cavern opening. But he was too late. There simply wasn't enough time to respond to the situation, considering how fast Anton could move.

The Dragon Master nosedived toward Anton like an arrow that couldn't miss. With his sword pointing toward the sky, the Warrior met the Dragon Master's wrath with proud determination. His fiery Methonian blood precluded fear; it never occurred to him how hopeless his predicament might be. For anyone else the mission would have seemed suicidal. But Anton was brave beyond reasonable limits—brave to the point of recklessness. He possessed incredible skills unknown even to the Dragon Master.

Diving toward his prey, the Dragon Master blasted a gust of fire from his gaping maw; Anton parried skillfully, but could not escape the talons as they swiftly reached toward him. The crushing claws dropped like the landing gear of an Aerocraft and snatched Anton from the ground; the momentum of the mighty serpent carried him aloft.

Anton looked like a caged animal held in the immense claws. His arms and sword had little freedom to move. Yet he struggled forcibly to reposition himself, hoping to strike a blow. The Dragon Master's jarring motions and razor-sharp claws made it impossible for Anton to attack.

Anton realized his folly—even if he could attack, the Dragon Master might drop him to the ground—and it was much too far a fall to survive. He knew he would pay with his life unless he found a solution, but he could only wait.

Vim felt helpless until he remembered he still had a trick up his sleeve. Quickly, he raised his staff and started to chant; instantly an invisible sphere formed around him and he levitated. But the Dragon Master had the advantage; he was far ahead of Vim. In a heartbeat, he disappeared behind the rim of the mountain, taking Anton with him. It would be a minute or two before Vim could catch up.

Desperately, Vim levitated toward the mountain's peak as quickly as he could; he feared losing yet another champion to his ancient foe, and it appeared as if he were once again too late. He couldn't wait another fifty years. Losing Anton so quickly would be a devastating blow his ancient heart couldn't bear. And the loss of the *Champion of One* would mean utter annihilation for humanity—it was absurd to assume he'd even have an opportunity for another champion.

"I *must* save him!" Vim yelled as he flew through the air. "That boy is beyond my comprehension; I *warned* him, and *still* he defied my command."

Vim recalled the words of Drogan the Djinni. *You're the Warrior spoken of in the Prophecy of One*, he had said. Vim knew everything was at stake, and feared it would all be over too soon. Failure wasn't an option. This time everything depended upon Anton's success; there were no alternatives.

"He must succeed, or all of Peruvious and the *universe* will be lost forever!" Vim said. His determination increased as he considered the extent of his peril. He poured all of his conviction and strength through the staff, and flew at breathtaking speed.

The Dragon Master dove inside the mountain's crater, accelerating at an incredible velocity, and then suddenly, before Anton expected it, he spread his enormous wings, shifted his body weight backward, and came to an almost instantaneous halt, lightly touching down in his inner mountain domain. Releasing his captive like a cat playing with a mouse, the Dragon Master confidently prepared to finish his prey.

The stresses of the shifting G-forces coupled with the compressing grasp of the Dragon had left Anton disoriented; a sudden dizziness caused him to slip and lose his footing, and he instantly stumbled and fell to his knees. His muscles ached and failed to respond properly after the crushing clutch of the Dragon's talons. To make things worse, the smell of the atmosphere nearly asphyxiated him—it was warm and heavy, and it stank like an amalgamation of sulfur and oily sweat. He felt like he might vomit.

However, now Anton had a chance to continue his fight. Scrambling to regain his feet, he again stumbled and fell on the loose gravel. But he was a Methonian Warrior, and failure wasn't an option. Again, he struggled to stand, stumbled, and took a couple of unsteady steps. Then the dizziness and instability melted away. His Methonian resilience fortified him and accelerated his recovery. As his vision cleared, he glanced at the whispering hints of early morning sky through the immense opening of the volcanic crater. He surveyed his surroundings while preparing for battle, feeling perplexed at how shallow the chamber seemed. It was just as he had seen it in Beelif's presentation—deep and long—yet it gave a sensation of shallowness due to its relative shape and size. It felt different from before, perhaps due to the dim sunlight peaking over the crater's rim.

After releasing his captive, the Dragon Master spoke again. "I s-see that my abilities-ss s-surpris-sse you foolis-sh little human!" His voice chuckled with a deep reptilian hiss. "I alls-so s-see you are without magic of your own and that magic ss-ssurpris-ess you. I wi-hill now free the la-hife from your p-huny human body! You shall fe-heel relief in itsss pass-ssing!"

Anton wondered what the point of this speech was; he also wondered what had happened to Vim. Would the wizard attempt a rescue? Or would he find it difficult to catch up with him? Assuming he must rely entirely upon himself, he found the challenge enticing. This was how he preferred to fight; his Methonian training and confidence precluded the need for help. At the same time, Vim's recent friendship left him feeling as though he *wanted* his support, as if he needed an audience to prove himself. This strange world seemed to disrupt his Methonian proficiencies—or did he simply need the audience he desired? Anton quickly cast off his self-analyzing and returned his attention to the current predicament.

Anton wasn't entirely sure what the Dragon Master's capabilities were, and he didn't want to be suddenly vulnerable at an inappropriate moment due to an unknown and unexpected variable. He wanted to make his first strike count, and he wanted it to put the circumstances in his favor. He wasn't about to end up like Boris—a chained and helpless meal.

The Dragon Master loomed over Anton; a lizard-like grin stretched across his face as he prepared to end Anton's life. For the first time, he got a look at how immense the giant serpent was; he towered over the trivial human like a titan.

Unwilling to allow the momentum of the battle to shift, Anton grasped his sword in both hands, summoned forth the blade of blue flame, and then raised it over his shoulder. Cobalt fire, argent at its core, lighted the area in which he stood, and made him appear mightier than his comparatively diminutive stature suggested.

The Dragon Master's eyes widened perceptibly as he chuckled. "This-s is-s my domain! I am mas-ster here! You think your lih-hittle toy is-ss a match for me?" He roared and hissed his hate.

Anton sprang into action. With unexpected speed and agility, he ran directly toward the enormous beast. The slippery shards and round pebbles beneath his feet didn't slow him down or hinder his efforts. As he ran, a light of intense power filled the cavern for an instant, as if lightning had struck. He wasn't sure where it emanated from, but it didn't stop his attack. Leaping into the air, he swung the blue blade and struck the Dragon in the side of his chest as hard as he could. A crackling electric sound came from the sword as it made contact. It easily pierced the Dragon between two plates of heavy reptilian armor, and buried itself clear to the hilt, surprising even Anton.

The Dragon Master exploded with a shriek of agony—a harrowing scream that boomed like a cannon firing next to Anton's ear, temporarily deafening him. Blood gushed from the open wound to the stone below.

Shutting off the Blue Flame Sword, Anton prepared his weapon for another blow; again, he summoned forth the fiery blade into action. Outraged, the Dragon Master gnashed his teeth at Anton, but missed his target widely; he pivoted his weight from one side to the other in an effort to improve his position for another strike. This gave Anton another opportunity to act. Without forethought, he parried and swung with blinding speed at the leg of the giant lizard. The fiery blade made contact exactly at the ankle. With the precision of a surgeon, the blue flame sliced through the heavy armor like a scalpel through tender flesh, instantly cleaving the enormous talon from the Dragon's limb. Blood gushed from the severed appendage and rapidly created a puddle on the ground; the stone surface beneath Anton's feet became as slippery as ice.

Shrieking, the mighty dragon blew fire in all directions as his head heaved uncontrollably from side to side. The gust singed Anton in the process, but the uncontrolled attack posed little peril. No longer having the support of one leg, the Dragon Master teetered, stumbled, and fell on his side, with a crash that shook solid stone; the crushing mass nearly squashed Anton as it came down all around him.

Scrambling to save himself, Anton cartwheeled over the neck of the mighty beast in order to miss the avalanche of armored flesh. He had another opportunity to strike. With unremitting determination, he prepared for a final blow.

Taking three quick paces and leaping at the Dragon's head, Anton turned his sword over and grasped it with both hands, like a dagger. The blade struck a third time with unequaled voracity, directly in the center of the Dragon's eye. The fiery blade buried itself to the hilt. Vitreous humor and brain matter sprayed like a momentary burst from a fire hose, and rained all around. Then, nothing moved. The Dragon Master was dead. To ensure his victory, Anton flipped his sword around, and in a swift single stroke, decapitated the limp monster.

"What have you done?" A familiar voice wailed behind him. "It's impossible to do what you have done!" It was Vim—smiling, and then frowning. In disbelief, he wasn't sure how to feel. "The Dragon Master is impossible to destroy!" he yelled at Anton while looking at the severed head. "He is a creature of immense power! The *balance* of your actions will exact a price we have yet to fathom. You've altered the fulcrum's position of the *Law of Balance*."

Puzzled, Anton looked over his shoulder at the wizard. "I did what I had to," he replied, with a sneer. "Didn't you want him dead? And you thought it was *beyond* my capabilities." Arrogantly, he ignored the Wizard's concern.

Not really knowing what to say, Vim slowly climbed up the loose shards and gravel toward his young friend. "The Dragon Master is a creature of immense power!" he said again, as if he needed to grasp the implications himself. "It's inevitable you'll pay for this with some loss, or perhaps something even worse. Even *I* have no way of knowing the outcome—but it will be a direct result of your actions."

"How can the death of such a creature cause *anything* bad to happen?" Anton scoffed. He wondered if the old man was scared or jealous of his success; his words sounded nonsensical.

"Everything here on Peruvious, and elsewhere in the universe, is subject to the laws of *cause and effect,* that is to say, the *Law of Balance!*" Vim elaborated. He knew Anton should already understand this, yet he seemed to require additional reinforcement to make his point. "Do you remember Drogan's story?" He looked at him closely.

"Yes, of course I remember—but what has *that* got to do with killing this big *lizard*?" Again, Anton's tone was scornful. "I got it: Drogan spoke of Peruvious as being the place where this God named *One* broke Himself to pieces, and of the *Law of Balance*."

"Didn't you understand the meaning of Drogan's tale?" Vim said, shaking his head. "You're so much like your brethren," he sighed, "I cannot guide you if you refuse to *listen* to me."

Anton looked at Vim with a perplexed expression. "You call this place Peruvious, the place where the good intelligence and bad intelligence are fighting for control of existence! What's your *point*?"

"Yes!" Vim said, looking at Anton, and waiting for him to grasp his point. He didn't feel like arguing. It seemed obvious that Anton did not comprehend.

Thinking about it for a minute, Anton tried to appease Vim's concern. "Well, then—what you're trying to say is that the *Staff of Balance* is the fulcrum used to control the scales between the two intelligences?" He shook his head as if he didn't believe his own question; it seemed ludicrous to assume this was possible.

"Precisely! All life—all people and creatures—are a part of the balance of nature and the universe. The Dragon Master was more than a simple creature; his creation came from dark magic, and magic was what he was. Who knows what effect his death will have upon the balance of nature and the universe! I believe that he exemplified the essence of evil. With him removed, good will be affected adversely in order to adjust the balance!"

"Why don't you just use your staff and rebalance everything the way you want it?" Anton said, rolling his eyes. He thought of how he'd felt the staff was somehow alive and he was confident Vim could do more than he attempted. "It seems you have the power to *control* the balance. Why not just *reset* it?"

Heaving a sigh, Vim shook his head. "I'm sorry; it simply doesn't work that way."

The two fell silent for a minute. Then, just as Vim had predicted, it happened. Suddenly, from deep within the gut rock, the very core of Peruvious, a loud screeching sound of stone shifting against stone resounded in a low rumble. The reverberation grew in amplitude for a moment, and then a violent shaking began under their feet, tossing them around. The vibrations increased substantially as each second passed, and the sound rose in tens of decibels proportionally. Within seconds, Vim could no longer stand. Anton fought to maintain his footing. He supported Vim with both hands. Together they danced on the loose rock under their feet. It felt as if they weighed more than they should—as if gravity itself had increased as the entire surface of Peruvious lifted into the air.

"We must flee!" Vim yelled, hoping Anton could hear him over the deafening sound. "The cavern may collapse at any moment!" He grasped Anton's wrist and raised the staff, enveloping them both in a golden sphere of energy. They swiftly floated into the air, flying beyond the rim of the crater. This gave them an interesting view of the mountain shifting beneath them as Vim raced through the opening toward the sky.

As they reached relative safety outside the mountain, everything seemed to settle down. Vim looked for a good place to land; he needed a little time to assess what had just occurred. Choosing a spot just beyond the base perimeter of the Barren Mountain, the two settled on an immense flat piece of obsidian.

"The tectonic plate of Upper Peruvious has shifted," Vim said. "It sits higher than it did before." Vim made a bold proclamation and watched Anton's reaction. "The separation between Upper and Lower Peruvious must've increased substantially."

"Just what does that mean?" Anton said, scoffing. "I don't understand." "There's a line—an edge between the two halves of Peruvious. Long ago, the staff, *this* staff, separated and raised Upper Peruvious in order to create a balancing effect between good and evil. It's like a fenced border drawn between two countries. Or, you may think of it as a set of balancing scales that evaluate good and evil."

Vim's explanation was less than helpful, but Anton seemed to understand what he was trying to say. He looked at him with disbelief. He sighed, and then nodded his acceptance.

"So, you're saying there's a physical change in altitude between the upper and lower halves? Is that why you refer to them as Upper and Lower Peruvious?" asked Anton.

"Yes. Long ago, the battle between Lothendus and Vile caused a cataclysmic event. Consequently, a clearly defined separation of what we now refer to as Upper and Lower Peruvious developed along an existing tectonic plate. The levels between the two halves shifted, creating a sheer cliff; nearly a mile high, it marks the boundary between the two halves."

"I see. And the distance of this separation increased as a result of the Dragon Master's death?" Anton looked at Vim in utter amazement and complete disbelief, and again he rolled his eyes.

"That is correct," Vim replied. He heaved a sigh. His patience was wearing thin.

"It did feel as though the ground was pushing up beneath our feet," Anton said, nodding.

It was obvious to Vim that Anton still didn't believe him. He didn't know how he could ever convince this young and skeptical hero the truth of what he refused to believe.

"I'm relieved you understand what you sensed; this is a tiny step forward. Good. Upper Peruvious is now higher than it was before. I don't know the extent of the change, but we will find out in due course. For now, we've more important things to accomplish." Vim decided to change the subject. "Let's set this discussion aside for now—there'll be more time to continue it later. Right now, we need to make our journey to the Castle of Amilius, so let's be on our way."

Vim motioned for Anton to grasp his arm so that they might levitate; he complied, and they rose into the air. The globe atop the Staff of Balance glowed brightly, lighting the morning with its golden energy.

A translucent aura of golden light surrounded the two travelers as they made their ascent; higher and higher, they rose into air and traveled northeast, and the Barren Mountain slowly faded into the distance.

"I'd like to know one thing," Anton asked. "What's the connection between Peruvious and the place Drogan referred to as *heaven*?"

Taken aback, Vim looked at Anton in surprise. Somehow, the question seemed out of context, but he was willing to answer anyway; he was happy that the Warrior wanted to know more on this particular subject.

"Peruvious *isn't* heaven. It's the so-called *magic plug* if you please, separating the two universes of existence and nonexistence. One divided Himself and put much of what He was into this great work. Because we live here with the Intelligence of Existence, how could we not absorb part of His essence? For it is all around us. If someone dares to use enough magic—that is to say, if someone chooses to use part of His essence— he in turn becomes more than just a mere human. In time—and it *has* happened—he may even become an entity of immeasurable power."

"How do you use this essence? Drogan mentioned prayer—is that how it's done? That seems so primitive—so abstract. That is all about *faith* and *religion*!" Anton scoffed cynically. He wasn't about to accept anything that required a belief system.

"Your skepticism is obvious," Vim replied. "But at least you're finally grasping the concept; this is a step in the right direction." Vim was pleased. "Using prayer—or more appropriately, *words of power*—anyone might learn to invoke the *Power of One*."

"So where did this dragon come from? How is it that such a creature existed?" Still not satisfied, Anton needed to know more.

"As I said before," Vim continued, "the Dragon Master was made from the perverse and dark magic of the Crystal Pyramid. His alignment was evil, and his creation came from pure evil; he was the embodiment of the dark side of magic." Vim paused, seeming taxed by Anton's questions. "Now—please, let us continue on our way. I need to concentrate on our travel." Because he had split his attention, the sphere had slowed and they'd descended significantly.

As Vim's concentration increased, the staff's globe emitted more light and the sphere surrounding them increased its height and speed; winds buffeted them around as they rode the currents of air like a ship on the ocean. To Anton, it seemed as though the staff pulsed and vibrated with energy, as if somehow it was capable of manufacturing it. He was enraptured with the runes glowing along the shaft. He still didn't understand how Vim's magic operated, but he was beginning to piece together what Drogan and Vim were teaching him; finally, a feeling of acceptance seeded itself inside his logical reasoning.

Watching the landscape below, Anton studied the rolling hills as they gradually transformed into flatter plains covered with early spring grass. Directly to the northeast, a vast lake was visible, and to the south and southwest was the tree line of the forest, where Anton had first arrived. Dotting the landscape in the rolling plains were herds of llamas, deer, and occasionally buffalo. Anton recognized that nature continued about its business even after the raising of the tectonic plate; all seemed as it should be.

Vim guided them along the edge of the forest and the rolling plains; after a time, he adjusted their trajectory directly north. Soon the forest dwindled to small thickets, and then the trees disappeared entirely, leaving nothing but the rolling hills.

The day waned, and the sun rose high and then began to sink into the west. Neither man spoke for what seemed hours as they traveled. It was natural for Anton to remain silent; this was a strict practice in his training, and he also preferred his own private thoughts as he digested all that had happened during the past two days; he found it superior to engaging in conversation with Vim at present; he'd always found contentment in the solitude of his own thoughts and Vim needed his silence in order to concentrate at working his magic.

As Vim continued focusing on the levitation, Anton contemplated the death of the Dragon Master. Repeatedly he considered having killed the mighty beast, and he wondered if he should feel remorse. But he felt nothing but pride at having achieved such an incredible feat. Yet the resulting fluctuation in the balance of the continent disturbed him. Was it conceivable he'd done some inestimable harm? How could that be possible?

It isn't just anyone who could kill such a creature, he thought to himself. *Vim must realize that I'm more than an average Warrior!* His ego swelled moment by moment, and his pride escalated exponentially—yet his heart felt empty and unfulfilled. Then he set these thoughts aside and considered the people he'd met.

Aside from Drogan and Beelif, Vim was the first human who had captivated Anton's intellect; only the teachings of his Methonian Masters had ever interested him in the past. Yet for some strange reason, his heart felt empty by Vim's perpetual silence as they traveled. Ultimately, he needed the wizard's thoughts and conversation after so much silence; he needed answers and was getting nothing.

Finally, Vim spoke. "We'll be arriving at the castle in just a few minutes. You can just see it in the distance."

It was true. Anton could see what appeared to be a stone wall, surrounding a large medieval-style castle. Within minutes, Vim guided their descent. The day grew late and the mountain range nearly eclipsed the sun on the western horizon; it painted the sky with a picturesque display of reds and yellows.

As they drew nearer to the castle, Anton studied its layout. It had many cylindrical turrets positioned at intervals around a perimeter wall, stretching nearly three hundred feet into the air. Within the main castle, many enormous towers dwarfed the perimeter turrets; they were more than twice as big, with conical points.

Before long, the two men touched down lightly outside the castle wall. The people in the vicinity declared surprise at the arriving sphere. Some of them appeared frightened. One man came up to Vim and greeted him respectfully, bowing.

Suddenly, several knights clad in golden armor charged toward them, with weapons drawn. One of the knights stepped forward and addressed Vim. "I'm Lord Vinicus, head of the Wardsman Alliance," he said, looking directly at Anton. "I've expected your arrival, and I'm instructed to take you to the throne room immediately."

Lord Vinicus stared at Anton with immense loathing. "King Amilius eagerly awaits your arrival, and he's given permission for you to enter. You'll follow me. Please feel as if you are our guests." He bowed his head slightly, but kept an eye on Anton, as if he didn't trust him. There was a note of disgust in his tone.

The three men looked at each other—Vim smiling hugely, Anton looking perplexed, and Lord Vinicus with concern and distrust radiating from his face, as the knights guided them toward the main gate of the castle. Vim observed Lord Vinicus's strange behavior toward Anton.

An Audience with the King

MANY THOUGHTS AND SUPPRESSED EMOTIONS filled Anton's mind and heart. They clouded his reasoning, yet he fought to ponder his present circumstances. He wondered how Lord Vinicus, or King Amilius, or anyone here at the castle could be expecting them. But then he remembered that Vim referred to Amilius as an entity, and this perhaps answered the question. He didn't comprehend precisely what an entity was, but he did know that they had special capabilities beyond his understanding. Furthermore, Drogan had mentioned that Amilius was once human and now existed somewhere beyond Peruvious. This seemed irrational and illogical, but Anton was determined to discover the truth.

Most likely, Anton thought, there is some form of technology that detected our arrival; I refuse to believe this too is metaphysical. Without a second thought he quickly cast the point aside. On the other hand, he hadn't seen any advanced engineering or science since his arrival; the primitive castle and the armored knights were yet more proof of an ancient lifestyle.

I wonder how many implausible people or creatures I'll meet today, Anton continued contemplating. Since I've arrived, the list of peculiarities hasn't stopped growing. It'd become routine at this point for him to encounter unusual creatures, or some magical being like Drogan. Everyone he'd confronted on Peruvious, human or otherwise, seemed so inexplicable and unique; none of them was anything he'd expected to stumble upon in an entire lifetime, let alone in such short order.

"Young one this time, aye, wizard?" Lord Vinicus looked over his shoulder at Vim, with a serious prodding glance. It seemed as though he was trying to provoke him into revealing Anton's secrets.

"Yes, he is," Vim replied casually, as if ignoring the substance of the inquiry. He combed his long beard slowly with his left hand, glanced out the corner of his eye at Anton, and then looked back at Vinicus. He was concerned how his young friend might react to the lord's pointed interrogatives.

"Bit of a troublemaker, is he?" Lord Vinicus continued. It was obvious he knew of Anton's exploits with the Dragon Master, and intended to goad him into rash behavior before they entered the castle.

"He has much to learn about Peruvious. He's a brave young lad, and yes, a bit reckless." Vim didn't care for the direction of the conversation, and he kept things as polite as possible. He looked disapprovingly at Lord Vinicus, as if to say he'd heard enough and he should stop.

As they followed the lord toward an enormous rampart surrounding the castle, Anton studied its defenses. A wide moat encircled the outer wall and was the first barrier he discerned; it was very deep, perhaps as much as a hundred yards, and fifty yards wide. Vinicus led them across a bridge spanning the moat at an unusually slow pace, as if he were waiting for something. The final section of the bridge slowly lowered from the palisade wall as they approached; Anton recognized it as a classic style drawbridge.

The palisade was over fifty yards tall, and had huge stone turrets positioned periodically at its many corners. These stood taller than the palisade wall, nearly three hundred feet above the ground, and they looked like chess pieces, round and topped with enormous rectangular stones evenly spaced for defense. Guards walked the perimeter, keeping watch over the countryside and the moat below; they carefully surveyed the visitors as they walked across the bridge.

After passing through the main gate of the keep, Anton noticed there were small wooden buildings scattered throughout the inner courtyard. With further observation, he saw that many of the buildings were guardhouses. These were adjacent to an extensive number of stables near the main gate and drawbridge. Some of the stables contained horses— Earth creatures that had long thought to be extinct, long before man ever ventured to the stars. He recognized them from the historical records back on Methonias. This was decidedly curious, and he was sure there was some good reason why he might see them here. Their purpose was unclear at this time; however, he assumed they were used for labor or transportation.

"Perhaps the King will have some suggestions to help the boy learn how to conduct himself more appropriately and respectfully." Lord Vinicus continued insulting Anton as he led the way into the Castle. It was apparent he disapproved of his recent exploit at the Barren Mountain. It seemed he knew that the balance of everything remained in the hands of someone new to Peruvious; obviously, he wanted his behavior to be recognized for what it was, and dishonored.

"A bit of a tenderfoot, I see," the lord continued. "Brash and lacking scruples he is."

"He's quick to fight, but his talent far exceeds even yours, lord." Vim defended his new friend though he risked losing an old one. He realized the lord didn't deserve this criticism, but Anton did deserve his complete support. "Perhaps you'll refrain from further criticism, or the Law of Balance may catch up with even *you*, my lord."

Vinicus stopped and gave Vim an ireful look. "You threaten me? The Law of Balance is on *my* side, wizard. All of us here train daily, and have done so for much longer than this *brash* youth has *lived*!" He pointed a finger at Vim, hesitated for a moment, and then quickly turned and continued on.

"The Law of Balance is on my side. It will not challenge me!" Again, Vinicus turned and faced Vim. Anger covered every feature of his face, and every muscle in his body tensed, as if he intended to fight. For a long moment he looked back and forth between the two.

"My lord! The king shall decide how brash this youth is! Now, lead us to the throne room!" Vim waved the back of his hand as if to dismiss

Vinicus; unstated meanings marked his face; it was clear he was finished listening to the lord's criticism.

Lord Vinicus turned around to lead them yet again, then suddenly turned around to face Vim, his finger pointing directly in his face. "I think you've made a mistake this time, wizard. I think this youth of yours is just another one of the necromancer's future puppets! You've only brought us one more enemy to add to the list. This one seems far more capable than the others; the army of the *Lords of Ruin* grows with your every effort!" Lord Vinicus spit the title, as if it were bile on his tongue.

"Enough!" Vim tapped the ground with his staff. Streaks of electric lightning fired in all directions through the solid stone beneath everyone's feet. The stone bucked and lurched. Everyone lost their footing— everyone, that is, but Anton, who endured the sudden convulsion unchallenged. His torso held steady as his legs rode the undulations beneath his feet, like a sailor on a ship buffeted on the ocean waves.

Trembling, with a look of fear in his eyes, Vinicus still didn't back down. "No, it's *not* enough, wizard! I'll hold you personally responsible for any further mishaps." Stabbing a finger towards Anton, Vinicus glared at Vim with fire in his eyes. "Do you deny he murdered that accursed beast and upset the balance of Peruvious? He intends to damn us all! Furthermore, your record of so-called help isn't exactly stellar!"

"I said, enough! The king shall decide whether he's evil, or is the one chosen by the prophecy! Drogan has already endorsed him." Vim held his ground and scowled back at Vinicus; he wasn't about to be intimidated.

For another long moment, the eyes of the two men locked in anger— each sizing up the other, like two rams ready to butt heads.

Tempering his emotions, Vim took a deep breath, and then continued. "Now, why don't you take us to the king?" He wanted to end the conversation; it gained nothing to argue, and their time grew shorter with every delay.

Lord Vinicus stood his ground for a moment longer without so much as a blink. His mouth started to form words—then, with a sudden thrust, he turned himself around and continued to lead the small party inside the castle ramparts.

Anton fumed at the way Vinicus had referred to him. He'd proven his superior skills by killing the Dragon Master single-handedly, and Vinicus only reacted with hatred and claimed he was evil! Furthermore, these people desired to challenge him, though they couldn't possibly hope to win! Still, he kept his feelings to himself; the tightness of his lips was the only sign of the turmoil that gnawed inside him.

The knights continued to guide the two unwelcome guests across a second bridge that spanned an inner moat; two towers anchored the bridge on either end. An arched opening through the base of each tower allowed people through. They had a heavy portcullis raised and held suspended in each of the arch openings; releasing them would instantly seal the bridge. Two rows of archers, one to either side of the far tower, defended the bridge; no one trapped between the portcullises would stand a chance at crossing.

The archers had their weapons drawn and pointed them directly at Anton as he passed through the first tower. Lord Vinicus raised his hand above his head, looked at each row in turn, and then quickly swiped his hand downward, signaling them to lower their weapons. They did, but their arrows remained nocked, pulled, and ready for use.

Combing at his long beard with increased speed, Vim looked around at the small army. Anton continued to assess the defenses and silently planned for his own resistance and the defense of Vim if necessary.

"That pig-human is unwanted here!" yelled a voice from atop the wall. "Take that *hogtrah* away!" he spat, a look of disgust on his face.

"Yes, return the creature to its own world! He's unwelcome here!" another called out. "He will damn us all! Make him leave!"

A sudden uproar of protests filled the air; all of the guards shouted with anger and hate. Anton carefully watched for the first signs of attack, expecting a volley of arrows.

"Dare you bring the Law of Balance to bear upon you?" Vim returned their challenges with one of his own. "My young Warrior friend sets the balance of the universe to nominal by the simple virtue of his *being* here— and you wish to upset this balance?" Raising his arms with the staff in one hand, he pointed toward the top of the rampart wall behind the moat; he too was prepared to meet any challenge. "You have but to gaze upon the moon and see it is white—it is no longer blue! What other evidence do you need?"

"Silence!" Lord Vinicus said, looking back and forth between his men and his unwanted guests. He quickly motioned for his guards to disarm.

"We'll let Amilius decide their fate; we have little choice. The first to attack will have to answer to me!"

Slowly, the guards seemed unsure for a moment and then deliberately un-nocked their arrows. Lord Vinicus cursed under his breath. Cautiously, he escorted Vim and Anton across the bridge to the second tower; again, guards appeared at the ready, lining the inner wall of the main keep. Lord Vinicus again cursed and again motioned for them to lower their weapons. Vim combed faster at his beard, frantically attempting to remove the unkempt knots from its lengths; his tension was plain for everyone to see. He closely watched Lord Vinicus as he disarmed his men.

Looking below them, Anton scrutinized the bottom of the second moat; scores of long steel-pointed spears covered its floor; they pointed toward the sky; the razor-sharp broadheads would quickly skewer any creature unfortunate enough to fall.

After crossing the bridge, Vinicus led them up a set of stairs toward the inner keep; it sat on higher ground, making the walls appear taller from the outside.

Again, a set of gates and a heavy portcullis together sealed the entrance in the wall. A massive crossbow on wheels sat ready to fire a tree-sized bolt through the opening of the gate if an enemy penetrated the portcullis.

Surprised, Anton marveled at the impressive design of this primitive stronghold and noted how well-defended it was. He wondered if it had some magical protection as well; everything here in Peruvious seemed magical. But he detected nothing.

The guests remained unchallenged as Lord Vinicus and his guards continued to guide them inside, but archers by the scores guarded their advance. Anton continued to observe everything, making mental notes of the number of guards, the architecture, and the locations and types of weaponry. He had been trained to do so when entering any hostile environment, especially a castle or fortification built for warfare. He noticed everyone in the inner keep wore some form of armor and carried a weapon, but the scores of archers concerned him the most; a foray would inevitably lead to someone's death.

Without question, the inner courtyard was a secondary line of defense. There were turret-style watchtowers attached to the main wall and placed strategically at defensive intervals; they gave the guards a perfect view in all directions.

As they traveled deeper into the keep, they came to a tertiary inner wall surrounded by yet another higher level of ground; it resembled the outermost wall on a slightly smaller scale. Again, a set of stairs provided the only access to this level. At this point, Vim, Anton, and their escorts were alone.

Anton considered how obsolete the medieval castle was. He wondered why these people used such a primitive method of defense. A simple Aerocraft with laser cannons could easily demolish all of the castle's defenses in minutes. Stone walls and moats seemed ridiculously antiquated, and almost made him laugh, yet he respected how effective the layout was for its purpose. It was very defensible, and any attack using the conventional weaponry found here on Peruvious could easily be defeated—yet the question remained why these people relied on such ancient contrivances and lived such a primitive lifestyle. Vim had said that in ancient times they too used technology; they most assuredly would have had a much more sophisticated set of weaponry.

Soon they approached the main castle. A long flight of stairs ascended nearly a hundred yards to an enormous foyer. It had Romanesque-style pillars placed around the perimeter, holding up a stone roof nearly fifty yards high. To Anton, it felt as if he was on ancient Earth at the height of the Roman Empire—or perhaps as if he was looking at an Egyptian temple. The two architectures seemed incongruous; the medieval outer walls and castle pillars conflicted, yet somehow tastefully blended. He wondered what had transpired to combine these two styles.

Climbing the stairs, they passed through the foyer into a tall hallway with small holes on the walls at intervals near the ceiling. These were large enough for a man to fire arrows through or drop hot liquid from and remain protected from the retaliation below. Before them stood a narrow bridge that spanned a deep dark pit. Any misstep would easily end in disaster. This passage was much smaller than the last two—merely fifteen yards across and less than three yards wide. It led into the main body of the castle.

At this point, it appeared that all of the guards and sentries were gone; apparently, they'd passed beyond the defended portion of the castle. Anton hadn't seen any of the guards since leaving the inner rampart. It gave him a sense of relief, yet his Methonian training kept him suspicious of unseen treachery.

"You needn't worry," Vim said quietly to Anton. "We're almost there, my friend." He spoke as if reassuring a frightened young child. He looked at Anton from the corner of his eye. The anger he'd seen earlier had subsided; only Anton's Methonian battle-readiness was apparent; Vim too was content that the lord's guards had disappeared.

Finally, they passed into an enormous indoor courtyard with monolithic pillars lining each side. These rested on a raised floor and supported a lower ceiling than that of the courtyard; it had a tiered set of wide stairs leading up to another room. The center ceiling of the outer chamber was higher than the pillar-supported sides, and a spherical dome arched between them. The room was long and narrow, and at its midpoint, an artfully exquisite fountain shot streams of water into the air; they oscillated around in sequences creating resplendent designs and intricate patterns, all lighted from the dome with a clever use of piped sunlight. The setting sun offered oranges and yellows to enhance the effect.

Large tapestries covered the sidewalls behind the pillars; ornate beyond anything Anton had ever seen before, he almost mistook them for giant photographs. They depicted vast unknown landscapes. Each included an image of the same man. On the first tapestry, he seemed young. In another, his stance seemed more mature, and somehow different. One oddity struck Anton—in each case the man's face was obscured. Anton didn't have time to study the tapestries so that he might uncover the mystery, and his attention quickly shifted to the next room.

Lord Vinicus quickly ushered them toward the far end of the courtyard and into a throne room; the entrance had a large archway and still another portcullis blocking it. When Vinicus approached the archway, the heavy iron bars slowly raised, allowing everyone passage.

As they entered the throne room, the first thing Anton noticed was that it sat at a forty-five-degree angle to the outer courtyard they'd just left. As he looked around, everything he saw stunned him. The throne room was an incredible feat of architecture. Painstakingly intricate mosaics covered the floor, and inlays of stone looked like paintings, covering portions of the ceiling—all of it handcrafted from exquisite colored marble, onyx, jade, granite, and obsidian.

Rows of pews were arranged in front of the stage. In the center of the stage sat a great throne that rested upon a semicircular dais; it was raised nearly two meters above the main floor. The throne was ornate, with extensive engravings inlayed with gold. It was made of solid white marble. A lavish red silk cushion covered its seat and back with an impressive intricate pattern of embroidery stitched with golden silk thread.

The area surrounding the enormous throne provided a perfect setting for artful handiwork. Long silken tapestries draped behind displays of traditional weaponry. Small raised daises sat on the stage floor to each side of the throne, where two people, perhaps guards, could stand.

Beautiful extravagant art covered everything from floor to ceiling. Incredible murals completely covered many of the walls. Each wall seemed to have a different theme—one of oceans, another of sunrises and sunsets, and another of burning forests and villages, and volcanoes erupting. Finally, Anton's attention fell on some enormous frescoes, depicting vast landscapes of mountains and valleys, forests and rivers. Looking at the center ceiling, he saw that stars, nebulas, and galaxies completely covered its surface. Its dome shape reminded him of the domes in ancient Roman architecture—extravagant, lavish, ornate, and beautiful. Anton realized that the many scenes he saw were really only one theme. They depicted earth, air, fire, and water. The center-domed ceiling depicted the vast universe.

Two large statues of beautiful naked women with large bowls on their shoulders sat on each corner of the stage; they mirrored each other to the subtlest detail. Carved from a splendid piece of flesh-colored marble, they seemed impressively lifelike, as if they were actual women frozen in time, not chiseled from stone. They dominated Anton's attention. The marble had extensive natural patterns that accentuated the women's best features in just the right places. The bowls contained golden fires that burned high into the air but didn't give off smoke, heat, or sound. They burned so brightly they nearly hurt his eyes. They provided the only lighting for the chamber. Anton wondered what type of fuel could burn this way. It seemed to defy physics.

The entire chamber was made of pure white marble with golden swirling patterns throughout. The throne stage offered the largest variety of artful things. Pillars lined the stage area much the same as they did outside of the castle, supporting a lower ceiling over the stage; a raised walkway encircled its perimeter. Great care had gone into the selection of the marble; master craftsmen had skillfully created every piece so that their natural tessellations and color matched the engravings on the throne.

In the floor's center mosaic was the symbol of a great shield and a gold ring encircling a golden sword that burned like fire. Anton immediately noticed the similarity between his ring and sword to those depicted in the floor's lavish inlay. Yet that sword had a golden flame, unlike the blue one he carried. He immediately looked at Vim and wondered if he had made the same connection, but the wizard seemed oblivious.

"The King will arrive momentarily," Lord Vinicus said, pointing to the kneeling area in front of the throne. "Please, relax for a few minutes until the King's arrival. When he does arrive, all subjects must kneel here. Yes, you are our... *guests*." His courtesy seemed genuine, and his voice sounded more relaxed than when they'd first met; however, obvious displeasure remained in his eyes.

Walking over to a uniformed man, obviously of a high rank, Vinicus kept one eye fixed upon Anton. The two men had a heated tete-a-tete, but Anton couldn't quite hear; even his heightened Methonian capabilities were insufficient. He wondered what might be at the root of the discord. Then, suddenly, Lord Vinicus bowed and turned around on one heel, leaving the chamber as if ordered away.

Many people arrived, filling the room. Vim and Anton stood front and center to the throne as requested. Vim waited patiently, with an enigmatic grin—as if he knew what to expect. Anton, on the other hand, continued his inspection of the chamber with efficient Methonian interest; he admired the details of the room with vigilant scrutiny. Everything appeared ornate; he had rarely seen such artful detail anywhere. The training facilities on Methonias didn't compare. Only the inner gardens of the Great Temple provided any beauty beyond its advanced architecture.

Presently, several people entered the chamber from concealed doors on either side of the throne. Each took what seemed to be an assigned position in a line in front of the throne. Each appeared to be a veteran soldier from a different region of Peruvious; each wore different attire and seemed to be from a different race. Anton was unaccustomed to such variety. After the men took their places, one of them addressed the audience.

"Welcome, honored guests, to the court of the Great Amilius—king of all regions of Peruvious, lord of all creatures dwelling in his domain, benevolent benefactor to all who are good and just. All bow and kneel before his greatness!"

With that command, everyone in the room, including Vim, quietly knelt on one knee, bowing their heads to avoid direct observation of the throne. The only one who didn't was Anton. He looked around the room with wonder; he'd never experienced royal pageantry before and it fascinated him, and seemed at a loss as to how he should respond.

Vim reached over, tugged at Anton's tunic, glared, and encouraged him to kneel and bow his head too. He raised his eyebrows and nodded at him, insisting he comply.

Blatantly, with an indifferent huff, Anton obeyed. Bowing his head, he put his wrists together and turned them up, kneeling in defined Methonian custom. This was the only way he knew how to show respect.

Suddenly, a blinding white glow emanated from the center of the throne. A moment later, the figure of a man was barely perceptible inside the light. Slowly, the intense brightness of the radiance around the throne subsided and a man stood there smiling at the audience kneeling before him.

"Greetings, Vim Alpenstock, keeper of the Staff of Balance, master wizard over all of Peruvious." His voice resounded throughout the room as if amplified electronically. "I see you have brought to my court young Anton, your latest Warrior from beyond our world!"

The surprises of Peruvious had become routine to Anton; he no longer felt impressed by them. Naturally, if this Amilius were some sort of a godlike entity, then it seemed reasonable to assume he would inherently know his name, and everything else about him. Yet he believed this so-called entity was simply informed of these facts prior to his unusual appearance. He was again feeling skeptical of all he witnessed—after all, how could these seemingly magical mysteries be possible? It defied reason! His upbringing and training hadn't prepared him to believe in supernatural beings! Such entities were obviously myths of Earth's past—part of Greek, Roman, Egyptian, or some other peculiar religious mysticism. Everyone he knew had long since dismissed them as legends. It seemed ridiculous that a simple light show could prove some mortal man to be a demi-god! All of the supposed magic he'd witnessed could only be some common science in disguise, not a mysterious power of mystical origin.

Silently, like a cat stalking its prey, lord Vinicus entered the room from behind a tapestry and stood quietly in the background. Anton noticed him from the corner of his eye the moment he made his appearance.

"I see that your friend is having a hard time adjusting to his new environment," continued the benevolent voice from the luminous throne. "Forgive the pervasive brightness—in a moment it will diminish as I complete the transformation from my ethereal form to my physical body." His voice continued to echo throughout the chamber as if electronically amplified.

"It's an absolute delight to again be in the presence of your majestic eminence," responded the kneeling Vim as he clasped his hands in front of him. It looked as if he were about to pray. The Staff of Balance rested awkwardly against his shoulder, and it shifted about as he spoke.

"Please stand, wise one." The King continued, as the luminosity diminished and he appeared more human. Still, an inexplicable aura of light persisted around him.

"You're more my equal than you realize, wizard." Amilius looked straight into Vim's eyes as he addressed him, holding his gaze for a moment or two.

Grasping the staff with both hands, Vim slowly rose to his feet; his every movement conveyed extreme age. Anton attempted to stand, too.

"Remain on your knees!" commanded Amilius. "You'll *earn* the privilege to stand before me, and you'll act only when given permission by *me!*" He pointed a finger at Anton; his hand glowed brightly as he did so.

An intense tingling sensation crawled on Anton's skin. He was unable to control his movements, and he felt compelled to return to the kneeling position. Even if he wanted to, he couldn't stand; his body was no longer under his control. Suddenly, his ring glowed with brilliant golden light, fluctuating in intensity as the king spoke.

Again, Amilius addressed Vim. "Your new champion is arrogant and young of mind—and these are the least of his faults. He believes that by successfully killing the Dragon Master, he's demonstrated greatness. Before I can bestow upon him that which is permitted by the Law of Balance, he must learn to respect his superiors, and to cherish *all* life—for every life is precious." Amilius looked around the room as he spoke; his eyes fell particularly upon Lord Vinicus.

"Therefore, you will take your new apprentice to the City of the Humans, and introduce him to Trepid Tantamount, so that he can begin his journey to maturity; there you and he will finish his education. When he's completed this task, return him to me, and I will bestow upon him a great gift, as is allowed by the Prophecy of One. His presence in my castle pains me. As you know, your time is short; you'll leave immediately! Now go!"

Suddenly the king vanished in a blaze of brilliant light. Then, one of the people standing near the throne stepped off the stage and approached the two visitors. He wore gold-plated armor, and had the markings of a leader of rank. Anton noticed he was the same man Lord Vinicus had exchanged words with before leaving the chamber.

Looking at Anton, he introduced himself. "My name is Thundaruss Rikin; I am champion to the king. All the great citizens here know me as first in command to King Amilius."

Looking directly at Vim, Thundaruss bowed slightly and raised his arm to point toward the entrance to the throne room. "I'll escort you to the drawbridge." Everyone knew Thundaruss's order was law, and several guards stood at the ready to enforce his command if necessary.

As the three of them prepared to leave, Anton wondered what precisely had just happened—one moment the king was exchanging pleasantries, and the next he was gone. The entire visit had lasted only a few minutes. Nothing made sense. Not only that—he felt insulted. The King had unexpectedly belittled his heroics, and this crushed him.

Young of mind? thought Anton. What a rude king! He doesn't understand my abilities at all! How could I be a pain to anyone" He silently fumed. The king obviously doesn't understand anything about me!

Anton had an overwhelming desire to challenge the king's champion, if only to prove his own superiority. But he thought better of it. After all, he'd sworn his servitude to Vim's cause and it wouldn't serve his needs if he did.

As Anton continued to seethe, their escort quickly ushered them along. It seemed to Anton that they reached the outer drawbridge in mere seconds; his angry thoughts overcame his perception of time, and it seemed to take mere moments to return to the outer ramparts— less time than it had taken to reach the inner throne room when he'd first arrived.

Feeling an overpowering need to retreat into himself, Anton longed for meditation so that he could contemplate the frustrating events of the day. He'd never felt so insulted. He'd never had anyone speak about him as if he were a mere child. On Methonias, his comrades had held him in reverence, respect, and admiration during his graduation. But on Peruvious people seemed to look down on him as if he were an ignorant youth and a mutant; this left him with unsettled emotions, and he ached to review his feelings.

"Still yourself—your emotions are evident to everyone, my young friend," Vim said. "Your face reveals much." Vim's voice was gentle and comforting; he understood the turmoil going on inside of Anton. "You will soon meet some very different people; try to calm yourself; your frustration serves you not!"

Putting a hand on his shoulder, Vim looked into Anton's eyes, gave him a warm smile, and tried to reassure him. "Much has happened today, I realize. It's too much for anyone—especially a fish out of water like you—to comprehend so quickly." Vim smiled and then looked around at the guards escorting them.

"I must meditate." Anton replied coldly, more to himself than Vim, but he nodded to let the wizard know he understood. Then he looked at the guards and realized their anger had changed. Their faces seemed to reveal a tolerance he hadn't seen when he'd arrived at the castle.

"Fish out of water," Anton mumbled to himself. "Guess I am. They just don't understand. Nobody here understands." He looked sheepishly at Vim, took a deep breath, let it out slowly, and then stared at the ground as they passed under the first portcullis.

The sun had long since set, and it was quite dark, making it difficult to see much of anything; the only light came from occasional Tiki torches along the path, and from lanterns carried by the guards. Even the moon hadn't risen far enough to aid them. This made Anton even more uncomfortable; he couldn't judge the hazards properly with his unsettled emotions and the lack of light.

When finally they arrived at the main gate of the outer keep, Thundaruss bade Vim farewell. "We shall await your return. Please, come as soon as your young champion has completed his training! We'll welcome the venerable Vim Alpenstock and his *improved* new champion at the appropriate time." Bowing his head slightly, Thundaruss turned and motioned for the guards to follow him as he returned inside the castle.

Anton continued to fume; he couldn't relinquish his anger over the fact that everyone viewed him as a mere child—not the superior Warrior that he knew he was. "Why does everyone here look down at me like this?" he thought, still aching for a chance to meditate.

Vim looked at Anton while leaning hard on his staff, grasping it with both hands. He contemplated Anton closely, objectively, and critically; he pondered the need for their visit to the City of the Humans. It would take much longer than he wanted to begin his campaign against the overlord, and this troubled him; he knew time was working against them, as Drogan and Amilius had both noted. The additional loss of time was unsettling. Everything rested on the shoulders of an impulsive youth. Vim feared it would take too long to inculcate the seed of maturity in Anton, and nurture it to fruition. Yet if anyone could show Anton the course to follow, it might indeed be Trepid Tantamount.

"Come now, my young friend," Vim said, speaking feebly and pointing past the outer gate. "It's time to eat and rest. I know you're as hungry as I am; I realize they should've fed us and given us time for rest, but alas, they didn't. This unsettles *me* as well." Winking at Anton, Vim smiled, lighting the globe on his staff.

Heaving a sigh, Anton replied quietly: "Thank you—I need time to refresh and reflect. This is all so confusing." With effort, he returned Vim's smile; it was a forced grimace, but it sufficed. He then nodded and scratched his head; his discomfort was apparent, and his hands simply needed something to do. "Lead on, I'll follow you."

Anton too wondered why nobody had invited them to refresh themselves inside the castle. But he knew things were far too complex for such hospitality; these people hadn't shown the slightest courtesy until they led them out of the castle. It seemed impossible to comprehend the unusual ways of the Peruvian people, and it had become tiresome to concern himself with their impertinence. Besides, he was a Methonian Warrior, not a philosopher, and he didn't want help from anyone to reflect upon and to understand their reasoning, he simply needed time to meditate.

Back on Methonias, nobody ever refused a Warrior a meal or a place to sleep. Warriors received admiration and respect. But Anton realized that only a handful of Warriors had come to Peruvious, and Peruvians had learned to hate them. Circumstances for him were quite different than he'd anticipated—different than any other Methonian had faced.

Aching for his next opportunity to rest and reflect, Anton allowed his confusion and emotions to overwhelm him; his thoughts whirled around in his head, uncontrolled. He needed to find solace the only way he knew how, and he needed to do it now.

Perhaps an hour or two might help me to resolve some of my new feelings, he thought. He'd come to the castle feeling unsettled, and he left feeling even more so. Meditation was not only essential—it was mandatory.

CHAPTER 17

Celestra and the Universe

IT WAS LATE IN THE evening. Anton and Vim traveled to the west and south of the castle on foot. Anton had no idea where they were going. The air felt cold. He could see his breath in the air as he trudged along. It chilled him, since he wore only a tunic and hakama. He hoped that soon they would find some shelter, or a warm place to appease his hunger and warm himself. In the meantime, he reached into his tunic and pulled out his EHD. Unfolding it, he quickly retrieved his haori and put it on; the added warmth made him more comfortable for the moment, but his emotions were still unsatisfied.

In contrast, Vim seemed content with the frigid breeze blowing down from the snowcapped mountains. He wore considerably more clothing— loose-fitting pants, a heavy jerkin over a thick shirt, and his tattered robe. Watching Anton, he puzzled over the sudden appearance of his haori from seemingly nowhere; the EHD seemed magical.

"I thought you didn't know what magic was?" Vim said. "Yet here you produce something magical!"

"It's a common device manufactured at the Great Temple on Methonias," Anton answered nonchalantly. "Every Warrior is issued one."

"I see. Well, it appears magical to me." Giving Anton a serious look, Vim adjusted the belt around his robe and then hastened his step down the trail. He seemed to know precisely where he was headed, and set a surprisingly brisk pace.

The exertion helped Anton fight off the chill of the night air. He appreciated that, but he wondered how long Vim would be able to maintain his vigorous stride. He recalled the journey they'd made down the side of the valley from Vim's home; the ancient wizard had seemed remarkably fit, particularly for his age, but subsequently he had tired quickly.

A brilliant argent glow radiated from the globe on Vim's staff, illuminating the way. The moon had just begun to rise as they came upon a very large stand of trees, nearly a mile from the main entrance of castle.

The two entered this small forest, following a heavily trodden path. Presently, they came upon a large clearing that seemed as if its only purpose was to provide a place for travelers to camp. It was large enough for a few dozen people to rest comfortably, and there was evidence that travelers had periodically done so. Near the center and just to the west there was a fire pit, and rocks roughly shaped for sitting upon.

Thankful for the modest windbreak the stand of trees provided, Anton regarded the fire pit with enthusiasm. After a moment, he looked around for loose wood so he could build a fire. Only the light of the staff illuminated the vicinity, making this a difficult task at first. But soon the moon had begun to illuminate the tops of the trees, aiding him in his effort.

Walking over to the fire pit, Vim held his staff up, and then spread his arms wide, preparing to perform his wizard's magic. Closing his eyes, he tipped his head back, stood quietly for a moment or two, and then shouted one word: "*Ignomiclis!*"

A brilliant fireball of energy burst from the globe, striking the fire pit, and filling it with conflagration. The energy was staggering, and in response, another fireball shot into the night sky, erupting from the pit like a signal flare. The entire atmosphere radiated a golden glow for just a few moments, and then faded to conventional firelight. Wood had mysteriously filled the empty pit, and there was a mighty crackling of fire. Heat drove the cool air away, inviting the two men to warm themselves.

The sound of crepitating wood engendered a primeval feeling in Anton. He was so surprised at the instant fire that his whole body tingled, as if a jolt of electricity had struck him. Without hesitation, he drew closer, held out the palms of his hands, and soaked in the warmth from the blaze. After a minute or two, he turned around slowly—allowing the heat to bathe his body, and finally alleviating his discomfort.

Satisfied that the fire was burning properly, Vim then created another of his wizard's dinners. Raising his staff, he began to chant in his archaic wizard's tongue. Golden fire swirled around the globe again, permeating the atmosphere. The light, combined with the yellow firelight and the white radiance of the rising moon, made the night seem to vanish around the encampment.

As Vim continued his work, several large rocks started to rise from the ground, creating a pile next to him. A few moments later, water started to bubble from the center like a fountain, and ran down the pile like a miniature waterfall, creating a small pool within the circular boarder of stones. The tiny lagoon stretched to a diameter of nearly fifteen feet, and had a depth of nearly six feet. Several small plants started to grow around the pool's edge at an accelerated rate; they stretched nearly six feet into the air and produced plump yellow and green fruit.

As if his magical efforts had exhausted him, Vim's hands trembled as he completed his magic. Struggling, he carefully picked two of the fruit, handing both of them to an intrigued Anton. "Eat," he said, pointing feebly. Then he picked two for himself. Stiffly, he sat upon one of the large rocks at the edge of the fountain and proceeded to assuage his hunger.

"Do you ever produce any meat other than fish? Protein is necessary to feed one's muscles." Anton made a clumsy attempt at humor, but his drollness fell short of its intent. Vim was too tired to acknowledge his poor attempt.

"I'm sorry, but I never provide more than simple fish, my young friend," Vim said. "The forest creatures would have difficulty accepting me if I fed upon animal flesh. Go ahead, enjoy your fruit—I think you'll be quite surprised." Vim's voice sounded more drained now; Anton noticed his labored tone immediately.

With hunger driving his actions and a look of curiosity on his face, Anton quickly tasted the fruit; he discovered that it did in fact taste very good—more so than the fruit he was accustomed to on Methonias, including the parita fruit he enjoyed so much in the village of Tooloo. A single fruit also satisfied his enormous hunger—just as the parita fruit had. But he didn't stop after the first. When he'd finished the second, savoring every bite, he took the hollowed-out skin and knelt at the edge of the pool. Using it like a ladle, he dipped it into the water, drew forth a portion of the ice-cold liquid, and drank his fill. To his surprise, it required very little to completely satisfy him; what was even more astonishing was that the water seemed to radiate a nearly imperceptible glow; in the dim light, it faintly lit his hands as he drank. When he was done, he felt refreshed and charged with energy, almost as if he'd enjoyed a complete night's sleep. He didn't understand why, but he appreciated the benefit.

As the day's exertions melted away, Anton was determined to meditate; picking a comfortable place near the fountain, he settled into his preferred lotus position. As he did so, something peculiar happened;

forest creatures of many types gathered around, lining the perimeter of the encampment. Their eyes glowed faintly, reflecting the firelight. They watched the two men going about their business with interest. Slowly, cautiously, they inched closer, positioning themselves a few feet away. They didn't seem particularly afraid, but they exhibited caution, adjusting to the two humans and the burning fire.

Anton was aware of them, yet he ignored them at first. Since arriving in Peruvious, his conception of normal behavior in both humans and creatures had been rewritten. It wasn't until the animals were nearly within reach that he pondered their behavior. He looked at Vim curiously when a deer nudged his shoulder with its nose.

Vim sat near Anton and continued to eat, quietly. The Staff of Balance rested against his shoulder, leaving both hands free, allowing him to consume his fruit. Noticing Anton's gaze, he quickly said between mouthfuls, "They're attracted to the staff." He finished his meal, watching his young friend to see if he understood.

Apathetic, Anton simply closed his eyes and returned to his meditation. His deep-seated need easily overcame the questions he had.

Vim remained silent while he finished his food. When his hunger was satisfied, he finally spoke. "I notice there's much anger and confusion in you, my young friend. I can feel your discomfort and distress; it radiates like an aura around you. The words Amilius spoke weigh heavily upon your heart; I believe this is why you choose to meditate. Your brothers did this too, but never to assuage their discomposure— they did it to prepare for battle." He carefully watched Anton and waited for a response.

Vim's reference to friendship disturbed Anton, and he ignored him. Growing up on Methonias precluded him from making any true friends. The Masters made sure personal bonding between students remained at a modicum. By keeping the students busy with training, they minimized their capacity for bonding, and only countenanced a strong sense of kinship or teamwork between the Warriors; they deemed this indispensable for the overall objectives of their education, and their inevitable deployment after graduation.

With a sigh, Vim again tried to reach Anton. "Please, allow me ease your heavy heart if I can," he continued. "I realize that we haven't spoken enough in the last day or two, but it *is* important for you to learn more about what you've experienced. When you meet Trepid Tantamount, you'll do little else *but* learn, and understand. As you know, this is the command of the king."

Opening his eyes for a moment, Anton looked at Vim with deliberate indifference. He closed them again and continued his efforts at meditation, as if to say, "Leave me alone—I've got more important things to do." He felt no particular reason to tell Vim anything about his feelings; as far as he was concerned, they were his alone to bear. They were also something he was ashamed to have. Besides, Vim seemed to know his mind and heart and many other things about him without his response. It was true that he felt perplexed and angry at the way Amilius had spoken to him; it disturbed him more than he wanted to admit, even to Vim.

Vim perceived Anton's apathy. Again, he heaved a sigh; he felt disgust mingled with patience, and he slowly shook his head. He knew Anton was just expressing another of his youthful attitudes, and he'd just have to work with it. Setting his concerns aside for the time being, he allowed Anton to continue his meditation. And then, after sitting quiet and motionless for a few moments, he attempted a different approach.

"I'd like to tell you a story," Vim said. "Not about the City of the Humans, but about a city anteceding it. It's where some the ancestors of the people you've just met—and the ones you're about to meet—came from. When you meet them tomorrow, it would be a good idea if you knew something about them."

Adjusting the staff resting against his shoulder, Vim freed his hands, looked directly at Anton, and then began his chronicle. "There was once a very large and beautiful city slightly to the north and far to the east of here, in what is now Lower Peruvious. Known as Celestra, it was the heart and soul of Peruvious. Those who lived there never knew drudgery. There was no mundane work; there was no pain, sickness, or unhappiness; and everyone pursued their interests with passion. Schools, libraries, research centers, and recreation and sports facilities filled the entire city. The people and culture had reached a level of enlightenment unparalleled by any other age of man. Government was minimal—almost nonexistent—and virtually unnecessary, since the people no longer needed to make very many decisions. Everything was self-sustaining, and was designed for everyone to have complete freedom to pursue spiritual enlightenment and fulfill their interests." Vim paused for a moment, hoping to see a spark of interest from Anton. Then he continued.

"Anyone was welcome to pursue any activity they wished. Art of all forms reached unparalleled levels. Painting, tapestry-making, sculpting, architecture, and all known artistry variants abounded. Education reached the highest level ever known. Life in Celestra was exceptional for everyone." Again, Vim paused; he expected Anton to open his eyes, but he remained motionless, as if disinterested.

"This city existed for more than a millennium in the time known as the *Golden Age of Mankind*. Naturally, I wouldn't be telling you this story if there weren't some reason other than how good things once were on Peruvious. As you may have guessed, tragedy eventually struck, and Lower Peruvious is now a place of destruction and ruin; this I've repeatedly mentioned." Adjusting his seat, Vim appeared to be uncomfortable as a result of these memories. Taking a deep breath, he continued.

"During this golden age, while all was pure enlightenment, something unprecedented happened. On a mountain to the south and east of Celestra arose a tower. In it dwelled a being that we later recognized as evil incarnate. Unknown to all that inhabited Celestra, this was Vile, and he emerged from that which does not exist." Again, Vim adjusted his seating as if uncomfortable. He stared at the ground, as if the images of his past played out like a movie in his memories. In a softer, more lamenting tone, he continued.

"Naturally, since all eyes either looked beyond Peruvious, or toward one's own interests, nobody was concerned when the tower arose; their thoughts were focused on their own lives. Therefore, no one even thought to search for this tower during the time of its construction; it was as though it remained shielded from their perception. By the time it was completed, it was too late."

As Vim continued, he noticed he'd slowly attracted Anton's attention. He understood the other's youthful attitudes, and knew precisely how to reach into the heart of one so young and frustrated.

On the other hand, Anton tried to conceal his increasing interest in Vim's tale; he disclosed little change outwardly, but his eyes had opened a slit, and then a little more, revealing his interest to the Wizard.

Closely monitoring Anton's change, Vim saw how his attention had slowly transformed from withdrawn and indifferent to ostensibly listening.

Suddenly, Anton interrupted. "Is this not part of the same story that the Djinni Drogan told us?" he said, smugly with impertinence.

"It may seem so, my young friend. But as it is with many stories, they overlap. I told you some of this when you arrived, and yes, Drogan told you more. But now it's important I complete it; you *need* to know what I have to say." Vim's response was gentle and understanding; he intended to minimize Anton's youthful brashness.

With infinite patience, Vim continued his narrative. "Now, as I was saying, the people of Celestra watched beyond Peruvious; their attention looked deep into the universe and pierced the many known dimensions. They accomplished this by using a magnificent structure they called the Observatory. Inside was the greatest device ever devised: the mighty Celestial Eye. As I mentioned, they used this device to look into the heavens, focusing on the far reaches of the universe and beyond. I will get to the significance of this device shortly."

Anton realized this wasn't simply a story from the past, but a story from Vim's past; he was somehow a part of the experience. Anton's thoughts raced as he pondered Vim's connection with the Celestial Eye, and his experiences in this faraway place.

"One day, this evil being arrived at the giant golden gates of Celestra. He'd disguised himself. This was unnecessary, for it was the tradition of the people of Celestra to grant access to anyone, and share all the wonders that the city had to offer. The people trusted anyone entering the city. Celestra was a place for *anyone* to learn, to practice, and to create anything they desired; the people shared all of what Celestra was with anyone who wished to find it. They referred to Celestra as the City of Enlightenment. Shortly after Vile's arrival, he proceeded to carry out his preconceived evil." Stopping for a moment, Vim smiled inwardly, seeing Anton's complete interest.

The fire crackled loudly, as if speaking for Vim; a large log slipped sideways and fell, shooting sparks into the night sky. While Vim hesitated, he stared into the fire as if watching the scenes of his story play out. It seemed as though he needed a moment to find the words to continue his recitation. Placing his forehead into the palms of his hands, he closed his eyes, took a deep breath through his teeth, and let it out slowly.

It was apparent to Anton that the telling of the story pained Vim deeply. Sitting motionless, he wondered what he was thinking as he revealed his troubled secrets. He hadn't seen such emotions since his visit to Tooloo.

After a few moments, Vim continued, but his tone was more disconsolate than before. "Vile spent little time carrying out the evil he'd prepared. He entered the great observatory as if interested in learning its purpose. Immediately, he gained control of the mighty Celestial Eye and turned it not outward at the universe, as was its design, but directly at the city itself. This allowed him to cast a great spell into and through the eye—a working of magic so potent and evil that it literally melted the entire city in one long sweeping onslaught. As the Celestial Eye slowly turned in a circle, it destroyed everything in its path, turning all things to rubble by burning them with magical black fire, melting them into a mass of ooze. Only the observatory remained intact."

"Then Vile stood outside of the Celestial Eye, reveling in his labors; it was as if he somehow fed upon the souls of the people he'd annihilated, and upon the destruction of everything. He raised his arms and chanted a guttural incantation; an invisible dome formed around the eye, sealing it forever from the rest of the world. With a final shout, Vile disappeared, returning to the tower atop the spire that we now call *Vile's End*."

"Today, all that remains of the inhabitants of Celestra are the descendants of those who weren't present during its destruction. Most of them attempted to return to Celestra after their wanderings brought them home, but naturally they couldn't. Others watched the catastrophe from afar and hid themselves lest the evil that brought the city to its demise should find *them* and complete the destruction of humanity. But in time, one by one, they came together, here, slowly gathering in what we now call Upper Peruvious; this process took many years." With his hands, Vim broadly indicated the area surrounding them. "It was arduous and perilous, and many died in the attempt—for evil creatures pursued them incessantly, killing many."

Taking a long deep breath and letting it out, he looked directly at Anton's open eyes. "As time went on, these few remaining people devised a plan to separate themselves from Peruvious. They preserved much of the knowledge they'd acquired, and they retained many of their skills, thus giving them the capability to continue their way of life in a place separated from the rest of Peruvious. This is where we are going—the home of the descendants of the people of Celestra. The City of the Humans."

As Vim completed his story, a single tear ran down his cheek, slowly traveling down his face. He clutched his staff, held it to his bosom, and trembled slightly. Reaching under his shirt, he produced a small cylindrical pendant on a chain, and grasped it tightly in the palm of his hand. For a second, it glowed ever so brightly. Then its light vanished and he quickly thrust it back under his shirt.

This simple act seemed familiar to Anton, but he gave it little attention and didn't attempt to recall where he may have seen it before. It disturbed his subconscious for just an instant, and then he ignored it entirely, shrugging the thought off.

"There's one more thing—some of the people you're going to meet are, well, shall we say, different. You will see. Everything will be explained at a more appropriate time." Vim's exhaustion was evident in his voice but it seemed as if he suddenly regained a modicum of his strength and control.

"You tell an interesting tale, old man," Anton said. "It seems everyone I meet, here on Peruvious and back home on Methonias, has experienced some sort of tragic loss; this is something I too understand, very well." Anton recalled the destruction of the cave in Tooloo, and the death of his wife. But he didn't want to explain more—at least not yet.

"Your tale is worse than my own," Anton said. It sounded as if he didn't care about the people Vim spoke of. Yet he understood intimately the pain in Vim's heart. He shook his head slightly to clear his thoughts and rid himself of the unpleasant knot in his stomach. But the imprinted visual memories of Tooloo continued to haunt him. Pondering his feelings further, he sat quietly in front of Vim with his legs crossed, as if he would return to his meditation at any moment.

Anton felt himself changing inside, in a way he wasn't sure he understood. His Masters had always taught: A Warrior must remain strong and free of emotion, yet not detached from the needs of those he serves. Emotions lead to failure; they ruin the decision-making process. He knew his deep-seated feelings were a weakness that festered inside him, and he wanted to remove them like a surgeon removes a tumor. But this was impossible. They were what made him different from all of his fellow Warriors, and he wasn't yet ready to give them up. Still, the fact that he had them frustrated him.

Finally, suppressing his discomposure, he realized there were things that were important enough to require his immediate attention. Abruptly standing, he looked for a place to sleep. On the far side of the fire, he found a flat bit of ground and prepared it by trampling down the new spring grass, creating a soft bed. The moon had risen over the tops of the trees and filled the sky above the clearing; along with the fire, it produced enough light to aid his efforts. He calculated it was nearly midnight, and he knew that both he and Vim needed to get some rest; daylight would come far too soon.

After completing this chore, Anton sat back down in front of Vim as if preparing to meditate. He looked at the older man differently, noticing that he seemed much older than before. Something in what Amilius had said —*you are more my equal than you realize*—preoccupied Anton. He desperately needed to find solace by meditating, but that would have to wait a little longer.

Vim saw that Anton was perplexed. He could see an understanding in his expression that he hadn't perceived before. Slowly stroking and combing his beard with his fingers, he considered what might have changed in the Warrior.

"I'd like to know, what was the fascination that the people of Celestra had with looking out into the universe?" Anton said. "I mean, what were they looking for?" The more Anton learned about Peruvious and its people, the more he needed to know more about them.

Smiling broadly, Vim nodded with pleasure.

"They looked deep into the universe, hoping to see beyond the galaxies and stars; they attempted to see into heaven itself! Even more, to see *The God, the Intelligence of Existence*; they wanted to see *One*! It was an extremely ambitious endeavor, and it seemed impossible." Vim watched for Anton's reaction, and then continued.

"The ultimate goal was to answer the ultimate question: What is the meaning and purpose of life? It was Lothendus's metier—an unprecedented calling. He met the challenge openly and anticipated success; he absolutely believed he couldn't fail."

This too, shocked Anton. He'd assumed it was simply a desire to explore the universe and study the cosmos, as was the way of things where he'd came from; a deep philosophical purpose never occurred to him.

I should have expected that, Anton thought. Everything I've experienced here seems ultimately to center on the issues of magic, monsters, God, and this Vile. It was true; he couldn't escape the omnipresent mythology—or was it mythology?

Giving Vim a look of skepticism, he challenged him. "How could *that be possible?*" he scoffed. "I mean, how could a telescope gaze into a mythical heaven and see *God Himself?*" Anton's sarcasm poured from him; his face expressed it even more than his words. "Besides, Drogan said that this *One* broke himself into pieces, and in part, *became* Peruvious. Wouldn't this preclude success? How much of this can I possibly accept or believe?"

Scowling, Vim again ignored Anton's impudence. "It is the God's truth that *One* did so, as you have witnessed in Drogan's testimonial. At that time, nobody knew about Drogan's revelation; *we* were the first to learn of it." Vim countered Anton's skepticism, hoping to end his distrust.

"So why did they need to do this in the first place? Couldn't they simply be content believing that God exists? What did they hope to gain?" Puzzled, Anton quizzed Vim; he wasn't satisfied with his simple answer. He couldn't believe anything intangible.

Taking a deep breath, Vim prepared as complete an answer as he could muster. "It's common knowledge that everything that is good and true comes from One. It's sooth that One is the Fountain of Life, and all life gushes from this fountain. There can be nothing without the hand of God creating it!" Vim spoke very clearly, hoping to impress the truth of his words. "Who wouldn't wish to see their true home, and the being that created them? Who wouldn't wish to know the purpose of their existence?"

For a moment, Vim raised an eyebrow and looked directly at Anton, as if expecting a response or sign of understanding. Then he went on.

"The people of Celestra wanted to find heaven so that they might understand better how to live, and what was expected of them. The desire to find the home of One became the aspiration of everyone in Celestra. After all that you have witnessed, don't you wish to see the being that created all things? Don't you wish to have the complete answer to the question: What is the meaning and purpose of life?"

Thinking, Anton tipped his head forward and nodded. Finally, taking it on faith rather seeing hard evidence, he accepted Vim's explanation. But he still had more questions. "How could they possibly expect to accomplish this? How could they possibly expect to find something based entirely in mythology?"

"Do you really believe that all you have witnessed thus far is mythological? Have you not witnessed entities and comprehended Drogan's revelation?" Vim was tired of Anton's lack of comprehension, and his refusal to accept his own experience.

"Lothendus had a plan," Vim continued. "He had developed an enormous resource of what you call technology, but hadn't completed the project by the time Celestra was destroyed. The Celestial Eye scoured the universe systematically as he feverishly attempted to complete his work. Given enough time, he believed he would've achieved his goal."

Giving Vim a baffled look, Anton shook his head again. He was unable to find a way to respond to his rationalization. He understood the implications of his story, but had no concept of the complexity of what he related to him; he'd never learned anything on this subject prior to his arrival on Peruvious. But he wanted to know the answer to Vim's questions.

In contrast, Anton's Masters had always taught him that *they* were the creators, and that *they* were the ones that gave life to the Warriors and all Methonians. Now, according to Vim, it was undeniable that this wasn't exactly true. So many things about his Masters had come into question in recent days; the mysteries that surrounded them continued to perplex him. He had always believed that his life belonged to his Masters, and it wasn't really his. If what Vim said was true, this too was erroneous.

"Now, as I was explaining to you," Vim continued, "Lothendus turned the Celestial Eye to the heavens, ceaselessly searching for God so that he could understand the meaning of life, the universe, and all things. Physics had long since conclusively proven that there could be no universe without creation! You needed to listen to Drogan's story. He was the voice of One!" Vim needed Anton to understand the challenges he would face soon, that his enemy was of equal power to the Creator of the universe, and that he, a mere mortal, would be required to defeat him.

Anton listened with growing interest. He was beginning grasp the message of the stories he'd heard, yet doubt filled his thoughts. Drogan and Vim were telling him more than he had first realized; it forced him to ponder the magnitude of these questions for himself. A fear of inadequacy filled his heart and left a tightening knot in his stomach. He worried that he couldn't succeed at the challenge set before him.

"Now, my young friend," Vim said. "Let us rest our bodies so that tomorrow we may complete our journey; it's very late." He stood up stiffly and proceeded toward the spot Anton had prepared for him; exhausted, he struggled to manage this simple effort. More than grateful for Anton's help, he settled himself down and closed his eyes.

Feeling fatigued too, Anton immediately followed Vim's example; it was past midnight and he knew they would get very little rest before daybreak.

Abruptly, all of the forest creatures in the vicinity scurried off, as if they understood the two were preparing for rest. Vim heard the commotion and raised his head; glancing around with interest, he watched them leave, but seemed unconcerned. Lighting his staff, he sat up, illuminated the entire area, and then looked around carefully. Seeing nothing, he extinguished his wizard's fire and lay down again.

Unexpectedly, a large wolf trotted into the encampment. He was an enormous creature, much larger than an average-sized wolf; shades of grey marked his long fur and he had yellow eyes that seemed to glow in the firelight. He positioned himself near Vim and sat down, panting heavily, as if he'd journeyed far.

Opening his eyes, Vim suddenly looked at the wolf and smiled. "Nice to see you, my friend. Welcome. We're going to rest; you're welcome to stay if you wish." Just as suddenly, Vim rolled over and fell fast asleep.

"Damn." Anton cursed to himself under his breath for not being more alert to danger. "How did I miss this creature's approach? This would never have happened to me back on Methonias," he grumbled with disgust.

Staring at the dispassionate yellow eyes of the enormous wolf, Anton was ready for battle, regardless of the fact that Vim seemed to know the creature. His hand twitched over the hilt of his sword; he had to concentrate hard to stop himself from springing into action. His body knew what to do, but he consciously forced himself not to comply, because Vim seemed unconcerned.

After a few moments, however, he realized the folly of his feelings. Vim's acceptance of the wolf reminded Anton of the last time he'd killed a creature, which had only brought him grief and the anger of everyone he met.

Anton then settled into his bed and tried to fall asleep, ignoring the wolf. It proved more difficult than he'd anticipated. After a few minutes, he looked over at Vim, listened to his snoring, and gave up. Something still troubled him and he needed to sort things out. Sitting up, he adopted the lotus position and prepared to meditate.

The wolf lingered nearby. He sat and panted. He walked around in circles and sniffed in various places. After Vim fell asleep, he moved further away, as if securing the area. He watched Anton carefully, as if waiting for something to happen, or perhaps an opportunity.

Ignoring the wolf as best he could, Anton delved deep inside himself and addressed the events of the day with more objectivity. He contemplated the folly of his pride after killing the Dragon Master; he'd received no praise from anyone, and he'd caused an upheaval of the balance of nature. This idea made him uncomfortable. It seemed ludicrous. He struggled for clarification from the teachings of his Masters; he considered their words of wisdom, but those only supported his killing of an enemy.

This was the crux of what was troubling him; realizing it, he was able to relax. He'd learned at the Great Temple that the destruction of evil was always the greater good. But here that wasn't necessarily true. This revelation perplexed him; it seemed a paradox. Wasn't Vim trying to get him to eliminate the ultimate evil from Peruvious? Furthermore, didn't his Masters teach that he should? How was he to answer this contradiction? In order to assess the issue fully, he needed more facts and more time.

After meditating for several minutes, Anton decided he was ready for sleep; he was simply too tired to solve this dilemma in one session. As his thoughts returned from deep inside himself, he turned toward the thicket's clearing. He slowly and methodically looked around, straining his senses as far as he could, until he finally felt satisfied that the area contained no hidden dangers other than the wolf. Only after this did he lay down to rest. He felt emotionally uneasy, yet content enough for sleep; his discordant feelings had finally subsided. This time, sleep came within seconds.

MORNING ARRIVED FAR TOO QUICKLY; the two men arose nearly simultaneously as the sunlight tinged the eastern sky. Still hidden behind the trees, its radiance stretched throughout most of the thicket, lighting everything in shades of grey. Dew covered the surrounding grass and its fresh smell permeated the atmosphere; Anton took a deep breath enjoying the sensation. He always relished the morning; it felt fresh and clean, and the crispness of the air revitalized his awareness.

Almost immediately after Vim stood, the wolf joined the two men. Vim's stiff old body required more warming up than Anton's; he stretched for a minute or two. When he was done, he moved over to the fire pit; little was left of the previous night's blaze, and the fountain had ceased bubbling forth. Only the pool endured, though most of the water had soaked into the ground. Raising his arms and holding the staff over his head, Vim chanted in his strange wizard's tongue, and worked his magic.

While Vim was casting his spell to provide the morning's meal, Anton waited impatiently. Uneasily, he kept an eye on the wolf, his hand twitching on his sword, ready for the slightest move the creature might make. It didn't take long before Vim finished his task and the morning's meal was ready.

Without hesitation, Anton knelt by the pool of water and took a long draft of the refreshing liquid. It sent a chill through his body, and he shivered. The morning mountain air was brisk, but not unbearable. Looking deeply into the pool, he pondered his reflection in the dim morning light; the water looked particularly inviting, and he thought of how long it'd been since his last hydro-sonic shower before leaving

Methonias. Several days had passed since his summoning, and his nose reported how his body emphatically reflected the issue.

Stripping off his clothes, he jumped into the pool; the water felt marvelous on his skin, invigorating every muscle in his body. Strength seemed to pour into him, as if he were a magnet drawing its energy. After completely scrubbing himself, he decided to wash his clothing as well. When he was done, he climbed out of the pool, laid his clothes out to dry by the fire, and warmed himself.

Vim's magic restored and replenished everything; the fire, and the plants and fruit seemed as if they'd always been there. Vim sat with his back to the fire, warming himself as he slowly ate some breakfast. The wolf sat nearby, looking more like a pet than a wild animal. His yellow eyes watched the two very carefully.

"Someday you're going to have to teach me how to do that little trick of yours; never have I witnessed a more useful skill!" Anton said, and he meant it.

Smiling, Vim chuckled. "It isn't a trick; the staff provides for my needs as I provide opportunities for it to act according to the Law of Balance. One hand washes the other, as it were."

Shaking his head and smiling, Anton laughed quietly, seated himself, and then proceeded to eat. The meal was the same as the night before, but it filled his stomach, assuaging his hunger. He was happy for it. "Food in is food in," he mumbled to himself.

For the first time since arriving in Peruvious, Anton felt modest contentment. The beauty of Peruvious was beginning to occupy his thoughts, and the uncomfortable events of the previous day seemed less important. A feeling of peace grew in his heart, and the simple sense of contentment eased his concerns; he needed to alleviate his perturbation if he was to continue Vim's mission. Looking around, he considered the splendor of nature. The trees were beautiful, and the spring flowers growing in clumps painted the landscape in beautiful colors that became more vivid as the sun continued to rise.

For no particular reason, Anton suddenly recalled the destruction of the village of Tooloo, unsettling his peaceful disposition. There was a knot in his stomach as his thoughts unexpectedly turned to Nelda; he missed her smile more than he cared to admit, and he gritted his teeth for a moment. Quickly, he clothed himself; the brisk chore distracted him from his discomfort, for now.

"Damn that *Virlaqueus*," he mumbled. "Even the Clone Masters can't remove my memory." He turned his attention toward Vim, wondering if he'd overheard him.

Seeing Anton's abrupt movements, and hearing his grumbling, Vim decided to distract him. "We must leave, *now*," he suddenly announced. Quickly standing, he conveyed a sense of urgency. "We can't waste any more time getting you to the City of the Humans and Trepid. Your training is vital." Grasping his staff, Vim cast a sudden bolt of energy at the fire, extinguishing it. Then he turned on his heel and walked a few paces toward the center of the clearing. "Over here, my young friend—I'm ready to depart."

As quickly as possible, Anton sprinted to Vim's side; he recognized that they were about to levitate. A certain reluctance filled him as he stood by the wizard; he'd enjoyed the morning here and wished to savor it a little longer. But duty called.

Grasping Anton's arm, Vim raised the staff over his head. Intense concentration marked his face as he closed his eyes and mumbled an incantation in his wizard's tongue. Instantly, argent fire burst from the staff's globe, and then slowly dimmed to a gentle glow of golden light. A golden sphere, transparent as glass and imperceptibly thin, enveloped them, and they rose straight up in the air.

Looking down at the ground, Anton saw the wolf as he howled into the air after them, pacing back and forth. His yellow eyes seemed to glow as he tried to watch the two ascend into the morning sky; soon it was obvious he could no longer see them.

The sun rose ever higher out of the east, lighting the low-level clouds from underneath with yellow and red pastels. As the two traveled higher, the thicket below quickly faded from view. They gained altitude more rapidly than Anton had anticipated—faster than the previous day—and as they pierced the low-lying cloud layer, a strong turbulent wind grabbed them and buffeted the sphere around. Vim strengthened his grip on the staff; his concentration was so intense it was as if he'd turned into a statue. He evoked immense power from the staff, and the golden light turned argent and blazed from the globe, like fire randomly licking and massaging its surface. Slowly, they dipped below the cloud layer, and their travel became more manageable.

Adjusting their direction, Vim put the sun behind them and headed directly west toward the mountain range, a few leagues away. Forest spread out below them, covering the ground like a carpet of green, dense and lush. As they approached the mountains, the terrain became markedly rugged; large rocky protuberances jutted randomly, towering over the trees, and many rocky cliffs overhung precipitously between. Occasionally Anton observed plateaus and lakes, streams and rivers. The topography was beautiful, and filled his heart with wonder. This new form of travel suited him; it allowed him to directly enjoy everything that passed below them—unlike traveling in an Aerocraft and viewing a holo-monitor.

Aided by a strong tailwind, they sped along quickly, and within a half hour, they'd reached the uppermost peaks of the mountain range. As before, Vim remained silent during their travels. The effort to levitate required his undivided attention, and he labored to push them along as quickly as he could. When they finally approached the jagged cliffs near the mountains' timberline, he adjusted his course, as if looking for a specific landmark or reference point. He reduced their altitude by several hundred yards, and after a short time, he seemed to find what he was looking for.

Vim's hands trembled from the strain of his exertion; Anton worried about the wizard's stamina; he realized that neither of them had gotten enough rest the previous night. If Vim lost his concentration, or even worse, his grip on his arm, the result would be disastrous.

Soon, to Anton's relief, they began their descent toward a plateau near the base of a high mountain peak; after a few minutes, they lightly touched down, and Vim released Anton's arm. As Vim powered down the staff, he nearly lost his footing. With instantaneous reflexes, Anton grasped his arm, supporting him.

Fatigued, Vim struggled to speak. "We're here," he said simply, and looked into Anton's eyes, nodding once to acknowledge his support. Taking a deep breath, he then stated: "let's find a place to rest. Trepid will send someone to greet us soon enough." Trembling all over, Vim supported himself and surveyed the area. After a few moments, he recognized what he sought, and proceeded down a narrow unused trail that led to a wide-open field.

Vim's ancient body conveyed his extreme age with each step; the efforts of the past few days weighed heavily upon him, and his feet slipped frequently on loose shale and slick mud; Anton supported him. Suddenly, without any noticeable reason, Vim stopped, leaning heavily upon his staff.

"Wait here, old man," ordered Anton. "I will seek a place for you to rest; you're exhausted." Quickly exploring the area, Anton looked for a soft place for Vim to lie down. He spotted a small patch of soft spring grass nearly a hundred yards off. Racing back to Vim, he picked him up and slung him over his shoulder like a sack of grain. Moving as quickly as he could, he carried him toward the soft green grass.

"Put me *down*, you impudent child!" Vim said. "I'm *tired*, not an *invalid*!"

"Sorry," Anton said. "I... I am at your service." Anton gently laid Vim down on the grass and stood over him as if protecting an infant from harm. "It seemed as though you needed my aid."

Scowling, Vim stared at the young Warrior. Then he closed his eyes. "Thank you," he drawled. "Just don't let it happen again! I know I'm old, and I know that I tire more easily than I used to—however, *never* remind me of it."

Taking a deep breath and letting out a huff, Anton gritted his teeth and examined his surroundings. Immensely fragrant flowers grew sporadically from the cracks in the granite; they were thick of stock, broad of leaf, and the color and shape of petunias; their early spring stems were short, and reached just above his ankles. Inhaling deeply, he smelled their delightful aroma and felt a relaxing sensation come over him. Kneeling down, he picked one, brought it to his nose, and drew in its redolence. Immediately it seemed to calm him like a drug. A calming numbness tranquilized his muscles. He felt compelled to sit next to Vim in the grass; he was surprised by the euphoric sensation that came over him.

After lying there for a few minutes enjoying the ebullience, a sudden desire for exploration drove Anton to have another look around the plateau. Standing up, he discovered that the ground was rough, uneven, and weather-worn, and the ground cover disguised the true hazards of the region. Everywhere the granite was smooth and damp, or in some places fractured and bumpy, and he felt like his feet could slide out from under him at any moment as he traversed its slippery surface; however, his

Methonian confidence made him imprudent of the many hazards. Cracks littered the area—some narrow, but some wide and deep enough to be of concern; a man could fall into them and quickly disappear from view. This made the weather-worn slippery stones even more treacherous.

Methonian Warriors practiced ceaselessly upon every conceivable surface during their years of training to prepare them for such hazards; Anton paid little heed to the hidden dangers, since he was confident of his skills. Something about the essence of the flowers seemed to numb his thoughts and his judgment though; therefore, he neglected to notice a subtle difference in the way he walked. As he strolled around, gauging the area, his anesthetized senses failed to prevent him from a sudden wrong turn. Stepping into a hidden fissure, he fell up to his waist, jamming his leg, twisting his ankle, and locking it securely into the crevice; it happened so quickly he hardly noticed until it was too late.

Shaking his head in disbelief, Anton let out an uncharacteristic moan of pain. "What the... ouch, damn!" he said. "Damnation!" Rarely did he use such language, but his state of shock prohibited restraint. After a moment, he took a deep breath, and then relaxed. "I must find a way out of this, and quickly!" he mumbled.

Interlacing his fingers together, he turned his palms out, stretched his arms, and cracked his knuckles. With great care, he tried to work his foot loose from the crevice by slowly and gently twisting it back and forth. It wouldn't budge. Without thinking, he positioned his hands to each side of the fissure, applied all of his strength to the granite, and pushed with all his strength and ability, as if he had any hope for success. While he strained against the solid rock, his emotions escalated; the intoxicating effect of the flowers reduced his capacity to withhold his anger.

Unexpectedly, Anton's ring and bracers burned like fire as he helplessly fought to pry apart the mountain. The sudden burst of golden flames startled him, but his determination to extricate himself overcame his shock, and he directed his attention upon his predicament. Hesitating, and then focusing his concentration, he again exerted one final heave; a sudden unmistakable sound of the granite cracking and popping reverberated through the air. An enormous piece of stone suddenly split free and he raised it over his head with both hands and heaved it away. It outweighed him tenfold, but in his stupor, he didn't give it a second thought. The enormous stone flew nearly thirty yards through the air and split into two halves with a muffled popping sound as it hit the ground. It sprayed several small pieces of shrapnel into the air.

Placing both palms together and pushing them with all his might, Anton closed his eyes, breathed deeply, and renewed his concentration. His ring and bracers continued to radiate a lustrous golden glow, and they cast a dazzling radiance all around him, enveloping him in fire. Carefully laying his hands against the stone, he continued his attempt to pry apart the fissure. As he heaved, he suddenly bellowed from the strain; it echoed off the nearby mountain walls and reverberated with unnatural amplification; he could feel an unexpected energy that seemingly came from his ring and bracers and filled his chest. Small pebbles scattered across the ground as if blown by a wind from the sheer magnitude of the audio vibrations. With all his might, he heaved again—and then the fissure slowly opened, easily allowing him to extricate himself.

Anton's liberation was a mixed blessing; he gasped a sigh of relief to be free, but his ankle was unable to support his weight. Scraped, bleeding, and obviously broken, he hobbled on one leg back toward Vim.

Hearing Anton's cry of desperation echo like thunder, Vim immediately awakened from his light sleep and stood with his mouth agape, shaking his head in disbelief at the magnitude of his bellow. When Anton's ring and bracers burned like fire, casting their power into the atmosphere, and his voice echoed across the mountain, it was clear no one could ignore him.

Softly and uneasily chuckling, Vim was nearly speechless. "Incredible," was all he said.

"You laugh at my predicament?" Anton seethed. "Thanks for your concern. It didn't occur to me you would laugh at an injured man." Anton fumed, sitting with his back to the wizard.

"I'm sorry, my young friend, it wasn't my intent to hurt your feelings. This is no small thing you've accomplished, even if it was at a great price."

A look of disgust marked Anton's face, but he reluctantly accepted Vim's concern. "Thanks. I don't know how it happened."

"You've demonstrated a use of magic that is utterly profound! Tell me exactly what you did! I mean, tell me the steps leading to your exhibition of strength so that we can discuss its relevance and importance!" Vim spoke with excitement and enthusiasm.

Carefully standing upon one leg, Anton slowly turned to face Vim, realizing that his anger was unwarranted. As he hobbled around, he gasped with pain when he applied a modest amount of weight to his ankle. It had already swollen to twice its normal size. Moaning to himself, he sat down to carefully examine the injury in more detail. He wasn't sure how extensive the damage was, but he knew he'd broken something.

Vim knelt next to him and placed his hand on Anton's broken ankle. Then he closed his eyes. "I'm sorry to say your ankle is fractured. It will require a healer to fix; I have little knowledge in this area. If we were at my cave I could give you a potion—alas, I'm not carrying one with me; my mistake."

"My injury is extensive; you should continue without me," Anton said, his dark mood deepening as he examined the damage. "On Methonias, when a Warrior sustains this level of injury during a training mission, he has little chance of returning to the Temple." He was insistent. "I will only slow you down; go on without me."

Vim gasped at this irresponsible assertion. "I will *not!*" he said, tapping his staff on the stone underneath his feet. The ground trembled as he did so. He looked angrily at Anton. "You're no longer *on* Methonias! Here, on Peruvious, you're the pivot point, the crux of all our hopes! I have waited my entire life for your arrival, I don't intend for it to end so quickly!"

Anton winced; he'd never expected that someone would offer to burden themselves on his behalf. "Very well, I'll do as you wish," he said. After a moment, he relaxed and decided to lie down on the soft grass.

"Now, young man," Vim continued. "Tell me what happened. Tell me how you managed to get yourself into this predicament. And most importantly, show me your ring!" Vim seemed almost excited.

Dismayed and angry, Anton thrust his hand into the air without acknowledging Vim's concern. His ring was clear—completely colorless.

Perplexed, Vim stared at the ring, and combed his beard very slowly; he wondered how the ring had shifted from its golden aura only moments before.

Relaxing his shoulders, Anton lowered his arm and quietly explained what had happened. "I decided to take a look around when you were resting. After a few minutes, I fell into one of the many cracks here. It was kind of a negligent thing to do; I'm not sure how I missed seeing the crack. Normally, I would never be so clumsy." Shaking his head, he gave a look of self-loathing.

Continuing to comb his long beard, Vim pondered Anton's account. Glancing around, he noticed the flowers growing around them.

"Did you inhale the fragrance of these flowers?" Vim asked. "That's wild dragon weed!" He let out a formidable chuckle, and then apologized. "I'm sorry, but one must *never* inhale the pollen from the flower of this plant; it can cause a sense of euphoria and make a man, as you said, *clumsy*; you apparently became intoxicated."

With that, Anton sat up. "*Damn* it! You mean I *drugged* myself?" He was disgusted. "Why didn't you *warn* me not to sniff these, umm, dragon weeds? I could've *killed* myself!"

Vim raised an eyebrow. "I'm sorry I didn't, I hadn't considered the issue. You're not responsible for your lack of skill or poor judgment; it simply wasn't your fault. It's a good thing the effects are very shortlived; they last only a few minutes."

Plucking one of the flowers, Anton tossed it as hard as he could. It flew through the air, much further than he'd expected it to, landing nearly thirty feet away. He suddenly thought of his experience with the *Virlaqueus* in the village of Tooloo; he couldn't believe he'd fallen into a similar unwelcome misfortune.

"I see you're finding those bracers quite useful," Vim said, watching the foliage as it passed through the air. "But it's your *ring* that interests me the most. Now, tell me the rest of what happened."

"Well, after jamming my leg in the crevice, I was unable to extricate myself. I don't know why, but it made me angry. I didn't think about it—I simply tried to pry the crack apart with my bare hands! Just dumb luck, I guess. Anyway, I tried as hard as I could to pry the crevice open. And then I noticed both my ring and the bracers burning as if on fire. For some reason, the stone easily gave way, and I freed myself."

Vim stroked his beard with increased vigor. "You're beginning to learn how to use your powers. This is unprecedented; I'm both surprised and overwhelmed by this development. Remember how you activated the magic; it's a critical point of learning to control your powers. You must master these skills before you return to see Amilius. Now, let me see if there's anything I can do to ease your discomfort."

Grasping his staff, Vim ignited its power; a minimal golden glow gently emanated from its globe, and it licked gently around the surface, like a flame nearly out of fuel. Placing the effluence over the broken ankle, he slowly increased the power until it enveloped Anton's entire leg to the knee. Chanting in his wizard's tongue, he slowly ran the globe up and down his leg. After a minute or two, he stopped, and then extinguished the staff's magic. Stepping back, he observed his handiwork.

A golden fire continued to glow around Anton's leg. It undulated to the rhythm of his breathing, and warmed him to the bone. The pain subsided, and the heat invigorated his ankle, as if he were receiving a massage. After a few moments, he started to feel drowsy, and then fell into unconsciousness.

Moments later, as if summoned, a band of four men with swords drawn surrounded the two; they were clearly prepared for an attack. Vim looked back and forth at them and quietly cursed under his breath.

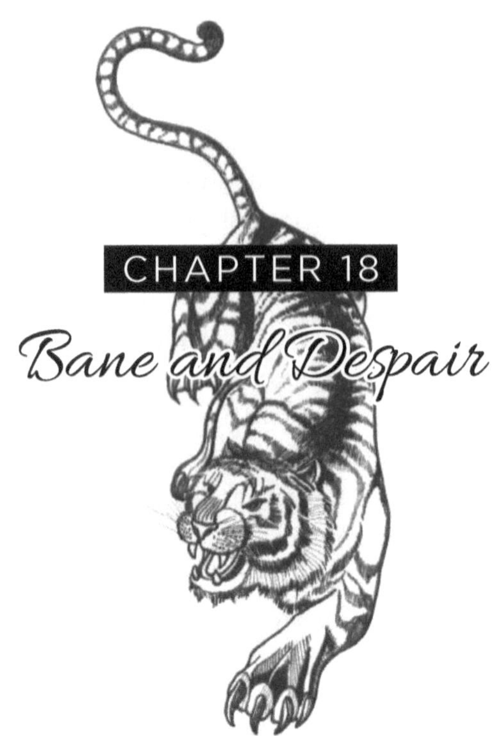

CHAPTER 18

Bane and Despair

VIM LOOKED AT THE FOUR men; he was puzzled as to why they approached with their swords unsheathed. Standing up slowly, he rested the staff against his shoulder, raised his arms, and spread his fingers wide apart.

"I do not wish to fight; why do you approach us with your weapons drawn?" Vim's tone suggested impatience—yet as he asked his question, he suddenly recognized the truth. The eyes of each man were blue, like the Crystal Pyramid—blasphemous and profane. This tore at his heart, for he knew they were somehow under the control of either Vile or one of the evil lords. He knew he couldn't save them—nobody could.

"We'll ask the questions here!" the largest of the four men responded insistently, pointing a finger at Vim accusingly. "You're scheduled for termination—the Evil One desires it."

All of the men wore heavy leather armor studded with pointed metal, a battered helmet, gauntlets that covered their hands to the elbow, and heavy boots; it was the uniform of the guards at the City of the Humans. All of them appeared ready for battle.

"Forgive me—I'm old, and you're *obviously* in command here," Vim said, trying to maintain his poise as he carefully studied the four; he wasn't in the best position to sound impertinent. "Where's Greyfwyn?" he demanded, trying to gain control of the situation.

The guard completely ignored Vim's question. "We know you," he said, "but who is this skinny boy on the ground here? We must make positive identification, there will be no mistakes." He poked Anton with the tip of his sword, piercing the flesh of his right arm. Fresh blood oozed from the cut and trickled to the ground, staining the grass.

"Hear me, you puppets of evil—you *will not* touch either of us!" Vim yelled at the men, scowling at the largest of them—distracting him, but only for an instant. His voice was stronger than it had been earlier, allowing him to intimidate the guard, if only for a moment. He was ready to defend himself and Anton, no matter the consequences.

"Your threats are meaningless to me, old man. Don't attempt to so much as move, or I'll cut both of you to shreds before you can speak again!" He stared back at Vim with a venomous glare; his dark blue eyes dared the older man to retaliate. With a wave of his arm, he motioned to his comrades; each man raised his sword and prepared to strike.

Lowering his arms, Vim slowly adjusted his grip on his staff; he wasn't about to let anyone get the upper hand on him—and certainly not these ill-tempered pawns of the overlord. He wondered how Vile had grown so powerful that his influence reached this far into Upper Peruvious, even though the staff was in control of the Balance of the Universe. He wondered if perhaps Anton had upset the staff's balance enough to break the great seal after killing the Dragon Master. He wasn't sure, but he was ready to fight, and wanted to know how they'd succumbed to the master of the Crystal Pyramid.

"You say you know who *I* am? Are you *sure*?" Vim carefully probed them anticipating that they might reveal any secrets they concealed. It seemed as though this whole situation was out of place; these men shouldn't be under the control of Vile, and they certainly shouldn't have access to the upper region of Peruvious if they were.

Vim hoped to persuade them into fighting to release the control of their minds from the enemy; he hoped he could persuade them to think for themselves, and most of all, hoped he could overcome the situation without the use of force. Yet he knew this wasn't to be. The control Vile had over their minds was produced by the Crystal Pyramid, the most powerful and destructive artifact of evil in the universe.

"Drop your weapon and get on your knees, immediately!" roared the first man. "Your life is forfeit, and I claim your soul in the name of the Evil One!" He looked ready to strike a blow.

Instantly, golden fire burst from the staff as Vim ignited its power; golden energy enveloped all four men so quickly they didn't have time to react. Vim intensified the energy by muttering an incantation in his wizard's tongue; the fire held the four captives in a magical stasis, paralyzing them.

While the magic held them, Vim steadied himself and prepared for a final move. The staff was vivid with power and he extracted a small portion of its energy to give him strength, if only for a few minutes. Moments passed as he absorbed its magical potency; life flowed into his ancient body and his eyes glowed pure gold. Years melted from his face, and his entire body gained a youthful stance. He appeared to be a man in his prime, confident and masterful.

Clutching the amulet inside his shirt, Vim drew it forth and touched it to the globe. It absorbed the energy like a magnet attracting steel; golden power streamed ever faster into it, as if sucked by a vacuum. With each passing moment, the energy grew in magnitude until the light it emitted was so intense it was impossible to gaze upon; it appeared as if Vim clutched a small star between his fingers. When he was done, he tucked it away under his shirt; even when covered beneath his robe it continued to glow and anyone in the vicinity could clearly see it.

When Vim finished, he enveloped Anton with a streamer of golden fire, lifted him into the air, moved him a safe distance from the four men, and laid him gently on the ground. He then encircled himself with the familiar golden sphere of light.

Returning his attention to the guards, Vim spoke one word: Ignomiclis!" The word of power released the guards from the staff's magic, and they flew through the air in different directions, as if a bomb had suddenly exploded under their feet. A silent concussion knocked the guards senseless, and each one grabbed his head, shrieking as if in torment, and then abruptly fell to the ground unconscious.

It wasn't Vim's intent to kill the men outright—their lives were too precious to waste. But he needed to prevent any bloodshed, and he needed time to decide what to do with them. In the meantime, he took a defensive posture. Magic fire still burned around the staff's globe, and he levitated down toward Anton and then knelt by his side. Grasping his arm, he created a carpet of conflagration beneath them, and then encircled him in his golden sphere. He then levitated high into the air, far from anyone's reach.

Vim wasn't sure what to do next. He gritted his teeth and decided to risk the exposure of the secret entrance of the City of the Humans. Concealed from any form of detection, the location could not be found by simply looking for it. But his decision to enter now worried him. He usually approached the entrance under the veil of darkness, to reduce the chance that someone would see. But he was desperate now, and knew he'd run out of time.

As quickly as possible, Vim headed directly toward the gateway. Other than the local inhabitants, he was the only person who knew where it was—for he was the holder of the Staff of Balance, and all such knowledge and insight was his to use. Without the staff, he too would succumb to the gateway's power of concealment; he wouldn't have a clue where to look. A seal similar to the one he'd placed upon Upper Peruvious guarded the entrance. It was a powerful magic that thwarted all perception; anyone who approached the gateway would find themselves inevitably avoiding it, without realizing their mistake.

Vim knew the gateway would still be impossible to cross until nightfall. Setting down about five hundred yards away, he discharged the power of the staff. He'd put nearly a league between him and Anton and the guards, and felt there was enough time to prepare for another assault, should one occur.

Finding a small grassy patch hidden between several large boulders, Vim tried to make Anton as comfortable as possible amidst the rocky terrain. He needed to staunch the cut on his arm as quickly as possible— blood continued to flow from the open wound.

"We'll be lucky to make it to the city *alive* at this rate." Vim spoke to an unconscious Anton as if comforting him, but he remained unconscious and completely oblivious to him.

Angrily, Vim wondered why fate worked against them; there was more going on than he could determine, and it nagged at him, and he tried to reason it through as best he could while he continued to work. Reaching into his robe, he removed a small leather pouch and untied its straps. From it, he produced a fine dark brown dust, sprinkling it over Anton's wound. He mumbled a few words, and the dust started to sparkle and glitter, as if it contained flakes of silver. Anton started to squirm, and rolled his head back and forth as if in pain. After a moment or two, his eyes opened, and he awoke, startled.

"What's going on?" Anton demanded, groggily. He looked around at the large rocks next to him, and the green grass he lay upon, and then up at Vim kneeling beside him. "Where are we? I don't recall being here! The last thing I remember was breaking my ankle." He saw the golden aura surrounding his leg. Feeling an itchy tingling sensation on his arm, he discovered the open wound covered with Vim's fine powder.

"Be still, my friend, much has transpired in the past few minutes." Vim hoped Anton wouldn't do something rash. He tried to calm him like a parent.

"I took the liberty of placing a spell of protection around your damaged leg; it will serve as a cast for the time being. Then four guards from the City of the Humans surrounded us. It was obvious they were under the control of the overlord; their eyes radiated a deep blue, and they intended to kill us. They damaged your arm while you were unconscious, and we barely escaped before they could do us more harm."

"As I slept? Why did I *sleep*? *What* humans? You should've awakened me if there was danger!" Anton felt anger for not being able to fulfill his designed purpose. A moment later, he realized he might not have had the capability to perform adequately against four opponents, but he could at least have tried.

Again, Anton noticed that his arm persistently itched. Scratching it, he looked at it and watched the wound disappear; only a bit of red skin remained where the cut had been. Wiping the sparkling dust from the area, he watched as the red coloration turned pink, and then vanished completely, leaving no scar.

"Your tricks continue to baffle me, old man. I thought you couldn't heal my leg—yet you're able to heal my arm?" Anton looked at Vim and shook his head. "I wish you could teach me this one too." He rubbed his arm with the palm of his hand.

Vim smiled hugely and stood up to have a look around. "We should concern ourselves with the present danger. The protection I placed on your leg should allow you to move about with a certain degree of freedom. My concern right now is whether those guards will return, and how many more of them we might expect."

"Harrumph," Anton mumbled and rolled over to his knees, carefully standing up. His leg felt stiff, as if the golden aura incasing it was an actual cast. But the pain was gone and he was able to move with relative freedom. Unfortunately, he couldn't bend his knee or ankle, and walking was clumsy. Scanning the region, he didn't perceive anything concerning. If the guards had decided to attack, they were still too far away to see.

"You say there were four guards?" Anton said. "And you think there may be more?"

"I'm only speculating—who knows how many are under Vile's control. However, my immediate concern is whether any of the Lords of Ruin are about; they would be much more of a challenge." Raising an eyebrow, Vim made sure Anton understood the gravity of their predicament. "A few guards are of little concern," Vim said, shrugging. "They have no magic." He expected Anton to come to the same conclusion, but realized he was still under the influence of his healing; therefore, his capacity to analyze the situation adequately was questionable.

Dissatisfied with Vim's response, Anton continued to scan the vicinity but still didn't see any immediate sign of danger. It was midafternoon, and his stomach growled. His healing body required additional sustenance, and he needed to do something soon. Rubbing his stomach unconsciously, he returned his attention to Vim.

"I'm hungry, how about some food? We haven't filled our stomachs for hours." He smiled, hoping for another of Vim's magical meals. But Vim only frowned.

"I dare not use any magic at this point; it may draw the notice of unwanted guests. We need to remain as concealed as possible. We're near the secret entrance to the City of the Humans, and I dare not risk its discovery." Vim pondered the implications of his choice to linger so close, but he also realized that nobody knew why they were there.

"Don't you think they already know where we are?" Anton raised his voice, scoffing. "If they attacked us once before, surely they'll find us *again*! It's best to be prepared and well rested, just in case."

"Yes, that's true," Vim replied. "But we've moved from our previous location—even if only by a modest amount, and I can sense the magical shielding of the entrance to the city. It should give us a degree of protection as long as I refrain from using the staff." Vim wasn't going to let Anton's need alter his decision; he knew it was too risky.

"I hardly think a little magic at this point will make any difference," Anton again scoffed, and waved his hand dismissively. He hoped to coax the older man into compliance, but then lowered his gaze and thought better of it.

Looking into Vim's eyes, Anton tried to read his thoughts; he was still unconvinced of any major risk. Besides, if anyone attacked, he knew he was still capable of matching their advance, even if he was injured. The magical cast seemed sufficient at protecting his leg, and he didn't feel any pain. After thinking about it for a minute or two he quickly brushed off his anger with a shrug.

Huffing, Anton put his hands on his hips and continued to scan the horizon. "I think we should at least *gather* some food then. Perhaps I can forage for something."

"You'll eat soon enough—trouble yourself not, my young friend. There's little in the area that might assuage your hunger." Vim sighed; he knew Anton required sustenance. Even more, he knew they needed to remain hidden so they wouldn't draw attention. He sat on a large stone, leaned his staff against an even larger rock next to him, and attempted to make himself as comfortable as possible.

"We must be patient until dark—that's the key to entering the city completely unnoticed." Taking little regard of Anton's outrage, Vim continued to comfort himself. He settled his tired body down on a soft patch of grass next to one of the large rocks, in order to be less visible. He hoped rest would appease Anton's hunger for now.

"Magic is out of the question." Vim said, waving his hand, mimicking Anton's dismissing gesture. He was eager to end the conversation, and did not want to argue further.

Again, Anton looked around and didn't see any cover to conceal his movements; if he were to forage, he'd have to do it in the open. Looking around, he could see that he'd have to travel at least a half mile to find sufficient concealment. After thinking about it for a few moments, he realized he needed camouflage. Searching the vicinity, he collected some small plants, water, and dirt. Mixing the water and dirt, he made mud and smeared it in patches and stripes on his exposed skin. He poked twigs and flowers in his clothing. The effect was surprising.

At first, Vim didn't think it would help much; then he was delightfully astonished.

"I find your methods crude, young man, but perhaps useful. It would appear that your disguise is adequate enough to allow you to gather us something to eat?" Raising his eyebrows and taking a deep breath, Vim had anticipated Anton's objective.

Smiling, Anton bowed and then said, "I'm at your service." Immediately he set off in search of food. After a few moments, he realized that the flora was a bit unfamiliar. It looked similar to what he was used to on Methonias, yet different enough that he wasn't sure it was edible. This irritated him; he wanted to be useful, and his stomach spoke to him loudly, making things worse. He was determined not to return empty-handed, and redoubled his efforts.

After considerable examination, Anton suddenly detected a lone tree in the distance to the west. He skillfully differentiated it from the lush forest that lay beyond it. The tree stood nearly a quarter mile away, and appeared as though it might bear fruit; this seemed unusual in the early spring, but was worth a closer examination. The craggy mountain features that stood tenuously in the distance beyond seemed to frame the tree. Slowly, he made his way toward it.

Wishing for smooth and stable terrain, Anton hoped the uneven surfaces wouldn't cause him further difficulties, considering the condition of his leg. Hurrying as quickly as his magical confinement allowed, his determination pushed him forward and he ignored his injury. Nothing would prevent him from obtaining his probable lunch. Fortunately, the span between him and the tree contained no fissures, and the hike was uneventful.

As he approached the tree, Anton heaved a sigh of relief. Yet as he drew nearer, something else interested him. There was a small lake that lay beyond and below it; only moments before it had been completely obscured from view by the terrain. The lake shimmered in the afternoon sun, glinting and sparkling as if enticing him to venture closer. He felt his attention drawn toward it, and nearly forgot about the tree entirely. A sudden stiff breeze started to blow and tossed his hair around; as if waking him from meditation, this simple sensation distracted him for just a moment and he then returned his attention to the tree.

Finally, Anton stood beside the tree. He gently touched its trunk, and noticed its age. The bark looked rough, but was incredibly soft; it appeared as if it flaked away when he rubbed his hand across its surface. It felt more like human skin, tender and warm, yet his eyes reported otherwise. This unusual texture gave him an odd sensation of hidden strength or energy or something indeterminable.

Standing under the tree's fruit-laden branches, Anton looked up and carefully examined the produce, noticing its unusual shape and color. The fruit was large and red with yellow spots, and shaped like an acorn squash. For a moment, he hesitated. Then hunger prevailed, and he carefully picked one.

Unexpectedly, a sense of foreboding shot like a bolt of electricity through Anton's system; he felt as though he shouldn't be there. His stomach suddenly knotted up, as if he was worried about something, or perhaps had violated something sacred. Hesitating, he considered this, but after a moment, he ignored the sensation, and he continued to pick another fruit with renewed enthusiasm.

The skin of the fruit felt tough, like that of a coconut. As Anton inspected it thoroughly, he noticed it had small silky hairs growing along its surface. Yet they seemed oddly translucent, or invisible; he had to blink his eyes to see them. Again, he puzzled over his actions, as if he'd violated something sacred, and then vigorously shook his head, and plucked a third fruit.

Satisfied that three would suffice, Anton returned his attention to the lake below the tree. Something about it tugged at him, as if it spoke to his soul, not his intellect, it seemed to draw him against his will toward its edge. This feeling left him pondering his intuition for a few moments. He shook his head yet again to clear the impression. All of these strong feelings and sensations seemed odd; rarely did he have such strong emotions coursing through him like a warning. Shaking his head again, he gritted his teeth and then turned around and started back toward Vim; he wanted to share his acquisition.

Suddenly, the atmosphere felt alive, and once again, a feeling of foreboding filled Anton. The hair on his arms and neck seemed to crawl against his skin, as if the air around him was charged with static electricity. He quickened his pace and looked carefully into the distance, scanning for any sign of trouble. He was sure something was about to happen, yet unsure of what it could be. The overwhelming feeling of foreboding increased with each step as he approached the patch of grass where Vim rested. Anxiety coursed through his nerves; he was certain something new and dangerous was imminent.

The globe of the Staff of Balance stuck in the air above the boulders that concealed Vim like a flag on a pole. Rolling his eyes at the wizard's blatant disregard for stealth, Anton quickened his pace; he traveled as fast as his burden would allow. His sense of foreboding increased with each moment, and he suddenly dropped the fruit to help speed him along even faster. Fifty yards remained as he redoubled his efforts, but he was too late.

Instantly, an unknown enemy appeared out of thin air answering Anton's trepidation. Five men suddenly materialized around Vim, in a flash of blue light neatly surrounding him.

Anton fumed at himself for yet another failure to ward off an unanticipated enemy. A merciless infuriation burst deep within him; his emotions flooded him with a desire for vengeance, and he was determined to correct this perpetual series of mistakes. He knew it was impossible to cross the distance to reach his friend in time, and this too fueled his outrage.

Suddenly, as if summoned intentionally, golden energy burst from his ring, enveloping his entire hand. Anton leapt into the air with all his might and screamed a barbaric roar as he flew through the air. The sound shook the atmosphere with a titanic concussion, scattering nearby stone and flattening the nearby foliage. The enormous stride carried him nearly twenty yards—just a few paces from his surprised opponents. He landed hard and unfaltering on the ground, and then stood in ready stance, prepared for combat.

Four of the five enemies whirled around to face Anton. Remembering Vim's description, he recognized them as the four humans Vim had dealt with earlier; they had the unmistakable attire and blue eyes. Each of them covered their ears as if injured by Anton's massive outburst.

The fifth man turned around to meet Anton's sudden and unexpected appearance. He alone was poised and unsurprised, as if he had anticipated Anton's arrival.

Vim grabbed his staff and pushed himself unsteadily to his feet. But he stumbled slightly as he stood erect. His incredible age was an impediment, making each effort clumsy. But he managed to recover in time.

The four guards each took a step back as Vim regained his footing. Unsheathing their swords, they pointed them menacingly. They looked unsure of what to do next and stood there waiting for an order; obviously, the fifth man was in command and had absolute control over their thoughts and actions. Their eyes darted around; fear and indecision covered their faces.

With absolute determination, Anton faced his enemy; concentrating, he ached to fulfill his design intent. Beyond doubt, he knew whom he needed to challenge, and he stood ready for the slightest movement of the fifth man; his hand hovered over the hilt of his hidden blue-flame sword. All he needed was a split-second to produce it.

The deep blue eyes of the fifth man pierced Anton's mind like a dagger, and impaled his heart, making his skin crawl. It was as if he could see into his soul, read his thoughts, and feel his emotions. Placing his left palm over his right fist in traditional Methonian fashion, Anton slowly bowed and sealed his thoughts for combat; his eyes never left the face of the fifth man. Anxiety filled every fiber of his being, and he was ready to respond to the slightest movement.

"Agonia," Vim snarled in disgust. "Lord of pain, and slave of eternal evil. You made a *mistake* coming here, and you're about to *fail*." Vim's tone embellished his intense loathing; hate and disgust radiated from him. With his arms spread wide, and his staff in hand, he too prepared to embrace battle.

"Your defeat is already written, wizard—stand aside while I eliminate your latest slave. I will easily remove you from Peruvious forever when I'm done with this child. Your failure is certain; you will allow destiny to occur." Agonia's voice sounded metallic, almost synthetic.

The hair on the back of Anton's neck stood erect and a shiver ran down his spine. Anger overrode reason, and he instantly sprang into action. As fast as a lightning bolt, he snatched his sword from its holster, took two enormous steps forward, and swung a four-foot length of blade at Lord Agonia. The blue flame passed within fraction of striking his breast; only a slight movement backward at the last second kept it from slicing his chest wide open. But Anton wasn't through with his attack. He parried on his heel and kicked with precise Methonian skill; his encased foot shot like a bullet at his opponent.

But his effort was foiled. At the last moment, Agonia raised his hand and defended himself by catching Anton's foot in his palm. Instantly, the magical cast encasing Anton's leg disappeared. Pain shot like an arrow up his leg as his foot returned to the ground to support him, and instantly he lost his balance. The unexpected recurrence of the agonizing pain sent him down hard, but he slapped the stone with his hands and arms, breaking his fall as best he could. Just as he hit the ground, the golden fire from his ring extinguished.

Vim was unable to aid Anton as he fell; he was preoccupied with the four other men. He easily overcame them, enveloping them in a golden aura. He held them captive in a magical stasis, just as he'd done earlier in the day. Anton was on his own for now.

Lord Agonia had an opportunity to strike. Out of nowhere, a long sword appeared in his hands and he raised it above his head to deliver a final blow to the fallen Warrior lying below him; only a heartbeat remained between life and death for Anton.

From Vim's perspective, everything happened in slow motion. He could see the fatal blow as it unfolded before him, but the effort it took to maintain his stasis around the four men precluded support for his champion. Without thinking, he unleashed a burst of energy that vaporized the men; golden energy crackled all around the vicinity, and the ground underneath his feet lurched and bucked as if an earthquake had struck.

Anton bounced on the ground as waves of energy buckled under him. He struggled to regain his feet to meet Agonia's attack, but failed; the vibrations were too much. For a moment, he found it impossible to defend himself; his injuries, combined with the tremors, made movement impossible, and prevented even his Methonian skills.

The evil lord seemed impervious to the tremors beneath his feet; they had absolutely no effect upon his stance or his swing; he stood there as if he were a permanent fixture in the atmosphere, separate from the stone beneath his feet and impervious to Vim's attack.

The lord's enormous sword sliced toward the fallen Anton, but the latter wasn't completely helpless. With the Blue Flame Sword in hand, he instinctively deflected the blow. Blue flame crashed into magic steel; golden fire burst from his ring and instantly traveled up his fiery blue blade, empowering it to slice through the evil sword and shattering it effortlessly; shards of steel burst like an explosion and rained all around. The sound of fractured metal boomed like a gun firing, impaling the air in an ear-piercing crack. The sword's hilt flew into the distance, landing with a dull thud against the ground.

The harmonics of the blow traveled up the bones of the mighty lord's arm and shattered them into hundreds of tiny fragments. His arm shot backwards and then dangled like a piece of rubber, hanging uselessly from his body. He stood expressionless, making no articulation of pain, or showing the slightest countenance that anything had occurred.

"You've won this battle," Agonia said, instantly disappearing.

Fumbling to his feet, Anton stood on one leg and hopped around to correct his balance; hobbling, he managed to face Vim and looked at him questioningly.

"What just happened? I mean, was that an... umm... some sort of an *entity*? He looked *Methonian*!"

Appearing sick to his stomach, Vim stared into Anton's face and simply replied, "You've defeated Lord Agonia, one of Vile's henchmen." He seemed oddly unenthusiastic. "Be assured, he *will* return, and he *will* bring help." Huffing, he continued. "An entity he is not! And yes, you should've recognized him—he *was* a Methonian Warrior just like you, but now Vile owns him."

Anton stood there, puzzled; he expected praise for his incredible triumph, yet Vim sounded angrier rather than pleased.

"Shouldn't he be happy and proud of me and this victory?" he mused under his breath. "Anyone else would be happy I'd saved them. Where's his *gratitude*?" Anton just stared at Vim, his eyes begging for recognition and approval. Quietly, dejectedly, he asked, "What happened to the other four men?"

Angrily, Vim responded. "I've *murdered* them! I'm ashamed. It was necessary, but I feel no need for praise!" A tear rolled down his cheek and he clutched at the amulet under his shirt. Again, he sat down on the grass, leaned against the large stone, and rested the staff against his shoulder. Covering his face with both hands, he sat there motionless and ignored Anton. "There will be a price to pay for this, too."

Suddenly, a strong breeze started to blow, and Anton's hair whipped into his face. He stood there for a few more moments staring at Vim, and then hobbled over to him, gritting his teeth with pain. He thought perhaps he could provide some wisdom or comfort, but before he could say anything, Vim uncovered his face and looked up at him. He sighed with compassion as he recalled Anton's injured ankle.

"That fracture must be very painful—let me immobilize it again; please, lie down." Grasping his staff to support himself, Vim clumsily stood over his champion. Closing his eyes, he chanted in a low tone in his wizard's tongue. As before, he ignited the staff's power, and the globe burned with his wizard's fire. As precisely as a surgeon using a scalpel, he placed the globe burning with magic over Anton's broken ankle, and slowly, gently, ran it up and down Anton's leg. Steadily, he increased the power until it completely encased his injured leg to the knee. Then, abruptly, he ceased his efforts.

"That will suffice for now. I don't think it will put you to sleep this time." He smiled warmly, like a father reassuring a child. "I think it's safe to use my magic to provide a meal; I doubt there will be any more attacks at this time. Besides, we have made ourselves known to anyone and everyone."

Once more, Vim raised his staff and chanted in his archaic wizard's tongue. Green iridescence mixed with golden fire filled the area surrounding the two men. A small pool of water formed, nearly encircling the patch of ground on which they stood. Plants grew at an impossible rate around its perimeter. Small silver fish formed and swam back and forth in the water, and a few moments later, they jumped into the air, as if offering themselves for sacrifice. Everything was much the same as the night before, but on a reduced scale.

The meal was simple, yet satisfying. It didn't take long for the two men to eat. As before, Anton felt invigorated when he partook of the water. It sent a vibrant, refreshing, and nearly electrifying sensation throughout his entire body, relaxing his nerves.

After Vim completed his meal, he still looked exhausted. More to the point, he seemed drained of his magical energy. Anton assumed his extreme age was responsible; it was as if it prevented him from exerting himself for any great length of time. He wondered why he didn't use the amulet under his shirt for more strength like he'd done earlier. Ever since they'd arrived atop the plateau, he'd struggled with continual fatigue and Anton was concerned that Vim wouldn't be much help when it came time for a real battle with a large number of enemies. Reflecting on Vim's capabilities in the caves of the Barren Mountain, and the battle they had just fought, Anton realized just how much he relied on his help.

"A couple of days ago I said: my service is not at your side," Anton said. "Now I see I was wrong; you have proven to me beyond all measure that it can *only* be at your side. You need more help than anyone I've ever known; forgive my shortsightedness." Stiffly, Anton stood up and bowed in full Methonian fashion.

"I must remain with you so that your purpose is fulfilled. It's obvious that your mission to save Peruvious is worthy of my service, and I'm bound—by my own choice at this point—to serve your request for my help. Regardless of Drogan's release, I'm bound by my design intent, and my life's purpose, if nothing else. I'm unable to alter this, because your cause is just. I will achieve all of your needs."

Kneeling in front of Vim, Anton again bowed his head and put his wrists together, forearms up, in obedient Methonian fashion. "My service is to you, and you alone." He then looked up into Vim's ancient eyes. "I'm glad that we are... *friends*."

Vim was shocked. He didn't expect to hear this from the arrogant youth. He looked deep into Anton's eyes and then smiled warmly and replied, "I'm proud that you consider me your friend; this is an honest and quite mutual friendship we share. Fear not! I'm old, yes, but I'll regain my strength once we've entered the City of the Humans, I have often gone there to recharge myself."

"I wish also to apologize," Anton went on, "for trying to make you use your magic earlier. My indiscretion was a disgrace. I shall heed your warnings better in the future." More than ever, Anton wished to do the right thing. Again, he stood and bowed very slowly, expressing his sincerity as decorously as he knew how.

With these new realizations, and insight into each other's character, the two men accepted their strengthened friendship; it went beyond simple needs or requests of service. Each would gladly give his life for the other to serve the single cause they now shared. Vim stood up, and for a few moments, the two looked at each other, contemplating their feelings. Vim noticed the seed of maturity beginning to grow in Anton, and Anton accepted and dedicated himself to Vim's profound cause. An undeniable connection bound the two men together in ways they were yet to test. No longer were they simply comrades out of mutual need—they were true friends. It was the first real friendship that Anton had ever made.

CHAPTER 19
The Portal Opens

THE AFTERNOON HOURS PASSED VERY quickly, and soon it was evening. While they waited, Anton decided to share the story of his assignment to Tooloo in order to pass the time. Now that he'd gained a greater respect for the ancient wizard, he genuinely desired to share his own story; he wanted Vim to understand who he was. He described how his Masters expected his ring to change from yellow to gold, and other minutiae of his ring's purpose.

In detail, he revealed his marriage to Nelda, and the subsequent decision that cost the lives of all the villagers. Perhaps his desire to share his recent past came from a need to vindicate the unusual color his ring emitted when he first arrived—or perhaps now that he had a true friend, he discovered it was possible to confide in him and relieve his heart of the heavy burden held within it. Either way, it contented him to share his story.

Sympathetically, and with great interest, Vim listened to Anton's entire narrative and rarely spoke a word. He heard the regret and the pain Anton had suffered, and he realized how difficult it had been for him to share his secrets. Finally, as the narrative reached its climax, the shocking end surprised him; he hadn't anticipated that all the villagers would meet such a fate. It reminded him of many such experiences he'd had, especially the destruction of Celestra.

Most significantly, when Anton described the feelings he had for Nelda, and how she had died along with the rest of the villagers, Vim understood the reason for Anton's bitterness and the pain he harbored in his heart. It helped to explain his temperament, and the reason he unconsciously pushed people away with his arrogance.

As Anton concluded, Vim reached over and patted him on the shoulder. "Not all stories have happy endings my friend. I could tell you of tragedies that have blackened my heart too; they've followed me for a lifetime. I could also tell you stories that brought me great joy—enough to reinforce anyone's beliefs that mankind is worthy of a brighter future! Try not to harbor ill feelings from the past. Rather, embrace the good times and remember what you fight for!" Smiling, he attempted to reassure Anton.

"I can avow that after enough time goes by, you will come to terms with your losses and your feelings of regret; it *does* get easier, bad memories *do* fade. But the truth is that you'll always remember how they made you feel." Hanging his head, Vim sighed and offered Anton a sincere look of comfort and understanding.

It was clear to Vim how Anton's recent tragedy had permanently altered his character. It was evident that the final test his Masters had given him tore deep into his heart, and the scars from the experience remained forever etched there.

However, Vim needed to tell Anton more of what was to occur shortly after dusk, so he decided to change the subject. Clearing his throat, he prepared to give him a description of the upcoming event.

But it would have to wait. Suddenly, for seemingly no reason, Anton stood up and headed back towards the tree he'd visited earlier in the day. He wanted to retrieve one of the odd fruit he'd dropped, hoping Vim would provide more information about it. He didn't have to go far before he found where he'd discarded them. Quickly retrieving one, he returned to Vim and sat back down.

Raising an eyebrow, Vim asked, "What have you there, young Warrior?" knowing quite well what he had. "There's only one place that

I know of to find something like *that* around here!" He looked at Anton knowingly from the corner of his eye.

"Well, when I decided to forage for something to eat, I saw in the distance…"

"You saw a *tree!*" Vim emphasized the word as if it meant something special, or unusual—as if to insinuate Anton had done something taboo. "Not just *any* old tree, mind you, but the *marker tree!*" His fervency escalated as he continued. "It's the *tree* that marks the entrance to the city!"

Speechless, Anton pondered Vim's implication; his words inferred more than they said; he wasn't used to such circumlocution. The Methonian Masters always spoke in precise logical phrases, never disguising their meaning, and they taught the Warriors to use speech as a tool for sharing thoughts, not for frivolous or emotional communication. They were to convey information as quickly as possible, and conversation between Warriors precluded abstract thought.

"I see you're not quite sure what I'm inferring. Most people never *see* that tree. As I explained to you before, the entrance to the city is guarded by magic, and anyone attempting to approach the point of entry is unwittingly guided away by this magical protection." Vim looked carefully into Anton's eyes, trying to see how well he understood.

"So you're saying that the tree only reveals itself after dark, and only to those who know it's there?" asked Anton. "And I shouldn't have been able to see it?"

"Correct! You shall see what I'm talking about shortly after dusk. It requires the presence of magic, which naturally the staff will provide." Vim was excited that Anton finally deduced his meaning.

"I hope you know you can't *eat* that fruit!" Chuckling for a moment or two, Vim took the fruit from Anton and stood up. Holding it high over his head, he then raised the staff, closed his eyes, and mumbled in his wizard's tongue. The globe slowly pulsated with argent power and emitted a faint glow. Then Vim carefully touched it to the fruit.

"Behold!" Vim proclaimed. The fruit started to scintillate, and golden sparks fired into the air. A sort of glitter or shimmering dust silently rained from the fruit, and it vibrated and writhed in his hand.

It was obvious to Anton that something completely unexpected and vastly significant was about to occur. He watched with anticipation and wonder as Vim worked his magic.

As Vim continued to chant in a low tone, he slowly moved the staff in a semi-circle back-and-forth, touching each end of the fruit in turn with the globe. Then, without warning, the fruit disappeared, and from his hand sprang what appeared to be a small girl with dragonfly wings attached to her back. She leapt into the air and fluttered around as if to gain her bearings.

First, she flew over to Anton—hesitating in front of him in midair, and then looked at his eyes closely. She did not wear a stitch of clothing which surprised him immensely. She was about eight inches tall, and had golden shoulder-length hair. Her four dragonfly wings flapped so quickly it was nearly impossible to see them, and they made a soft tinkling musical sound as she darted about, sounding almost like the striking of uppermost keys of a xylophone, or a piano. The music was so soft and delicate, and it was only perceptible at very close range; as she flew further away, it became inaudible even to Anton's ears.

After having a good look at Anton, she flew over to Vim. There she hesitated for a moment with her arms folded across her chest; it was as if she were standing in mid-air, with her wings continuously flapping.

"Why have you released me, wizard? I should *not* be about until the sun sinks behind the mountains!" She scowled at Vim, shaking her tiny finger at him as if scolding a small child for bad behavior.

"Your fruit was removed from the tree by my young companion; he was hungry and looking for food; unfortunately, he didn't realize his error," replied Vim with a defensive snarl; it was as if he expected this reaction from the little faerie and was entirely unconcerned about her accusations.

"As you can see, evening is nigh, and you would've been released shortly anyway." Vim waved the back of his hand at the little faerie, as if shooing an insect. "Go meet our new champion—he's more your concern than I, and I'm sure he's much more interested in faeries than I."

"Humph," she retorted, closing her eyes and throwing her nose into the air. Quickly she flew over to Anton and once again hovered near his face. "Was *my* fruit the only one you picked, or did you eat some of my sisters? I hope you become violently ill!"

"There are two more of your... umm... *sisters*, over there." Anton pointed in the direction of the fruit he'd discarded.

"So! You *did* eat one of us! You're a *horrible* man! I hope your stomach hurts!" She fumed and flew off in search of the fruit. Sparkling dust floated lightly behind her as she fluttered about, and her wings glistened in the evening sunlight.

"I did no such thing!" Anton yelled after her. "I didn't have a chance!"

Following behind, Anton's eyes never left her. Within seconds, she discovered the other two fruit he'd dropped, as if she knew exactly where to look. Instantly, she spun around in a high-speed pirouette over one of the fruits, glowing like the globe on Vim's staff. In a heartbeat, the light increased. Soon she scintillated like a tiny star; the setting of the sun behind the nearby peak of Loomspire enhanced the effect.

It didn't take long for the other fruits to transform into faeries. Then three of them fluttered about, and each one in turn flew over to Anton, examining him closely. They all appeared identical except in one way; each had a different color and style of hair. The first faerie was blonde, the second had wavy green hair, and the third a deep shade of red that was both longer and straighter than the other two.

Anton admired each one as they stopped for a moment to examine his face. The blonde faerie came last; she'd already inspected him previously, but looked again as if to follow a ritual. As she took her turn, Anton held out his hand as if to create a perch for her to land on. She started to laugh.

"You think I'm a bird! Oh, what a *silly* human you are!" She flew around in a circle, laughing, and nearly clobbered Anton as she fluttered about; she seemed to be out of control. "You're *cute!*" she went on, laughing. "I think you're *funny!*"

In a synchronized chorus, the other two faeries also laughed, and all three flew in a circle around Anton. They spiraled around him at a dizzying speed, like electrons around the nucleus of an atom; not even a Methonian Warrior could follow their flight. Then they all stopped in front of his face, as if standing on an invisible surface.

Faerie dust filled the air and sifted gently to the ground, and then all three of them bowed to Anton as if to honor him; again, he was stunned at their behavior.

Looking directly at the blond faerie, Anton stammered, "I... I think *you're* really cute too!" The three little faeries astonished him beyond words.

"You think I'm *cute*?" said the blond faerie, smiling and fluttering about randomly. "He thinks *I* am *cute*! Tee hee hee, he thinks that *I'm cute*!" She held her nose high with pride, as if Anton had raised her status above the other two faeries.

"I believe it's time to introduce my young friend to your queen," Vim said, interrupting the antics of the faeries, returning everyone's attention to more important concerns. "If you'll notice, the sun has set behind the mountains, and in short time we should be able to enter the City of the Humans." Grasping his staff, he set off toward the tree Anton had visited earlier in the day.

"The *queen*!" all three faeries said in unison.

"Let *us* lead the way, old man!" said the red-haired faerie.

Quickly, all three faeries flew off in the direction of the tree, outdistancing the humans with ease. Vim fired up a moderate glow from his staff in order to light their path as the sun set.

Anton was thankful for the light; he remembered all too well how treacherous the terrain could be. His leg glowed with a golden aura; this helped to light his own way, and he had little fear of repeating his earlier mistake.

The companions covered the distance quickly; Vim's pace seemed faster than before, as if in anticipation of entering the city, or perhaps to visit with an old friend.

Within a few minutes, everyone arrived at the tree, and Vim and Anton watched the faeries flying around it in a wide circle, like bees around a flower. Each faerie in turn flew over to a fruit and pirouetted over it, glowing like a tiny star; sparks seemed to ignite from each of their concealed sisters as they did so. Faerie dust rained silently everywhere. Within moments, three more faeries joined the others. Soon there were so many that Anton could no longer count them. They flew around the tree at an ever-increasing speed, and the entire knoll was alight with their activities. Anton gawked at their exploits.

Suddenly, all of their fluttering ceased; all of the fruit had transformed into tiny faeries, leaving only leaves upon the tree's branches. To Anton's wonder, all of them joined hands and flew in a clockwise direction around the freshly harvested tree. As if on cue, they started to sing a song in unison. Anton was mesmerized by the beautiful tune; he couldn't imagine such a wonderful sound coming from these tiny creatures. Standing with his mouth agape, he watched them dance and sing in midair.

It's time to share our Mother's love, her appearance we will soon see. We cherish her like heaven above, our hearts replete with glee!

She is our sight, our guiding light, our compass in life it's true.

Come join us now and show us all, you're the one that gets us through.

Her magic is strong, so don't be long, we dance so eagerly.

She will show us all the way to go, her love is pure, you'll see!

After a time, they split into two chains, each dancing in opposite directions, one above the other—then they broke into three. The dance increased in complexity; every faerie knew exactly what to do, executing each move in an intricate choreography.

Soon the tree started to sparkle and glow. The sun had disappeared entirely behind Loomspire, leaving the region completely eclipsed and dark; the tree shone so brightly that the entire knoll blazed with argent light. The faeries continued their dance, and it didn't take long until the tree transformed from a simple trunk and branches to a humanlike form. Within minutes, a half-human sized faerie stood upon the stump of a tree; she stretched her arms wide, looked around, and smiled.

She was an exquisite beauty, a perfect example of femininity unlike anything Anton had ever seen; he was instantly captivated with her stunning pulchritude. She had sterling platinum hair, and large faerie wings that were translucent like her daughters'; they had a structural framework of red colored fluorescent lines that glowed. Her face was remarkably youthful, as if she were approximately Anton's age. Just like the smaller faeries that grew as fruit from her branches, she wore nothing at all.

"Good evening, everyone!" she said with a delicate feminine voice. "And I extend a particular hello to you, savior!" She looked directly at Anton as she spoke. "Wizard! My friend, you're *most* welcome!"

Her resplendent voice reminded Anton of the voice he'd heard on the Aerocraft when he left Methonias; the soft tone sent a shiver down his spine; he was speechless.

"I'm pleased to see you again my queen." Vim bowed slightly to honor the queen faerie. "As always, it's a pleasure."

Vim grinned from ear to ear, something Anton hadn't seen him do before; it was in direct contrast to the way he'd treated the smaller faeries earlier; Anton wondered why.

The queen turned around with arms extended, and smiled lovingly to each one of the faeries, as if to hug them all. "How are all of my children tonight?" she inquired.

"We're all fine," they sang in unison as they darted and circled around the knoll. Each one hesitated in front of her and curtsied, as if to acknowledge her transformation and show their respect.

Every movement the queen made flowed smoothly and delicately. She was gracefully feminine, as if performing a ballet. She brought one foot to the side of her knee, stood impossibly on one leg with only her toes touching the stump, as if she were weightless, and continued to reach out elegantly with each hand to greet all of the small faeries.

Watching with wonderment, Anton stood motionless. The queen unequivocally captivated him as she performed her greetings. Gradually, she pirouetted and gracefully reached out to touch each faerie one by one. She did not miss any as she performed her ritual. Anton felt as though he'd stepped out of time; everything around him seemed to disappear as he watched her performance. This took a few minutes, as there were so many of the smaller faeries to acknowledge. Finally, she turned toward the two humans and stood flat-footed upon the stump.

Quickly looking around, she spoke again. "We all know Vim well— but by what name shall I address this handsome young man you've brought to visit me?" She smiled sweetly at Anton, closed her eyes, and then tittered girlishly.

"He's Vim's new friend," all the faeries replied in unison after fluttering about and changing positions.

"Well, he sure is a fine looking young man, isn't he?" the queen said. "By what name shall I address you, savior?" Her smile compelled everyone's attention; Anton stood there utterly entranced and was unable to respond.

Nudging Anton, Vim raised his eyebrows and nodded, encouraging him to reply.

"I, um, I'm Anton Seven, a Methonian Warrior," Anton said. He pointed generally at the faeries, his eyes never leaving the queen. "And as they said, I'm Vim's new friend." His reaction was stiff and softly spoken; he stammered as he struggled to sound charming—but he failed in the attempt.

"Anton Seven," she repeated slowly, as if to memorize the name. "You *are* a fine-looking young man—welcome!"

Suddenly, the blonde faerie flew up to the queen, as if she had something urgent to say. "He said *I* was really *cute!*" She laughed her giggly faerie laugh, and then flew back to join the rest of her sisters, disappearing into the multitude.

The queen smiled and giggled cheerfully like a young girl. "You think one of my faeries is *cuter* than the *others*, young Anton?" She smiled softly and put her hand over her chest.

"Umm, I, ah, think that *all* of you are… well… very nice looking," Anton replied awkwardly. He again stammered, not really knowing what to say. The whole situation overwhelmed his capacity to handle fundamental conversation.

"Ahem," Vim interjected, in an effort to move events along. "It's delightful as always to see you, my dear queen, but there's a small matter of business to attend to." He pointed toward the lake below the knoll. "Please forgive me for interrupting, but we *do* need to enter." He was very impatient, but tried to be polite and respectful by bowing stiffly.

"My dear wizard, what is so important that we forget to properly introduce our new friend?" The queen looked displeased. "We must not forget proper introductions! I really *must* get to know young Anton. I too have… *business*, as you say. After all, he *admires* my darling little faeries. I see in him a desire!" She smiled at Vim, politely but assertively.

"Very well," Vim said. "Proceed. However, I will remind you that the window of opportunity is short and time is already running out." Vim had no need for faerie formalities. He waved the back of his hand as if giving her permission to continue. He respected the queen immensely, but his impatience was clear.

Looking directly at Vim, the queen addressed his restlessness. "Fear not, my friend, we have plenty of time to fulfill both of our needs. You know time is irrelevant here!" Her smile disappeared; it seemed as though she was warning Vim.

The queen quickly returned her attention to Anton, smiled warmly, and stepped off the stump, walking over to him. Her feet never seemed to quite touch the ground, yet they skimmed through the short wild grass as she flew. Her wings flapped at a very high speed making them nearly impossible to see. An aura of light emanated from her; as she drew closer to Anton, it followed along with her and lit the entire knoll; each of the little faeries cast a glow as well, but on a much smaller scale.

"Your eyes tell me you're unfamiliar with faeries, and our faerie customs. Do you find me *attractive*, young Anton?" She knew all human men had a natural attraction for her beauty, and she easily perceived Anton's intense desire, burning in him like an ebullient fire.

"Do you seek friendship with me and my faeries?" The queen asked, trying to unmask Anton's innermost feelings. She knew very well what they were, but wished to hear him articulate them.

Completely incapable of suppressing his reply, Anton answered before he thought. "Oh yes—I find you *very* attractive, and I thirst for your friendship." His response came from somewhere deep inside him, a place he didn't know he had until he'd spoken. It surprised him. He looked longingly at the queen's beautiful features; they stirred his primordial propensity. He found it impossible to keep his eyes politely upon hers, and couldn't control his male responses, as nature overrode and eliminated his restraint.

"Faeries are unable to clothe themselves, as do humans; our wings would be confined and useless if we did. If it would please you, I can cover myself lightly with leaves and vines." She sensed Anton's youthful impetuousness, and she needed his attention, and enjoyed his concupiscence. Instantly, small leaves tethered together by a single vine wound around her and barely covered her body in the most appropriate places. Looking up at Anton, she smiled and asked, "Do you *desire* me, young Anton?"

He was embarrassed beyond measure. He knew that his Methonian self-discipline should restrain him from his intense male yearnings— but his experience with the *Virlaqueus* had forever altered him, and his restraint was entirely lacking. He was afraid to admit to her his lasciviousness, and he struggled to suppress his natural urges.

"Yes and no. You are beautiful, but I cannot..."

"There is no disgrace, young Anton. *All* human men are enchanted by us at first. Feel not ashamed—I'm not displeased with your feelings. On the contrary, they are *expected!*" She smiled, attempting to comfort him. "Enjoy—you can give in to your infatuations; be not embarrassed! However, if you are uncomfortable, allow me to help."

Somehow, as if she'd released his inner yearnings, Anton felt his male concupiscence diminish, and was then able to relax. He pondered the change for a just a moment, and then set it aside. It was impossible for her to control his lustful desires—wasn't it?

"I can see inside your heart, young Anton—your thoughts are entirely transparent to me. Your desires are not for me—they stem from someone else! I'm simply *available* at this time." She took a step closer, standing within arm's length. "Please, allow me to see you more clearly, more deeply; I need to feel your heart, and what resides within it."

"More clearly?" Anton looked puzzled; he didn't understand what the queen meant. "You may do as you wish, I have no fear."

"Fear? You silly boy! It's as clear as a summer day that you fear only failure!" She laughed sweetly, and smiled up into his eyes. "You're brave—brave to the point of foolishness!" Tittering like a small girl, she held her hand over her mouth, feigning graciousness—but a look of seriousness was in her eyes.

Reaching out, she touched Anton's chest. As she did so, her hand became translucent and it passed inside of him. The sensation took his breath away, and he struggled for a moment to catch his wind. Suddenly, a feeling of warmth filled his heart and an impression of joy and love filled his soul as if he were once again under the influence of the *Virlaqueus*. But this time it was different—he didn't feel intoxicated or concupiscent. The sensation of happiness was so intense it made every nerve in his body tingle. He felt dizzy. His thoughts reeled, and he felt faint, yet his footing remained unfaltering. He hungered to absorb as much of the sensation as he could.

"I can see inside your heart a longing for love—no, a *thirst* for love—no, a *loneliness* for love. It stems from a recent event in your life." Smiling, the queen closed her eyes, took a deep breath, and then let it out slowly, sensually. "I feel the goodness of your heart—it's pure, but a sharp point pricks my finger like a thorn as it passes through." Suddenly she opened her eyes with a shocked look. Her smile disappeared. Then it tenderly returned as if it had never gone.

The queen's words returned Anton's thoughts to the village of Tooloo. Images of his experiences there flashed through his mind. Trepidation suddenly surged through him, but the gentle touch of the queen squelched it. A crisp awareness of his surroundings—as if he were part of nature, as if he were part of the knoll he stood upon—sharpened his senses; intense joy replaced his fear and sang like a melody in his heart.

"There is a great secret of life I wish to share with you," the queen said. "Love is the key; it's the answer to everything. Your every experience, your every thought should always come from your heart; you can only obtain success through honest *true* love." She looked directly into Anton's eyes, slowly gazing back and forth from one to the other as she spoke, making sure he heard and comprehended the profundity of her meaning. "Promise me you'll remember this."

"I—I will. I feel you speak the truth." Anton felt as if he was in a dream as he replied. His eyes were transfixed upon the queen, as if she had hypnotized him.

Carefully, slowly, the queen removed her hand from Anton's chest; it became solid once again but there was a drop of blood that formed on her fingertip. Looking at it for just a moment, she held it up for all to see. Suddenly, the blond faerie flew over to her and placed both of her hands upon the drop of blood, closed her eyes, and cried silently. Instantly, golden glitter burst forth from her hand and rained silently to the ground. The blood vanished, and the finger spontaneously healed.

The queen smiled at the tiny faerie. "Thank you, my darling! Please, rejoin your sisters."

She then spoke to Anton: "With this tiny sacrifice of blood, I have forgiven your lustful sins, savior; they are absolved, you're free of them. Now it's *your* turn to absolve the sins of humanity." She studied him carefully, and then gave him a gentle hug.

"You've never known *true love*, my dear; yours was induced, and born of lust. This love is fading, but it shall remain a part of you forever; this is good, but you need to know what *true love* is." Placing her cheek against Anton's chest, she continued to hug him.

"Never fear, you *will* love again. It will find you when you least expect it. Only then will you comprehend the true meaning of my words. There's so much good in you. I feel it deep in my heart; it touches my soul."

The sense of joy lingered in Anton's heart as the queen maintained her embrace. He had never experienced an emotion in this way before; he thought his heart was about to burst with delight. A smile stretched across his face and he closed his eyes, trying to preserve the sensation.

"Your feelings of love originate from your good nature," the queen said. "I'm merely the facilitator to bring them forth and reveal them to you. If you were evil, and had a cold heart, you would feel only fear and abhorrence for me, not warmth. You've passed the test." She gently let go of Anton and took a half step backwards. "I see tremendous pain in you for the loss of your friends. This must be left in your past if you're to succeed in your mission—otherwise you will fail."

"I *can't* let it go!" Anton countered suddenly. He didn't want to reveal his personal secrets, but his capacity to conceal them was forfeit; the queen had purposefully exposed his privacy for all to see. "My mission to Tooloo was a terrible incident; I wish it hadn't ended the way it did." Feebly, he tried to disguise his discomfort, but only confirmed his hidden emotions in the attempt. "I *loved* Nelda."

"I've touched your heart, my dear—I know your secrets, and know the truth of your love. But fear not, I *will* help you." The queen again raised her hand and reached toward Anton. This time she cupped his chin and smiled. "My sweet boy, you have a wonderful heart, but you won't allow yourself to move beyond the pain of your past. You must let these feelings go so that you can move forward; they will *destroy* you if you preserve them! In time, you'll become bitter and hateful. This only plays into the hands of the enemy. It's a powerful tool for him to use against you—to recruit you."

"She's correct," interjected Vim. "You *must* focus on the mission, not on your past. It's imperative that you do so now." Vim drew closer and looked back and forth at them as he spoke. He leaned heavily on his staff, needing its support in order to remain standing.

"My queen, I remind you that we *must* enter the portal!" Looking directly at her, Vim's impatience was unmistakable. He pointed toward the lake.

"You're correct, wizard—my friend Vim." Turning to face her stump, the Queen floated to her place upon the knoll. As she did, she looked at all the little faeries fluttering about, and held her hand out, apportioning her love for each one.

As she neared the stump, she flapped her wings. They hummed a beautiful rich melody. Up into the night sky she flew, and in a trice, she dropped down the other side of the knoll, approaching the lake Anton had examined earlier in the day. All of the small faeries flew after her, leaving streams of light and golden dust behind them as if they'd suddenly accelerated into light speed. Every couple of yards one would stop to brighten the path, like two rows of Tiki torches for the two humans to follow.

"Where's she going, what's she doing?" asked Anton. He looked at Vim with a puzzled expression. "Where's this portal you spoke of?"

"It should be clear—especially to *you,* young man! She's going to open the seal to the City of the Humans! Cast your eye upon the lake below—there's little time to witness the event. Hurry!" Vim's tone was urgent, and he briskly walked down the hillside, between the two rows of faeries and after the queen.

Faster than Anton anticipated, Vim sped toward the lake; he seemed unexpectedly revivified as he approached. As quickly as he could, he followed behind his friend. It was nearly four hundred yards down and across the lower plateau, but it didn't take them long to traverse the distance. When they approached the water, Anton took particular notice of the well-groomed grass that covered the area surrounding the lake—it made the landscape feel smooth but slippery under his feet, requiring him to take care with his footing. His magically encased leg made traveling awkward, but he skillfully managed it.

The lake was dark and picturesque in the dim light of the late evening. Anton felt enraptured by the sight. Suddenly, a crisp breeze started to blow off the nearby snowcapped mountains; it whipped his hair around and into his face, sending a shiver up and down his spine. An odd, unexpected foreboding stabbed his heart like the point of a dagger. It was like something he'd never felt before—as if somehow, he knew that a critical phenomenon was about to commence. It was clear that a subtle yet fundamental change had occurred inside of him after the queen had touched his heart; somehow, he could empathetically feel the impending event.

The Queen Faerie seemed to stand floating in midair; she was ready to perform her magic and open the gate. As she circled around the lake's edge, it seemed as if she was looking for an exact spot. Presently, she stopped and spun in a pirouette—with one arm curved over her head, the other held under her bosom, and her toes pointed straight down as if again performing ballet. Faster and faster she whirled, until it was impossible to see her—only a silhouette of pure white light indicated she was there at all. Rapidly, a small tornado encircled her, veiling her radiance; it sent a tail down to the lake that slowly gyrated in a circle where it made contact with the water. It spiraled for what seemed like minutes. And then, finally, from inside the convolution, she emerged, flying straight up into the air as if expelled from a cannon.

The queen flew over to where Vim and Anton stood, and landed lightly between them. Smiling at Vim, she nodded and pointed directly at the swirling disturbance she'd left behind. "The entrance emerges; I have removed the protective seal." As she spoke, the twister diminished in intensity, and then quietly disappeared, leaving an entirely different landscape.

Directly to the west, a large heavy ring of roughly hewn stone stood on its side; obviously, it was the portal. To each side of the ring was a semi-circular wall of stone that tapered down at an angle and stretched to each side of the beach. At each end of the semicircle, a small tower stood like a monolith. A blue flame burned from its pointed peak. Unfamiliar foliage sporadically littered the walls: short bushes that looked like miniature palm trees and leaned slightly toward the people standing nearby, as if somehow aware of them and reaching out to them. A faint florescent light radiated from them, softly lighting the wall from which they grew. A pathway of sand inlaid with stone stretched toward the ring, inviting travelers to walk its path.

A mysterious dense churning turbulence of fog filled the center hole of the stone ring; it boiled, misted, and whirled silently, as if a violent storm raged in its core. It was silent, yet it seethed quickly.

Turning around to face Anton, the Queen embraced him, laid her head against his chest, and gave him a gentle loving hug. She was warm and soft, and Anton's primeval desires returned, burning passionately in his heart. The effect of her touch was pleasurable, and he returned the hug enthusiastically. After a few moments, she released him, and took a step back.

"I have a gift for you, young Anton; I think you will find it to be the greatest gift you've ever received." Raising her left hand high, palm up, she daintily spread her fingers and rotated her wrist in a circle. When she did so, the blonde faerie quickly flew over to her and hovered in front of her.

"My Queen!" she said, excitedly, and then curtsied. "What is your wish?" She darted around nervously, as if she were prepared to perform anything the queen might ask.

Looking at Anton, she continued. "I bestow upon you a single gift of *true* friendship. By the power of The Law of Balance, I'm permitted this, for I am the Heart of One!" As she said this, faerie dust burst from her in all directions; it shimmered in the dim light and gently showered all around. She then closed her eyes and stretched out both arms, as if to embrace the world.

Her personal revelation shocked Vim. He watched, dumbfounded, and when the queen announced her secret, he shouted: "By all the Gods, if I had ever known!" He subtly tapped the ground with the staff, and it rumbled underfoot. Power lit the staff's globe, and in turn the night, with a golden radiance. Looking at the queen, he bowed stiffly and leaned on the staff to maintain his balance.

"I'm forever at your disposal, my Queen! Your revelation comes at an unexpected time indeed!" Vim looked at her seriously, as if she'd hidden many secrets from him, and he wanted her to know how he felt.

"Control yourself, Wizard!" With a serious mien, the queen looked at Vim and held his gaze for just a moment, as if to impress her deportment. Then she returned her attention to Anton and smiled.

"This blonde faerie is known as Tania, and she will be with you always; she will *never* leave you." The queen continued to look into Anton's eyes and again smiled in her enamoring way.

"This is no small gift, and I wish for you to learn to love her with all your heart. Remember, love is the key to everything; only *true* love will give you the strength to fulfill your mission." Her expression lingered as she gazed deeply into Anton's eyes, as if looking to see if he completely understood her inference.

"I'm going with you!" Tania proclaimed gleefully, and flew in a circle around Anton's head. After orbiting a few times, she landed on his shoulder and hugged him around the neck. "I will be your friend— never doubt me!"

"Tania is one of my oldest faeries," the queen said, "and she is quite sensible. I'm sure you'll grow to respect her just as we do. Protect her, and let no harm come to her. She will help you in ways you might never imagine."

Anton was shocked; things were happening too quickly. He wondered why anyone would give him a gift such as this! Furthermore, what was he to do with a tiny faerie for a friend? He didn't feel as if he needed a little girl flying and fluttering about, but he was pleased nonetheless. Placing his right palm over his left fist, he bowed in Methonian fashion; his eyes never left the queen's, as he demonstrated his appreciation the only way he knew how.

"Thank you my, uh, queen—I shall not disappoint you, and I will honor your wishes. I'm always at your service." He stammered, and his response sounded hollow. He had no idea what challenges the future might offer, but he fully intended to fulfill the queen's wishes. Any agreement made by a Methonian Warrior was an unbreakable promise. Most of all, he wondered how he would keep Tania alive in the face of unknown dangers—especially when he was to confront an enemy he didn't yet comprehend and whose strength had yet to be measured.

"The moon will be rising shortly," Vim interjected, as if he needed to change the subject. "The door will open soon." He turned due west to look at the portal with expectant eyes. Slightly to the north of the portal, Loomspire towered over the company, as if watching over them, and Vim looked up at it as if searching for something. A few moments passed when suddenly in the east the slightest hint of light reached from below the horizon; it was the moon rising.

Quickly looking from east to west and back again, Anton wondered what was about to happen. Everyone stood silently, as if expecting a momentous event. He particularly wondered what role the moon was to play. He fidgeted as he waited.

Suddenly, the first arch of the moon peeked over the eastern edge of the plateau. As if on cue, the faeries flew out into the semicircle around the edge of the portal, lining each side of the pathway like Tiki torches—just as they'd done before. Vim stood directly in front of the first stepping stone, and the queen stood next to him. Both had their backs to the moon. Anton continued to look around impatiently, examining everything with great interest. His anticipation filled him with anxiety.

Minutes passed as the moon continued to rise. Then it finally dominated the night sky; silently, everyone held their positions. Anton's anxieties continued to escalate and he wondered how long it would take before they could leave.

Tania sat on Anton's shoulder as if it was a chair. She seemed completely disinterested, and huffed each time Anton stirred and shuffled. Be patient," she exclaimed, trying to encourage him to relax. "It's about to happen! You'll see; it'll be fun!"

Suddenly, the moon fired a beam of light directly at the swirling mass of turbulent fog. The cloud dissipated, as if burned away by the natural phenomenon. As if it were a holo-monitor, the stone circle showed the image of a pyramid in the distance. The portal had opened, the doorway was unbarred and the questers could finally continue their journey to the City of the Humans.

Smiling, Anton looked at the queen and then at Vim. Without a second glance, he took a step down the stone path. He knew his destiny lay beyond the stone ring, and he was ready to move forward to the next leg of his adventure.

HERE ENDS Enter: The Champion, book one of Tales of a Methonian Warrior: The Chronicles of Anton Seven. Be ready for the next installment: Transformations.

GLOSSARY

AELFWYN A high-ranking guard in the City of the Humans; he is also known as "Trepid's right hand."

AEROCRAFT A small flying taxi used primarily as a shuttle for training missions on Methonias.

AEROPORT A small airport used by Aerocrafts.

AGONIA, LORD One of the Lords of Ruin, sometimes called the "Lord of Pain." A former Methonian Warrior captured and controlled by Vile the necromancer.

ALPENSTOCK, VIM A man known as "The Wizard of Peruvious" and "Bearer of the Staff of Balance"; the man responsible for summoning Anton to Peruvious.

AMBADEDO AULA Latin in origin for a room (aula) in which to consume (ambadedo) food; also described as a "mess hall."

AMILIUS, KING An entity that rules as king over all of Upper Peruvious.

AUTO-CART A small self-propelled device used to deliver items throughout the Great Temple on Methonias.

AUTO-GURNEY An automatic self-propelled gurney used to move patients throughout the Great Temple.

BARNABAS SIX A young Warrior Anton met at the Great Temple.

BARREN MOUNTAIN, THE A volcano located in the northwest region of Upper Peruvious, home of the Dragon Master.

BEELIF Leader of the Primords.

BERRYBREW A heavy liqueur made of berries and honey, and made by the Primords. It is brewed in a cauldron like a potion.

BORIS THREE One of the Warriors Anton accompanied on his first mission to the Badlands of Methonias to rescue a Chief's daughter from the Troglodyte caves.

BORIS TWO The Warrior that Vim brought to Peruvious prior to Anton. He died at the Barren Mountain, eaten by the Dragon Master.

BREAKFEAST A term used by the Primords to describe a large celebration accompanying the first meal of the day.

CELESTE The young girl saved by Boris and Anton from the *Lapillusaurus* in the Troglodyte's caves.

CELESTIAL EYE A telescope found in Celestra that is capable of seeing the entire universe and all dimensions.

CLONE MASTERS A specific group of Masters responsible for the advanced science of genetic engineering on Methonias. They were solely responsible for the designs of the specialized genetically engineered Methonian life.

CRYSTALLOGRAPHIC HOLO-PROJECTOR A small device made of unique crystal resembling a jeweler's ring-sizing bar that can project a Warrior's past events using holographic imaging.

CUDBWYN A high-ranking guard in the City of the Humans; he is also known as "Trepid's eyes and ears."

DEIDRA One of the last Katrahs. A half-cat, half-human hybrid.

DRAGON MASTER A large dragon living inside the crater of the Barren Mountain.

DUKE One of the Warriors Anton accompanied on his first mission to the Badlands of Methonias to rescue a Chief's daughter from the Troglodyte caves.

EDGAR SIX One of the Warriors Anton accompanied on his first mission to the Badlands of Methonias to rescue a Chief's daughter from the Troglodyte caves.

EADWYN A high-ranking guard in the City of the Humans; he is also known as "The Incorrigible."

ENOCH A large man from Trieos Three; Anton encounters him on MB-1 when he departs Methonias.

ETHERISCOPE A fifteen-foot diameter sphere that holds a virtual representation of the entire universe, and is operated by a supercomputer; it is used to view of all time, from the "Big Bang" to the present, anywhere in the universe.

EHD (EHD) An EHD is a small device, lightweight and able to fold like a handkerchief. A small black bag closes at the top with a string laced across the opening. It has the capacity of a cubic yard, yet when completely filled it weighs only ounces. Inside the device is a dimension outside of normal three-dimensional space. This device remains the same size in this dimension regardless of the space used within.

FOOD REPLICATION UNIT (FRU) A device that creates food from a supply of base elements, and then offers the nutrition in the form of pills, or as simple nondescript food items.

FRACKNOID A small creature created in Lower Peruvious. Fracknoids are covered with black fur, and have glowing red eyes and many razor-sharp teeth made of steel. They are vicious, deadly, and nearly impossible to kill.

GEM LIZARD Descriptive name of the *Lapillusaurus*, used by Methonian natives. (See *Lapillusaurus*.)

GLOWROD A clear cylinder about eighteen inches long, made from a polymer. Its core is lined with Methonian Crystal. It is used as a weapon, tool, or light source.

GREAT TEMPLE Home of the Methonian Masters and their Methonian Warriors. It is located in the northern icy mountains of Methonias.

GREAT SEAL, THE A clear magical dome that stretches over the entire land of Upper Peruvious. It protects it from entry by any living creature.

GREYFWYN A high-ranking guard in the City of the Humans; he is also known as "The Organizer."

HAKAMA Japanese traditional formal clothing for men; it is a divided or undivided skirt, which resembles a wide pair of pants.

HAORI Also known as a "long jacket," a haori is a hip-length or thigh-length kimono jacket worn traditionally by Japanese men over a kimono.

HEAD COUNCIL The leading group of Masters located on Saurian Five.

HOGTRAH A portmanteau or blend word for Hog Transformed Human. A human-pig hybrid developed before the eugenic wars; there were hundreds living under the City of the Humans during Anton's visit there.

INTERSTELLAR SIXTEEN An intergalactic bus used to transport people from one star system to another. It was the most advanced craft built until the Pleceivious M-60 later replaced it.

IVAN One of the Warriors Anton accompanied on his first mission to the Badlands of Methonias, to rescue a chief's daughter from the Troglodyte caves.

KACATU An acronym for: Knowledge-Accelerated Computer Aided Transfer Unit. A device found in Celestra.

KANZA One of the natives of the village of Tooloo; he was a very disagreeable and outspoken man.

KATRAH A portmanteau or blend word for Cat Transformed Human. A human-cat hybrid developed before the eugenic wars; there were only two left in the City of the Humans during Anton's visit there.

KIMONO A Japanese traditional garment worn by women, men, and children—a T-shaped, straight-lined robe.

Lapillusaurus A large genetically created dinosaur with the capability to create crystal gems like an oyster creates pearls. They are found on Methonias and provide the specialized crystals for the Methonian Masters' usage. The natives refer to them as gem lizards.

LAVACIA Wife of Mahkeetah.

LORCA A Primord living in the City of the Humans. He is the healer, doctor, and alchemist working directly for Trepid.

LORING FOUR A Methonian Warrior sent on a mission to the village of Tooloo many years before Anton's visit. He first discovered the effects of the *Virlaqueus* flower.

LOTHENDUS The scientist known as "the great genius"; he was the first Wizard of Peruvious and the creator of the Staff of Balance; Vim's mentor and teacher.

LUKE One of the Warriors Anton accompanied on his first mission to the Badlands of Methonias, to rescue a chief's daughter from the Troglodyte caves.

LUTHIAN The leader a group of men that committed crimes against the village of Tooloo; he was formerly an Aerocraft pilot for the Great Temple.

MAHKEETAH A former Methonian Warrior and temporary chief of the village Tooloo; father of Nelda.

MARPITAS A purple pear-shaped tropical fruit with an incredibly sweet flavor found in the jungle regions of southern Methonias.

MB-1 An acronym for "Methonian Base One," a space station in orbit around Methonias, used as a spaceport for interstellar travel.

METHONIAN CLONING LABS The laboratories used by the Methonian Masters for creating advanced genetic humans and clones.

METHONIAN MASTERS The genetic engineers and trainers of the Methonian Warriors, and the Governing Council of Galactic Peace living on the terraformed planet of Methonias.

METHONIAN WARRIOR Genetically engineered highly trained super-humans, designed and created to control peace in the known universe.

MOUNTAIN OF HARVEST A large hill in Lower Peruvious; this is the location the Intelligence of Non-Existence uses to harvest human souls.

MUZOKE A young boy Anton met in the village of Tooloo; Tok's older brother; Son of Tyrell.

NANOBOTS Tiny robots constructed of nanometer-sized components; robots of a microscopic scale.

NAOMIE A teenage girl who lived in the village of Tooloo; she was the daughter of Tarna, and the first young girl killed by the outsiders.

NEKELMUSE Large spherical creature(s) with one eye, one mouth, and two pointed horns that float through the air like hot air balloons and shoot fireballs from their mouths. Derived from the Sumerian word for "Evil Eye."

NELDA A beautiful young girl who lived in the village of Tooloo; she was the daughter of the former Chief Mahkeetah, and briefly Anton's wife.

NEO-KUKULCAN The pyramid structure in the City of the Humans; it is the home of Trepid Tantamount.

NONE The self-proclaimed name of the Intelligence of NonExistence. The destroyer of the known universe and ruler of the Negative Universe.

NOOTKA An old frail man that lived in the village of Tooloo; he was the former chief, and Tyrell's father.

ONE The self-proclaimed and contemporary name of God; the Intelligence of Power, Wisdom, and Goodness; the creator and ruler of heaven, the universe, Peruvious, and all living things.

OBSERVATORY, THE A structure in the city of Celestra that housed a device known as the Celestial Eye.

ODIOUS, LORD One of the Lords of Ruin, sometimes called the "The Detestable Lord." A former Methonian Warrior captured and controlled by Vile the necromancer.

PERTHUS One of the tiny Primords who lived in the Primord hamlet; he was a friend of Vim Alpenstock.

PICURIS A village in the southern equatorial tropical region of Methonias, located near the village Tooloo.

PLECEIVIOUS M-60 A luxury interstellar star cruiser used to travel between star systems.

PRIMORDS A small group of tiny humans living in Upper Peruvious near Vim's cave; they have the special ability to talk to both plants and animals.

PUTUCU RIVER A wide fast-running river located in the valley below Vim's cave. The island of the Primords is located in the center of the river below the cave.

RIKIN, THUNDARUSS The champion and lieutenant to King Amilius.

RULER The Master holding the position of Chief of the Head Council of Masters residing on Saurian Five; the original or first Master.

SAURIAN FIVE A planet in the Saurian system on the outer reaches of the galaxy. The Warriors assigned there never return.

SERPOTAUR Giant muscular creatures with the body of a man and the head of a snake; each wields a magical staff with a large ruby attached to the top.

SINISTER, LORD One of the Lords of Ruin, sometimes called the "Lord of Evil." A former Methonian Warrior captured and controlled by Vile the necromancer.

SLIPSTREAM DRIVE An advanced propulsion drive defining the Pleceivious M-60's unique design and speed capabilities.

SPOTTER DROPS A powerful potion manufactured by the Primords. It gives the user the ability to locate an object of their desire. This potion is used one drop at a time.

STAR CRUISER A passenger ship used in interstellar travel.

SUPERGRIP TSUKA The handle of a Methonian katana, made from a material that clings to the user's hands. It helps to prevent slippage or have it torn from the user's hand in battle. The term "mekugi" is the Japanese name for the handle of a katana.

TANIA A small faerie given to Anton as a companion and friend by the queen faerie.

TARA FRUIT A yellow tough-skinned fruit with an orange-red inside and a tangy-sweet flavor. It has the shape of an acorn squash and grows in the tropical region of Methonias. Reportedly, it can sustain a man for long periods of time when no other food is available.

TARA WINE A wine made from tara fruit. It is quite potent in alcohol content, more closely related to liqueur than wine.

TARNA One of the men living in the village of Tooloo; His daughter Naomie was the first of the young girls killed by the outlaws.

TAUN One of the last katrahs. A half-cat, half-human genetic hybrid.

THORIK Chief of the village Picuris, a village in the southern equatorial tropical region of Methonias located near the village Tooloo.

TILLICH One of the tiny Primords who lived in the Primord hamlet; he was a friend of Vim Alpenstock.

TOK A small boy in the village of Tooloo; Anton saved him from drowning; son of Tyrell.

TOOLOO A village located in the southern equatorial tropical region of Methonias. Anton completed his final training there.

TOWERS OF TOR Two large towers positioned on the absolute edge of Upper Peruvious, looking over the Lower Lands. Each is octagonal, and resembles a lighthouse; each houses an octahedron of crystal, and uses it to project the energy of the Great Seal.

TREPID TANTAMOUNT An alias for the *Eye of One*; He used this to disguise Himself from Evil.

TRIEOS THREE One of the human colony planets located near the heart of the galaxy; it is the origin world to a race of taller-than-average humans.

TRINARY CODE Advanced binary code used by computers of Anton's time; it is an advanced instruction set developed for predictable Boolean instructions.

TRITANIUM An advanced alloy of titanium, aluminum, and other metals; unique to Methonias. Typically used in the construction of spacecraft, transportation vehicles, the superstructures of buildings, and weaponry.

TROGLODYTES A group of genetically specialized humanoids living in caves in the desolate Badland region of Methonias. They are highly aggressive by nature and use humans as slaves.

TSUBA A Japanese term referring the collar located above the tsuka (grip or handle) on a katana.

TYBALT One of the Warriors Anton accompanied on his first mission to the Badlands of Methonias, to rescue a Chief's daughter from the Troglodyte caves.

VALDE DOMUS, MOUNT The "Great Home Mountain" found in the northern region of Methonias. It is where the Great Temple was constructed.

VINICUS, LORD Captain of the Wardsman Alliance.

VIPERCRAFT A single-pilot flying vehicle used on Methonias for planetary and civil defense.

WARDSMAN ALLIANCE The battalion of guards at the castle of Amilius; they defend the castle and protect the last of humanity.

WARRIOR Genetically engineered highly trained super-humans designed and created to control peace in the known human universe. See also *Methonian Warrior*.

XENOSTEMORPHOLOGY LABORIA The cloning science used on Methonias to adjust brain chemistry, behavior, and mental disciplines. Part of the overall sciences used in the development and construction of Warriors and related super-humans.

YOR The commander of the Hogtrah army.